ASHES
TO
ASHES

TAMI HOAG

ASHES TO ASHES

WHEELER
PUBLISHING, INC.
ROCKLAND, MA

★ AN AMERICAN COMPANY ★

L.T.
(1)

NORTH

Published in Large Print by arrangement with Bantam Books, a division of Bantam Doubleday Dell Publishing Group, Inc., in the United States and Canada.

Wheeler Large Print Book Series.

Set in 16 pt Plantin.

Library of Congress Cataloging-in-Publication Data

Hoag, Tami.
    Ashes to ashes / Tami Hoag.
        p. (large print) cm.(Wheeler large print book series)
    ISBN 1-56895-713-0 (hardcover)
    1. Large type books.
I. Title. II. Series
[PS3558.O333A94   1999b]
813'.54—dc21   99-18710
                                                                  CIP

AUTHOR'S NOTE AND ACKNOWLEDGMENT

MY THANKS AND HEARTFELT GRATITUDE first and foremost to Special Agent Larry Brubaker, FBI, for so generously sharing his time and expertise. I state unequivocally he was *not* the pattern for Vince Walsh! (Sorry about that, Bru.) I will also note here that between beginning this book and finishing it, a number of changes have taken place in the FBI units formerly—and within this story—known as Investigative Support and CASKU (Child Abduction Serial Killer Unit). Now under the blanket heading of the National Center for the Analysis of Violent Crime, the agents in this unit no longer work sixty feet below ground at the FBI Academy in Quantico. Literally moving up in the world, they get to have windows in their new place. Not as interesting for writers, but the agents appreciate it.

My sincere gratitude also to the following law enforcement and legal services professionals for graciously giving their time to answer my many questions. As always, I've done my best to bring a feeling of authenticity to the jobs depicted within this book. Any mistakes made or liberties taken in the name of fiction are my own.

Frances James, Hennepin County Victim/Witness Program
Donna Dunn, Olmsted County Victim Services
Sergeant Bernie Martinson, Minneapolis PD
Special Agent in Charge Roger Wheeler, FBI
Lieutenant Dale Barsness, Minneapolis PD
Detective John Reed, Hennepin County Sheriff's Office

Andi Sisco: A million thanks for making connections for me! You're a star.
Diva Karyn, aka Elizabeth Grayson: Special thanks for some inspired suggestions regarding a particularly gruesome fetish used herein. Who says suspense writers have cornered the market on disgusting knowledge?
Brain Dead author Eileen Dreyer: Thanks for the usual support, technical and otherwise.
Diva Bush, aka Kim Cates: For more of the same.
And special thanks, Rocket, for your support, empathy, encouragement, and the occasional necessary kick in the ass. Misery loves company.

1
CHAPTER

SOME KILLERS are born. Some killers are made. And sometimes the origin of desire for homicide is lost in the tangle of roots that make an ugly childhood and a dangerous youth, so that no one may ever know if the urge was inbred or induced.

He lifts the body from the back of the Blazer like a roll of old carpet to be discarded. The soles of his boots scuff against the blacktop of the parking area, then fall nearly silent on the dead grass and hard ground. The night is balmy for November in Minneapolis. A swirling wind tosses fallen leaves. The bare branches of the trees rattle together like bags of bones.

He knows he falls into the last category of killers. He has spent many hours, days, months, years studying his compulsion and its point of origin. He knows what he is, and he embraces that truth. He has never known guilt or remorse. He believes conscience, rules, laws, serve the individual no practical purpose, and only limit human possibilities.

"Man enters into the ethical world through fear and not through love."—Paul Ricoeur, Symbolism of Evil.

1

His True Self adheres only to his own code: domination, manipulation, control.

A broken shard of moon glares down on the scene, its light faint beneath the web of limbs. He arranges the body to his satisfaction and traces two intersecting X's over the left upper chest. With a sense of ceremony, he pours the accelerant. Anointing the dead. Symbolism of evil. His True Self embraces the concept of evil as power. Fuel for the internal fire.

"Ashes to ashes."

The sounds are ordered and specific, magnified by his excitement. The scrape of the match against the friction strip, the pop as it bursts with flame, the whoosh of the fire as it comes alive and consumes. As the fire burns, his memory replays the earlier sounds of pain and fear. He recalls the tremor in her voice as she pleaded for her life, the unique pitch and quality of each cry as he tortured her. The exquisite music of life and death.

For one fine moment he allows himself to admire the drama of the tableau. He allows himself to feel the heat of the flames caress his face like tongues of desire. He closes his eyes and listens to the sizzle and hiss, breathes deep the smell of roasting flesh.

Elated, excited, aroused, he takes his erection out of his pants and strokes himself hard. He brings himself nearly to climax, but is careful not to ejaculate. Save it for later, when he can celebrate fully.

His goal is in sight. He has a plan, meticulously thought out, to be executed with perfection. His name will live in infamy with all the great ones—Bundy, Kemper, the Boston Strangler, the Green River Killer. The press here has already given him a name: the Cremator.

It makes him smile. It makes him proud. He lights another match and holds it just in front of him, studying the flame, loving the sinuous, sensuous undulation of it. He brings it closer to his face, opens his mouth, and eats it.

Then he turns and walks away. Already thinking of next time.

MURDER.

The sight burned its impression into the depths of her memory, into the backs of her eyeballs so that she could see it when she blinked against the tears. The body twisting in slow agony against its horrible fate. Orange flame a backdrop for the nightmare image.

Burning.

She ran, her lungs burning, her legs burning, her eyes burning, her throat burning. In one abstract corner of her mind, she was the corpse. Maybe this was what death was like. Maybe it *was* her body roasting, and this consciousness was her soul trying to escape the fires of hell. She had been told repeatedly that was where she would end up.

In the near distance she could hear a siren and see the weird flash of blue and red lights against the night. She ran for the street, sobbing, stumbling. Her right knee hit the frozen ground, but she forced her feet to keep moving.

Run run run run run run—

"Freeze! Police!"

The cruiser still rocked at the curb. The door was open. The cop was on the boulevard, gun drawn and pointed straight at her.

"Help me!" The words rasped in her throat.

"Help me!" she gasped, tears blurring her vision.

Her legs buckled beneath the weight of her body and the weight of her fear and the weight of her heart that was pounding like some huge swollen thing in her chest.

The cop was beside her in an instant, holstering his weapon and dropping to his knees to help. Must be a rookie, she thought dimly. She knew fourteen-year-old kids with better street instincts. She could have gotten his weapon. If she'd had a knife, she could have raised herself up and stabbed him.

He pulled her up into a sitting position with a hand on either shoulder. Sirens wailed in the distance.

"What happened? Are you all right?" he demanded. He had a face like an angel.

"I saw him," she said, breathless, shaking, bile pushing up the back of her throat. "I was there. Oh—Jesus. Oh—shit. I saw him!"

"Saw who?"

"The Cremator."

2

CHAPTER

"WHY AM I always the one in the wrong place at the wrong time?" Kate Conlan muttered to herself.

First day back from what had technically been a vacation—a guilt-forced trip to visit her parents in hell's amusement park (Las Vegas)—she was late for work, had a headache, wanted to strangle a certain sex crimes sergeant for spooking one of her clients—a screw-up *she* would pay for with the prosecuting attorney. All that and the fashionably chunky heel on a brand new pair of suede pumps was coming loose, thanks to the stairs in the Fourth Avenue parking ramp.

Now this. A twitcher.

No one else seemed to notice him prowling the edge of the spacious atrium of the Hennepin County Government Center like a nervous cat. Kate made the guy for late thirties, no more than a couple of inches past her own five-nine, medium-to-slender build. Wound way too tight. He'd likely suffered some kind of personal or emotional setback recently—lost his job or his girlfriend. He was either divorced or separated; living on his own, but not homeless. His clothes were rumpled, but

5

not castoffs, and his shoes were too good for homeless. He was sweating like a fat man in a sauna, but he kept his coat on as he paced around and around the new piece of sculpture littering the hall—a symbolic piece of pretension fashioned from melted-down handguns. He was muttering to himself, one hand hanging on to the open front of his heavy canvas jacket. A hunter's coat. His inner emotional strain tightened the muscles of his face.

Kate slipped off her loose-heeled shoe and stepped out of the other one, never taking her eyes off the guy. She dug a hand into her purse and came out with her cell phone. At the same instant, the twitcher caught the interest of the woman working the information booth twenty feet away.

Damn.

Kate straightened slowly, punching the speed-dial button. She couldn't dial security from an outside phone. The nearest guard was across the broad expanse of the atrium, smiling, laughing, engaged in conversation with a mailman. The information lady came toward the twitcher with her head to one side, as if her cotton-candy cone of blond hair were too heavy.

Dammit.

The office phone rang once...twice. Kate started moving slowly forward, phone in one hand, shoe in the other.

"Can I help you, sir?" the information woman said, still ten feet away. Blood was going to wreck the hell out of her ivory silk blouse.

6

The twitcher jerked around.

"Can I help you?" the woman asked again.

...fourth ring...

A Latina woman with a toddler in tow cut through the distance between Kate and the twitcher. Kate thought she could see the tremors begin—his body fighting to contain the rage or the desperation or whatever was driving him or eating him alive.

...fifth ring. "Hennepin County Attorney's Office—"

"Dammit!"

The movement was unmistakable—planting the feet, reaching into the jacket, eyes going wider.

"Get down!" Kate shouted, dropping the phone.

The information woman froze.

"Someone fucking pays!" the twitcher cried, lunging toward the woman, grabbing hold of her arm with his free hand. He jerked her toward him, thrusting his gun out ahead of her. The explosion of the shot was magnified in the towering atrium, deafening all ears to the shrieks of panic it elicited. Everyone noticed him now.

Kate barreled into him from behind, swinging the heel end of her shoe against his temple like a hammer. He expelled a cry of startled shock, then came back hard with his right elbow, catching Kate in the ribs.

The information woman screamed and screamed. Then lost her feet or lost con-sciousness, and the weight of her falling body

7

jerked down on her assailant. He dropped to one knee, shouting obscenities, firing another round, this one skipping off the hard floor and going God knew where.

Kate fell with him, her left hand clutching the collar of his coat. She couldn't lose him. Whatever beast he'd had trapped inside was free now. If he got away from her, there'd be a hell of a lot more to worry about than stray bullets.

Her nylons giving her no purchase on the slick floor, she scrambled to get her feet under her, to hang on to him as he fought to stand. She swung the shoe again and smacked him in the ear. He twisted around, trying to backhand her with the gun. Kate grabbed his arm and forced it up, too aware as the gun went off again that there were more than twenty stories of offices and courtrooms above.

As they struggled for control of the gun, she hooked a leg around one of his and threw her weight against him, and suddenly they were falling, down and down, tumbling over each other down the biting metal treads of the escalator to the street level—where they were met by half a dozen shouts of "Freeze! Police!"

Kate looked up at the grim faces through the haze of pain and muttered, "Well, it's about damn time."

"HEY LOOK!" ONE of the assistant prosecutors called from his office. "It's Dirty Harriet!"

"Very funny, Logan," Kate said, making her way down the hall to the county attorney's office. "You read that in a book, didn't you?"

"They have to get Rene Russo to play you in the movie."

"I'll tell them you said so."

Aches bit into her back and hip. She had refused a ride to the emergency room. Instead, she had limped into the ladies' room, combed her mane of red-gold hair into a ponytail, washed off the blood, ditched her ruined black tights, and gone back to her office. She didn't have any wounds worth an X ray or stitches, and half the morning was gone. The price of being a tough: She would have to make do tonight with Tylenol, cold gin, and a hot bath, instead of real painkillers. She could already tell she was going to be sorry.

The thought occurred to her that she was too old to be tackling lunatics and riding them down escalators, but she stubbornly resisted the idea that forty-two was too old for anything. Besides, she was only five years into what she termed her "second adulthood." The second career, the second stab at stability and routine.

The only thing she had wished for all the way home from the weirdness of Las Vegas was a return to the nice, normal, relatively sane life she had made for herself. Peace and quiet. The familiar entanglements of her job as a victim/witness advocate. The cooking class she was determined not to fail.

But no, she had to be the one to spot the twitcher. She was always the one who had to spot the twitcher.

9

Alerted by his secretary, the county attorney opened his office door for her himself. A tall, good-looking man, Ted Sabin had a commanding presence and a shock of gray hair, which he swept back from a prominent widow's peak. A pair of round steel-rimmed glasses perched on his hawkish nose gave him a studious look and helped camouflage the fact that his blue eyes were set too deep and too close together.

While he had once been a crack prosecutor himself, he now took on only the occasional high-profile case. His job as head honcho was largely administrative and political. He oversaw a bustling office of attorneys trying to juggle the ever-increasing workload of the Hennepin County court system. Lunch hours and evenings found him moving among the Minneapolis power elite, currying connections and favor. It was common knowledge he had his eye on a seat in the U.S. Senate.

"Kate, come in," he invited, the lines of his face etched deep with concern. He rested a big hand on her shoulder and guided her across the office toward a chair. "How are you? I've been brought up to speed about what happened downstairs this morning. My God, you could have been killed! What an astonishing act of bravery!"

"No, it wasn't," Kate protested, trying to ease away from him. She slipped into the visitor's chair and immediately felt his gaze on her bare thighs as she crossed her legs. She tugged discreetly at the hem of her black skirt, wishing to hell she'd found the spare panty hose she'd thought were in her desk drawer. "I just reacted, that's all. How's Mrs. Sabin?"

"Fine." The reply was absent of thought. He focused on her as he hitched his pinstriped trousers and perched a hip on the corner of his desk. "Just reacted? The way they taught you at the Bureau."

He was obsessed with the fact that she had been an agent in what she now deemed a past life. Kate could only imagine the lewd fantasies that crawled like slugs through his mind. Dominatrix games, black leather, handcuffs, spanking. *Bleeehhhh.*

She turned her attention to her immediate boss, the director of the legal services unit, who had taken the chair next to hers. Rob Marshall was Sabin's opposite image—doughy, dumpy, rumpled. He had a head as round as a pumpkin, crowned with a thinning layer of hair cropped so short, it gave more the appearance of a rust stain than a haircut. His face was ruddy and ravaged by old acne scars, and his nose was too short.

He'd been her boss for about eighteen months, having come to Minneapolis from a similar position in Madison, Wisconsin. During that time they had tried with limited success to find a balance between their personalities and working styles. Kate flat-out didn't like him. Rob was a spineless suckup and he had a tendency to micromanage that rubbed hard against her sense of autonomy. He found her bossy, opinionated, and impertinent. She took it as a compliment. But she tried to let his concern for victims offset his faults. In addition to his administrative duties, he often sat in on conferences with victims, and put in time with a victim's support group.

He squinted at her now from behind a pair of rimless glasses, his mouth pursing as if he'd just bitten his tongue. "You could have been killed. Why didn't you just call for security?"

"There wasn't time."

"Instinct, Rob!" Sabin said, flashing large white teeth. "I'm sure you and I could never hope to understand the kind of razor-sharp instincts someone with Kate's background has honed."

Kate refrained from reminding him yet again that she had spent most of her years with the FBI at a desk in the Behavioral Sciences Unit at the National Center for the Analysis of Violent Crime. Her days in the field were longer ago than she cared to remember.

"The mayor will want to give you an award," Sabin said brightly, knowing he would get in on the photo op.

Publicity was the last thing Kate wanted. As an advocate, it was her job to hold the hands of crime victims and witnesses, to shepherd them through the justice system, to reassure them. The idea of an advocate being chased down by media hounds was likely to spook some of her clients.

"I'd rather she didn't. I don't think it's the best idea for someone with my job. Right, Rob?"

12

"Kate's right, Mr. Sabin," he said, flashing his obsequious smile—an expression that often overtook his face when he was nervous. Kate called it the bootlicker's grin. It made his eyes nearly disappear. "We don't want her picture in the paper...all things considered."

"I suppose not," Sabin said, disappointed. "At any rate, what happened this morning isn't why we've called you in, Kate. We're assigning you a witness."

"Why all the fanfare?"

Most of her client assignments were automatic. She worked with six prosecuting attorneys and caught everything they charged—the exception being homicides. Rob assigned all homicides, but an assignment never warranted anything more than a phone call or a visit to her office. Sabin certainly never involved himself with the process.

"Are you familiar with the two prostitute murders we've had this fall?" Sabin asked. "The ones where the bodies were burned?"

"Yes, of course."

"There's been another one. Last night."

Kate looked from one grim face to the other. Behind Sabin she had a panoramic view of downtown Minneapolis from twenty-two stories up.

"This one wasn't a prostitute," she said.

"How did you know that?"

Because you'd never take time out of your day if it was.

"Lucky guess."

"You didn't hear it on the street?"

13

"On the street?" Like he was in a gangster movie. "No. I wasn't aware there'd been a murder."

Sabin walked around behind his desk, suddenly restless. "There's a chance this victim was Jillian Bondurant. Her father is Peter Bondurant."

"Oh," Kate said with significance. Oh, no, this wasn't just another dead hooker. Never mind that the first two victims had fathers somewhere too. This one's father was *important*.

Rob shifted uncomfortably in his chair, though whether it was the case or the fact that he insisted on wearing his pants too small around the waist was unclear. "Her driver's license was left near the body."

"And it's been confirmed that she's missing?"

"She had dinner with her father at his home Friday night. She hasn't been seen since."

"That doesn't mean it's her."

"No, but that's the way it worked with the first two," Sabin said. "The ID left with each hooker's body matched up."

A hundred questions shot through Kate's mind, questions about the crime scene, about what information the police had released about the first two murders and what had been held back. This was the first she'd heard about the IDs being left at the scene. What did that mean? Why burn the bodies beyond recognition, yet leave the victim's identity right there?

"I assume they're checking dental records," she said.

The men exchanged looks.

"I'm afraid that's not an option," Rob said carefully. "We have a body *only*."

"Jesus," Kate breathed as a chill ran through her. "He didn't decapitate the others. I never heard that."

"No, he didn't," Rob said. He squinted again and tipped his head a little to one side. "What do you make of it, Kate? You've had experience with this kind of thing."

"Obviously, his level of violence is escalating. It could mean he's gearing up for something big. There was some sexual mutilation with the others, right?"

"The cause of death on the other two was ruled strangulation by ligature," Sabin said. "I'm sure I don't need to tell you, Kate, that while strangulation is certainly a violent enough method of murder, a decapitation will throw this city into a panic. Particularly if the victim was a decent, law-abiding young woman. My God, the daughter of one of the most prominent men in the state. We need to find this killer fast. And we can make that happen. We've got a witness."

"And this is where I come in," Kate said. "What's the story?"

"Her name is Angie DiMarco," Rob said. "She came running out of the park just as the first radio car arrived."

"Who called it in?"

"Anonymous caller on a cell phone, I'm told," Sabin said. His mouth tightened and twisted as if he were sucking at a sore tooth.

15

"Peter Bondurant is a friend of the mayor's. I know him as well. He's beside himself with grief at the idea that this victim is Jillian, and he wants this case solved ASAP. A task force is being put together even as we speak. Your old friends at the Bureau have been called. They're sending someone from the Investigative Support Unit. We clearly have a serial killer on our hands."

And a prominent businessman up your butts.

"Rumors are already flying," Sabin muttered darkly. "The police department has a leak big enough to drain the Mississippi."

The phone on his desk was lighting up like the switchboard on a disease telethon, though it never audibly rang.

"I've spoken with Chief Greer and with the mayor," he continued. "We're grabbing this thing by the short hairs right now."

"That's why we've called you in, Kate," Rob said, shifting in his chair again. "We can't wait until there's been an arrest to assign someone to this witness. She's the only link we have to the killer. We want someone from the unit attached to her right away. Someone to sit with her during police interviews. Someone to let her know not to talk to the press. Someone to maintain the thread of contact between her and the county attorney's office. Someone to keep tabs on her."

"It sounds like what you want is a baby-sitter. I've got cases ongoing."

"We'll shift some of your caseload."

"Not Willis," she said, then grimaced. "As

16

much as I'd like to dump him. And absolutely not Melanie Hessler."

"I could take Hessler, Kate," Rob insisted. "I sat in on the initial meeting. I'm familiar with the case."

"No."

"I've worked with plenty of rape victims."

"No," she said as if she were the boss and the decision was hers to make.

Sabin looked annoyed. "What case is this?"

"Melanie Hessler. She was raped by two men in the alley behind the adult bookstore she works in downtown," Kate explained. "She's very fragile, and she's terrified about the trial. She couldn't take me abandoning her—especially not to a man. She needs me. I won't let her go."

Rob huffed a sigh.

"Fine," Sabin declared impatiently. "But this case is priority one. I don't care what it takes. I want this lunatic out of business. Now."

Now that the victim would garner more than a minute and a half on the six o'clock news. Kate had to wonder how many dead prostitutes it would have taken to get Ted Sabin to feel that same level of urgency. But she kept the question to herself and nodded, and tried to ignore the sense of dread that settled in her stomach like a lead weight.

Just another witness, she told herself. Just another case. Back to the usual, familiar entanglements of her job.

Like hell.

A dead billionaire's daughter, a case full of

politicos, a serial killer, and someone winging in from Quantico. Someone from ISU. Someone who hadn't been there five years ago, she had to hope—but knew that hope was a flimsy shield.

Suddenly, Las Vegas didn't seem so bad after all.

3

CHAPTER

THIS HAPPENED in the night. It was dark. How much could she have seen?" Kate asked.

The three of them walked together through the underground concourse that ran beneath Fifth Street and connected the government center to the depressing Gothic stone monstrosity that housed the Minneapolis city government offices and the Minneapolis police department. The underground corridor was busy. No one was going out onto the street voluntarily. The gloomy morning had turned dour as a leaden sky sank low above the city and let loose with a cold, steady rain. November: a lovely month in Minnesota.

"She told the police she saw him," Rob said, trundling along beside her. His legs

18

were short for his body, and hurrying gave him the toddling gait of a midget, even though he was of average height. "We have to hope she saw him well enough to identify him."

"I'd like a composite sketch in time for the press conference," Sabin announced.

Kate ground her molars. Oh, yeah, this was going to be a peach of a case. "A good sketch takes time, Ted. It pays to get it right."

"Yes, well, the sooner we get a description out there, a picture out there, the better."

In her mind's eye she could envision Sabin wringing information out of the witness, then tossing her aside like a rag.

"We'll do everything we can to expedite the situation, Mr. Sabin," Rob promised. Kate shot him a dirty look.

The city hall building had at one time in its history been the Hennepin County court-house, and had been constructed with a sense of sober grandiosity to impress visitors. The Fourth Street entrance, which Kate seldom had cause to pass through, was as stunning as a palace, with a marble double grand staircase, incredible stained glass, and the enormous *Father of the Waters* sculpture. The main body of the building had always reminded her of an old hospital with its tiled floor and white marble wainscoting. There was forever a vacant feeling about the place, although Kate knew it was all but bursting at the seams with cops and crooks, city officials and reporters and citizens looking for justice or a favor.

The criminal investigative division of the PD had been crammed into a gloomy warren of rooms at the end of a cavernous hall while remodeling went on in their usual digs. The reception area was cut up with temporary partitions. There were files and boxes stacked everywhere, beat-up dingy gray metal file cabinets had been pushed into every available corner. Tacked to the wall beside the door into the converted broom closet that now housed sex crimes investigators was a sign that proclaimed:

TURKEY WAKE
NOVEMBER 27
PATRICK'S
1600HRS

Sabin gave the receptionist a dismissive wave and took a right into the homicide offices. The room was a maze of ugly steel desks the color of dirty putty. Some desks were occupied, most were not. Some were neat, most were awash in paperwork. Notes and photographs and cartoons were tacked and taped to walls and cabinets. A notice on one side of the door ordered: HOMICIDE—LOCK UP YOUR GUNS!

Telephone receiver pressed to his ear, Sam Kovac spotted them, scowled, and waved them over. A twenty-two-year veteran, Kovac had that universal cop look about him with the requisite mustache and cheap haircut, both sandy brown and liberally threaded with silver.

20

"Yeah, I realize you're dating my second wife's sister, Sid." He pulled a fresh pack of Salems from a carton on his desk and fumbled with the cellophane wrapper. He had shed the jacket of his rumpled brown suit and jerked his tie loose. "That doesn't entitle you to inside information on this murder. All that'll get you is my sympathy. Yeah? Yeah? She said that? Well, why do you think I left her? Uh-huh. Uh-huh. Is that right?"

He bit at the tab on the cigarette wrapper and ripped the pack open with his teeth. "You hear that, Sid? That's the sound of me tearing you a new one if you print a word of that. You understand me? You want information? Come to the press conference with everybody else. Yeah? Well, same to you."

He slammed the receiver down and turned his scowl on the county attorney. His eyes were the green-brown of damp bark, bloodshot, and hard and bright with intelligence. "Damn newsies. This is gonna get uglier than my aunt Selma, and she has a face that could make a bulldog puke."

"Do they have Bondurant's name?" Sabin asked.

"Of course they do." He pulled a cigarette from the pack and let it dangle from his lip as he rummaged through the junk on his desk. "They're all over this like flies on dog crap," he said, glancing back at them over his shoulder. "Hi, Kate— Jesus, what happened to you?"

"Long story. I'm sure you'll hear it

at Patrick's tonight. Where's our witness?"

"Down the hall."

"Is she working with the sketch artist yet?" Sabin asked.

Kovac blew air between his lips and made a sound like a disgusted horse. "She's not even working with *us* yet. Our citizen isn't exactly overjoyed to be the center of attention here."

Rob Marshall looked alarmed. "She's not a problem, is she?" He flashed the bootlicker's smile at Sabin. "I suppose she's just shaken up, Mr. Sabin. Kate will settle her down."

"What's your take on the witness, Detective?" Sabin asked.

Kovac snatched up a Bic lighter and a messy file and started for the door. World-weary and nicked up, his build was at once solid and rangy, utilitarian rather than ornamental. His brown pants were a little baggy and a little too long, the cuffs puddling over the tops of his heel-worn oxfords.

"Oh, she's a daisy," he said with sarcasm. "She gives us what's gotta be a stolen out-of-state driver's license. Tells us she's living at an apartment in the Phillips neighborhood but she's got no keys for it and can't tell us who has. If she hasn't got a sheet, I'll shave my ass and paint it blue."

"So, you ran her and what?" Kate asked, forcing herself to keep pace with him, so that Sabin and Rob had to fall in behind. She had learned long ago to cultivate friendships with the cops who worked her cases. It was to her advantage to have them as allies rather than adversaries. Besides, she liked the good ones, like Kovac. They did a hard job for little credit and not enough pay for the plain old-fashioned reason that they believed in the necessity of it. She and Kovac had built a nice rapport in five years.

"I tried to run the name she's using today," he qualified. "The fucking computer's down. Swell day this is gonna be. I'm on nights this rotation, you know. I oughta be home in bed. My *team* is on nights. I hate this team-concept crap. Give me a partner and leave me the hell alone. You know what I mean? I got half a mind to transfer out to sex crimes."

"And turn your back on all this fame and glamour?" Kate teased, bumping him with a subtle elbow.

He gave her a look, tilting his head down in conspiracy. A spark of wry humor lit his eyes. "Shit, Red. I like my stiffs uncomplicated, you know."

"I've heard that about you, Sam," she joked, knowing he was the best investigator in the PD, a straight-up good guy who lived the job and hated the politics of it.

He huffed a laugh and pulled open the door to a small room that looked into another through the murky glass of a one-way mirror. On the other side of the glass, Nikki Liska, another detective, stood leaning against one wall, eyes locked in a staredown with the girl who sat on the far side of the fake-woodgrain table. A bad sign. The situation had already

23

become adversarial. The table was littered with soda cans and paper coffee cups and doughnut chunks and fragments.

The sense of dread in Kate's belly gained a pound as she stared through the glass. She put the girl at maybe fifteen or sixteen. Pale and thin, she had a button nose and the lush, ripe mouth of a high-priced call girl. Her face was a narrow oval, the chin a little too long, so that she would probably look defiant without trying. Her eyes tilted at an exotic Slavic angle, and looked twenty years too old.

"She's a kid," Kate declared flatly, looking to Rob with confusion and accusation. "I don't do kids. You know that."

"We need you to do this one, Kate."

"Why?" she demanded. "You've got a whole juvenile division at your disposal. God knows they deal with murder on a regular basis."

"This is different. This isn't some gang shoot-'em-up we're dealing with," Rob said, seemingly relegating some of the most violent crime in the city to the same category as shoplifting and traffic mishaps. "We're dealing with a serial killer."

Even in a profession that dealt with murder as a matter of routine, the words *serial killer* struck a chord. Kate wondered if their bad guy was aware of that, if he reveled in the idea, or if he was too completely bound up in his own small world of hunting and killing. She had seen both types. All their victims ended up equally dead.

She turned from her director and looked again

24

at the girl who had crossed paths with this latest predator. Angie DiMarco glared at the mirror, resentment pulsing from her in invisible waves. She picked up a fat black pen from the table and very deliberately drew the cap end slowly back and forth along her full lower lip in a gesture that was both impatient and sensuous.

Sabin gave Kate his profile as if he were posing for a currency engraver. "You've dealt with this kind of case before, Kate. With the Bureau. You have a frame of reference. You know what to expect with the investigation and with the media. You may well know the agent they send from the Investigative Support Unit. That could be helpful. We need every edge we can get."

"I studied victims. I dealt with dead people." She didn't like the anxiety coming to life inside her. Didn't like having it, didn't want to examine its source. "There's a big difference between working with a dead person and working with a kid. Last I heard, dead people were more cooperative than teenagers."

"You're a witness advocate," Rob said, his voice taking on a slight whine. "She's a witness."

Kovac, who had propped himself up against the wall to watch the exchange, gave her a wan smile. "Can't pick your relatives or your witnesses, Red. I would have liked Mother Teresa to come running out of that park last night."

"No, you wouldn't," Kate returned. "The defense would claim she had cataracts and

Alzheimer's, and say anyone who believes a man can rise from the dead three days after the fact is a less than credible witness."

Kovac's mustache twitched. "Scum lawyers."

Rob looked bemused. "Mother Teresa's dead."

Kate and Kovac rolled their eyes in unison.

Sabin cleared his throat and looked pointedly at his watch. "We need to get going with this. I want to hear what she has to say."

Kate arched a brow. "And you think she'll just tell you? You don't get out of the office enough, Ted."

"She'd damn well better tell us," he said ominously, and started for the door.

Kate stared through the glass for one last moment, her eyes meeting those of her witness, even though she knew the girl couldn't see her. A teenager. Christ, they could just as well have assigned her a Martian. She was nobody's mother. And there was a reminder she didn't need or want.

She looked into the girl's pale face and saw anger and defiance and experience no kid that age should have. And she saw fear. Buried beneath everything else, held as tight inside her as a secret, there was fear. Kate didn't let herself acknowledge what it was inside her own soul that let her recognize that fear.

In the interview room, Angie DiMarco flicked a glance at Liska, who was looking at her watch. She turned her eyes back to the one-way glass and slipped the pilfered pen inside the neckline of her sweater.

26

"A kid," Kate muttered as Sabin and Rob Marshall stepped out into the hall ahead of her. "I wasn't even good at being one."

"That's perfect," Kovac said, holding the door open for her. "Neither is she."

LISKA, SHORT, BLOND, and athletic with a boy's haircut, rolled away from the wall and gave them all a weary smile as they entered the interview room. She looked like Tinker Bell on steroids— or so Kovac had declared when he christened her with the nickname Tinks.

"Welcome to the fun house," she said. "Coffee, anybody?"

"Decaf for me and one for our friend at the table, please, Nikki," Kate said softly, never taking her eyes off the girl, trying to formulate a strategy.

Kovac spilled himself into a chair and leaned against the table with one arm, his blunt-tipped fingers scratching at chocolate sprinkles that lay scattered like mouse turds on the tabletop.

"Kate, this is Angie DiMarco," he said casually. "Angie, this is Kate Conlan from the victim/witness program. She's being assigned to your case."

"I'm not a case," the girl snapped. "Who are they?"

"County Attorney Ted Sabin and Rob Marshall from victim/witness." Kovac pointed to one and then the other as the men took seats across the table from their prized witness.

27

Sabin gave her his best Ward Cleaver expression. "We're very interested in what you have to say, Angie. This killer we're after is a dangerous man."

"No shit." The girl turned back to Kovac. Her glare homed in on his mouth. "Can I have a smoke?"

He pulled the cigarette from his lips and looked at it. "Hell, *I* can't even have one," he confessed. "It's a smoke-free building. I was going outside with this."

"That sucks. I'm stuck in this fucking room half the fucking night and I can't even have a fucking cigarette!"

She sat back and crossed her arms over her chest. Her brown hair was oily and parted down the middle, falling loose around her shoulders. She wore too much mascara, which had smudged beneath her eyes, and a faded Calvin Klein denim jacket that had once belonged to someone named Rick. The name was printed in indelible ink above the left breast pocket. She kept the jacket on despite the fact that the room was warm. Security or hiding needle tracks, Kate figured.

"Oh, for godsake, Sam, give her a cigarette," Kate said, shoving up the sleeves of her sweater. She took the vacant chair on the girl's side of the table. "And give me one too, while you're at it. If the PC Nazis catch us, we'll all go down together. What're they gonna do? Ask us to leave this rat hole?"

She watched the girl out of the corner of her eye as Kovac shook two more cigarettes out of the pack. Angie's fingernails were bitten to the quick and painted metallic ice blue. Her hand trembled as she took the gift. She wore an assortment of cheap silver rings, and two small, crude ballpoint tattoos marred her pale skin—a cross near her thumb, and the letter A with a horizontal line across the top. A professional job circled her wrist, a delicate blue ink bracelet of thorns.

"You've been here all night, Angie?" Kate asked, drawing on the cigarette. It tasted like dried shit. She couldn't imagine why she had ever taken up the habit in her college days. The price of cool, she supposed. And now it was the price of bonding.

"Yes." Angie fired a stream of smoke up at the ceiling. "And they wouldn't get me a lawyer either."

"You don't need a lawyer, Angie," Kovac said congenially. "You're not being charged with anything."

"Then why can't I blow this shithole?"

"We got a lot of complications to sort out. For instance, the matter of your identification."

"I *gave* you my ID."

He pulled it from the file and handed it to Kate with a meaningful lift of his eyebrows.

"You're twenty-one," Kate read deadpan, flicking ashes into an abandoned cup of oily coffee.

"That's what it says."

"It says you're from Milwaukee—"

"*Was*. I left."

"Any family there?"

"They're dead."

"I'm sorry."

"I doubt it."

"Any family here? Aunts, uncles, cousins, half-related circus freaks? Anyone at all we could call for you—to help you through this?"

"No. I'm an orphan. Poor me." She bluffed a sarcastic laugh. "Trust me, I don't need any family."

"You've got no permanent address, Angie," Kovac said. "You have to realize what's happened here. You're the only one who can identify a killer. We need to know where you're at."

She rolled her eyes in the way only teenage girls can, imparting both incredulity and impatience. "I *gave* you my address."

"You gave me the address for an apartment you don't have keys for and you can't tell me the name of who it is you're staying with."

"I *told* you!"

She pushed up out of her chair and turned away from Kovac, the cigarette in her hand raining ashes on the floor. The blue sweater she wore beneath her jacket was either cropped short or shrunken, revealing a pierced navel and another tattoo—three drops of blood falling into the waistband of her dirty jeans.

"Her name is Molly," she said. "I met her at a party and she said that I could crash at her place until I get my own."

Kate caught the hint of a tremor in the girl's voice, the defensive body language as she pulled in on herself and turned away from them.

Across the room, the door opened and Liska came in with the coffee.

"Angie, no one's trying to jam you up here," Kate said. "Our first concern is that you're safe."

The girl wheeled on her, her eyes dark blue and glittering with anger. "Your *concern* is that I testify against this psycho Cremator creep. You think I'm nuts? He'll track me down and kill me too!"

"Your cooperation is imperative, Angie," Sabin said with authority. The man in command. "You're our only witness. This man has killed three women that we know of."

Kate shot a dagger look at the county attorney.

"Part of my job is to see to it that you're safe, Angie," she explained, keeping her voice even and calm. "If you need a place to stay, we can make that happen. Do you have a job?"

"No." She turned away again. "I been looking," she added almost defensively. She gravitated toward the corner of the room, where a dirty backpack had been discarded. Kate was willing to bet everything the kid owned was in that bag.

"It's tough coming into a new town," Kate said quietly. "Don't know your way around. Don't have any connections. Hard to get set up, get your life going."

The girl bowed her head and chewed at a thumbnail, her hair swinging down to obscure her face.

"It takes money to set yourself up," Kate went

31

on. "Money to eat. Money for a place. Money for clothes. Money for everything."

"I get by."

Kate could imagine just how. She knew how it worked with kids on the street. They did what they had to do to survive. Beg. Steal. Sell a little dope. Turn a trick or two or ten. There was no shortage of depraved human scum in the world more than willing to prey on kids with no homes and no prospects.

Liska set the steaming coffee cups on the table and leaned down to murmur in Kovac's ear. "Elwood tracked down the building manager. The guy says the apartment's vacant and if this kid is living there, then he wants a five-hundred-dollar deposit or he'll press charges for criminal trespass."

"What a humanitarian."

"Elwood says to him: 'Five hundred? What's that? A buck a cockroach?'"

Kate absorbed the whispered remarks, her eyes still on Angie. "Your life's tough enough right now without having to become a witness to a murder."

Head still down, the girl sniffed and brought the cigarette to her lips. "I didn't see him kill her."

"What *did* you see?" Sabin demanded. "We need to know, Miss DiMarco. Every minute that passes is crucial to the investigation. This man is a serial killer."

"I think we're all aware of that, Ted," Kate conceded with a razor's edge in her voice. "You really don't have to remind us every two minutes."

32

Rob Marshall twitched hard. Sabin met her gaze, his own impatience showing. He wanted a revelation before he bolted for his meeting with the mayor. He wanted to be able to step in front of the cameras at the press conference and give the monster loose among them a name and a face and announce that an arrest was imminent.

"Angie seems to be having some difficulty deciding whether to cooperate or not," he said. "I think it's important she realize the gravity of the situation."

"She watched someone set a human body on fire. I think she understands the gravity of the situation perfectly."

In the corner of her eye, Kate could see she had caught the girl's attention. Maybe they could be friends living on the street together after Sabin fired her for challenging him in front of an audience. What was she thinking? She didn't even want this mess in her lap.

"What were you doing in that park at that hour of night, Angie?" Rob asked, mopping at his forehead with a handkerchief.

The girl looked him square in the face. "Minding my own fucking business."

"You can take your coat off if you want," he said with a brittle smile.

"I don't want."

His jaw clenched and the grin became more of a grimace. "That's fine. If you want to keep it on, that's fine. It just seems hot in here. Why don't you tell us in your own way how you came to be in that park last night, Angie."

She stared at him with venom in her eyes. "I'd tell you to kiss my ass, but you're so fucking ugly, I'd make you pay in advance."

His face flushed as red as a bad rash.

A beeper went off and everyone in the room except the witness reached for theirs. Sabin scowled darkly as he read the message in the display window of his. He checked his watch again.

"Did you get a good look at the man, Angie?" Rob asked in a tight voice. "You could be such a help here. I know you've gone through something terrible—"

"You don't know shit," the girl snapped.

A vein popped out in Rob's left temple and sweat beaded on his shiny forehead.

"That's why we're asking you, kiddo," Kate said calmly. She blew a lazy stream of smoke. All the time in the world. "Did you get a good look at the guy?"

Angie studied her for a moment, the time and the silence stretching, then looked to Sabin to Liska to Kovac, and back to Rob Marshall. Gauging. Assessing.

"I saw him in the flames," she said at last, dropping her gaze to the floor. "He lit the body on fire and he said, 'Ashes to ashes.' "

"Would you know him if you saw him again?" Sabin demanded.

"Sure," she murmured, bringing the cigarette to her lips for one final drag. The tip of it glowed like an ember from hell against the pale white of her face. When she spoke again, it was on a breath of smoke. "He's the devil."

"**WHAT WAS THAT** about?" Kate went on the offensive the second they stepped from the interview room into the hall.

Sabin turned on her, his expression furious. "I was about to ask you the same thing, Kate. We need this girl's cooperation."

"And you think you're going to get it by coming down on her like a ton of bricks? In case you didn't notice, she wasn't responding."

"How could she respond with you butting in every time I started making some headway?"

"Force meets resistance, Ted. And it's my job to butt in—I'm an advocate," she said, realizing she was inviting the wrath of a very powerful man. He had the power to take her off this case.

I should be so lucky, she thought. Already this investigation had the makings of a world-class cluster fuck. She couldn't possibly want to be stuck in the middle of it.

"You're the one who dragged me into this," she said. "You want me to be this girl's friend, remember? That's going to be a tough enough job without you setting us up as a group force against her.

"She has to want to tell us what she saw. She has to believe we'll take care of her. Do you honestly think she trusts you not to take what she has to give and cut her loose? How do you think a kid like Angie ends up in a mess like this in the first place?"

"You didn't want this case because she's a kid," Sabin said irritably. "Now suddenly you're an authority."

"You wanted me on this because of my expertise, my frame of reference," she reminded him. "Then you have to trust me to do the job. I know how to interview a witness."

Sabin dismissed her by turning to Kovac. "You said the girl was apprehended fleeing the scene?"

"Not exactly."

"She ran out of the park as the first unit arrived," he said impatiently. "She was running away from a burning body. That makes her a suspect. Shake her down. Rattle her. Threaten her. Scare the truth out of her. I don't care how you do it. I've got a meeting in two minutes with the chief and the mayor. The press conference is set for five. I want a description of a killer by then."

He walked away from them, straightening his jacket, moving his shoulders like a boxer who'd just gone five rounds. Kate looked to Kovac, who made a sour face.

"See the kind of shit I have to put up with?" he said.

"*You?*" Kate sniffed. "He could fire my ass. And still I don't care if he's on his way to a tryst with Janet Reno. Power doesn't give him license to harass a witness—or for you to do it for him. If you run over this kid with hobnail boots, I'll make your life a misery, Sam."

Kovac grimaced. "Jesus, Kate, the big dog says toss her in the can. What am I gonna do?

36

Thumb my nose at him? He'll have my *cojones* in his nutcracker for Christmas."

"I'll use 'em for tennis."

"Sorry, Kate. You're overruled. Sabin can castrate me *and* my pension. Look on the bright side: The tank'll be like Club Med to this chick."

Kate turned to her boss for support. Rob shifted his weight from one foot to the other. "These circumstances are extraordinary, Kate."

"I realize that. I also realize that if this kid had watched our psycho light up one of those hookers, there wouldn't be a press conference pending and Ted Sabin wouldn't even know her name. But that doesn't change what she saw, Rob. It doesn't change who she is or how she needs to be handled. She expects to be treated badly. It gives her an excuse to be uncooperative."

His expression was a cross between wry and wrenched. "I thought you didn't want this case."

"I don't," Kate said flatly. "I have no personal desire to be ass-deep in alligators, but if I'm in this thing, then I'm in it all the way. Let me do my job with her or assign me elsewhere. I won't be a puppet and I won't have my hands tied. Not even by his high and mightiness."

It was a bluff of sorts. She may not have wanted the job, but she was the best advocate for the job—or so Ted Sabin thought. Sabin with his hard-on for the idea of her as an FBI agent. As much as the obsession disgusted her, Kate knew it gave her a certain amount of leverage with him and therefore with Rob.

The real question was: What would it cost her? And why should she care enough to pay the price? She could smell the stench of this case a block away, could feel the potential entanglements touching her like the tentacles of an octopus. She should have cut and run. If she'd had any sense. If she hadn't looked past Angie DiMarco's defenses and glimpsed the fear.

"What's Sabin gonna do, Rob?" she questioned. "Cut off our heads and set us on fire?"

"That's not even remotely funny."

"I didn't mean for it to be. Have some backbone and stand up to him, for Christ's sake."

Rob sighed and discreetly pried a thumb inside the waistband of his slacks. "I'll talk to him and see what I can do. Maybe the girl will come up with an ID from the mug books by five," he said without hope.

"You must still have connections in Wisconsin," Kate said. "Maybe you can get a line on her, find out who she really is."

"I'll make some calls. Is that all?" he asked pointedly.

Kate pretended innocence. She was well aware of her tendency to lead the dance, and perfectly unapologetic about it where her boss was concerned. He never inspired her to follow.

Rob walked away looking defeated.

"Ever the man of action, your boss," Kovac said dryly.

"I think Sabin keeps his *cojones* in a jar in his medicine cabinet."

"Yeah, well, I don't want mine added to the collection. See if you can get something out of this kid besides lies and sarcasm before five." He clamped a hand on Kate's shoulder in congratulations and consolation. "Way to go, Red. The job's all yours."

Kate frowned as she watched him retreat to the men's room. "And I ask yet again: Why do I always have to be the one in the wrong place at the wrong time?"

4

CHAPTER

SUPERVISORY SPECIAL AGENT John Quinn walked out of the jetway and into the Minneapolis-St. Paul airport. It looked like nearly every other airport he'd ever seen: gray and cheerless, the only sign of emotion rising above the grim and travel-weary being the celebration of a family welcoming home a boy with a buzz cut and a blue air force uniform.

He felt a flicker of envy, a feeling that seemed as old as he was—forty-four. His own family had been geared for contention, not celebration. He hadn't seen them in years. Too busy, too distant, too detached. Too ashamed of them, his old man would have said...and he would have been right.

He spotted the field agent standing at the edge of the gate area. Vince Walsh. According to the file, he was fifty-two with a solid record. He would retire in June. He looked an unhealthy sixty-two. His complexion was the color of modeling clay, and gravity had pulled the flesh of his face down, leaving deep crevices in his cheeks and across his forehead. He had the look of a man with too much stress in his life and no way out but a heart attack. He had the look of a man who would rather have been doing something other than picking up some hotshot mind hunter from Quantico.

Quinn forced his energy level up along with the corners of his mouth. React accordingly: look apologetic, nonaggressive, nonthreatening; just a touch of friendliness, but not overly familiar. His shoulders were drooping naturally with fatigue; he didn't bother to square them up. "You're Walsh?"

"You're Quinn," Walsh declared flatly as Quinn started to pull his ID from the interior pocket of his suit coat. "Got luggage?"

"Just what you see." A bulging garment bag that exceeded regulation carry-on dimensions and a briefcase weighed down with a laptop computer and a ream of paperwork. Walsh made no offer to take either.

"I appreciate the ride," Quinn said as they started down the concourse. "It's the quickest way for me to get right in the game. Eliminates me driving around lost for an hour."

"Fine."

Fine. Not a great start, but there it was. He'd work the guy around as they went. The important thing here was to hit the ground running. The case was the priority. Always the case. One after another, on top of another, with another and another around the bend...The fatigue shuddered down through him, giving his stomach a kick as it went.

They walked in silence to the main terminal, took the elevator up one floor, and crossed over the street to the parking ramp where Walsh had left his Taurus parked illegally in a handicapped slot. Quinn dumped his stuff in the trunk and sat back for the ride out to the highway. Cigarette smoke had permeated the car's interior and gave the beige upholstery the same gray cast as the car's driver.

Walsh reached for a pack of Chesterfields as they hit state highway five. He hooked his lip over the cigarette and pulled it out of the pack. "You mind?"

He flicked a lighter without waiting for a reply.

Quinn cracked the window a slit. "It's your car."

"For seven more months." He lit up, sucked

in a lungful of tar and nicotine, and stifled a cough. "Christ, I can't shake this damn cold."

"Filthy weather," Quinn offered. Or lung cancer.

The sky seemed to press down over Minneapolis like an anvil. Rain and forty-three degrees. All vegetation had gone dormant or had died and would stay that way until spring—which he suspected was a depressingly long way off in this place. At least in Virginia there were signs of life by March.

"Could be worse," Walsh said. "Could be a goddamn blizzard. Had one here on Halloween a few years back. What a mess. Must have been ten feet of snow that winter and it wasn't gone till May. I hate this place."

Quinn didn't ask why he stayed. He didn't want to hear the common litany against the Bureau or the common complaints of the unhappily married man with in-laws in the vicinity, or any other reason a man like Walsh hated his life. He had his own problems—which Vince Walsh would not want to hear about either. "There's no such place as Utopia, Vince."

"Yeah, well, Scottsdale comes close enough. I never want to be cold again as long as I live. Come June, I'm out of here. Out of this place. Out of this thankless job."

He glanced at Quinn with suspicion, as if he figured him for some Bureau stoolie who would be on the phone to the special agent in charge the second he was left alone.

"The job can wear on a man," Quinn commiserated. "The politics is what gets to me," he said, picking the hot nerve with unerring accuracy. "Working in the field, you get it from both ends—the locals *and* the Bureau."

"That's a fact. I wish to hell I could have blown out of here for good yesterday. This case is gonna be nothing but one kick in the ass after another."

"Has that started already?"

"You're here, aren't you?"

Walsh picked up a file folder from the seat between them and handed it over. "The crime scene photos. Knock yourself out."

Quinn took the file without taking his dark eyes off Walsh. "You have a problem with me being here, Vince?" he asked bluntly, softening the question with an expression that was part I'm-your-buddy smile, part confusion that he didn't feel. He'd been in this situation so many times, he knew every possible reaction to his arrival on the scene: genuine welcome, hypocritical welcome, cloaked annoyance, open hostility. Walsh was a number three who would have claimed he said exactly what he thought.

"Hell no," he said at last. "If we don't nail this scumbag ASAP, we're all gonna be running around with targets on our backs. I got no problem with you having a bigger one than me."

"It's still your case. I'm here as support."

"Funny. I said the same thing to the homicide lieutenant."

Quinn said nothing, already starting to lay

out a team strategy in his mind. It looked like he might have to work around Walsh, although it seemed unlikely that the ASAC (assistant special agent in charge) here would have assigned a less than stellar agent to this case. If Peter Bondurant could make top dogs in Washington bark, the locals weren't apt to antagonize the man. According to the faxes, Walsh had a solid rep that spanned a lot of years. Maybe a few too many years, a few too many cases, a few too many political games.

Quinn already had a picture of the political situation here. The body count was three—just meeting the official standard to be considered serial murders. Ordinarily he would have been consulted by phone at this stage—if he was consulted at all. In his experience, locals usually tried to handle this kind of thing themselves until they were slightly deeper in dead bodies. And with a caseload of eighty-five, he had to prioritize worst to least. A three-murder case rarely made his travel schedule. His physical presence here seemed unnecessary—which aggravated his frustration and his exhaustion. He closed his eyes for two seconds, reining the feelings back into their corral.

"Your Mr. Bondurant has friends in very high places," he said. "What's the story with him?"

"He's your basic nine-hundred-pound gorilla. Owns a computer outfit that has a lot of defense contracts—Paragon. He's been making noises about moving it out of state, which has the governor and every other politician in the state lining up to kiss his ass. They say he's worth a billion dollars or more."

"Have you met him?"

"No. He didn't bother to go through our office to get to you. I hear he went straight to the top."

And in a matter of hours the FBI had Quinn on a plane to Minneapolis. No consideration to the normal assignment of cases by region. No consideration to the cases he had ongoing. None of the usual bureaucratic bullshit entanglements over travel authorizations.

He wondered sourly if Bondurant had asked for him by name. He'd been in the spotlight a hell of a lot in the last year. Not by his own choosing. The press liked his image. He fit their profile of what a special agent from the Investigative Support Unit should look like: athletic, square-jawed, dark, intense. He took a good picture, looked good on television, George Clooney would play him in the movies. Some days the image was useful. Some days he found it amusing. More and more it was just a pain in the ass.

"He didn't waste any time," Walsh went on. "The girl's not even cold yet. They don't even know for a fact it's his kid—what with the head gone and all. But you know, people with money don't screw around. They don't have to."

"Where are we at with the ID on the victim?"

"They've got her DL. They're going to try to get her fingerprints, but the hands were pretty badly burned, I'm told. The ME has requested

45

Jillian Bondurant's medical history regarding any distinguishing marks or broken bones to see if anything matches up. We know the body is the right size and build. We know Jillian Bondurant had dinner with her father Friday night. She left his house around midnight and hasn't been seen since."

"What about her car?"

"No one's found it yet. Autopsy's scheduled for tonight. Maybe they'll get lucky and be able to match the body's stomach contents with the meal Bondurant and her father had that night, but I doubt it. She'd have had to have been killed almost right away. That's not how this sicko operates.

"The press conference is at five—not that the press is waiting for it," he went on. "They've been all over the air with the story. They've already given this scumbag a nickname. They're calling him the Cremator. Catchy, huh?"

"I'm told they're drawing correlations to some murders from a couple of years ago. Is there any connection?"

"The Wirth Park murders. No connection, but a couple of similarities. Those victims were black women—and one Asian transvestite he got by mistake. Prostitutes or supposed prostitutes—and this guy's first two vics were prostitutes. But there's always someone killing prostitutes. They're easy targets. Those vics were mostly black and these are white. That right there points to a different killer—right?"

"Sexual serial killers generally stay within their own ethnic group, yes."

"Anyway, they got a conviction on one of those Wirth Park murders and closed the books on the others. They got their killer, there just wasn't enough physical evidence to go to trial on all the cases. Besides, how many life sentences can a guy serve?

"I talked to one of the homicide dicks this morning," Walsh said, crushing out the stub of his cigarette in the filthy ashtray. "He says there's no doubt about it, this is definitely a different scumbag. But to tell you the truth, I don't know much more about these murders than you. Until this morning all they had were two dead hookers. I read about them in the paper just like everyone else. I sure as hell know the other guy never cut anybody's head off. That's a new twist for this neck of the woods."

The dark play on words struck him belatedly, and he made a little huffing sound and shook his head at the bad joke.

Quinn looked out the window at the gray and the rain, the winter-dead trees as black and bleak as if they'd been charred, and observed a moment of sympathy for the nameless, faceless victims not important enough to warrant anything but a label. In their lives they had known joy and sorrow. On the way to their deaths they had likely known terror and pain. They had families and friends who would mourn them and miss them. But the press and society at large whittled their lives and their

47

deaths down to the lowest, lowliest common denominator: two dead hookers. Quinn had seen a hundred...and he remembered every one.

Sighing, he rubbed at the dull headache that had taken up semipermanent residence in his frontal lobes. He was too tired for the kind of diplomacy needed at the start of a case. This was the kind of tired that went to the marrow of his bones and weighed him down like lead. There had been too many bodies in the last few years. Their names scrolled through his mind at night when he tried to sleep. Counting corpses, he called it. Not the kind of thing that inspired sweet dreams.

"You want to go to your hotel first or to the office?" Walsh asked.

As if what he wanted had anything to do with it. What he wanted in life had gone out of sight for him long ago.

"I have to go to the crime scene," he said, the unopened folder of photographs as heavy as a steel plate on his lap. "I need to see where he left her."

THE PARK LOOKED like a campsite the day after a Cub Scout jamboree. The charred ground where the fire had been, the yellow tape strung from tree to tree like bunting to fence off the area; the dead grass trampled down, leaves pressed into the ground like wet paper cutouts. Crumpled paper coffee cups had blown out of the trash can that sat just off the blacktop trail on the hillside and skittered across the ground.

Walsh parked the car and they got out and stood on the blacktop, Quinn scanning the entire area from north to south. The crime scene was slightly below them in a shallow bowl of ground that had afforded excellent cover. The park was studded with trees, both deciduous and evergreen. By dead of night this would be a small world all its own. The nearest residences—neat middle-class single-family homes—were well away from the crime scene, the skyscrapers of downtown Minneapolis several miles to the north. Even the small service lot where they were parked was obscured from view by trees and what was likely a beautiful row of lilacs in the spring—camouflage to hide a small locked utility shed and the park maintenance vehicles that came and went as needed.

Their UNSUB (unknown subject) had likely parked here and carried the body down the hill for his little ceremony. Quinn looked up at the sodium vapor security light that topped a dark pole near the utility shed. The glass had been shattered, but there were no visible fragments of it on the ground.

"We know how long that light's been out?"

Walsh looked up, blinking and grimacing as the rain hit him in the face. "You'll have to ask the cops."

A couple of days, Quinn bet. Not long enough that the park service would have gotten around to fixing it. If the damage was the work of their man in preparation for his midnight call...If he had come here in advance, knocked out the light, cleaned up the glass to help avoid detection of the vandalism and thereby improve his odds that the security light would not be replaced quickly...if all of that was true, they were dealing with a strong degree of planning and premeditation. And experience. MO was learned behavior. A criminal learned by trial and error what to do and what not to do in the commission of his crimes. He improved his methods with time and repetition.

Ignoring the rain that pelted down on his bare head, Quinn hunched his shoulders inside his trench coat and started down the hill, conscious that the killer would have taken this route with a body in his arms. It was a fair distance—fifty or sixty yards. The crime scene unit would have the exact measurements. It took strength to carry a dead weight that far. The time of death would have determined how he had carried her. Over the shoulder would have been easiest—if rigor had not yet set in, or if it had come and gone already. If he had been able to carry her over his shoulder, then his size could vary more; a smaller man could accomplish the task. If he had to carry her in his arms, he would had to have been larger. Quinn hoped they would know more after the autopsy.

"What did the crime scene unit cover?" he asked, the words coming out of his mouth on a cloud of steam.

Walsh hustled along three paces behind him, coughing. "Everything. This whole section of park, including the parking area and the utility shed. The homicide guys called in their own Bureau of Investigation crime scene people and the mobile lab from the Minnesota Bureau of Criminal Apprehension as well. They were very thorough."

"When did this rain start?"

"This morning."

"Shit," Quinn grumbled. "Last night—would the ground have been hard or soft?"

"Like a rock. They didn't get any shoe prints. They picked up some garbage—scraps of paper, cigarette butts, like that. But hell, it's a public park. The stuff could have come from anyone."

"Anything distinguishing left at the first two scenes?"

"The victims' driver's licenses. Other than that, nothing to my knowledge."

"Who's doing the lab work?"

"BCA. Their facilities are excellent."

"I've heard that."

"They're aware they can contact the FBI lab if they need help or clarification on anything."

Quinn pulled up just short of the charred ground where the body had been left, a thick, dark sense of oppression closing tight around his chest as it always did at a crime scene. He had never tried to discern whether the feeling was anything as mystical or romantic as the notion of a malingering sense of evil or something as psychologically profound as displaced guilt. The feeling was just a part of him.

51

He supposed he should have welcomed it as some proof of his humanity. After all the bodies he'd seen, he had yet to become totally hardened.

Then again, he might have been better off if he had.

For the first time, he opened the folder Walsh had given him and looked at the photographs someone had had the foresight to slip into plastic protectors. The tableau presented might have made the average person recoil. Portable halogen lights had been set up near the body to illuminate both the night and the corpse, giving the photo a weirdly artistic quality. As did the charring of the flesh, and the melted fabric of the woman's clothing. Color against the absence of color; the fanciful vibrance of a triangle of undamaged red skirt against the grim reality of its wearer's violent death.

"Were the others wearing clothes?"

"I don't know."

"I'll want to see those photos too. I'll want to see everything they've got. You have my list?"

"I faxed a copy to the homicide detectives. They'll try to have it all together for the task force meeting. Hell of a sight, isn't it?" Walsh nodded to the photograph. "Enough to put a person off barbecue."

Quinn made no comment as he further studied the photo. Because of the heat of the fire, the muscles and tendons of the limbs had contracted, pulling the victim's arms and legs into what was technically known as a pugilistic attitude—a position that suggested animation. A suggestion made macabre by the absence of the head.

Surreal, he thought. His brain wanted to believe he was looking at a discarded mannequin, something that had been dragged too late out of the incinerator at Macy's. But he knew what he was looking at had been flesh and bone, not plastic, and she had been alive and walking around three days earlier. She had eaten meals, listened to music, talked with friends, attended to the boring minutae of the average life, never imagining that hers was nearly over.

The body had been positioned with the feet pointing toward downtown, which Quinn thought might have been more significant if the head had also been posed or buried nearby. One of the more infamous cases he had studied years before had included the decapitation of two victims. The killer, Ed Kemper, had buried the heads in the backyard of his family home, beneath his mother's bedroom window. A sick private joke, Kemper had later admitted. His mother, who had emotionally abused him from boyhood, had "always wanted people to look up to her," he'd said.

The head of this victim had not been found and the ground was too hard for the killer to have buried it here.

"There're a lot of theories on why he's burning them," Walsh said. He bounced a little on the balls of his feet, trying unsuccessfully to keep the cold from knifing into his bones.

53

"Some people think he's just a copycat of the Wirth Park murders. Some people think it's symbolism: Whores of the world burn in hell—that kind of thing. Some think he's trying to obscure the forensic evidence and the victim's identity at the same time."

"Why leave the DL if he doesn't want them identified?" Quinn said. "Now he takes this one's head. That makes her pretty damn hard to recognize—he didn't have to burn her up. And still he leaves the driver's license."

"So you think he's trying to get rid of trace evidence?"

"Maybe. What's he use for an accelerant?"

"Alcohol. Some kind of high-test vodka or something."

"Then the fire is more likely part of his signature than it is part of his MO," Quinn said. "He might be getting rid of trace evidence, but if that's all he wanted, why wouldn't he just use gasoline? It's cheap. It's easily had with little or no interaction with another person. He chooses alcohol for an emotional reason rather than a practical one. That makes it part of the ritual, part of the fantasy."

"Or maybe he's a big drinker."

"No. A drinker doesn't waste good booze. And that's exactly what he'd call this: a waste of good liquor. He may be drinking prior to the hunt. He may drink during the torture and murder phase. But he's no drunk. A drunk would make mistakes. Sounds like this guy hasn't made any so far."

None that anyone had noticed, at any rate.

He thought again of the two hookers whose death had preceded this woman's and wondered who had caught their cases: a good cop or a bad cop. Every department had its share of both. He'd seen cops shrug and sleepwalk through an investigation if they didn't feel the victim was worth their time. And he'd seen veteran cops break down and cry over the violent death of someone most taxpaying citizens wouldn't sit next to on the bus.

He closed the file. Rain ran down his forehead and dripped off the end of his nose.

"This isn't where he left the others, is it?"

"No. One was found in Minnehaha Park and one in Powderhorn Park. Different parts of the city."

He would need to see maps, to see where each dumping site was in relation to the others, where each abduction had taken place—to try to establish both a hunting territory and a killing and/or dumping territory. The task force would have maps in their command center, posted and flagged with little redheaded pins. Standard op. There was no need to ask. His mind was already full of maps bristling with pins. Manhunts that ran together like tag-team events, and command centers and war rooms that all looked alike and smelled alike, and cops who tended to look alike and sound alike, and smell like cigarettes and cheap cologne. He couldn't separate the cities anymore, but he could remember every single one of the victims.

The exhaustion poured through him again,

and he wanted nothing more than to lie down right there on the ground.

He glanced over at Walsh as the agent fell into another spasm of deep, phlegm-rattling coughing.

"Let's go," Quinn said. "I've seen enough here for now."

He'd seen enough, period. And yet it took him another moment to move his feet and follow Vince Walsh back to the car.

5

CHAPTER

THE TENSION in the mayor's conference room was high and electric. Grim excitement, anticipation, anxiety, latent power. There were always those who saw murder as tragedy and those who sensed career opportunity. The next hour would sort out one type from the other, and establish the power order of the personalities involved. In that time Quinn would have to read them, work them, decide how to play them, and slot them into place in his own scheme of things.

He straightened his back, squared his aching shoulders, lifted his chin, and made his entrance.

Show time. The heads turned immediately as he walked in the door. On the plane he had memorized the names of some of the principal players here, scouring the faxes that had come into the office before he'd left Virginia. He tried to recall them now, tried to sort them from the hundreds of others he'd known in hundreds of conference rooms across the country.

The mayor of Minneapolis detached herself from the crowd when she spotted him, and came toward him with purpose, trailing lesser politicians in her wake. Grace Noble resembled nothing so much as an operatic Valkyrie. She was fifty-something and large, built like a tree trunk, with a helmet of starched blond hair. She had no upper lip to speak of, but had carefully drawn herself one and filled it in with red lipstick that matched her suit.

"Special Agent Quinn," she declared, holding out a broad, wrinkled hand tipped with red nails. "I've been reading all about you. As soon as we heard from the director, I sent Cynthia to the library for every article she could find."

He flashed what had been called his *Top Gun* smile—confident, winning, charming, but with the unmistakable glint of steel beneath it. "Mayor Noble. I should tell you not to believe everything you read, but I find there is an advantage to having people think I can see into their minds."

"I'm sure you don't have to be able to read minds to know how grateful we are to have you here."

57

"I'll do what I can to help. Did you say you'd spoken with the director?"

Grace Noble patted his arm. Maternal. "No, dear. Peter spoke with him. Peter Bondurant. They're old friends, as it happens."

"Is Mr. Bondurant here?"

"No, he couldn't bring himself to face the press. Not yet. Not knowing..." Her shoulders slumped briefly beneath the weight of it all. "My God, what this will do to him if it *is* Jillie..."

A short African American man with a weightlifter build and a tailored gray suit stepped up beside her, his eyes on Quinn. "Dick Greer, chief of police," he said crisply, thrusting out his hand. "Glad to have you on board, John. We're ready to *nail* this creep."

As if he would have anything to do with it. In a metropolitan police department the chief was an administrator and a politician, a spokesman, an idea man. The men in the trenches likely said Chief Greer couldn't find his own dick in a dark room.

Quinn listened to the list of names and titles as the introductions were made. A deputy chief, a deputy mayor, an assistant county attorney, the state director of public safety, a city attorney, and a pair of press secretaries—too damn many politicians. Also present were the Hennepin County sheriff, a detective from the same office, a special agent in charge from the Minnesota Bureau of Criminal Apprehension with one of his agents,

58

the homicide lieutenant from the PD— representatives from three of the agencies that would comprise the task force.

He met each with a firm handshake and played it low key. Midwesterners tended to be reserved and didn't quite trust people who weren't. In the Northeast he would have given more of the steel. On the West Coast he would have turned up the charm, would have been Mr. Affable, Mr. Spirit of Cooperation. Different horses for different courses, his old man used to say. And which one was the real John Quinn—even he didn't know anymore.

"...and my husband, Edwyn Noble," the mayor finished the introductions.

"Here in a professional capacity, Agent Quinn," Edwyn Noble said. "Peter Bondurant is a client as well as a friend."

Quinn's attention focused sharply on the man before him. Six five or six six, Noble was all joints and sinew, an exaggerated skeleton of a man with a smile that was perfectly square and too wide for his face. He looked slightly younger than his wife. The gray in his hair was contained to flags at the temples.

"Mr. Bondurant sent his attorney?" Quinn said.

"I'm Peter's personal counsel, yes. I'm here on his behalf."

"Why is that?"

"The shock has been terrific."

"I'm sure it has been. Has Mr. Bondurant already given the police his statement?"

Noble leaned back, the question physically

putting him off. "A statement regarding what?"

Quinn shrugged, nonchalant. "The usual. When he last saw his daughter. Her frame of mind at the time. The quality of their relationship."

Color blushed the attorney's prominent cheekbones. "Are you suggesting Mr. Bondurant is a suspect in his own daughter's death?" he said in a harsh, hushed tone, his gaze slicing across the room to check for eavesdroppers.

"Not at all," Quinn said with blank innocence. "I'm sorry if you misunderstood me. We need all the pieces of the puzzle we can get in order to form a clear picture of things, that's all. You understand."

Noble looked unhappy.

In Quinn's experience, the parents of murder victims tended to camp out at the police department, demanding answers, constantly underfoot of the detectives. After the description Walsh had given of Bondurant, Quinn had expected to see the man throwing his weight around city hall like a mad bull. But Peter Bondurant had reached out and touched the director of the FBI, called out his personal attorney, and stayed home.

"Peter Bondurant is one of the finest men I know," Noble declared.

"I'm sure Agent Quinn didn't mean to imply otherwise, Edwyn," the mayor said, patting her husband's arm.

The lawyer's attention remained on Quinn.

"Peter was assured you're the best man for this job."

"I'm very good at what I do, Mr. Noble," Quinn said. "One of the reasons I'm good at my job is that I'm not afraid to *do* my job. I'm sure Mr. Bondurant will be glad to hear it."

He left it at that. He didn't want to make enemies of Bondurant's people. Offend a man like Bondurant and he'd find himself called on the carpet before the Bureau's Office of Professional Responsibility—at the very least. On the other hand, after having Peter Bondurant jerk him out here like a dog on a leash, he wanted it made clear he wouldn't be manipulated.

"We're running short on time, people. Let's take our seats and get started," the mayor announced, herding the men toward the conference table like a first-grade teacher with a pack of little boys.

She stood at the political end of the table as everyone fell into rank, and drew breath to speak just as the door opened again and four more people walked in.

"Ted, we were about to start without you." The mayor's doughy face creased with disapproval at his lack of punctuality.

"We've had some complications." He strode across the room directly toward Quinn. "Special Agent Quinn. Ted Sabin, Hennepin County attorney. I'm glad to meet you."

Quinn rose unsteadily to his feet. His gaze glanced off the man's shoulder to the woman trailing reluctantly behind him. He mum-

61

bled an adequate reply to Sabin, shaking the county attorney's hand. A mustached cop stepped up and introduced himself. Kovac. The name registered dimly. The pudgy guy with them introduced himself and said something about having once heard Quinn speak somewhere.

"...And this is Kate Conlan with our victim/witness program," Sabin said. "You may—"

"We've met," they said in unison.

Kate looked Quinn in the eye for just a moment because it seemed important to do so, to recognize him, acknowledge him, but not react. Then she glanced away, stifling the urge to sigh or swear or walk out of the room.

She couldn't say she was surprised to see him. There were only eighteen agents assigned to Investigative Support's Child Abduction/Serial Killer Unit. Quinn was the current poster boy for CASKU, and sexual homicide was his specialty. The odds had not been in her favor, and her luck today was for shit. Hell, she should have *expected* to see him standing in the mayor's conference room. But she hadn't.

"You've worked together?" Sabin said, not quite certain whether he should be pleased or disappointed.

An awkward silence hung for a second or three. Kate sank into a chair.

"Uh—yes," she said. "It's been a long time."

Quinn stared at her. No one took him by surprise. Ever. He'd spent a lifetime building that level of control. That Kate Conlan could walk in the door and tilt the earth beneath his feet after all this time did not sit well. He ducked his head and cleared his throat. "Yeah. You're missed, Kate."

By whom? she wanted to ask, but instead she said, "I doubt it. The Bureau is like the Chinese Army: The personnel could march into the sea for a year and there'd still be plenty of warm bodies to fill the posts."

Oblivious of the discomfort at the other end of the table, the mayor brought the meeting to order. The press conference was less than an hour away. The politicians needed to get their ducks in a row. Who would speak first. Who would stand where. Who would say what. The cops combed their mustaches and drummed their fingers on the table, impatient with the formalities.

"We need to make a *strong* statement," Chief Greer said, warming up his orator's voice. "Let this creep know we *won't rest* until we get him. Let him know right up front we've got the FBI's leading profiler here, we've got the combined resources of *four* agencies working on this thing day and night."

Edwyn Noble nodded. "Mr. Bondurant is establishing a reward of one hundred fifty thousand for information leading to an arrest."

Quinn pulled his attention away from Kate and rose. "Actually, Chief, I wouldn't advise any of that just yet."

Greer's face pinched. Edwyn Noble glared

at him. The collective expression from the political end of the table was a frown.

"I haven't had the opportunity to thoroughly go over the case," Quinn began, "which is reason enough to hold off. We need to get a handle on just who this killer might be, how his mind works. Making a blind show of strength at this point could be a move in the wrong direction."

"And that would be based on what?" Greer asked, his bulky shoulders tensing beneath the weight of the chip he was carrying. "You've said yourself, you haven't reviewed the case."

"We've got a killer who's putting on a show. I've seen the photos from this last crime scene. He brought the body to a public place, intending to shock. He drew attention to the scene with a fire. This probably means he wants an audience, and if that's what he wants, we have to be careful of just how we give it to him.

"My advice is to hold off today. Minimize this press conference. Assure the public you're doing everything you can to identify and arrest the killer, but don't go into details. Keep the number of people behind the podium down—Chief Greer, Mayor Noble, Mr. Sabin, that's it. Don't get into the specifics of the task force. Don't talk about Mr. Bondurant. Don't bring up the FBI. Don't mention my name at all. And don't take any questions."

Predictably, eyebrows went up all around the table. He knew from experience some of them had been expecting him to try to take the limelight: the FBI bully jumping in to grab the headlines. And undoubtedly, some of them wanted to show him off at the press conference like a trophy—*Look who we've got on our side: It's Super Agent!* No one ever expected him to downplay his role.

"At this stage of the game we don't want to set up an adversarial situation where he may see me as a direct challenge to him," he said, resting his hands at his waist, settling in for the inevitable arguments. "I'm in the background as much as I can be. I'll maintain a low profile with the media for as long as I can or until I deem it advantageous to do otherwise."

The politicians looked crestfallen. They loved nothing so much as a public forum and the undivided attention of the media and thereby the masses. Greer obviously resented having his thunder stolen. The muscles in his jaw pulsed subtly.

"The people of this city are ready to panic," the chief said. "We've got three women dead, one of them *beheaded*. The phones in my office are ringing off the hook. A *statement* needs to be made. People want to know we're going after this *animal* with everything we've got."

The mayor nodded. "I'm inclined to agree with Dick. We've got business conferences in town, tourists coming in for plays, for concerts, for holiday shopping—"

"To say nothing of the anxiety of the general population over the growing crime rate in the city," said the deputy mayor.

"It was bad enough with the two prostitute killings making the news," a press secretary added. "Now we've got the daughter of a very prominent citizen dead. People start thinking if it could happen to her, it could happen to anyone. News like this creates an environment of fear."

"Give this guy a sense of importance and power and this city may well have a reason to panic," Quinn said bluntly.

"Isn't it just as likely that minimizing the case in the media could enrage him? Drive him to commit more crimes in order to draw more attention to himself?" Greer questioned. "How do you know coming out with a strong and public offensive won't scare him and flush him out?"

"I don't. I don't know what this guy might do—and neither do you. We need to take the time to try to figure that out. He's murdered three women that you know of, getting progressively bolder and more flamboyant. He won't scare easily, I can tell you that. We may eventually be able to draw him into the investigation—he's sure as hell watching—but we need to maintain tight control and keep our options open." He turned toward Edwyn Noble. "And the reward is too large. I'd advise you to cut it back to no more than fifty thousand to start."

"With all due respect, Agent Quinn," the lawyer said tightly, "the choice is Mr. Bondurant's."

"Yes, it is, and I'm sure he feels information about his daughter's murder is worth any price. My reasoning is this, Mr. Noble: People will come forward for a lot less than one hundred fifty thousand. An amount that extraordinary is going to bring in a flood of kooks and money-grubbing opportunists willing to sell their own mothers down the river. Start with fifty. Later we may want to use raising the amount as a strategic move."

Noble breathed a measured sigh and pushed his chair back from the table. "I'll need to speak with Peter about this." He unfolded his long body and walked across the room to a side table with a telephone.

"We've got every reporter in the Twin Cities camped out on the steps of city hall," the mayor pointed out. "They're anticipating something more than a simple statement."

"That's their problem," Quinn said. "You have to think of them as tools rather than guests. They're not entitled to the details of an ongoing investigation. You called a press conference, you didn't promise them anything."

The mayor's expression suggested otherwise. Quinn tightened his grip on the fraying threads of his patience. *Play diplomat. Go easy. Don't lose your cool.* Christ, he was tired of it.

"Did you?"

Grace Noble looked to Sabin. "We had hoped to have a composite sketch..."

Sabin cut a nasty look at Kate. "Our witness is being less than cooperative."

"Our witness is a scared kid who saw a psychopath set fire to a headless corpse," Kate said sharply. "The last thing on her mind is accommodating your timetable...sir."

"She got a good look at the guy?" Quinn asked.

Kate spread her hands. "She says she saw him. She's tired, she's afraid, she's angry—and rightfully so—at the treatment she's been given. Those factors tend not to create a spirit of cooperation."

Sabin began to position himself for rebuttal. Quinn blocked the argument. "Bottom line: We have no composite."

"We have no composite," Kate said.

"Then don't bring it up," Quinn said, turning back to the mayor. "Divert their attention to something else. Give them a photograph of Jillian Bondurant and one of her car and make an appeal for people to call the hotline if they've seen either one since Friday evening. Don't talk about the witness. Your first concern here has to be with how your actions and reactions will be perceived by the killer, not how they'll be perceived by the media."

Grace Noble pulled in a deep breath. "Agent Quinn—"

"I don't normally come into a case this early on," he interrupted, the control slipping a little more. "But since I'm here, I want to do everything I can to help defuse the situation and bring a swift and satisfactory conclusion to the investigation. That means advising you all on proactive investigative strategies and how to handle the case in the press. You don't have to listen to me, but I'm drawing on a wealth of past experience. The director of the FBI personally chose me for this case. You might want to consider why before you disregard my suggestions."

Kate watched him as he took two steps back from the table and the argument, and turned his profile to her, pretending to look out the window. A subtle threat. He had established his own importance and now dared them to challenge it. He had attached the director of the FBI to his position and indirectly dared them to defy *him*.

Same old Quinn. She had known him as well as anyone could know John Quinn. He was a master manipulator. He could read people in a heartbeat and change colors like a chameleon. He played both adversaries and colleagues with the brilliance of Mozart at the keyboard, turning them to his side of an argument with charm or bullying or guile or the brute force of his intelligence. He was smart, he was sly, he was ruthless if he needed to be. And who he really was behind all the clever disguises and razor-sharp strategies—well, Kate wondered if *he* knew. She'd thought she had once upon a time.

Physically, he had changed some in five years. The thick, dark hair was salted with gray and cropped almost military short. He looked leaner, worn thin by the job. Ever the clotheshorse, he wore a suit that was Italian and expensive. But the coat hung a little loose off the broad shoulders, and the pants were a little baggy. The effect, though, created elegance rather than an eroding of his physical presence. The planes and angles of his face were sharp. There were circles under the brown eyes. Impatience vibrated in the air around him, and she wondered if it was real or manufactured for the moment.

Sabin turned toward her suddenly. "Well, Kate, what do you think?"

"Me?"

"You worked for the same unit as Special Agent Quinn. What do you think?"

She could feel Quinn's eyes on her, as well as the gazes of everyone else in the room. "No. I'm just the advocate here. I don't even know what business I have being at this meeting. John is the expert—"

"No, he's right, Kate," Quinn said. He planted his hands on the tabletop and leaned toward her, his dark eyes like coals—she thought she could feel the heat of them on her face. "You were a part of the old Behavioral Sciences Unit. You've got more experience with this kind of case than anyone else at this table besides me. What's your take?"

Kate stared at him, knowing her resentment had to be plain in her eyes. Bad enough to have Sabin put her on the spot, but for Quinn to do it struck her as a betrayal. But then, why she should have been surprised at that, she couldn't imagine.

"Regarding this case, I have no basis on which to form an educated opinion," she began woodenly. "However, I am well aware of Special Agent Quinn's qualifications and expertise. Personally, I think you would be making a mistake not to follow his advice."

Quinn looked to the mayor and the chief of police.

"You can't unring a bell," he said quietly. "Put too much information out there now, there's no taking it back. You can call another press conference tomorrow if you need to. Just give the task force this chance to muster their resources and get a running start."

Edwyn Noble returned from his phone call, his face sober. "Mr. Bondurant says he'll do whatever Agent Quinn suggests. We'll set the reward at fifty thousand."

THE MEETING ADJOURNED at four forty-eight. The politicos moved into the mayor's office for last-minute preparations before facing the press. The cops gathered in a cluster at the far end of the conference room to talk about setting up the task force.

"Sabin isn't happy with you, Kate," Rob said in a tone of confidentiality, as if anyone else in the room would be interested.

"I'd say Ted Sabin can kiss my ass, but he'd be on his knees in a heartbeat."

Rob blushed and frowned. "Kate—"

"He dragged me into this, he can live with the consequences," she said, moving toward the door. "I'm going to go check on Angie. See if she's come up with anything from the mug

71

books yet. You're going to the press conference?"

"Yes."

Good. She had a witness to spring while everyone else was looking the other way. Where to take the girl was the next problem. She belonged in a juvenile facility, but they had as yet been unable to prove she was a juvenile.

"So you worked with Quinn?" Rob said, still with the voice of secrecy, following her toward the door. "I heard him speak at a conference once. He's very impressive. I think his focus on victimology is dead on."

"That's John, all right. *Impressive* is his middle name."

Across the room, Quinn turned away from his conversation with the homicide lieutenant and locked on her, as if he'd picked up her comment on his radar. At the same instant, Rob Marshall's pager beeped and he excused himself to use the phone, looking disappointed at the lost opportunity to speak with Quinn again.

Kate wanted no such opportunity. She turned away and started again for the door as Quinn came toward her.

"Kate."

She glared at him and jerked her arm away as he moved to take hold of her.

"Thanks for your help," he said softly, ducking his head in that way he had that made him seem boyish and contrite when he was neither.

"Yeah, right. Can I have the cervical collar concession tomorrow when you march in here and tell them to challenge this son of a bitch in order to trap him?"

He blinked innocently. "I don't know what you mean, Kate. You know as well as I do how important it is to be proactive in a situation like this—when the time is right."

She wanted to ask him if he was talking about the killer or the politicians, but she stopped herself. Quinn's proactive theories extended to all aspects of his life.

"Don't play your little mind games with me, John," she whispered bitterly. "I didn't mean to help you. I didn't offer you anything. You took, and I don't appreciate it. You think you can just manipulate people like pawns on a chessboard."

"The end justified the means."

"It always does, doesn't it?"

"You know I was right."

"Funny, but that doesn't make you seem any less of a jerk to me." She took a step back toward the door. "Excuse me. I've got a job to do. You want to make power plays, you leave me out of the game plan, thank you very much."

"Good to see you too, Kate," he murmured as she walked away, thick red-gold hair swinging softly across her back.

It struck Quinn only belatedly that she had a nasty bruise on her cheek and a split lip. He'd seen her as he remembered her: as an ex-friend's wife...as the only woman he'd ever truly loved.

6

CHAPTER

THE CROWD is large. The Twin Cities are overrun with reporters. Two major daily newspapers, half a dozen television stations, radio stations too numerous to keep track of. And the story has brought in still more reporters from other places.

He has captured their attention. He relishes the sense of power that brings. The *sounds* in particular excite him—the urgent voices, the angry voices, the scuffle of feet, the whirl of camera motor drives.

He wishes he hadn't waited so long to go public. His first murders were private, hidden, far between in both time and space, the bodies left buried in shallow graves. This is so much better.

The reporters jockey for position. Videographers and photographers set the perimeter of the gathering. Blinding artificial lights give the setting an otherworldly white glow. He stands just outside the media pack with the other spectators, caught on the fringe of a headline.

The mayor takes the podium. The spokeswoman for the community expressing the collective moral outrage against senseless acts of violence. The county attorney parrots the mayor's remarks and promises punishment. The chief of police makes a statement regarding the formation of a task force.

They take no questions, even though the reporters are clamoring for confirmation of the victim's identity and for the gruesome details of the crime, like scavengers drooling for the chance to pick the carcass after the predator's feast. They bark out questions, shout the word *decapitation*. There are rumors of a witness.

The idea of someone watching the intimacy of his acts excites him. He believes any witness to his acts would be aroused by those acts, as he was. Aroused in a way just beyond understanding, as he had been as a child locked in the closet, listening to his mother having sex with men he didn't know. Arousal instinctively known as forbidden, irrepressible just the same.

Questions and more questions from the media.

No answers. No comment.

He sees John Quinn standing off to one side among a group of cops, and feels a rush of pride. He is familiar with Quinn's reputation, his theories. He has seen him on television, read articles about him. The FBI has sent their best for the Cremator.

He wants the agent to take the podium, wants to hear his voice and his thoughts, but Quinn doesn't move. The reporters seem not to recognize him standing out of reach of the spotlight. Then the principals walk away from the podium, surrounded by uniformed police officers. The press conference is over.

Disappointment weighs down on him. He had expected more, wanted more. Needs more. He had predicted *they* would need more.

With a jolt he realizes he has been waiting to react, that for a moment he allowed his feelings to hinge on the decisions of others. Unacceptable behavior. He is *pro*active, not *re*active.

The reporters give up and hurry for the doors. Stories to write, sources to pump. The small crowd in which he stands begins to break up and move. He moves with them, just another face.

"LET'S GO, KIDDO. We're out of here."

Angie looked up from the mug books on the table, wary, her stringy hair hiding half her face. Her gaze darted from Kate to Liska as she rose from her chair, as if she were expecting the detective to pull a gun and prevent her escape. Liska's attention was on Kate.

"You got the okay to go? Where's Kovac?"

Kate looked her in the eye. "Yeah...uh, Kovac's tied up with the lieutenant at the press conference. They're talking task force."

"I want in on that," Liska said with determination.

"You should. A case like this makes careers." And breaks them, Kate thought, wondering just how much trouble she was making for herself springing Angie DiMarco—and how much trouble she would be making for Liska.

The end justifies the means. She thought of Quinn. At least her goal was noble rather than self-serving manipulation.

Rationalization: the key to a clear conscience.

"Are the cameras rolling?" Liska asked.

"Even as we speak." Kate watched out of the corner of her eye as her client palmed a Bic lighter someone had left on the table and slipped it into her coat pocket. Christ. A kid *and* a kleptomaniac. "Seems like a good time to split."

"Run for it while you can," Liska advised. "You're a double bonus today. I hear your name attached to a certain act of heroic lunacy at the government center this morning. If the newsies don't nail you for one thing, they'll nail you for another."

"My life is much too exciting."

"Where are you taking me?" Angie demanded as she came to the door, slinging her backpack over one shoulder.

"Dinner. I'm starving, and you look like you've been starving for a while."

"But your boss said—"

"Screw him. I want to see somebody lock Ted Sabin in a room for a day or two. Maybe he'd develop a little empathy. Let's go."

Angie shot one last glance at Liska and scooted out the door, hiking her backpack up as she hurried after Kate.

"Will you get in trouble?"

"Do you care?"

"It's not my problem if you get fired."

"That's the spirit. Listen, we've got to go up to my office. If anyone stops me on the way, do us both a favor and pretend we're not together. I don't want the media putting two and two together, and you don't want them knowing who you are. Trust me on that one."

Angie gave her a sly look. "Could I get on *Hard Copy*? I hear they pay."

"You fuck this up for Sabin and he'll get you on *America's Most Wanted*. That is if our friendly neighborhood serial killer doesn't put you on *Unsolved Mysteries* first. If you don't hear anything else I tell you, kiddo, hear this. You do *not* want to be on television, you do *not* want your picture in a newspaper."

"Are you trying to scare me?"

"I'm just telling you how it is," she said as they entered the concourse to the government center.

Kate put on her don't-fuck-with-me face and walked as quickly as she could, considering the aches and stiffness from her morning wrestling match were beginning to sink in deep. Time was a-wasting. If the politicians took John's advice and somehow managed to contain themselves, the press conference would break up fast. Some of the reporters would dog Chief Greer, but most would split between the mayor and Ted Sabin, liking their odds better with elected officials than with a cop. Any minute now the concourse could be swarming with them.

If they followed Sabin into the concourse

and caught sight of her, if someone called her name or pointed her out within earshot of the ravenous pack, she was bound to get cornered about the government center gunman. Eventually someone might make the mental leap and connect her to rumors of a witness in the latest homicide, and then the last few hours would truly deserve listing in the annals of all-time shitty days. Somewhere on the lower third of the list, she figured, leaving plenty of room above for the string of rotten days to come.

But luck was with her for once today. Only three people tried to intercept her on their way to the twenty-second floor. All making clever comments on Kate's morning heroics. She brushed them off with a wry look and a smart remark, and never broke stride.

"What's that about?" Angie asked as they got off the elevator, her curiosity overcoming her show of indifference.

"Nothing."

"He called you the Terminator. What'd you do? Kill somebody?" The question came with a look that mixed disbelief with wariness with a small, grudging flicker of admiration.

"Nothing that dramatic. Not that I haven't been tempted today." Kate keyed the access code into the security panel beside the door to the legal services department. She unlocked the door to her own office and motioned Angie inside.

"You know, you don't *have* to take me anywhere," the girl said, flopping into the spare chair. "I can take care of myself. It's a free country and I'm not a criminal...or a kid," she added belatedly.

"Let's not even touch on that subject for the moment," Kate suggested, glancing through her unopened mail. "You know what the situation is here, Angie. You need a safe place to stay."

"I can stay with my friend Michele—"

"I thought her name was Molly."

Angie pressed her mouth into a line and narrowed her eyes.

"Don't even try to bullshit me," Kate advised—for all the good it would do. "There is no friend, and you don't have a place to crash in the Phillips neighborhood. That was a nice touch, though, picking a rotten neighborhood. Who would claim they lived there if they didn't?"

"Are you calling me a liar?"

"I think you've got your own agenda," Kate said calmly, her attention on a memo that read: *Talked w/Sabin. Wit to Phoenix House— RM.* Permission. Odd Rob hadn't mentioned this in the mayor's office. The note was in a receptionist's hand. No time notation. The decision had probably come just before the press conference. All that subterfuge on her part for nothing. Oh, well.

"An agenda that probably centers on staying out of jail or a juvenile facility," she went on.

"I'm not a—"

"Save it."

She hit the message button on her phone and listened to the voices of the impatient and the forlorn who had tried to reach her during the afternoon. Reporters hot on the trail of the government center shootout heroine. She hit fast forward through each of them. Mixed in with the news hounds was the usual assortment. David Willis, her current pain-in-the-butt client. A coordinator of a victims' rights group. The husband of a woman who had allegedly been assaulted, though Kate had the gut feeling it was a scam, that the couple was looking to score reparation money. The husband had a string of petty drug arrests on his record.

"Kate." The gruff male voice coming from the machine made her flinch. "It's Quinn—um—John. I, ah, I'm staying at the Radisson."

As if he expected her to call. Just like that.

"Who's that?" Angie asked. "Boyfriend?"

"No, um, no," Kate said, scrambling to pull her composure together. "Let's get out of here. I'm starving."

She drew in a long breath and released it as she pushed to her feet, feeling caught off guard, something she had always worked studiously to avoid. Another offense to add to the list against Quinn. She couldn't let him get to her. He'd be here and gone. A couple of days at most, she figured. The Bureau had sent him because Peter Bondurant had friends in high places. It was a show of good faith or ass kissing, depending on your point of view.

He didn't need to be here. He wouldn't be

here long. She didn't have to have any contact with him while he was here. She wasn't with the Bureau anymore. She wasn't a part of this task force. He had no power over her.

God, Kate, you sound like you're afraid of him, she thought with disgust as she turned her Toyota 4Runner out of the parking ramp onto Fourth Avenue. Quinn was past history and she was a grown-up, not some adolescent girl who'd broken up with the class cool guy and couldn't bear to face him in homeroom.

"Where are we going?" Angie asked, dialing the radio to an alternative rock station. Alanis Morissette whining at an ex-boyfriend with bongos in the background.

"Uptown. What do you want to eat? You look like you could use some fat and cholesterol. Ribs? Pizza? Burgers? Pasta?"

The girl made the snotty shrug that had driven parents of teenagers from the time of Adam to consider the pros and cons of killing their young. "Whatever. Just as long as there's a bar. I need a drink."

"Don't push it, kid."

"What? I have a valid driver's license." She flopped back against the seat and put her feet up against the dash. "Can I bum a smoke?"

"I don't have any. I quit."

"Since when?"

"Since 1981. I fall off the wagon every once in a while. Get your feet off my dashboard."

The big sigh as she rearranged herself sideways in the bucket seat. "Why are you taking me to dinner? You don't like me. Wouldn't you rather go home to your husband?"

"I'm divorced."

"From the guy on the answering machine? Quinn?"

"No. Not that it's any of your business."

"Got kids?"

A beat of silence before answering. Kate wondered if she would ever get over that hesitation or the guilt that inspired it. "I have a cat."

"So do you live in Uptown?"

Kate cut her a sideways look, taking her eyes briefly off the heavy rush hour traffic. "Let's talk about you. Who's Rick?"

"Who?"

"Rick—the name on your jacket."

"It came that way."

Translation: name of the guy she stole it from. "How long have you been in Minneapolis?"

"A while."

"How old were you when your folks died?"

"Thirteen."

"So you've been on your own how long?"

The girl glared at her for a beat. "Eight years. That was lame."

Kate shrugged. "Worth a shot. So what happened to them? Accident?"

"Yeah," Angie said softly, staring straight ahead. "An accident."

There was a story in there somewhere, Kate thought as she negotiated the twisted transition from 94 to get to Hennepin Avenue. She could probably guess at some of the key plot ingredients—alcohol, abuse, a cycle of unhappy

83

circumstances, and dysfunction. Virtually every kid on the street had lived a variation of that story. So had every man in prison. Family was a fertile breeding ground for the kind of psychological bacteria that warped minds and devoured hope. Conversely, she knew plenty of people in law enforcement and social work who came from that same set of circumstances, people who had come to that same fork in the road and turned one way instead of the other.

She thought again of Quinn, even though she didn't want to.

The rain had thickened to a misty, miserable fog. The sidewalks were deserted. Uptown, contrary to its name, was some distance south of downtown Minneapolis. A gentrified area of shops, restaurants, coffee bars, art house movie theaters, it centered on the intersection of Lake Street and Hennepin. Just a stone's throw—and a world—west of the tough Whittier neighborhood, which in recent years had become the territory of black gangs, driveby shootings, and drug raids.

Uptown was edged to the west by Lake Calhoun and Lake of the Isles, and was currently inhabited by yuppies and the terribly hip. The house Kate had grown up in and now owned was just two blocks off Lake Calhoun, her parents having purchased the solid prairie-style home decades before the area became trendy.

Kate chose La Loon as their destination, a pub away from the lively Calhoun Square area, parking in the nearly empty side lot.

She wasn't in the mood for noise or a crowd, and knew both could be used as a shield by her dinner companion. Just being a teenager was enough of a barrier to overcome.

Inside, La Loon was dark and warm, all wood and brass with a long, old-fashioned bar and few patrons. Kate shunned a booth in favor of a corner table, where she took the corner chair, which gave her a view of the entire dining room. The paranoid seat. A habit Angie DiMarco had already picked up for herself. She didn't sit across from Kate with her back to the room; she took a side seat with her back to a wall so she could see anyone approaching the table.

The waitress brought menus and took drink orders. Kate longed for a stout glass of gin, but settled for chardonnay. Angie ordered rum and Coke.

The waitress looked at Kate, who shrugged. "She's got ID."

A look of sly triumph stole across Angie's face as the waitress walked away. "I thought you didn't want me to drink."

"Oh, what the hell," Kate said, digging a bottle of Tylenol out of her purse. "It's not like it's going to corrupt you."

The girl had clearly expected a confrontation. She sat back, a little bemused, slightly disappointed. "You're not like any social worker I ever knew."

"How many have you known?"

"A few. They were either bitches or so goody-goody, I wanted to puke."

"Yeah, well, plenty of people will tell you I qualify on one count."

"But you're different. I don't know," she said, struggling for the definition she wanted. "It's like you've been around or something."

"Let's just say I didn't come into this job via the usual route."

"What's that mean?"

"It means I don't sweat the small stuff and I don't take any shit."

"If you don't take any shit, then who beat you up?"

"Above and beyond the call of duty." Kate tossed the Tylenol back and washed it down with water. "You should see the other guy. So, any familiar faces in those mug books today?"

Angie's mood shifted with the subject, her pouty mouth turning down at the corners, her gaze dropping to the tabletop. "No. I would have said."

"Would you?" Kate muttered, earning a sullen glance. "They'll want you to work with the sketch artist in the morning. How do you think that'll go? Did you see him well enough to describe him?"

"I saw him in the fire," Angie murmured.

"How far away were you?"

Angie traced a gouge mark in the tabletop with one bitten fingernail. "I don't know. Not far. I was cutting through the park and I had to pee, so I ducked behind some bushes. And then he came down the hill...and he was carrying that—"

Her face tightened and she bit her lip,

hanging her head lower, obviously in the hope that her hair would hide the emotion that had rushed to the surface. Kate waited patiently, keenly aware of the girl's rising tension. Even to a streetwise kid like Angie, seeing what she had seen had to be an unimaginable shock. The stress of that and the stress of what she had been through at the police station, compounded by exhaustion, would all have to eventually take a toll.

And I want to be there when the poor kid breaks down, she thought, never pleased with that aspect of her job. The system was supposed to champion the victim, but it often victimized them again in the process. And the advocate was caught in the middle—an employee of the system, there supposedly to protect the citizen who was being dragged into the teeth of the justice machine.

The waitress returned with their drinks. Kate ordered cheeseburgers and fries for both of them and handed the menus back.

"I—I didn't know what he was carrying," Angie whispered when the waitress was out of earshot. "I just knew someone was coming and I needed to hide."

Like an animal that knew too well the night was stalked by predators of one kind or another.

"A park's a scary place late at night, I suppose," Kate said softly, turning her wineglass by the stem. "Everybody loves to go in daylight. We think it's so pretty, so nice to get away from the city. Then night comes, and suddenly it's like the evil forest out of *The Wizard of Oz*. Nobody wants to be there in the dead of night. So what were you doing there, Angie?"

"I told you, I was just cutting through."

"Cutting from where to where at that hour?" She kept her tone casual.

Angie hunkered over her rum and Coke and took a long pull on the straw. Tense. Forcing the anger back up to replace the fear.

"Angie, I've been around. I've seen things even you wouldn't believe," Kate said. "Nothing you tell me could shock me."

The girl gave a humorless half-laugh and looked toward the television that hung above one end of the bar. Local news anchor Paul Magers was looking grave and handsome as he related the story of a madman run amok in the county government center. They flashed a mug shot and told about the recent breakup of the man's marriage, his wife having taken their children and gone into hiding in a shelter a week before.

Precipitating stressors, Kate thought, not surprised.

"Nobody cares if you were breaking the law, Angie. Murder overrules everything—burglary, prostitution, poaching squirrels—which I personally consider a service to the community," she said. "I had a squirrel in my attic last month. Vermin menace. They're nothing but rats with furry tails."

No reaction. No smile. No overblown teenage outrage at her callous disregard for animal life.

"I'm not trying to lean on you here, Angie. I'm telling you as your advocate: The sooner you come clean about everything that went down last night, the better for all concerned— yourself included. The county attorney has his shorts in a knot over this case. He tried to tell Sergeant Kovac he should treat you as a suspect."

Alarm rounded the girl's eyes. "Fuck him! I didn't do anything!"

"Kovac believes you, which is why you're not sitting in a cell right now. That and the fact that I wouldn't allow it. But this is serious shit, Angie. This killer is public enemy number one, and you're the only person who's seen him and lived to tell the tale. You're in the hot seat."

Elbows on the table, the girl dropped her face into her hands and mumbled between her fingers, "God, this sucks!"

"You've got that right, sweetie," Kate said softly. "But here's the deal, plain and simple. This nut job is going to go on killing until somebody stops him. Maybe you can help stop him."

She waited. Held her breath. Willed the poor kid over the edge. She could see through the bars of Angie's fingers: the girl's face going red with the pressure of holding the emotions in. She could see the tension in the thin shoulders, feel the anticipation that thickened the air around her.

But nothing in this situation was going to be plain or simple, Kate thought as her pager began to shrill inside her purse. The moment, the opportunity, was gone. She swore silently as she dug through the bag, cursing the inconvenience of modern conveniences.

"Think about it, Angie," she said as she rose from her chair. "You're *it,* and I'm here to help you."

That makes me IT by association, she thought as she headed to the pay phone in the alcove by the bathrooms.

No. Nothing about this would be plain or simple.

7

CHAPTER

"**WHAT THE HELL** did you do with my witness, Red?" Kovac leaned against the wall of the autopsy suite, the receiver of the phone jammed between his shoulder and his ear. He slipped a hand inside the surgical gown he wore over his clothes, pulled a little jar of Mentholatum from his jacket pocket, and smeared a gob around each nostril.

"I thought it'd be nice to treat her like a human being and feed her a real meal as opposed to the crap you give people at the cop shop," Kate said.

"You don't like doughnuts? What kind of American are you?"

"The kind who has at least a partial grasp of the concept of civil liberties."

"Yeah, fine, all right, I get it." He plugged his free ear with a finger as the blade of a bone saw whined against a whetstone in the background. "Sabin asks, I'm gonna tell him you nabbed her before I could throw her in the slammer—which is true. Better your lovely tit in a wringer than my johnson."

"Don't worry about Sabin. I've got his okay on a memo."

"Do you have a picture of him signing it? Is it notarized?"

"God, you're a raving paranoid."

"How do you think I've lived this long on the job?"

"It wasn't from kissing ass and following orders. That's for damn sure."

He had to laugh. Kate called a spade a spade. And she was right. He handled his cases as he thought best, not with an eye to publicity or promotion. "So where are you taking the angel after this grand feast?"

"The Phoenix House, I'm told. She belongs in a juvie facility, but there you go. I've got to put her somewhere, and her ID says she's an adult. Did you get a Polaroid of her?"

"Yeah. I'll show it around juvenile division. See if anyone knows her. I'll give a copy to Vice too."

"I'll do the same on my end of things if you get me a copy."

"Will do. Keep me posted. I want a short leash on that chick." He raised his voice briefly as water pounded into a stainless steel sink. "I gotta go. Dr. Death is about to crack open our crispy critter."

"Jesus, Sam, you're so sensitive."

"Hey, I gotta cope. You know what I'm saying."

"Yeah, I know. Just don't let the wrong people hear you doing it. Is the task force set up?"

"Yeah. As soon as we get the brass out of our hair, we'll be good to go." He looked across the room to where Quinn stood in discussion with the ME and Hamill, the agent from the BCA, all of them in surgical gowns and booties. "So what's the story with you and the Quantico hotshot?"

There was the briefest of hesitations on the other end of the line. "What do you mean?"

"What do you mean, what do I mean? What's the deal? What's the story? What's the history?"

Another pause, just a heartbeat. "I knew him, that's all. I was working on the research side in Behavioral Sciences. The people in BSU and Investigative Support regularly cross paths. And he used to be a friend of Steven's—my ex."

This tossed in at the end, as if he might believe it was an afterthought. Kovac filed it all away for future rumination. *Used to be* a friend of Steven's. There was more to that story, he thought as Liska came toward him from the crowd around the corpse, looking impatient and nauseated. He gave Kate his pager number and instructions to call, and hung up.

"They're ready to rock and roll," Liska said, pulling a travel-size jar of Vicks VapoRub from the pocket of her boxy blazer. She stuck her nose over the rim and breathed deep.

"God, the smell!" she whispered as she turned and fell in step with him, heading back toward the table. "I've had floaters. I've had drunks in Dumpsters. I once had a guy left in the trunk of a Chrysler over the Fourth of July weekend. I never smelled anything like this."

The stench was an entity, a presence. It was an invisible fist that forced its way into the mouths of all present, rolled over their tongues, and jammed at the backs of their throats. The room was cold, but not even the constant blast of clean, frigid air from the ventilation system or the cloying perfume of chemical air fresheners could kill the smell of roasted human flesh and organs.

"Nothing like posting Toasties," Kovac said.

Liska pointed a finger at him and narrowed her eyes. "No internal-organ jokes or I puke on your shoes."

"Wimp."

"And I'll kick your ass later for calling me that."

There were three tables in the room, the ones at either end occupied. They walked past one as an assistant eased a plastic bag full of organs back into the body cavity of a man with thick yellow toenails. A scale hung over each table, like the kind for weighing grapes and sweet peppers in the supermarket. These were for weighing hearts and brains.

"Did you want me to start the party without you?" the ME queried with an arch of her brow.

Maggie Stone was generally considered by her staff to have a few nuts rattling loose in the mental machine. She suspected everyone of everything, rode a Harley Hog in good weather, and had been known to carry weapons. But when it came to the job, she was the best.

People who had known her in her tamer years claimed her hair was naturally mouse brown. Sam had never been good at remembering such details for long, which was one of many reasons he had two ex-wives. He did notice Dr. Stone, on the far side of forty, had recently gone from flame-red to platinum. Her hair was chopped short and she wore it in a style that looked as if she'd just rolled out of bed and gotten a bad scare.

She stared at him as she adjusted the tiny clip-on microphone at the neck of her scrub suit. Her eyes were a spooky translucent green.

"Get this bastard," she ordered, pointing a scalpel at him, the implication in her tone being that if he didn't, she would. She then turned her attention to the charred body that lay on the stainless steel table, curled up like a praying mantis. A deep calm settled over her.

"Okay, Lars, let's see if we can't straighten her out a bit."

Moving to one end of the table, she took hold of the corpse firmly but gently while her assistant, a hulking Swede, took hold of the ankles and they began to pull slowly. The resulting sound was like snapping fried chicken wings.

Liska turned away with a hand over her mouth. Kovac stood his ground. On the other side of the table, Quinn's expression was granite, his eyes on the body that had yet to give up its secrets. Hamill, one of two agents from the BCA assigned to the task force, cast his gaze up at the ceiling. He was a small, tidy man with a runner's wire-thin body and a hairline that was rapidly falling back from a towering forehead.

Stone stood back from the table and picked up a chart.

"Dr. Maggie Stone," she said quietly for the benefit of the tape, though she appeared to be addressing the deceased. "Case number 11-7820, Jane Doe. Caucasian female. The head has been severed from her body and is currently missing. The body measures 55 inches in length and weighs 122 pounds."

The measurement and weight had been obtained earlier. A thorough set of X rays and photographs had been taken, and Stone had gone over the body carefully with a laser to illuminate and collect trace evidence. She now went over every inch of the body visually, describing in detail everything she saw, every wound, every mark.

The burned clothing remained on the corpse. Melted to the body by the heat of the fire. A cautionary tale against wearing synthetic fabrics.

Stone made note of the "severe trauma" to the victim's neck, speculating the damage had been done by a blade with a serrated edge.

"Postmortem?" Quinn asked.

Stone stared at the gaping wound as if she were trying to see down into the dead woman's heart. "Yes," she said at last.

Lower down on the throat were several telltale ligature marks—not a single red furrow, but stripes that indicated the cord had been loosened and tightened over the course of the victim's ordeal. This was likely the manner of death—asphyxiation due to ligature strangulation—though it would be difficult to prove because of the decapitation. The most consistent indicator of a strangulation death was a crushed hyoid bone at the base of the tongue in the upper part of the trachea—above the point of decapitation. Nor was there any opportunity to check the eyes for petechial hemorrhaging, another sure sign of strangulation.

"He played with the others this way?" Quinn asked, referring to the multiple ligature marks on the throat.

Stone nodded and moved down the body.

"Is this roughly the same amount of fire damage as the other bodies?"

"Yes."

"And the others were clothed."

"Yes. After he killed them, we believe. There were wounds on the bodies with no corresponding damage to the clothing—what clothing wasn't destroyed by the fire."

"And not in their own clothes," Kovac said. "Stuff the killer picked out for them. Always synthetic fabrics. Fire melts the fabric. Screws trace evidence on the body."

Undoubtedly it meant more to the mind hunter, he thought with a twinge of impatience. As valuable as he knew profiles of murderers could be, the flatfoot cop in him held the reservation that the brainiacs sometimes gave these monsters a little too much credit. Sometimes killers did things just for the hell of it. Sometimes they did things out of curiosity or pure evil or because they knew it would jam up the investigation.

"We gonna get any fingerprints?" he asked.

"Nope," Stone said as she examined the back of the left hand. The top layer of skin had turned a dirty ivory color and was sloughing off. The underlayer was red. Knuckle bones gleamed white where the skin had seared away entirely.

"Not good ones anyway," she said. "My guess is he positioned the body with the hands crossed over the chest or stomach. The fire instantly melted the blouse and the resulting goo melted into the fingertips before the tendons in the arms began to constrict and pull the hands away from the body."

"Is there any chance of separating the fabric residue from the fingertips?" Quinn asked. "The fabric itself might bear an impression of the friction ridges."

"We don't have the capability here," she said. "Your people back in Washington might be game to try. We can detach the hands, bag them, and send them in."

"I'll have Walsh call ahead."

Coughing like he had tuberculosis, Walsh had begged off from the autopsy. There was no need for the whole task force to attend. They would all be briefed in the morning and would all have access to the reports and photographs.

Stone moved methodically down the length of the body. The victim's legs were bare, the skin seared and blistered in an irregular pattern where the accelerant had burned away in a flash.

"Ligature marks at the right and left ankles," she said, her small, gloved hands moving tenderly, almost lovingly, over the tops of the victim's feet—as much emotion as she would show during the process.

Kovac took in the appearance of the wounds the bindings had made around the victim's ankles, trying hard not to picture this woman tied to a bed in some maniac's chamber of horrors, struggling so frantically to get free that the ligatures had cut grooves into her flesh.

"The fibers have already gone to the BCA lab," Stone said. "They seemed consistent with the others—a white polypropylene twine," she specified for the benefit of Quinn and Hamill. "Tough as hell. You can buy it in any office supply store. The county buys enough every month to wrap around the moon. It's impossible to trace.

"Deep lacerations in a double-X pattern to the bottoms of both feet." She went on with the exam. She measured and catalogued each cut, then described what appeared to be cigarette burns to the pad of each toe.

"Torture or disfigurement to conceal her identity?" Hamill wondered aloud.

"Or both," Liska said.

"Looks like all of this was done while she was alive," Stone said.

"Sick bastard," Kovac muttered.

"If she got free, she couldn't have run," Quinn said. "There was a case in Canada a few years ago where the victim's Achilles tendons were severed for the same reason. Did the other victims have similar wounds?"

"They had each been tortured in a variety of ways," Stone answered. "Neither exactly the same. I can get you copies of the reports."

"That's already being taken care of, thank you."

There was no hope of removing the victim's clothing without taking skin with it. Stone and her assistant snipped and peeled, coaxing the melted fibers gently away with forceps, Stone swearing under her breath every few minutes.

Anticipation tightened in Kovac's gut as the destroyed blouse and a layer of flesh were worked away from the left side of the chest.

Stone looked across the body at him. "Here it is."

"What?" Quinn asked, moving to the head of the table.

Kovac stepped in close and surveyed the killer's handiwork. "The detail we've managed to keep away from the stinking reporters. This pattern of stab wounds—see?"

A tight cluster of eight marks, half an inch to an inch in length, perforated the dead woman's chest roughly in the vicinity of the heart.

"The first two had this," Kovac said, glancing at Quinn. "They were each strangled and the stabbing was done after the fact."

"In that exact pattern?"

"Yep. Like a star. See?" Holding his hand three inches above the corpse, he traced the pattern in the air with his index finger. "The longer marks form one X. The shorter marks form another. Smokey Joe strikes again."

"Other similarities too," Stone said. "See here: amputation of the nipples and areola."

"Postmortem?" Quinn asked.

"No."

Stone looked to her assistant. "Lars, let's turn her over. See what we find on the other side."

The body had been positioned on its back before being set ablaze. Consequently, the fire damage was contained to the front side. Stone removed the undamaged pieces of clothing and bagged them for the lab. A piece of red spandex skirt. A scrap of chartreuse blouse. No underwear.

"Uh-huh," Stone murmured to herself,

then glanced up at Kovac. "A section of flesh missing from the right buttock."

"He did this with the others too?" Quinn asked.

"Yes. With the first victim he took a chunk from the right breast. With the second, it was also the right buttock."

"Eliminating a bite mark?" Hamill speculated aloud.

"Could be," Quinn said. "Biting certainly isn't unusual with this kind of killer. Any indication of bruising in the tissue? When these guys sink their teeth in, it isn't any love nip."

Stone took up her little ruler to measure the wounds precisely. "If there was any bruising, he's cut it out. There's considerable muscle gone."

"Jesus," Kovac muttered with disgust as he stared at the shiny dark red square on the victim's body, the flesh cut out precisely with a small sharp knife. "Who does this guy think he is? Hannibal Fucking Lecter?"

Quinn gave him a look from the headless end of the body. "Everybody's got a hero."

CASE NUMBER 11-7820, Jane Doe, Caucasian female, had no organic reason to die. She had been healthy in all respects. Well fed, carrying the extra ten or fifteen pounds most people did. Although what her last meal had been, Dr. Stone had not been able to determine. If this was Jillian, she had digested the dinner she'd eaten with her father before her death. Her body was free of disease and natural defect. Stone had judged her to be between the ages of twenty and twenty-five. A young woman with most of her life ahead of her—until she crossed the path of the wrong man.

This type of killer rarely chose a victim who was ready to die.

Quinn reviewed this fact as he stood on the wet tarmac of the morgue's delivery bay. The damp cold of the night seeped into his clothes, into his muscles. Fog hung like a fine white shroud over the city.

There were too damn many victims who were young women: pretty young women, ordinary young women, women with everything going for them, and women with nothing in their lives but a sliver of hope for something better. All of them broken and wasted like dolls, abused and thrown away as if their lives had meant nothing at all.

"Hope you're not attached to that suit," Kovac said as he walked up, fishing a cigarette out of a pack of Salem Menthols.

Quinn looked down at himself, knowing the stench of violent death had permeated every fiber of his clothing. "Professional hazard. I didn't have time to change."

"Me neither. Used to drive my wives crazy."

"Wives—plural?"

"Consecutive, not concurrent. Two. You know how it is—the job and all....Anyway, my second wife used to call them corpse clothes—

whatever I had to wear to a really putrid death scene or an autopsy or something. She made me undress in the garage, and then you'd think she'd maybe burn the clothes or stick 'em in the trash or something, 'cause she sure as hell wouldn't let me wear them again. But no. She'd box the stuff up and take it to the Goodwill—on account of it still had wear in it, she'd say." He shook his head in amazement. "Underprivileged people all over Minneapolis were walking around smelling like dead bodies, thanks to her. You married?"

Quinn shook his head.

"Divorced?"

"Once. A long time ago."

So long ago, the brief attempt at marriage seemed more like a half-remembered bad dream than a memory. Bringing it up was like kicking a pile of ashes, stirring old flecks of emotional debris inside him—feelings of frustration and failure and regret that had long since gone cold. Feelings that came stronger when he thought of Kate.

"Everybody's got one," Kovac said. "It's the job."

He held the cigarettes out, Quinn declined.

"God, I gotta get that smell out of my mouth." Kovac filled his lungs and absorbed the maximum amount of tar and nicotine before exhaling, letting the smoke roll over his tongue. It drifted away to blend into the fog. "So, you think that's Jillian Bondurant in there?"

"Could be, but I think there's a chance it's

not. The UNSUB went to a hell of a lot of trouble to make sure we couldn't get prints."

"But he leaves Bondurant's DL at the scene. So maybe he nabbed Bondurant, then figured out who she was and decided to hang on to her, hold her for ransom," Kovac speculated. "Meanwhile, he picks up another woman and offs her, leaves Bondurant's DL with the body to show what might happen if Daddy doesn't cough up."

Kovac narrowed his eyes as if he were playing the theory through again for review. "No ransom demand we know of, and she's been missing since Friday. Still, maybe...But you don't think so."

"I've never seen it happen that way, that's all," Quinn said. "As a rule, with this type of murder you get a killer with one thing on his mind: playing out his fantasy. It's got nothing to do with money—usually."

Quinn turned a little more toward Kovac, knowing this was the member of the task force he most needed to win over. Kovac was the investigative lead. His knowledge of these cases, of this town, and of the kind of criminals who lived in its underbelly would be invaluable. Trouble was, Quinn didn't think he had the energy left to pull out the old I'm-just-a-cop-like-you routine. He settled for some truth, instead.

"The thing about profiling is that it's a proactive tool based on the reactive use of knowledge gained from past events. Not a perfect science. Every case could potentially present something we've never seen before."

"I hear you're pretty good though," the detective conceded. "You nailed that child-killer out in Colorado right down to his stutter."

Quinn shrugged. "Sometimes all the pieces fit. How long before you can get your hands on Bondurant's medical records for comparison with the body?"

Kovac rolled his eyes. "I oughta change my name to Murphy. Murphy's Law: Nothing's ever easy. Turns out, most of her medical records are in *France*," he said as if France were an obscure planet in another galaxy. "Her mom divorced Peter Bondurant eleven years ago and married a guy with an international construction firm. They lived in France. The mother's dead, stepfather still lives there. Jillian came back here a couple of years ago. She was enrolled at the U—University of Minnesota."

"The Bureau can help get the records via our legal attaché offices in Paris."

"I know. Walsh is already on it. Meantime, we'll try to talk to anyone who was close to Jillian. Find out if she had any moles, scars, birthmarks, tattoos. We'll get pictures. We haven't turned up any close friends yet. No boyfriend anyone knows of. I gather she wasn't exactly a social butterfly."

"What about her father?"

"He's too distraught to talk to us." Kovac's mouth twisted. "'Too distraught'—that's what his lawyer says. If I thought somebody whacked my kid, I'd be fucking distraught, all right. I'd be climbing all over the cops. I'd be living in their back pockets, doing anything I could to nail the son of a bitch." He cocked an eyebrow at Quinn. "Wouldn't you?"

"I'd turn the world upside down and shake it by its heels."

"Damn right. I go over to Bondurant's house to break the news this might be Jillian. He gets a look like I'd hit him in the head with a ball bat. 'Oh, my God. Oh, my God,' he says, and I think he's gonna puke. So I don't think much of it when he excuses himself. The son of a bitch goes and calls his lawyer and he never comes out of his study again. I spend the next hour talking to Bondurant via Edwyn Noble."

"And what did he tell you?"

"That Jillian had been to the house Friday night for dinner and he hadn't seen her since. She left around midnight. A neighbor corroborates. The couple across the street were just getting home from a party. Jillian's Saab pulled onto the street just as they turned onto the block at eleven-fifty.

"Peter Filthy Fucking Rich Bondurant," he grumbled. "My luck. I'll be writing parking tickets by the time this thing is through."

He finished his cigarette, dropped it on the tarmac, and ground out the butt with the toe of his shoe.

"Too bad DNA tests take so damn long," he said, jumping back to the matter of identification. "Six weeks, eight weeks. Too damn long."

"You're checking missing persons reports?"

"Minnesota, Wisconsin, Iowa, the Dakotas. We've even called Canada. Nothing fits yet. Maybe the head'll turn up," he said with optimism the way he might hope for the return of a pair of eyeglasses or a wallet.

"Maybe."

"Well, enough of this shit for tonight. I'm starving," he said abruptly, pulling his suit coat shut as if he had confused hunger for cold. "I know a place with great Mexican takeout. So hot it burns the corpse taste out of your mouth. We'll swing by on the way to your hotel."

They walked away from the delivery bay as an ambulance pulled up. No lights, no siren. Another customer. Kovac fished his keys out of his pocket, looking at Quinn from the corner of his eye. "So, you knew our Kate?"

"Yeah." Quinn stared into the fog, wondering where she was tonight. Wondering if she was thinking about him. "In another lifetime."

8
CHAPTER

KATE EASED her aching body down into the old claw-foot tub and tried to exhale the tension she had stored up during the day. It worked its way from the core of her through her muscles in the form of pain. She envisioned it rising from the water with steam and the scent of lavender. The brass wire tray that spanned the tub before her held a Bad Monday-size glass of Bombay Sapphire and tonic. She took a deep drink, lay back, and closed her eyes.

The stress management people frowned on alcohol as an answer to tension and preached that it would set a person on the road to alcoholism and doom. Kate had been up and down the road to doom. She figured if she was ever to become an alcoholic, it would have happened years before. Five years before. It hadn't, and so tonight she drank gin and waited for the pleasant numbness it would bring.

For just the briefest of moments the montage of faces from that bleak period of her life flashed through her mind's eye: Steven's changing face over the passing of that terrible year—distant, cold, angry, bitter; the doctor's regret, worn tired and bland by too many tragedies; her daughter's sweet face, there and gone in a single painful heartbeat. Quinn's face—intense, compassionate, passionate...angry, dispassionate, indifferent, a memory.

It never failed to amaze her, the sudden sharpness of that pain as it stabbed through the cotton batting of time. A part of her wished fervently it would dull, and another part of her hoped that it never would. The endless cycle of guilt: the need to escape it and the equally desperate need to cling to it.

She opened her eyes and stared at the window beyond the foot of the tub. A rectangle of night peered in above the half-curtain, blackness beyond the steamed glass.

She had at least healed over the surface of the old wounds and moved on with her life, which was as much as anyone could ever honestly hope to do. But how easily torn, that old scar tissue. How humbling the reality that she hadn't really grown past that pain attached to the memory of John Quinn. She felt like a fool and a child, and blamed the element of surprise.

She would do better tomorrow. She would have a clear head and keep her focus. She would allow no surprises. There was no sense in dredging up the past when the present demanded all her attention. And Kate Conlan had never been anything if not sensible...with the exception of a few brief months during the worst year of her life.

She and Steven had grown apart. A tolerable situation, had all things remained equal.

Then Emily had contracted a virulent strain of influenza, and in a matter of days their sweet, sunny child was gone. Steven had blamed Kate, feeling she should have recognized the seriousness of the illness sooner. Kate had blamed herself despite the doctors' assurances that it wasn't her fault, that she couldn't have known. She had been so in need of someone to hold her, someone to offer comfort and support and absolution....

Pulling the end of the towel over her shoulder from the towel bar behind her, she dabbed at her eyes, wiped her nose, then took another drink. The past was out of her control. She could at least delude herself into believing she had some control of the present.

She steered her thoughts to her client. Idiotic word—*client*. It implied the person had chosen her, hired her. Angie DiMarco would have done neither. What a piece of work that kid was. And Kate was far too experienced in the ways of the real world to believe there was a heart of gold under all that. There was more likely something warped and mutated by a life less kind than that of the average stray cat. How people could bring a child into the world and let her come to this... The notion brought indignation and an unwelcome stab of jealousy.

It wasn't her job, really, finding out who Angie DiMarco was or why she was that sadly screwed-up person. But the more she knew about a client, the better able she was to understand that client, to act and react accordingly. To manipulate. To get what Sabin wanted out of the witness.

Draining the tub, she dried off, wrapped herself in a fat terry robe, and took the last of her drink to the small antique writing desk in her bedroom. Her feminine sanctuary. Peach tones and rich deep green gave the room a sense of warmth and welcome. Nanci Griffith's quirky sweet voice drifted from the speakers of the small stereo system on the bookshelf. Thor, the Norwegian forest cat who held dominion over the house, had claimed Kate's bed as his rightful throne and lay in all his regal, hairy splendor dead center on the down comforter. He gazed at her with the bored supremacy of a crown prince.

Kate curled a leg beneath her on the chair, pulled a sheet of paper from a cubbyhole in the desk, and began to write.

Angie DiMarco

Name? Probably phony. Belongs to some woman in Wisconsin. Get someone to run it through Wisconsin DMV.

Family dead—figuratively or literally? Abuse? Likely. Sexual? Strong probability.

Tattoos: multiple—professional and amateur. Significance? Significance of individual designs? Body piercing: fashion or something more?

Compulsive behaviors: Nail biting. Smokes.
Drinks: How much? How often?
Drugs? Possibly. Thin, pale, unkempt. But
seems too focused in behavior.

She could make only a thumbnail sketch of Angie's personality. Their time together had been too brief and too strongly influenced by the stress of the situation. Kate hated to think what conclusions some stranger would draw of *her* if she were thrust in a similar position. Stress triggered those old fight-or-flight instincts in everyone. But understanding didn't make the kid any more pleasant to deal with.

Luckily, the woman who ran the Phoenix House was accustomed to a wide range of bad attitudes. Residents at the house were women who had chosen or been forced down some of life's rougher roads and now wanted out.

Angie had been less than appreciative for the roof over her head. She had lashed out at Kate in a way that struck Kate as being way out of proportion.

"So what if I don't want to stay here?"

"Angie, you've got no place else to go."

"You don't know that."

"Don't make me go through this again," Kate said with an impatient sigh.

Toni Urskine, director of the Phoenix, lingered in the doorway for that much of the exchange, watching with a frown. Then she left them to have it out in the otherwise deserted den, a small room with cheap paneling and cast-off furnishings. Mismatched rummage sale "art" on the walls gave the place the ambiance of a fleabag hotel.

"You have no permanent address," Kate said. "You tell me your family is dead. You haven't managed to come up with a single real-live person who would take you in. You need a place to stay. This is a place to stay. Three squares, bed, and bath. What's the problem?"

Angie swatted at a stained throw pillow on a worn plaid love seat. "It's a fucking sty, that's the problem."

"Oh, excuse me, you've been living at the Hilton? Your fake address wasn't in this good a house?"

"You like it so much, then you stay here."

"I don't have to stay here. I'm not the homeless witness to a murder."

"Well, I don't fucking want to be!" the girl cried, her eyes shining like crystal, sudden tears poised to spill down her cheeks. She turned away from Kate and jammed the heels of her hands against her eyes. Her thin body curled in on itself like a comma.

"No, no, no," she mewed softly to herself. "Not now..."

The swift break in emotions caught Kate flat-footed. This was what she had wanted, wasn't it? To have the hard shell crack. Now that it had, she wasn't quite sure what to do about it. She hadn't been expecting the break to come now, over this.

Hesitantly, she stepped toward the girl, feeling awkward and guilty. "Angie..."

"No," the girl whispered more to herself than to Kate. "Not now. Please, please..."

"You don't have to be embarrassed, Angie," Kate said softly, standing close, though she made no attempt to touch the girl. "You've had a hell of a day. I'd cry too. I'll cry later. I'm no good at it—my nose runs, it's gross."

"Why c-c-can't I j-j-just stay with you?"

The question came from way out in left field, hit Kate square in the temple, and stunned her to her toes. As if this girl had never been away from home. As if she had never stayed among strangers. She'd likely been living on the street for God only knew how long, doing God only knew what to survive, and suddenly this dependence. It didn't make sense.

Before Kate could respond, Angie shook her head a little, rubbed the tears from her face with the sleeve of her jacket, and sucked in a ragged breath. That fast the window of opportunity shut and the steel mask was back in place.

"Never mind. Like you fucking care what happens to me."

"Angie, I care what happens to you or I wouldn't have this job."

"Yeah, right. Your job."

"Look," Kate said, out of energy for the argument, "it beats sleeping in a box. Give it a couple of days. If you hate it here, I'll see about making some other arrangements. You've got my cell phone number: Call me if you need me or if you just need to talk. Anytime. I meant what I said—I'm on your side. I'll pick you up in the morning."

114

Angie said nothing, just stood there looking sullen and small inside her too-big denim jacket that belonged to someone else.

"Try to get some sleep, kiddo," Kate said softly.

She had left the girl standing in the den, staring out a window at the lights of the house next door. The poignant picture brought a sense of sympathy to Kate. The symbolism of a kid on the outside of a family looking in. A child with no one.

"This is why I don't work with kids," she said now to the cat. "They'd just ruin my reputation as a hard-ass."

Thor trilled deep in his throat and rolled onto his back, offering his hairy belly for rubbing. She complied, enjoying the contact with another living being who appreciated and loved her in his own way. And she thought of Angie DiMarco lying awake in the night, in a house filled with strangers, the one connection in her life that meant anything to anyone being her connection to a killer.

A BLINKING MESSAGE light greeted Quinn as he let himself into his room at the Radisson Plaza Hotel. He tossed the sack of Mexican takeout in the wastebasket beneath the writing table, called room service, and ordered wild rice soup and a turkey sandwich he probably wouldn't eat. His stomach couldn't deal with Mexican anymore.

He stripped out of his clothes, crammed

115

everything but his shoes into a plastic laundry bag, tied the bag shut, and set it by the door. Someone down in laundry was in for an unpleasant surprise.

The water pounded out of the showerhead like a hail of bullets, as hot as he could stand it. He scrubbed his hair and body and let the water work on the knots in his shoulders, then he turned and let it pelt him in the face and chest. Images from the day tumbled through his head, out of order: the meeting, Bondurant's lawyer, the rush to the airport, the crime scene tape fluttering around the trunks of sturdy maple trees, Kate.

Kate. Five years was a long time. In five years she had established herself in a new career, she had a new life—which she deserved after all that had gone wrong in Virginia.

And what had he built in five years besides his reputation and a lot of unused vacation time?

Nothing. He owned a town house and a Porsche and a closet full of designer suits. He socked the rest of his money away for a retirement that would probably end in a massive coronary two months after he left the Bureau because he had nothing else in his life. If the job didn't kill him first.

He turned the water off, climbed out of the shower, and toweled himself dry. He had an athlete's body, solid, roped with muscle, leaner than it used to be—the reverse of most men in their mid-forties. He couldn't remember when his enjoyment of food had become indifference. Once upon a time he had considered himself a gourmet cook. Now he ate because he had to. The exercise he used to burn off tension burned off all the calories as well.

The greasy, spicy smell of the discarded Mexican food was permeating the bedroom. A smell preferable to a burned corpse, though he knew from experience it wouldn't be so welcome when it turned stale and he woke up to it at three in the morning.

The thought brought on a tumble of unpleasant memories of other hotel rooms in other cities and other dinners bought to fight off the aftertaste and smell of death. Of lying awake, alone in a strange bed in the middle of the night, sweating like a horse from nightmares, his heart racing.

The panic hit him in the gut like a sledgehammer, and he sat down on the edge of the bed in sweat pants and a gray FBI Academy T-shirt. He put his head in his hands for a moment, dreading the attack—the hollowness, the dizziness; the tremors that started in the core of him and rattled outward, down his arms and legs; the sense that there was nothing left of who he really was, the fear that he wouldn't know the difference.

He cursed himself and reached down deep for the strength to fight it off as he had done again and again in the last year. Or was it two now? He measured time by cases, measured cases by bodies. He had a recurring dream that he was locked away in a white room, pulling the hair out of his head one by one and naming each after the victims, pasting the hairs to the wall with his saliva.

He clicked the television on for noise to drown out the voice of fear in his head, then dialed the phone for his voice mail messages. Seven calls regarding other cases he had dragged here with him: a string of robberies and torture murders of gay men in Miami; the poisoning deaths of five elderly women in Charlotte, North Carolina; a child abduction case in Blacksburg, Virginia, that had, as of 8:19 P.M. eastern standard time, become a homicide with the discovery of the little girl's body in a wooded ravine.

Goddamn, he should have been there. Or maybe he should have been in rural Georgia, where a mother of four had been beaten to death with a ball peen hammer in a fashion reminiscent of three other murders in the last five years. Or maybe he should have been in England, consulting with Scotland Yard on the case that had turned up nine mutilated bodies in the yard of an abandoned slaughterhouse, the eyes gouged out of each and the mouths sewn shut with waxed thread.

"Special Agent Quinn, this is Edwyn Noble—"

"And you got this number how?" Quinn asked aloud as the message played.

He wasn't thrilled with Noble's in with this investigation. Being married to the mayor gave him a foot in the door no other lawyer in the city would have had. Being Peter Bondurant's attorney forced the door open wider.

118

"I'm calling on behalf of Mr. Bondurant. Peter would very much like to meet with you tomorrow morning if possible. Please give me a call back tonight."

He left the number, then a seductive taped voice informed Quinn he had no further messages. He recradled the receiver with no intention of picking it up again to call Noble. Let him stew. If he had something pertinent to the case, he could call Kovac or Fowler, the homicide lieutenant. Quinn called no one back, preferring to wait until after he didn't eat his dinner.

The ten o'clock news led with the latest murder, flashing taped footage of the crime scene unit combing over the dumping site in the park, then going to the tape of the press conference. A photo of Jillian Bondurant came up with another of her red Saab. A good three and a half minutes of coverage, total. The average news story ran less than half that.

Quinn dug the files for the first two murders out of his briefcase and stacked them on the writing desk. Copies of investigative reports and crime scene photos. Autopsy reports, lab reports, initial and follow-up investigative reports. News clippings from both the *Minneapolis Star Tribune* and the *St. Paul Pioneer Press*. Descriptions and photos of the crime scenes.

He had stated very clearly he wanted no information on possible suspects if there were any, and none had been included. He couldn't let anyone's speculation about a possible suspect cloud his judgment or steer his analysis in one direction or another. This was yet another reason he would have preferred to put the profile together from his office in Quantico. Here he was too close; the case was all around him. The personalities involved in the cases could spur reactions he would not have looking at a collection of adjectives and facts. There was too much worthless input, too many distractions.

Too many distractions—like Kate. Who hadn't called and had no reason to, really. Except that they had once shared something special...and walked away from it...and let it die....

Nothing in a Quinn life had the power to be quite so distracting as the irreparable past. The only cure Quinn had found for the past was to try to control the present, which meant pouring himself into the case at hand. Focus with intensity on maintaining control of the present. And on maintaining control of his sanity. And when the nights stretched long— as they all did—and his mind raced with the details of a hundred murders, he could feel his grip slipping on both.

ANGIE SAT AT the head of the small, hard twin bed, her back pressed into the corner so that she could feel the nubby plaster wall biting through the baggy flannel shirt she had chosen to sleep in. She sat with her knees pulled up beneath her chin, her arms wrapped tight around her legs. The door was closed; she was alone. The only light coming in through the window came from a distant streetlamp.

The Phoenix was a house for women "rising to a new beginning." So said the sign on the front lawn. It was a big, rambling old house with squeaky floors and no frills. Kate had brought her there and dumped her among the ex-hookers and ex-dopers and women trying to escape boyfriends who beat the shit out of them.

Angie had looked in at some of them watching TV in a big living room full of ratty furniture, and thought how stupid they must be. If there was one thing she had learned in life, it was that you could escape circumstance, but you could never escape who you were. Your personal truth was a shadow: There was no denying it, no changing it, and no getting rid of it.

She felt the shadow sweep over her now, cold and black. Her body trembled and tears rose in her eyes. She had been fighting it off all day, all night. She had thought it was going to swallow her whole right in front of Kate—an idea that only added to the panic. She couldn't lose control in front of anyone. Then they'd know that she was crazy, that she was defective. They'd ship her off to the nuthouse. She'd be alone then.

She was alone now.

The tremor began at the very core of her, then opened up wider and wider into a weird, hollow feeling. At the same time, she felt her consciousness shrinking and shrinking until she felt as if her body was just a shell and she was a tiny being locked inside it, in danger of falling off a ledge into some dark chasm inside and never being able to climb out.

She called this feeling the Zone. The Zone was an old enemy. But as well as she knew it, it never failed to terrify her. She knew if she didn't fight it off, she could lose control, and control was everything. If she didn't fight it off, she could lose whole blocks of time. She could lose herself, and what would happen then?

It shook her now, and she started to cry. Silently. Always silently. She couldn't let anyone hear her, she couldn't let them know how afraid she was. Her mouth tore open, but she strangled the sobs until her throat ached. She pressed her face against her knees, closing her eyes tight. The tears burned, fell, slid down her bare thigh.

In her mind, she could see the burning corpse. She ran from it. She ran and ran but didn't get anywhere. In her mind, the corpse became her, but she couldn't feel the flames. She would have welcomed the pain, but she couldn't conjure it up with just her mind. And all the while she felt herself growing smaller and smaller inside the shell of her body.

Stop it! Stop it! Stop it! She pinched her thigh hard, digging the ragged edge of her fingernails into the skin. And still she felt herself being sucked deeper and deeper into the Zone.

You know what you have to do. The voice unfurled in her mind like a black ribbon. She shivered in response to it. It twined itself through vital parts of her, a strange matrix of fear and need.

You know what you have to do.

Frantically, she pulled her backpack to her, fumbled with the zipper, and dug through an inner pocket for the thing she needed. Her fingers curled around the box cutter, which was disguised as a small plastic key.

Shaking, choking back the sobs, she crawled to a wedge of light on the bed and shoved up the left sleeve of the flannel shirt, exposing a thin white arm that was striped with narrow scars, one beside another and another, lining her arms like bars in an iron fence. The razor emerged from the end of the box cutter like a serpent's tongue and she drew it across a patch of tender skin near her elbow.

The pain was sharp and sweet, and seemed to short-circuit the panic that had electrified her brain. Blood blossomed from the cut, a shiny black bead in the moonlight. She stared at it, mesmerized as the calm flowed through her.

Control. Life was all about control. Pain and control. She had learned that lesson long ago.

•   •   •

"I'M THINKING OF changing my name," he says. "What do you think of Elvis? Elvis Nagel."

His companion says nothing. He picks up a pair of panties from the pile in the box and presses them to his face, burying his nose in the crotch and sniffing deep the scent of pussy. Nice. Smell is not as good a stimulant as sound for him, but still...

"Get it?" he says. "It's an anagram. Elvis Nagel—Evil's Angel."

In the background, three televisions are running videotapes of the local six o'clock newscasts. The voices blend together in a discordant cacophony he finds stimulating. The common thread that runs through them all is urgency. Urgency breeds fear. Fear excites him. He especially enjoys the sound of it. The tight, quivering tension underlying a controlled voice. The erratic changes in pitch and tone in the voice of someone openly afraid.

The mayor appears on two screens. The ugly cow. He watches her speak, wondering what it might be like to cut her lips off while she is still alive. Maybe make her eat them. The fantasy excites, as his fantasies always have.

He turns up the volume on the televisions, then crosses to the stereo system set into the bookcase, selects a cassette from the rack, and slips it into the machine. He stands in the center of the basement room, staring at the televisions, at the furrowed brows of anchormen and the faces of the people at the press conference shot from three different angles, and

124

lets the sounds wash over him—the voices of the reporters, the background echo in the cavernous hall, the urgency. At the same time from the stereo speakers comes the voice of raw, unvarnished fear. Pleading. Crying for God. Begging for death. His triumph.

He stands in the center of it. The conductor of this macabre opera. The excitement builds inside him, a huge, hot, swelling, sexual excitement that builds to a crescendo and demands release. He looks to his companion for the evening, considering, but he controls the need.

Control is all. Control is power. *He* is the action. *They* are the reaction. He wants to see the fear in all their faces, to hear it in their voices—the police, the task force, John Quinn. Especially Quinn, who hadn't even bothered to speak at the press conference, as if he wanted the Cremator to think he didn't warrant his personal attention.

He will have Quinn's attention. He will have their respect. He will have whatever he wants because he has control.

He turns the televisions down to a dull mumble but leaves them on so he won't return to silence. Silence is something he abhors. He turns off the stereo system but pockets a microcassette recorder loaded with a tape.

"I'm going out," he says. "I've had enough of you. You're boring me."

He goes to the mannequin he has been playing with, trying different combinations of the clothes of his victims.

"Not that I don't appreciate you," he says quietly.

He leans forward and kisses her, putting his tongue in her open mouth. Then he lifts the head of his last victim off the shoulders of the mannequin, puts it back into its plastic bag, takes it to the refrigerator in the laundry room, and sets it carefully on a shelf.

The night is thick with fog and mist, the streets black and gleaming wet in the glow of the streetlights. A night reminiscent of the Ripper's London. A night for hunting.

He smiles at the thought as he drives toward the lake. He smiles wider as he presses the play button on the microcassette recorder and holds the machine against his ear, the screams a twisted metamorphosis of a lover's whispered words. Affection and desire warped into hatred and fear. Two sides of the same emotions. The difference is control.

9
CHAPTER

"IF THE NEWSIES find us here, I'll eat my shorts," Kovac declared, turning around in a circle in the middle of the floor.

One wall was papered in a montage of naked women engaged in various erotic pursuits, the other three in cheap red flocked paper that best resembled moth-eaten velvet.

"Something tells me you could have gotten that done here for you," Quinn remarked dryly. He sniffed the air, identifying the smells of mice, cheap perfume, and damp underwear. "For a bargain price."

"The newsies find us here, our careers are toast," Elwood Knutson said. The big homicide sergeant pulled a giant ceramic penis out of a drawer behind the counter and held it up for all to see.

Liska made a face. "Jesus, Sam. You sure know how to pick 'em."

"Don't look at me! You think I hang out in massage parlors?"

"Yeah."

"Very funny. These lovely accommodations are courtesy of Detective Adler, Hennepin County Sheriff's Office. Chunk, take a bow."

Adler, a chunk of muscle with ebony skin and a tight cap of steel-gray curls, gave a sheepish grin and a wave to the rest of the task force. "My sister works for Norwest Banks. They foreclosed on the building after sex crimes shut the place down last summer. The location is perfect, the price is right—meaning free—and the press lost interest in the place after the hookers moved out. No one's going to suspect this is where we're meeting."

Which was the main point, Quinn thought as he followed Kovac down the narrow hall, the detective turning on lights in the succession of four smaller rooms—two on either side of the hall. It was essential that the task force be allowed to do their jobs without interruption or distraction, without having to run a gauntlet of reporters. A place where the case could be contained and leaks kept to a minimum.

And if the leaks continued, Elwood was right. The press would roast their careers on a public bonfire.

"I love it!" Kovac declared, striding back down the hall to the front room. "Let's set up."

Liska wrinkled her nose. "Can we hose it down with Lysol first?"

"Sure, Tinks. You can redecorate the place while the rest of us are solving these murders."

"Oh, fuck you, Kojak. I hope you're the first to catch the cooties from the toilet seat."

"Naw, that'll be Bear Butt in there with the *Reader's Digest*. Cooties see his hairy ass and come running. He's probably got a whole civilization living in that pelt."

Elwood, who was roughly the size and shape of a small grizzly, raised his head with dignity. "On behalf of hairy people everywhere, I take umbrage."

"Yeah?" Kovac said. "Well, take your umbrage outside and grab some stuff. We're burning daylight."

Two unmarked utility vans from the PD fleet were parked in the alley, loaded with the necessary office furniture and equipment. All of it was carried into the former Loving Touch

Massage Parlor, along with boxes of office supplies, a coffeemaker, and, most important, the boxes containing the files on all three murders attributed to the killer the detectives privately called Smokey Joe.

Quinn worked alongside the others. Just one of the guys. Trying to blend into another team like a free agent cleanup hitter drifting from one baseball park to another. Brought in by management to hit a dinger in the big game, then cut loose and sent on to the next crucial moment. The jokes felt forced, the attempts at camaraderie false. Some of these people would feel they knew him by the time all this was over. They wouldn't really know him at all.

Still, he went through the motions as he always did, knowing none of the people around him could tell the difference—the same way people working side by side with this serial killer wouldn't know or suspect. People in general had a myopic view of their own small worlds. They focused on what was important to them. The rotting soul of the guy in the next cubicle didn't matter to them—until his disease touched their lives.

In short order, the Loving Touch had been transformed from a brothel to a tactical war room. By nine o'clock the entire task force had assembled: six detectives from the Minneapolis PD, three from the Sheriff's Office, two from the state Bureau of Criminal Apprehension, Quinn, and Walsh.

Walsh looked like he had malaria.

129

Kovac briefed them on all three murders, finishing with the autopsy of the Jane Doe victim, complete with photographs that had been rushed through the lab for processing and enlarging.

"We'll have some of the preliminary lab results today," he said as he passed the gruesome pictures around the table. "We've got a blood type—O positive—which happens to be Jillian Bondurant's—and a gazillion other people's.

"I want you to note the photographs of wounds where sections of flesh have been cut from the body. We had similar wounds on the first two vics. We're speculating the killer may be cutting away bite marks. But with this latest, he might have cut away any identifying marks that could prove or disprove the victim's identity: scars, moles, et cetera."

"Tattoos," someone said.

"Bondurant's father is unaware of Jillian having any tattoos. According to his lawyer, he couldn't come up with any distinguishing marks at all. Jillian had been out of his life for about half of hers, so I guess it's not surprising. We're trying to come up with photographs of her in a bathing suit or something, but no luck so far.

"We're proceeding on the assumption that Jillian Bondurant is the vic," he said, "but staying open to other possibilities. There've been a few calls to the hotline, people claiming they've seen her since Friday, but none of them have panned out yet."

"Are you going to bring up the K word?" asked Mary Moss from the BCA. She looked like a soccer mom from the suburbs in a turtleneck and tweed blazer. Oversize glasses dominated her oval face. Her thick gray-blond pageboy seemed in need of a serious thinning.

"There haven't been any ransom demands that we know of," Kovac said, "but it's not beyond the realm."

"Big Daddy Bondurant sure never jumped to the kidnapping conclusion," Adler said. "Anyone find that strange besides me?"

"He heard about the driver's license found with the body and accepted the probability the body was hers," Hamill concluded.

Adler spread hands the size of catcher's mitts. "I say again: Anyone find that strange besides me? Who wants to believe their child is the decapitated victim of a homicidal maniac? Man as rich as Bondurant, isn't he gonna think kidnapping before murder?"

"Is he talking yet?" Elwood asked, chowing down a bran muffin as he perused the autopsy photos.

"Not to me," Kovac said.

"I don't like the smell of that either."

"His attorney called me last night and left a message," Quinn said. "Bondurant wants to see me this morning."

Kovac stepped back, nonplussed. "No shit? What'd you tell him?"

"Nothing. I let him hang overnight. I don't particularly want to meet him at this stage of

131

the game, but if it helps you get a foot in his door..."

Kovac smiled like a shark. "You need a lift over to the Bondurant house, don't you, John?"

Quinn tipped his head, wincing. "Do I have time to call and up my life insurance?"

Laughter erupted around the table. Kovac made a face.

"He gave me a lift from the morgue last night," Quinn explained. "I thought I'd be going back in a black bag."

"Hey," Kovac barked with false annoyance. "I got you there in one piece."

"Actually, I think my spleen is over on Marquette somewhere. Maybe we can pick it up on the way."

"He's been here a day and already he's got your number, Sam," Liska joked.

"Yeah, like you should talk, Tinks," someone else countered.

"I drive like Kovac only when I've got PMS."

Kovac held up a hand. "Okay, okay, back to business. Back to the bite marks. We ran that feature through the database back when we were looking at the first murder, searching for any known offenders in the metro—murderers or sex offenders—who had bitten or cannibalized victims, and came up with a list. We also ran it through VICAP and came up with another list." He lifted a sheaf of computer printouts.

"How long before we can confirm or deny this body is Bondurant's?"

Gary "Charm" Yurek of the PD had been designated media spokesman for the task force, giving the line of official bullshit to the press every day. He had a face worthy of a soap star. People tended to become distracted by the utter perfection of his smile and miss that he hadn't really told them anything.

Kovac looked now to Walsh. "Vince, any word on the girl's health records?"

Walsh hacked a phlegm-rattling cough, shaking his head. "The Paris office is tracking them down. They've been trying to contact the stepfather, but he's somewhere between construction sites in Hungary and Slovakia."

"Apparently, she's been the picture of health since her return to the States," Liska said. "She's had no serious injuries or illness, nothing to warrant X rays—except her teeth."

"He screwed us up but good taking her head," Elwood complained.

"You come up with any ideas on that, John?" Kovac asked.

"Could be he meant to jam up the investigation. Could be that the body isn't Jillian Bondurant and he's sending some kind of message or playing a game," Quinn suggested. "Maybe he knew the victim—whoever she was—and decapitated her to depersonalize her. Or the decapitation could be the new step in the escalation of his violent fantasies and how he plays them out. He could be keeping the head as a trophy. He could be using it to further act out his sexual fantasies."

133

"Judas," Chunk muttered.

Tippen, another of the sheriff's detectives, scowled. "You're not exactly narrowing it down."

"I don't know enough about him yet," Quinn said evenly.

"What *do* you know?"

"Basics."

"Such as?"

He looked to Kovac, who motioned him to the head of the table.

"This is *not* by any means the completed analysis. I want that made clear. I did a quick read-through of the reports last night, but it takes more than a couple of hours to build a solid, accurate profile."

"Okay, you've covered your ass," Tippen said impatiently. "So who do you think we're looking for?"

Quinn held his temper in check. It was nothing new to have a skeptic in the crowd. He had learned long ago how to play them, how to pull them around a little at a time with logic and practicality. He leveled his gaze on Tippen, a lean, homely man with a face like an Irish wolfhound—all nose and mustache and shaggy brows over sharp, dark eyes.

"Your UNSUB is a white male, probably between the ages of thirty and thirty-five. Sadistic sexual serial killers hunt within their own ethnic group as a rule." Pointing to the close-ups of wounds from the crime scene photos, he said, "You've got a very specific pattern of wounds, carefully repeated on each

134

victim. He's spent a long time perfecting this fantasy. When you find him you'll find a collection of S&M pornography. He's been into it for a long while. The sophistication of the crimes, the care taken to leave no usable physical evidence, suggests maturity and experience. He may have an old record as a sex offender. But record or no, he's been on this course from when he was in his late teens or early twenties.

"He likely started with window peeping or fetish burglaries—stealing women's underwear and so forth. That may still be a part of his fantasy. We don't know what he's doing with the victims' clothing. The clothes he dresses them in after he's killed them are clothes he's chosen for them from his own source."

"You suppose he played with Barbie dolls as a kid?" Tippen said to Adler.

"If he did, you can bet they ended up with limbs missing," Quinn said.

"Jesus, I was kidding."

"No joke, Detective. Aberrant fantasies can begin as young as five or six. Particularly in a home with sexual abuse or open sexual promiscuity going on—which is almost a sure bet in this case.

"He's likely murdered long before your first victim and gotten away with it. Escaping detection will make him feel bold, invulnerable. His presentation of the bodies in a public area where he could have been seen and where the bodies would certainly be found is risky and suggests arrogance. It also suggests the type of killer who can be drawn to the investigation. He wants attention, he's watching the news, clipping articles from the paper."

"So Chief Greer was right yesterday when he said we should make a statement to this creep," Kovac said.

"He'll be just as right today or tomorrow, when we're ready to make a move."

"And it looks like your idea," Tippen muttered.

"I'll be happy to let you suggest it to the brass, Detective," Quinn said. "I don't give a rat's ass who gets credit. I don't want my name in the paper. I don't want to see myself on TV. Hell, I'd just as soon be doing this job in my office sixty feet underground back in Quantico. I have one objective here: helping you nail this son of a bitch and take him out of society forever and ever, amen. That's all this is about for me."

Tippen dropped his gaze to his notepad, a nonbeliever still.

Kovac huffed a little sigh. "You know, we got no time for fence pissing. I'm sure no one in the general public gives a rip which one of us has the biggest dick."

"I have," Liska chirped, snatching the giant ceramic penis away from Elwood, who had set it on the table as a centerpiece. She held it up as proof of her claim.

Laughter broke the tension.

"Anyway," Quinn went on, sliding his hands into his pants pockets and cocking a leg, settling in, subtly letting Tippen know he wasn't going anywhere and wasn't bothered by his opinions. "We have to be careful about how we draw him in. I'd suggest starting with a heavily publicized community meeting held in a location central between the dumping sites. You're asking for help, for community participation. It's nonaggressive, nonthreatening. He can come into that scenario feeling anonymous and safe.

"It won't be easy to trick him unless his arrogance gets out of hand. He's organized. He's of above-average intelligence. He's got a job, but it may be beneath his capabilities. He knows the city parks system, so if you haven't done so already, you'll want to get a parks service employee roster, see if anyone has a criminal record."

"Already happening," Kovac said.

"How do you know he has a job at all?" Tippen challenged. "How do you know he's not some drifter, familiar with the parks because that's where he hangs out?"

"He's no drifter," Quinn said with certainty. "He's got a house. The crime scenes are not the death scenes. The women were abducted, taken someplace, and held there. He needs privacy, a place where he can torture his victims without having to worry about anyone hearing.

"Also, he may have more than one vehicle. He probably has access to a Suburban-type truck or a pickup. A basic package, older, dark in color, fairly well kept. Something to transport the bodies in, a vehicle that wouldn't seem out of place pulling into the service lot of a city park. But this may not be what he's picking them up in, because a big vehicle would be conspicuous and memorable to witnesses."

"How do you know he's an underachiever?" Frank Hamill asked.

"Because that's the norm for this type of killer. He has a job because it's necessary. But his energies, his *talents,* are applied to his hobby. He spends a lot of his time fantasizing. He lives for the next kill. A corporate CEO wouldn't have that kind of free time."

"Even though they're mostly psychopaths," someone joked.

Quinn flashed a shark smile. "Be glad some of them like their day jobs."

"What else?" Liska asked. "Any guesses on appearance?"

"I've got mixed feelings on this because of the conflicting victimology."

"Hookers go for cash, not flash," Elwood said.

"And if all three victims were hookers, I'd say we're looking for a guy who's unattractive, maybe has some kind of problem like a stutter or a scar, something that would make it difficult for him to approach women. But if our third vic is the daughter of a billionaire?" Quinn arched a brow.

"Who knows what she might have been into."

"Is there any reason to think she was involved in prostitution?" Quinn asked. "On the surface she wouldn't seem to have much in common with the first two victims."

"She doesn't have a record," Liska said. "But then, her father is Peter Bondurant."

"I need more extensive victimology on all three women," Quinn said. "If there's any kind of common link between them, that's a prime spot for you to start developing a suspect."

"Two hookers and a billionaire's daughter— what could they possibly have in common?" Yurek asked.

"Drugs," Liska said.

"A man," Mary Moss offered.

Kovac nodded. "You two want to work that angle?"

The women nodded.

"But maybe the guy just nabbed these women from behind," Tippen suggested. "Maybe he didn't need to finesse them. Maybe he picked them because they were in the wrong place at the wrong time."

"It's possible. It just doesn't feel that way to me," Quinn said. "He's too smooth. These women just vanished. No one saw a struggle. No one heard a scream. Logic tells me they went with him willingly."

"So where's Bondurant's car?" Adler asked. Jillian's red Saab had yet to be located.

"Maybe *she* picked *him* up," Liska said. "It's the nineties. Maybe he's still got her car."

"So we're looking for a killer with a three-car garage?" Adler said. "Hell, I am in the wrong line of work."

"You want to start whacking ex-wives for a living, you could fill the damn garage with Porsches," Kovac joked.

Liska punched him in the arm. "Hey! *I'm* an ex-wife."

"Present company excluded."

Quinn took a long drink of his coffee while the jokes ran through the group. Humor was a safety valve for cops, releasing measured bursts of pressure the job built up inside them. The members of this team were standing at the start of what would undoubtedly be a long, unpleasant gauntlet. They would need to squeeze a joke in wherever they could. The better their rapport as a unit, the better for the investigation. He usually tossed in a few jokes himself to bend the image of the straitlaced G-man.

"Sizewise," he went on, "he'll probably be medium height, medium build—strong enough to tote a dead body around but not so big as to seem a physical threat when he's approaching his victims. That's about as much as I can give you for now."

"What? Can't you just close your eyes and conjure up a psychic photograph or something?" Adler said, only half joking.

"Sorry, Detective," Quinn said with a grin and a shrug. "If I were psychic, I'd be making my living at the racetrack. Not a psychic cell in my body."

"You would have if you was on TV."

"If we were on TV, we'd have solved these crimes in an hour," Elwood said. "TV is why

140

the public gets impatient with an investigation that lasts more than two days. The whole damn country lives on TV time."

"Speaking of TV," Hamill said, holding up a videocassette. "I've got the tape from the press conference."

A television with a built-in VCR sat atop a wheeled metal cart near the head of the table. Hamill loaded the cassette and they all sat back to watch. At Quinn's request, a videographer from the BCA special operations unit had been stationed discreetly among the cameramen from the local stations with instructions to capture not the event, but the people gathered to take it in.

The voices of the mayor, Chief Greer, and the county attorney droned in the background as the camera scanned the faces of reporters and cops and news photographers. Quinn stared at the screen, tuned to pick up the slightest nuances of expression, the glint of something knowing in a pair of eyes, the hint of something smug playing at the corners of a mouth. His attention was on the people at the periphery of the crowd, people who seemed to be there by accident or coincidence.

He looked for that intangible, almost imperceptible something that set a detective's instincts on point. The knowledge that their killer might have been standing there among the unsuspecting, that he could have been looking at the face of a murderer without knowing, stirred a deep sense of frustration within. This killer wouldn't stand out. He wouldn't appear to be nervous. He wouldn't have the wild-eyed edginess that would give him away as disorganized offenders often did. He'd killed at least three women and gotten away with it. The police had no viable leads. He had nothing to worry about. And he knew it.

"Well," Tippen said dryly. "I don't see anyone carrying an extra head with them."

"We could be looking right at him and not know it," Kovac said, hitting the power button on the remote control. "But if we come up with a possible suspect, we can go back and look again."

"We gonna get that composite from the wit today, Sam?" Adler asked.

Kovac's mouth twisted a little. "I sure as hell hope so. I've already had calls from the chief and Sabin about it." And they would ride his ass until they got it. He was the primary. He ran the investigation and took the heat. "In the meantime, let's make assignments and hit the bricks before Smokey Joe decides to light up another one."

PETER BONDURANT'S HOME was a sprawling old Tudor with an expensive view of Lake of the Isles beyond its tall iron bar fence. Tall bare-branched trees studded the lawn. One broad wall of the stucco home was crazed with a net-work of vines, dry and brown this time of year. Just a few miles from the heart of Min-neapolis, it discreetly displayed signs of city life paranoia along the fence and on the closed driveway gate in the form of blue-and-white security company signs.

Quinn tried to take it all in visually and still pay attention to the call on his cell phone. A suspect had been apprehended in the child abduction in Blacksburg, Virginia. The CASKU agent on site wanted to confirm a strategy for the interrogation. Quinn was sounding board and guru. He listened, agreed, made a suggestion, and signed off as quickly as he could, wanting his focus on the matter at hand.

"The man in demand," Kovac remarked as he swung the car into the drive too fast and hit the brakes, rocking to a stop beside the intercom panel. His gaze moved past Quinn to the news vans parked on either side of the street. The occupants of the vans stared back. "Lousy vultures."

A voice crackled from the intercom speaker. "Yes?"

"John Quinn, FBI," Kovac said with drama, flashing a comic look at Quinn.

The gate rolled open, then closed behind them. The reporters made no move to rush in. Midwestern manners, Quinn thought, knowing full well there were places in this country where the press would have stormed the place and demanded answers as if they had a right to tear apart the grief that belonged to the victim's family. He'd seen it happen. He'd seen promotion-hungry reporters dig through people's garbage for scraps of information that could be turned into speculative headlines. He'd seen them crash funerals.

A black Lincoln Continental polished to a hard shine sat in the driveway near the house. Kovac pulled his dirt-brown Caprice alongside the luxury car and turned the key. The engine rattled on pathetically for half a minute.

"Cheap piece of crap," he muttered. "Twenty-two years on the job and I get the worst fucking car in the fleet. You know why?"

"Because you won't kiss the right ass?" Quinn ventured.

Kovac huffed a laugh. "I'm not kissing anything that's got a dick on the flip side." He chuckled to himself as he dug through a pile of junk on the seat, finally coming up with a mini-cassette recorder, which he offered to Quinn.

"In case he still won't talk to me...By Minnesota law, only one party to a conversation needs to grant permission to tape that conversation."

"Hell of a law for a state full of Democrats."

"We're practical. We've got a killer to catch. Maybe Bondurant knows something he doesn't realize. Or maybe he'll say something that won't ring a bell with you because you're not from here."

Quinn slipped the recorder into the inside breast pocket of his suit coat. "The end justifies the means."

"You know it."

"Better than most."

"Does it ever get to you?" Kovac asked as

144

they got out of the car. "Working serial murders and child abductions twenty-four/seven. I gotta think that'd get to me. At least some of the stiffs I get deserved to get whacked. How do you cope?"

I don't. The response was automatic—and just as automatically unspoken. He didn't cope. He never had. He just shoveled it all into the big dark pit inside him and hoped to hell the pit didn't overflow.

"Focus on the win column," he said.

The wind cut across the lake, kicking up whitecaps on water that looked like mercury, and chasing dead leaves across the dead lawn. It flirted with the tails of Quinn's and Kovac's trench coats. The sky looked like dirty cotton batting sinking down on the city.

"I drink," Kovac confessed amiably. "I smoke and I drink."

A grin tugged at Quinn's mouth. "And chase women?"

"Naw, I gave that up. It's a bad habit."

Edwyn Noble answered the door. Lurch with a law degree. His expression froze at the sight of Kovac.

"Special Agent Quinn," he began as they moved past him into an entry hall of carved mahogany paneling. A massive wrought iron chandelier hung from the second-story ceiling. "I don't remember you mentioning Sergeant Kovac when you called."

Quinn flashed him innocence. "Didn't I? Well, Sam offered to drive me, and I don't know my way around the city, so..."

"I've been wanting to talk to Mr. Bondurant myself anyway," Kovac said casually, browsing the artwork on display in the hall, his hands stuffed into his pockets as if he were afraid of breaking something.

The lawyer's ears turned red around the rim. "Sergeant, Peter's just lost his only child. He'd like to have a little time to collect himself before he has to be subjected to any kind of questioning."

"Questioning?" Kovac's brows arched as he glanced up from a sculpture of a racehorse. He exchanged a look with Quinn. "Like a suspect? Does Mr. Bondurant think we consider him a suspect? Because I don't know where he would have gotten that idea. Do you, Mr. Noble?"

Color streaked across Noble's cheekbones. "Interview. Statement. Whatever you'd like to call it."

"I'd like to call it a conversation, but, hey, whatever you want."

"What I want," came a quiet voice from beyond an arched doorway, "is to have my daughter back."

The man who emerged from the dimly lit interior hall was half a foot shy of six feet, with a slight build and an air of neatness and precision even in casual slacks and a sweater. His dark hair was cropped so close to his skull it looked like a fine coating of metal shavings. He stared at Quinn with serious eyes through the small oval lenses of wire-framed glasses.

"That's what we all want, Mr. Bondurant," Quinn said. "There may still be a chance of making that happen, but we'll need all the help we can get."

The straight brows drew together in confusion. "You think Jillian might still be alive?"

"We haven't been able to conclusively determine otherwise," Kovac said. "Until we can positively identify the victim, there's a chance it's not your daughter. We've had some unsubstantiated sightings—"

Bondurant shook his head. "No, I don't think so," he said softly. "Jillie is dead."

"How do you know that?" Quinn asked. Bondurant's expression was somber, tormented, defeated. His gaze skated off somewhere to Quinn's left.

"Because she was my child," he said at last. "I can't explain it any better than that. There's a feeling—like a rock in my gut, like some part of me died with her. She's gone.

"Do you have children, Agent Quinn?" he asked.

"No. But I've known too many parents who've lost a child. It's a terrible place to be. If I were you, I wouldn't be in any hurry to get there."

Bondurant looked down at Quinn's shoes and breathed a sigh. "Come into my study, Agent Quinn," he said, then turned to Kovac, his mouth tightening subtly. "Edwyn, why don't you and Sergeant Kovac wait for us in the living room?"

Kovac made a sound of dissatisfaction.

Concern tightened the lawyer's features. "Perhaps I should sit in, Peter. I—"

"No. Have Helen get you coffee."

Clearly unhappy, Noble leaned toward his client across the hall like a marionette straining against its strings. Bondurant turned and walked away.

Quinn followed. Their footfalls were muffled by the fine wool of a thick Oriental runner. He wondered at Bondurant's strategy. He wouldn't talk to the police, but he banished his attorney from a conversation with an FBI agent. It didn't make sense if he was trying to protect himself. Then again, anything incriminating he said in the absence of his attorney would be worthless in court, audiotape or no audiotape.

"I understand you have a witness. Can she identify the man who did this?"

"I'm not at liberty to discuss that," Quinn said. "I'd like to talk about you and your daughter, your relationship. Forgive me for being blunt, but your lack of cooperation with the police thus far comes across as puzzling at best."

"You think I'm not reacting in the typical way of a parent of a murdered child? *Is there* a typical reaction?"

"*Typical* is maybe not the word. Some reactions are more common than others."

"I don't know anything that would be pertinent to the case. Therefore, I have nothing further to tell the police. A stranger abducted and murdered my daughter. How could they expect me to have any information relevant to such a senseless act?"

Bondurant led the way into a spacious office and closed the door. The room was dominated by a massive U-shaped mahogany desk, one wing of which was devoted to computer equipment, one to paperwork. The center section was meticulously neat, the blotter spotless, every pen and paper clip in its place.

"Take your coat off, Agent Quinn. Have a seat." He gestured a thin hand toward a pair of oxblood leather chairs while he went around the desk to claim his own place in a high-backed executive's throne.

Putting distance and authority between them, Quinn thought, shrugging out of his top-coat. *Putting me in my place.* He settled into a chair, realizing immediately that it squatted just a little too low to the ground, just enough to make its occupant feel vaguely small.

"Some maniac murdered my daughter," Bondurant said again calmly. "In the face of that, I can't really give a good goddamn what anyone thinks of my behavior. Besides, I *am* helping the investigation: I brought you here."

Another reminder of the balance of power, softly spoken.

"And you're willing to talk to me?"

"Bob Brewster says you're the best."

"Thank the director for me the next time you speak to him. Our paths don't cross that often," Quinn returned, deliberately unimpressed by the man's implied cozy familiarity with the director of the FBI.

"He says this type of murder is your specialty."

"Yes, but I'm not a hired gun, Mr. Bondurant. I want to be very clear on that. I'll do what I can in terms of building a profile and advising as to investigative techniques. If a suspect is brought in, I'll offer an interview strategy. In the event of a trial, I'll testify as an expert witness and offer my expertise to the prosecution regarding the questioning of witnesses. I'll do my job, and I'll do it well, but I don't work for you, Mr. Bondurant."

Bondurant absorbed this information expressionless. His face was as bony and severe as his attorney's, but without the relief of the too-wide smile. A hard mask, impossible to see past.

"I want Jillian's killer caught. I'll deal with you because you're the best and because I've been told I can trust you not to sell out."

"Sell out? In what way?"

"To the media. I'm a very private man in a very public position. I hate the idea that millions of strangers will know the intimate details of my daughter's death. It seems like it should be a very private, personal thing— the ending of a life."

"It should be. It's the *taking* of a life that can't be kept quiet—for everyone's sake."

"I suppose what I really dread isn't people knowing about Jillie's death so much as their ravenous desire to tear apart her life. And mine—I'll admit that."

Quinn shifted in his chair, casually crossing his legs, and offered the barest hint of a sympathetic smile. Settling in. The I-could-be-your-friend guise. "That's understandable. Has the press been hounding you? It looks like they're camped out front."

"I refuse to deal with them. I've pulled in my media relations coordinator from Paragon to handle it. The thing that angers me most is their sense of entitlement. Because I'm wealthy, because I'm prominent, they think they have some right to invade my grief. Do you think they parked their news vans in front of the homes of the parents of the two prostitutes this maniac killed? I can assure you they didn't."

"We live in a society addicted to sensationalism," Quinn said. "Some people are deemed newsworthy and some are considered disposable. I'm not sure which side of the coin is worse. I can just about guarantee you the parents of those first two victims are sitting at home wondering why news vans *aren't* parked in front of their houses."

"You think they'd like people to know how they failed as parents?" Bondurant asked, a slim shadow of anger darkening his tone. "You think they'd like people to know why their daughters became whores and drug addicts?"

Guilt and blame. How much of that was he projecting from his own pain? Quinn wondered.

"About this witness," Bondurant said again, seeming a little shaken by his last near-revelation. He moved a notepad on his desk a quarter of an inch. "Do you think she'll be able to identify the killer? She doesn't sound very reliable."

"I don't know," Quinn said, knowing exactly where Bondurant had gotten his information. Kovac was going to have to do his best to plug that leak, which would mean stepping on some very sensitive, influential toes. The victim's family was entitled to certain courtesies, but this investigation needed as tight an environment as possible. Peter Bondurant couldn't be allowed total access. He in fact had not been ruled out as a viable suspect.

"Well...we can only hope..." Bondurant murmured.

His gaze strayed to the wall that held an assortment of framed photographs, many of himself with men Quinn had to assume were business associates or rivals or dignitaries. He spotted Bob Brewster among the crowd, then found what Bondurant had turned to: a small cluster of photographs on the lower left-hand corner.

Quinn rose from his chair and went to the wall for a closer inspection. Jillian at various stages of her life. He recognized her from a snapshot in the case file. One photograph in particular drew his eye: a young woman out of place in a prim black dress with a white Peter Pan collar and cuffs. Her hair was cut boyishly short and bleached nearly white. A striking contrast to the dark roots and brows. Half a dozen earrings ornamented one ear. A tiny ruby studded one nostril. She resembled her father in no way at all. Her body, her face, were softer, rounder. Her eyes were huge and sad, the camera catching the vulnerability she felt at not being the politely feminine creature of someone else's expectations.

"Pretty girl," Quinn murmured automatically. It didn't matter that it wasn't precisely true. The statement was made for a purpose other than flattery. "She must have felt very close to you, coming back here from Europe for college."

"Our relationship was complicated." Bondurant rose from his chair and hovered beside it, tense and uncertain, as if a part of him wanted to go to the photographs but a stronger part held him back. "We were close when she was young. Then her mother and I divorced when Jillie was at a vulnerable age. It was difficult for her—the antagonism between Sophie and me. Then came Serge, Sophie's last husband. And Sophie's illness—she was in and out of institutions for depression."

He was silent for a stretch of time, and Quinn could feel the weight of everything Bondurant was omitting from the story. What had precipitated the divorce? What had driven Sophie's mental illness? Was the distaste in Bondurant's voice when he spoke of his successor's bitterness over a rival or something more?

"What was she studying at the university?" he asked, knowing better than to go directly for the other answers he wanted. Peter Bondurant wouldn't give up his secrets that easily, if he gave them up at all.

"Psychology," he said with the driest hint of irony as he stared at the photo of her in the black dress and bleached boy-cut, the earrings and pierced nose and unhappy eyes.

"Did you see her often?"

"Every Friday. She came for dinner."

"How many people knew that?"

"I don't know. My housekeeper, my personal assistant, a few close friends. Some of Jillian's friends, I suppose."

"Do you have additional staff here at the house or just the housekeeper?"

"Helen is full-time. A girl comes in to help her clean once a week. There's a grounds crew of three who come weekly. That's all. I prefer my privacy to a staff. My needs aren't that extravagant."

"Friday's usually a hot night on the town for college kids. Jillian wasn't into the club scene?"

"No. She'd grown past it."

"Did she have many close friends?"

"Not that she spoke about with me. She was a very private person. The only one she mentioned with any regularity was a waitress at a coffee bar. Michele something. I never met her."

"Did she have a boyfriend?"

"No," he said, turning away. French doors behind his desk led out to a flagstone courtyard of vacant benches and empty planters. He stared through the glass as if he were looking through a portal into another time. "Boys didn't interest her. She didn't want temporary relationships. She'd been through so much...."

His thin mouth quivered slightly, and a deep pain came into his eyes. The strongest sign of inner emotion he had shown. "She had so much life ahead of her," he murmured. "I wish this hadn't happened."

Quinn quietly moved in alongside him. His voice was low and soft, the voice of sad experience and understanding. "That's the hardest thing to cope with when a young person dies—especially when they've been murdered. The unfulfilled dreams, the unrealized potential. The people close to them—family, friends—thought they had so much time to make up for mistakes, plenty of time down the road to tell that person they loved them. Suddenly that time is gone."

He could see the muscles of Bondurant's face tighten against the pain. He could see the suffering in the eyes, that hint of desperation at the knowledge the emotional tidal wave was coming, and the fear that there may not be enough strength to hold it back.

"At least you had that last evening together," Quinn murmured. "That should be some comfort to you."

Or it could be the bitter, lasting reminder of every unresolved issue left between father and daughter. The raw wound of opportunity lost. Quinn could almost taste the regret in the air.

"How was she that night?" he asked quietly. "Did she seem up or down?"

"She was"— Bondurant swallowed hard and searched for the appropriate word—"herself. Jillie was always up one minute and down the next. Volatile."

The daughter of a woman in and out of institutions for psychiatric problems.

"She didn't give any sign something was

bothering her, that she was worried about anything?"

"No."

"Did you discuss anything in particular, or argue about—"

Bondurant's explosion was sudden, strong, surprising. "My God, if I'd thought there was anything wrong, if I'd thought something was going to happen, don't you think I would have stopped her from leaving? Don't you think I would have kept her here?"

"I'm sure you would have," Quinn said softly, the voice of compassion and reassurance, emotions he had stopped giving out in full measure long ago because it took too much from him and there was no one around to help him refill the well. He tried to keep his focus on his underlying motive, which was to get information. Manipulate, coax, slip under the guard, draw out the truth a sliver at a time. Get the info to get the killer. Remember that the first person he owed his allegiance to was the victim.

"What did you talk about that night?" he asked gently as Bondurant worked visibly to gather his composure.

"The usual things," he said, impatient, looking out the window again. "Her classes. My work. Nothing."

"Her therapy?"

"No, she—" He stiffened, then turned to glare at Quinn.

"We need to know these things, Mr. Bondurant," Quinn said without apology. "With every victim we have to consider the possibility that some part of their life may have a link to their death. It may be the thinnest thread that ties one thing to the other. It might be something you don't think could be important at all. But sometimes that's all it takes, and sometimes that's all we have.

"Do you understand what I'm telling you? We'll do everything in our power to keep details confidential, but if you want this killer apprehended, you have to cooperate with us."

The explanation did nothing to soften Bondurant's anger. He turned abruptly back to the desk and pulled a card from the Rolodex. "Dr. Lucas Brandt. For all the good it will do you. I'm sure I don't have to tell you that anything Jillian related to Lucas as a patient is confidential."

"And what about anything she related to you as her father?"

His temper came in another quick flash, boiling up and over the rigid control. "If I knew anything, *anything* that could lead you to my daughter's murderer, don't you think I would tell you?"

Quinn was silent, his unblinking gaze steady on Peter Bondurant's face, on the vein that slashed down across his high forehead like a bolt of lightning. He pulled the Rolodex card from Bondurant's fingers.

"I hope so, Mr. Bondurant," he said at last. "Some other young woman's life may depend on it."

• • •

"**WHAT'D YOU GET?**" Kovac asked as they walked away from the house. He lit a cigarette and went to work sucking in as much of it as he could before they reached the car.

Quinn stared down the driveway and past the gate where two cameramen stood with eyes pressed to viewfinders. There was no long-range audio equipment in sight, but the lenses on the cameras were fat and long. His period of anonymity was going into countdown.

"Yeah," he said. "A bad feeling."

"Jeez, I've had that from the start of this deal. You know what a man like Bondurant could do to a career?"

"My question is: Why would he want to?"

"'Cause he's rich and he's hurting. He's like that guy with the gun in the government center yesterday. He wants someone else to hurt. He wants someone to pay. Maybe if he can make someone else miserable, he won't feel his own pain so much. You know," he said in that offhand way he had, "people are nuts. So what'd he say? Why won't he talk to us locals?"

"He doesn't trust you."

Kovac straightened with affront and tossed his cigarette on the driveway. "Well, fuck him!"

"He's paranoid about details leaking to the media."

"Like what details? What's he got to hide?"

Quinn shrugged. "That's your job, Sherlock. But I got you a place to start."

They climbed into the Caprice. Quinn pulled the cassette recorder from his coat pocket and laid it on the seat between them with the Rolodex card on top of it.

Kovac picked up the card and frowned at it. "A shrink. What'd I tell you? People are nuts. *Especially* rich people—they're the only ones who can afford to do anything about it. It's like a hobby with them."

Quinn stared up at the house, half expecting to see a face at one of the windows, but there was no one. All the windows were blank and black on this dreary morning.

"Was there ever any mention in the press about either of the first two victims being drug users?" he asked.

"No," Kovac said. "The one used to be, but we held it back. Lila White. 'Lily' White. The first vic. She was a basehead for a while, but she got herself straightened out. Went through a county program, lived at one of the hooker halfway houses for a while—only that part didn't take, I guess. Anyway, the drug angle didn't develop. Why?"

"Bondurant made a reference. Might have just been an assumption on his part, but I don't think so. I think either he knew something about the other victims or he knew something about Jillian."

"If she was using anything around the time of her death, it'll show up in the tox screen. I went through her town house. I didn't see anything stronger than Tylenol."

"If she was using, you might have a con-

159

nection to the other victims." And thereby a possible connection to a dealer or another user they could develop into a suspect.

The feral smile of the hunter on a fresh scent lifted the corners of Kovac's mustache. "Networking. I love it. Corporate America thinks they're on to something new. Crooks have been networking since Judas sold Jesus Christ down the river. I'll call Liska, have her and Moss nose around. Then let's go see what Sigmund Fraud here has to say about the price of loose marbles." He tapped the Rolodex card against the steering wheel. "His office is on the other side of this lake."

10

CHAPTER

"SO WHAT do you think of Quinn?" Liska asked.

Mary Moss rode shotgun, looking out the window at the Mississippi. Barge traffic had given up for the year. Along this stretch, the river was a deserted strip of brown between ratty, half-abandoned industrial and warehouse blocks. "They say he's hot stuff. A legend in the making."

160

"You've never worked with him?"

"No. Roger Emerson usually works this territory out of Quantico. But then, the vic isn't usually the daughter of a billionaire captain of industry with contacts in Washington.

"I liked the way he handled Tippen," Moss went on. "No bully-boy, I'm-the-fed-and-you're-a-hick nonsense. I think he's a quick study of people. Probably frighteningly intelligent. What'd you think?"

Liska sent her a lascivious grin. "Nice pants."

"God! Here I was being serious and professional, and you were looking at his ass!"

"Well, not when he was talking. But, come on, Mar, the guy's a total babe. Wouldn't you like a piece of that if you could get it?"

Moss looked flustered. "Don't ask me things like that. I'm an old married woman! I'm an old married *Catholic* woman!"

"As long as the word *dead* doesn't figure into that description, you're allowed to look."

"Nice pants," Moss muttered, fighting chuckles.

"Those big brown eyes, that granite jaw, that sexy mouth. I think I could have an orgasm watching him talk about proactive strategies."

"Nikki!"

"Oh, that's right, you're a married woman," Liska teased. "You're not allowed to have orgasms."

"Do you talk this way when you're riding around with Kovac?"

"Only if I want to get him crazy. He twitches

like a gigged frog. Tells me he doesn't want to know anything about my orgasms, that a woman's G spot should just remain a mystery. I tell him that's why he's been divorced twice. You should see how red he gets. I love Kovac—he's such a guy."

Moss pointed through the windshield. "Here it is—Edgewater."

The Edgewater town homes were a collection of impeccably styled buildings designed to call to mind a tidy New England fishing village—gray clapboard trimmed in white, cedar shake roofs, six-over-six paned windows. The units were arranged like a crop of wild mushrooms connected by meandering, landscaped paths. All of them faced the river.

"I've got the key to Bondurant's unit," Liska said, piloting the car into the entrance of the town house complex, "but I called the caretaker anyway. He says he saw Jillian leaving Friday afternoon. I figure it won't hurt to talk to him again."

She parked near the first unit and she and Moss showed their badges to the man waiting for them on the stoop. Liska pegged Gil Vanlees for mid-thirties. He was blond with a thin, weedy mustache, six feet tall, and soft-looking. His Timberwolves starter jacket hung open over a blue security guard's uniform. He had that look of a marginal high school jock who had let himself go. Too many hours spent watching professional sports with a can in his hand and a sack of chips beside him.

"So, you're a detective?" His small eyes gleamed at Liska with an almost sexual excitement. One was blue and one the odd, murky color of smoky topaz.

Liska smiled at him. "That's right."

"I think it's great to see women on the job. I work security down at the Target Center, you know," he said importantly. "Timberwolves, concerts, truck pulls, and all. We've got a couple gals on, you know. I just think it's great. More power to you."

She was willing to bet money that when he was sitting around drinking with the boys, he called those women names even she wouldn't use. She knew Vanlees's type firsthand. "So you work security there and look after this complex too?"

"Yeah, well, you know my wife—we're separated—she works for the management company, and that's how we got the town house, 'cause I'm telling you, for what they charge for these places...It's unreal.

"So I'm kind of like the super, you know, even though I'm not living here now. The owners here count on me, so I'm hanging in until the wife decides what to do. People have problems—plumbing, electrical, whatnot— I see it gets taken care of. I've got the locksmith coming to change the locks on Miss Bondurant's place this afternoon. And I keep an eye out, you know. Unofficial security. The residents appreciate it. They know I'm on the job, that I've got the training."

"Is Miss Bondurant's unit this way?" Moss

163

inquired, gesturing toward the river, leaning, hinting.

Vanlees frowned at her, the small eyes going smaller still. "I talked to some detectives yesterday." As if he thought she might be an impostor with her mousy-mom looks, not the real deal like Liska.

"Yeah, well, we're following up," Liska said casually. "You know how it is." Though he clearly didn't have a clue other than what he'd picked up watching *NYPD Blue* and reading cheesy detective magazines. Some people would cooperate better when they felt included. Others wanted all kinds of assurances neither the crime nor the investigation would taint their lives in any way.

Vanlees dug a ring of keys out of his jacket pocket and led the way down the sidewalk. "I applied to the police department once," he confided. "They had a hiring freeze on. You know, budgets and all."

"Jeez, that's tough," Liska said, doing her best Frances McDormand in *Fargo* impersonation. "You know, it seems like we always need good people, but that budget hang-up, that's a kicker...."

Vanlees nodded, the man in the know. "Political BS—but I don't need to tell you, right?"

"You got that right. Who knows how many potential great cops like yourself are working other jobs. It's a shame."

"I could have done the job." Years-old bitterness colored his tone like an old stain that wouldn't quite wash out.

"So, did you know this Bondurant girl, Gil?"

"Oh, sure, I saw her around. She never had much to say. Unfriendly type. She's dead, huh? They wouldn't say it for sure on the news, but it's her, right?"

"We've got some questions unanswered."

"I heard there was a witness. To what—that's what I'm wondering. I mean, did they see him kill her or what? That'd be something, huh? Awful."

"I can't really get into it, you know?" Liska said, apologetic. "I'd like to—you being in a related field and all—but you know how it is."

Vanlees nodded with false wisdom.

"You saw her Friday?" Moss asked. "Jillian Bondurant?"

"Yeah. About three. I was here working on my garbage disposal. The wife tried to run celery through it. What a mess. Little Miss College Graduate. You'd think she'd have more brains than to do that."

"Jillian Bondurant..." Moss prompted.

He narrowed his mismatched eyes again. "I was looking out the kitchen window. Saw her drive out."

"Alone?"

"Yep."

"And that was the last time you saw her?"

"Yeah." He turned back to Liska. "That nutcase burned her up, didn't he? The Cremator. Jeez, that's sick," he said, though morbid fascination sparked bright in his expression. "What's this town coming to?"

"Your guess is as good as mine."

"I think it's the millennium. That's what I think," he ventured. "World's just gonna get crazier and crazier. The thousand years is over and all that."

"*Millennium,*" Moss muttered, squinting down at a terra-cotta pot of dead chrysanthemums on the deck of Jillian Bondurant's small front porch.

"Could be," Liska said. "God help us all, eh?"

"God help us," Moss echoed sarcastically.

"Too late for Miss Bondurant," Vanlees said soberly, turning the key in the brass lock. "You need any help here, Detective?"

"No, thanks, Gil. Regulations and all..." Liska turned to face him, blocking his entrance to the house. "Did you ever see Miss Bondurant with anyone in particular? Friends? A boyfriend?"

"I saw her dad here every once in a while. He actually owns the unit. No boyfriend. A girlfriend every once in a while. A friend, I mean. Not *girlfriend*—at least I don't think so."

"One particular girl? You know her name?"

"No. She wasn't too friendly either. Had a mean look to her. Almost like a biker chick, but not. Anyway, I never had anything to do with her. She—Miss Bondurant—was usually alone, never said much. She didn't really fit in here. Not too many of the residents are students, and then she dressed kind of strange. Army boots and black clothes and all."

"Did she ever seem out of it to you?"

"Like on drugs, you mean? No. Was she into drugs?"

"I'm just covering my bases, you know, or else my lieutenant..."

She let the suggestion hang, the impression being that Vanlees could empathize, blood brother that he was. She thanked him for his help and gave him her business card with instructions to call if he thought of anything that might be helpful to the case. He backed away from the door, reluctant, craning his neck to see what Moss was doing deeper into the apartment. Liska waved good-bye and closed the door.

"Eew, Christ, let me go take a shower," she whispered, shuddering as she came into the living room.

"Jeez, you didn't like him, then, Margie?" Moss said with an exaggerated north country accent.

Liska made a face at her and at the odd combination of aromas that hung in the air—sweet air freshener over stale cigarette smoke. "Hey, I got him talking, didn't I?"

"You're shameless."

"In the line of duty."

"Makes me glad I'm menopausal."

Liska sobered, her gaze on the door. "Seriously, those cop wanna-bes creep me out. They always have an authority thing. A need for power and control, and a deep-seated poor self-image. More often than not, they've got a thing against women. Hey!" She brightened again suddenly. "I'll have to bring this theory to the attention of Special Agent Quite Good-looking."

"Hussy."

"I prefer *opportunist.*"

Jillian Bondurant's living room had a view of the river. The furnishings looked new. Overstuffed nubby sofa and chairs the color of oatmeal. Glass-topped rattan coffee table and end tables dirty with the fine soot of fingerprint dust left behind by the Bureau of Investigation team. An entertainment center with a large televison and a top-line stereo system. In one corner a desk and matching bookshelves held textbooks, notebooks, everything pertaining to Jillian's studies at the U, all of it ridiculously neat. Along another wall sat the latest in shiny black electronic pianos. The kitchen, easily seen from the living room, was immaculate.

"We'll need to find out if she had maid service."

"Not the digs of the average flat-broke college student," Liska said. "But then, I gotta think nothing much about this kid was average. She had a pretty atypical childhood trotting all over Europe."

"And yet she came back here for college. What's with that? She could have gone anywhere—to the Sorbonne, to Oxford, to Harvard, to Southern Cal. She could have gone somewhere warm and sunny. She could have gone somewhere exotic. Why come here?"

"To be close to Daddy."

Moss walked the room, her gaze scanning for anything that might give a clue about their victim. "I guess that makes sense. But still...My daughter Beth and I have a great relationship, but the second that girl graduated high school, she wanted out of the nest."

"Where'd she go?"

"University of Wisconsin at Madison. My husband isn't Peter Bondurant. She had to fly somewhere with tuition reciprocity," Moss said, checking through the magazines. *Psychology Today* and *Rolling Stone.*

"If my old man had a billion bucks and would spring for a place like this, I'd want to spend time with him too. Maybe I can get Bondurant to adopt me."

"Who was here yesterday?"

"They sent a couple of uniforms after the body was found with Bondurant's DL—just to make sure she wasn't here, alive and oblivious. Then Sam came over with Elwood to look around. They canvassed the neighbors. Nobody knew anything. He picked up her address book, credit card receipts, phone bills, and a few other things, but he didn't come up with any big prizes. Gotta think if she had a drug habit, the B of I guys would have found something."

"Maybe she carried everything with her in her purse."

"And risk losing her stash to a purse snatcher? I don't think so. Besides, this place is way too clean for a druggie."

Two bedrooms with two full baths on the

second level. In her small house in St. Paul, Liska had the cozy pleasure of sharing one small crummy bathroom with her sons, ages eleven and nine. She made good pay as a detective, but things like hockey league and orthodontists cost bucks, and the child support her ex had been directed by the courts to pay was laughable. She often thought she should have had sense enough to get knocked up by a rich guy instead of by a guy *named* Rich.

Jillian's bedroom was as eerily tidy as the rest of the house. The queen-size bed had been stripped bare by the B of I team, the sheets taken to the lab to be tested for any sign of blood or seminal fluid. There was no discarded clothing draped over chairs or trailing on the floor, no half-open dresser drawers spilling lingerie, no pile of abandoned shoes—nothing like Liska's own crowded room she never had the time or desire to clean. Who the hell ever saw it but herself and the boys? Who ever saw Jillian Bondurant's room?

No snapshots of a boyfriend tucked into the mirror above the oak dresser. No photos of family members. She pulled open the drawers in the nightstands that flanked the bed. No condoms, no diaphragm. A clean ashtray and a tiny box of matches from D'Cup Coffee House.

Nothing about the room gave away any personal information about its occupant— which suggested to Liska two possibilities: that Jillian Bondurant was the princess of repression, or that someone had come through the house after her disappearance and sanitized the place.

Matches and the smell of cigarettes, but every ashtray in the place was clean.

Vanlees had a key. Who else could they add to that list? Peter Bondurant. Jillian's mean-looking girlfriend? The killer. The killer now had Jillian's keys, her address, her car, her credit cards. Kovac had immediately put a trace on the cards to catch any activity following the girl's disappearance Friday night. So far, nothing. Every cop in the greater metro area had the description and tag numbers on Bondurant's red Saab. Nothing yet.

The master bath was clean. Mauve and jade green with decorative soaps no one was supposed to actually use. The shampoo in the bathtub rack was Paul Mitchell with a sticker from a salon in the Dinkydale shopping center. A possible source of information if Jillian had been the kind to confess all to her hairdresser. There was nothing of interest in the medicine cabinet or beneath the sink.

The second bedroom was smaller, the bed also stripped. Summer clothes hung in the closet, pushed out of the master bedroom by the rapid approach of another brutal Minnesota winter. Odds and ends occupied the dresser drawers—a few pair of underpants: black, silky, size five; a black lace bra from Frederick's of Hollywood: skimpy, wash-worn, 34B; a pair of cheap black leggings with a hole in one knee, size S. The clothes were not folded, and Liska had the feeling they did not belong to Bondurant.

The friend? There wasn't enough stuff to indicate a full-time roommate. The fact that this second bedroom was being used discounted the idea of a lover. She went back into the master suite and checked the dresser drawers again.

"You coming up with anything?" Moss asked, stepping into the bedroom doorway, careful not to lean against the jamb, grimy with fingerprint powder.

"The willies. Either this chick was incredibly anal or a phantom house fairy got here before anyone else. She went missing Friday. That gave the killer a good two days with her keys."

"But there've been no reports of anyone unknown or suspicious coming around."

"So maybe the killer wasn't unknown or suspicious. I wonder if we could get a surveillance team to watch the place for a couple days," Liska mused. "Maybe the guy'll show up."

"Better chance he's already been here and gone. He'd be taking a big risk coming back after the body had been found."

"He took a pretty big risk lighting up that body in the park."

Liska pulled her cell phone out of a coat pocket and dialed Kovac's number, then listened impatiently while it rang unanswered. Finally she gave up and stuffed the phone back in her pocket. "Sam must have left his coat in the car again. He oughta wear that phone on a chain like a trucker's wallet. Well, you're probably right anyway. If Smokey Joe wanted to come back here, he'd do it after he'd killed her but before her body had been discovered. And if he's been here already, maybe his prints are being run even as we speak."

"We should get that lucky."

Liska sighed. "I found some clothes that probably belong to a girlfriend in the second bedroom, found the name of Jillian's hair salon and a book of matches for a coffeehouse."

"D'Cup?" Moss said. "I found one too. Should we try it on for size?"

Liska smirked. "A D cup? In my ex-husband's dreams. You know what I found in his sock drawer once?" she said as they walked down into the living room together. "One of those dirty magazines full of women with big, huge, giant, gargantuan tits. I'm talking hooters that would hang to your knees. Page after page of this. Tits, tits, tits the size of the *Hindenburg*. And men think *we're* bad because we want six inches to *mean* six inches."

Moss made a sound between a groan and a giggle. "Nikki, after a day with you, I'm going to have to go to confession."

"Well, while you're there, ask the priest what it is about boys and boobs."

They let themselves out of the apartment and locked the place behind them. The wind blew down the river, sweeping along the scents of mud and decaying leaves and the metallic tinge of the city and the machines that inhabited it. Moss pulled her jacket tight around her.

173

Liska shoved her hands deep in her pockets and hunched her shoulders. They walked back to the car, complaining in advance about how long winter was going to be. Winter was always too long in Minnesota.

As they backed out of the parking slot, Gil Vanlees stood looking out the door of the house he no longer lived in, watching them with a blank expression until Liska raised a hand and waved good-bye.

"**WHY DON'T WE** try again, Angie?" the forensic artist said gently.

His name was Oscar and he had a voice the consistency of warm caramel. Kate had seen him lull people nearly to sleep with that voice: Angie DiMarco wasn't about to be lulled.

Kate stood behind the girl and a good six feet back, near the door. She didn't want her own impatience compounding Angie's nervousness. The girl sat in her chair, squirming like a toddler in a pediatrician's waiting room, unhappy, uncomfortable, uncooperative. She looked like she hadn't slept well, though she had taken advantage of the bathroom facilities at the Phoenix and showered. Her brown hair was still limp and straight, but it was clean. She wore the same denim jacket over a different sweater and the same dirty jeans.

"I want you to close your eyes," the artist said. "Take a slow, deep breath and let it out—"

Angie heaved an impatient sigh.

"—slooowly..."

Kate had to give the man credit for his tolerance. She personally felt on the verge of slapping someone, anyone. But then, Oscar hadn't had the pleasure of picking up Angie from Phoenix House, where Toni Urskine had yet again unleashed her frustration with the Cremator cases on Kate.

"Two women brutally murdered and nothing gets done because they were prostitutes. My God, the police even went so far as to say there was no threat to the general public—as if these women didn't count as citizens of this city! It's outrageous!"

Kate had refrained from attempting to explain the concept of high-risk and low-risk victim pools. She knew too well what the reaction would be—emotional, visceral, without logic.

"The police couldn't care less about women who are driven by desperation into prostitution and drugs. What's another dead hooker to them—one less problem off the street. A millionaire's daughter is murdered and suddenly we have a crisis! My God, a *real* person has been victimized!" she had ranted sarcastically.

Kate made an effort to loosen the clenching muscles in her jaw even now. She had never liked Toni Urskine. Urskine worked around the clock to keep her indignation cooking at a slow burn. If she or her ideals or "her victims," as she called the women at the Phoenix, hadn't been slighted outright, she would find some way of perceiving an insult so she could climb up on her soapbox and shriek at anyone within hearing distance. The Cremator murders would give her fuel for her own fire for a long time to come.

Urskine had a certain amount of justification for her outrage, Kate admitted. Similar cynical thoughts about these cases had run through Kate's own mind. But she knew the cops had been working those first two murders, doing the best they could with the limited manpower and budget the brass allowed for the average violent death.

Still, the only thing she'd wanted to say to Toni Urskine that morning was "Life's a bitch. Get over it." Her tongue still hurt from biting it. Instead, she'd offered, "I'm not a cop, I'm an advocate. I'm on your side."

A lot of people didn't want to hear that either. She worked with the police and was considered guilty by association. And there were plenty of times when the cops looked at her and saw her as an enemy because she worked with a lot of bleeding-heart liberals who spent too much time bad-mouthing the police. Stuck in the middle.

Good thing I love this job, or I'd hate it.

"You're in the park, but you're safe," Oscar said gently. "The danger is past, Angie. He can't hurt you now. Open your mind's eye and look at his face. Take a good long look."

Kate moved slowly to a chair a few feet from her witness and eased herself down. Angie caught Kate's steady gaze and shifted the other way to find Oscar watching her too, his kindly eyes twinkling like polished onyx in a face that was drowning in hair—a full beard and mustache and a bushy lion's mane worn loose around his thick shoulders.

"You can't see if you won't look, Angie," he said wisely.

"Maybe I don't want to see," the girl challenged.

Oscar looked sad for her. "He can't hurt you here, Angie. And all you have to look at is his face. You don't have to look inside his mind or his heart. All you have to see is his face."

Oscar had sat across from a lot of witnesses in his time, all of them afraid of the same two things: retribution by the criminal sometime in the vague future, and the more immediate fear of having to relive the crime over and over. Kate knew a memory or a nightmare could cause as much psychological stress as an event taking place in real time. As evolved as people liked to believe the human race had become, the mind still had difficulty differentiating between actual reality and perceived reality.

The silence went on. Oscar looked at Kate.

"Angie, you told me you'd do this," she said.

The girl scowled harder. "Yeah, well, maybe I changed my mind. I mean, what the hell's in it for me?"

"Keeping safe and taking a killer off the street."

"No, I mean *really*," she said, suddenly all business. "What's in it for me? I hear there's a reward. You never said anything about a reward."

"I haven't had time to talk to anyone about it."

"Well, you'd better. 'Cause if I'm gonna do this, then I damn well want something for it. I deserve it."

"That remains to be seen," Kate said. "So far you haven't given us squat. I'll check into the reward. In the meantime, you're a witness. You can help us and we can help you. Maybe you don't feel ready for this. Maybe you don't think your memory is strong enough. If that's what's really going on here, then fine. The cops have mug books stacked to the rafters. Maybe you'll run across him in there."

"And maybe I can just get the fuck out of here." She shoved herself up out of the chair so hard, the legs scraped back across the floor.

Kate wanted to choke her. This was why she didn't work juvenile: Her tolerance for drama and bullshit was too low.

She studied Angie, trying to formulate a strategy. If the kid really wanted to leave, she would leave. No one was barring the door. What Angie wanted was to make a scene and have everyone fuss over her and beg her to come back. Begging was not an option as far as Kate was concerned. She wouldn't play a game where she didn't have a shot at control.

If she called the kid's bluff and Angie walked, Kate figured she could just as well follow the girl out the door. Sabin would put her career through the shredder if she lost his star and only witness. She was already on her second career. How many more could she have?

She rose slowly and went to lean against the doorjamb with her arms crossed.

"You know, Angie, I gotta think there's a reason you told us you saw this guy in the first place. You didn't have to say it. You didn't know anything about a reward. You could have lied and told us he was gone when you came across the body. How would we know any different? We have to take your word for what you saw or didn't see. So let's cut the crap, huh? I don't appreciate you jerking me around when I'm on your side. I'm the one who's standing between you and the county attorney who wants to toss your ass in jail and call you a suspect."

Angie set her jaw at a mulish angle. "Don't threaten me."

"That's not a threat. I'm being straight with you because I think that's what you want. You don't want to be lied to and screwed over any more than I do. I respect that. How about returning the favor?"

The girl gnawed on a ragged thumbnail, her hair swinging down to obscure her face, but Kate could tell she was blinking hard, and felt a swift wave of sympathy. The mood swings this kid inspired were going to drive her to Prozac.

"You must think I'm a real pain in the ass," Angie said at last, her lush mouth twisting at one corner in what looked almost like chagrin.

"Yeah, but I don't consider that a fatal or irreversible flaw. And I know you've got your reasons. But you've got more to be afraid of if you don't try to ID him," Kate said. "Now you're the only one who knows what he looks like. Better if a couple hundred cops know too."

"What happens if I don't do it?"

"No reward. Other than that, I don't know. Right now you're a potential witness. If you decide that's not what you are, then it's out of my hands. The county attorney might play rough or he might just cut you loose. He'll take me out of the picture either way."

"You'd probably be glad."

"I didn't take this job because I thought it would be simple and pleasant. I don't want to see you alone in all this, Angie. And I don't think that's what you want either."

Alone. Goose bumps chased themselves down Angie's arms and legs. The word was a constant hollowness in the core of her. She remembered the feeling of it growing inside her last night, pushing her consciousness into a smaller and smaller corner of her mind. It was the thing she feared most in the world and beyond it. More than physical pain. More than a killer.

"We'll leave you alone. How would you like that, brat? You can be alone forever. You just sit in there and think about it. Maybe we'll never come back."

She flinched at the remembered sound of the door closing, the absolute darkness of the closet, the sense of aloneness swallowing

180

her up. She felt it rising up inside her now like a black ghost. It closed around her throat like an unseen hand, and she wanted to cry, but she knew she couldn't. Not here. Not now. Her heart began beating harder and faster.

"Come on, kiddo," Kate said gently, nodding toward Oscar. "Give it a shot. It's not like you've got anything better to do. I'll make a phone call about that reward money."

The story of my life, Angie thought. *Do what I want or I'll leave you. Do what I want or I'll hurt you.* Choices that weren't choices.

"All right," she murmured, and went back to the chair to give instructions on drawing a portrait of evil.

11

CHAPTER

THE BUILDING that housed the offices of Dr. Lucas Brandt, two other psychotherapists, and two psychiatrists was a Georgian-style brick home of gracious proportion. Patients seeking treatment here probably felt more like they were going to high tea than to pour out their innermost secrets and psychological dirty laundry.

Lucas Brandt's office was on the second floor. Quinn and Kovac were left to cool their heels in the hall for ten minutes while he finished with a patient. Bach's Third Brandenburg Concerto floated on the air as soft as a whisper. Quinn stared out the Palladian window that offered a view of Lake of the Isles and part of the larger Lake Calhoun, both as gray as old quarters in the gloom of the day.

Kovac prowled the hall, checking out the furniture. "Real antiques. Classy. Why is it rich crazies are classy and the kind I have to haul into jail just want to piss on my shoes?"

"Repression."

"What?"

"Social skills are founded and couched in repression. Rich crazies want to piss on your shoes too," Quinn smiled, "but their manners hold them back."

Kovac chuckled. "I like you, Quinn. I'm gonna have to give you a nickname." He looked at Quinn, taking in the sharp suit, considering for a moment, then nodded. "GQ. Yeah, I like that. GQ, like the magazine. G like in G-man. Q like in Quinn." He looked enormously pleased with himself. "Yeah, I like that."

He didn't ask if Quinn liked it.

The door to Brandt's business office opened, and his secretary, a petite woman with red hair and no chin, invited them in, her voice a librarian's whisper.

The patient, if there had been one, must have escaped out the door of the second room.

Lucas Brandt rose from behind his desk as they entered the room, and an unpleasant flash of recognition hit Kovac. *Brandt.* The name had rung a bell, but he wouldn't have equated the Brandt of his association with the Brandt of *Neuroses of the Rich and Famous.*

They went through the round of introductions, Kovac waiting for that same recognition to dawn on Brandt, but it didn't—which served only to further sour Kovac's mood. Brandt's expression was appropriately serious. Blond and Germanically attractive with a straight nose and blue eyes, he was of medium build with a posture and presence that gave the impression he was bigger than he really was. *Solid* was the word that came to mind. He wore a trendy silk tie and a blue dress shirt that looked professionally ironed. A steel-gray suit coat hung on one of those fancy-ass gentleman's racks in the corner.

Kovac smoothed a hand self-consciously over his J. C. Penney tie. "Dr. Brandt. I've seen you in court."

"Yes, you probably have. Forensic psychology—a sideline I picked up when I was first starting out," he explained for Quinn. "I needed the money at the time," he confessed with a conspiratorial little smile that let them in on the joke that he didn't need it now. "I found I enjoyed the work, so I've kept a hand in it. It's a good diversion from what I see day to day."

Kovac arched a brow. "Take a break from rich girls with eating disorders and go testify for some scumbag. Yeah, there's a hobby."

"I work for who needs me, Detective. Defense or prosecution."

You work for who pulls his wallet out first. Kovac knew better than to say it.

"I'm due in court this afternoon, as a matter of fact," Brandt said. "And I've got a lunch date first. So, while I hate to be rude, gentlemen, can we get down to business here?"

"Just a few quick questions," Kovac said, picking up the toy rake that went with the Zen garden on the credenza by the window. He looked from the rake to the box as if he expected it was for digging up cat feces.

"You know I can't be of much help to your investigation. Jillian was my patient. My hands are tied by doctor-patient confidentiality."

"Your patient is dead," Kovac said bluntly. He picked up a smooth black stone from the sand and turned to lean back against the credenza, rolling the stone between his fingers. A man settling in, making himself comfortable. "I don't think her expectations for privacy are quite what they were."

Brandt looked almost amused. "You can't seem to make up your mind, Detective. Is Jillian dead or not? You implied to Peter she may still be alive. If Jillian is alive, then she still has the expectation of privacy."

"There's a high probability the body found is Jillian Bondurant's, but it's not a certainty," Quinn said, moving back toward the conversation, taking the reins diplomatically from Kovac. "Either way, we're working against the clock, Dr. Brandt. This killer will kill again. That's an absolute. Sooner rather than later, I think. The more we can find out about his victims, the closer we will be to stopping him."

"I'm familiar with your theories, Agent Quinn. I've read some of your articles. In fact, I think I have the textbook you coauthored somewhere on those shelves. Very insightful. Know the victims, know their killer."

"That's part of it. This killer's first two victims were high risk. Jillian doesn't seem to fit the mold."

Brandt sat back against the edge of his desk, tapped a forefinger against his lips, and nodded slowly. "The deviation from the pattern. I see. That makes her the logical centerpiece to the puzzle. You think he's saying more about himself in killing Jillian than with the other two. But what if she were just in the wrong place at the wrong time? What if he didn't choose the first two because they were prostitutes? Perhaps all the victims were situational."

"No," Quinn said, studying the subtle, curious light of challenge in Brandt's eyes. "There's nothing random in this guy's bag of tricks. He picked each of these women for a reason. The reason should be more apparent with Jillian. How long had she been seeing you?"

"Two years."

"How had she come to you? By referral?"

"By golf. Peter and I are both members at Minikahda. An excellent place to make connections," he confessed with a smile, pleased with his own clever business acumen.

"You'd make more if you lived in Florida," Quinn joked. *Aren't we buddies—so smart, so resourceful.* "The season here has to be— what?—all of two months?"

"Three if we have spring," Brandt shot back, settling into the rhythm of repartee. "A lot of time spent in the clubhouse. The dining room is lovely. You golf?"

"When I get the chance." Never because he enjoyed it. Always as an opportunity for a contact, a chance to get his ideas through to his SAC or the unit chief, or supposed downtime with law enforcement personnel he was working cases with across the country. Not so different from Lucas Brandt after all.

"Too bad the season's over," Brandt said.

"Yeah," Kovac drawled, "damned inconsiderate for this killer to work in November, if you look at it that way."

Brandt flicked him a glance. "That's hardly what I meant, Detective. Though, now that you've brought it up, it's a shame you didn't catch him this summer. We wouldn't be having this conversation.

"Anyway," he said, turning back to Quinn. "I've known Peter for years."

"He doesn't strike me as a very social man."

"No. Golf is serious business with Peter. Everything is serious with Peter. He's very driven."

"How did that quality impact his relationship with Jillian?"

"Ah!" He held up a finger in warning and shook his head, still smiling. "Crossing the line, Agent Quinn."

Quinn acknowledged the breach with a tip of his head.

"When did you last speak with Jillian?" Kovac asked.

"We had a session Friday. Every Friday at four."

"And then she'd go over to her father's house for supper?"

"Yes. Peter and Jillian were working very hard on their relationship. They'd been separated for a long time. A lot of old feelings to deal with."

"Such as?"

Brandt blinked at him.

"All right. What about a general statement, say, about the root of Jillian's problems? Give us an impression."

"Sorry. No."

Kovac gave a little sigh. "Look, you could answer a few simple questions without breaching anyone's trust. For instance, whether or not she was on any medication. We need to know for the tox screen."

"Prozac. Trying to even out her mood swings."

"Manic depressive?" Quinn asked.

The doctor gave him a look.

"Did she have any problem with drugs that you knew of?" Kovac tried.

"No comment."

"Was she having trouble with a boyfriend?"

Nothing.

"Did she ever talk about anyone abusing her?"

Silence.

Kovac rubbed a hand over his mouth, petting his mustache. He could feel his temper crumbling like old cork. "You know this girl two years. You know her father. He considers you a friend. You could maybe give us a direction in this girl's murder. And you waste our time with this bullshit game—pick and choose, hot and cold."

Quinn cleared his throat discreetly. "You know the rules, Sam."

"Yeah, well, fuck the rules!" Kovac barked, flipping a book of Mapplethorpe photographs off the end table. "If I was a defense attorney waving a wad of cash, you can bet he'd find a loophole to ooze through."

"I resent that, Detective."

"Oh, well, yeah, I'm sorry I hurt your feelings. Somebody tortured this girl, Doctor." He pushed away from the credenza, his expression as hard as the stone he shot into the wastebasket. The sound was like a .22 popping. "Somebody cut her head off and kept it for a souvenir. If I knew this girl, I think I would care about who did that to her. And if I could help catch the sick bastard, I would. But you care more about your social status than you care about Jillian Bondurant. I wonder if her father realizes that."

He gave a harsh laugh as his pager went off. "What the hell am I saying? Peter Bondurant doesn't even want to believe his daughter could be alive. The two of you probably deserve each other."

The pager trilled again. He checked the readout, swore under his breath, and went out of the office, leaving Quinn to deal with the aftermath.

Brandt managed to find something amusing in Kovac's outburst. "Well, that was quick. It generally takes the average cop a little longer to lose his temper with me."

"Sergeant Kovac is under a great deal of stress with these murders," Quinn said, moving to the credenza and the Zen garden. "I apologize on his behalf."

The stones in the box had been arranged to form an X, the sand raked in a sinuous pattern around them. His mind flashed on the lacerations in the victim's feet—a double X pattern—and on the stab wounds to the victim's chest—two intersecting Xs.

"Is the pattern significant?" he asked casually.

"Not to me," Brandt said. "My patients play with that more than I do. I find it calms some people, encourages the flow of thought and communication."

Quinn knew several agents at the NCAVC who kept Zen gardens. Their offices were sixty feet below ground—ten times deeper than the dead, they joked. No windows, no fresh air, and the knowledge that the weight of the earth pressed in on the walls were all symbolic enough to give Freud a hard-on. A person needed something to relieve the tension. Personally, he preferred to hit things—hard. He spent hours in the gym punishing a punching bag for the sins of the world.

"No apology needed on Kovac's behalf." Brandt bent down to pick up the Mapplethorpe book. "I'm an old hand at dealing with the police. Everything is simple to them. You're either a good guy or a bad guy. They don't seem to understand that I find the boundaries of my professional ethics frustrating at times too, but they are what they are. You understand."

He set the book aside and sat back against his desk, his hip just nudging a small stack of files. The label read BONDURANT, JILLIAN. A microcassette recorder lay atop the file, as if perhaps he had been at work or would still work on his notes from his last session with her.

"I understand your position. I hope you understand mine," Quinn said carefully. "I'm not a cop here. While our ultimate goal is the same, Sergeant Kovac and I have different agendas. My profile doesn't require the kind of evidence admissible in court. I'm looking for impressions, feelings, gut instinct, details some would consider insignificant. Sam's looking for a bloody knife with fingerprints. You see what I mean?"

Brandt nodded slowly, never taking his eyes from Quinn's. "Yes, I believe I do. I'll have to think about it. But at the same time, you should consider that the problems Jillian brought to me may have had nothing whatsoever to do with her death. Her killer may not have known anything at all about her."

"And then again, he might have known the

one thing that set him off," Quinn said. He took a business card from a slim case in his breast pocket and handed it to Brandt. "This is my direct line at the Bureau office downtown. I hope to hear from you."

Brandt set the card aside and shook his hand. "With due consideration for the circumstances, it was a pleasure meeting you. I have to confess, I'm the one who suggested your name to Peter when he told me he wanted to call your director."

Quinn's mouth twisted as he started for the door. "I'm not so sure I should thank you for that, Dr. Brandt."

He left the office through the reception area, glancing at the woman waiting on the camelback sofa with her feet perfectly together and her red Coach bag balanced on her knees, her expression a carefully blank screen over annoyance and embarrassment. She didn't want to be seen there.

He wondered how Jillian had felt coming here and confiding all to one of her father's sycophants. Had it been a choice or a condition of Peter's support? She'd shown up every week for two years, and only God and Lucas Brandt knew why. And very possibly Bondurant. Brandt could preen for them and display his ethics like a peacock fanning his tail feathers, but Quinn suspected Kovac was right: When it came down to it, Brandt's first obligation would be to himself. And keeping Peter Bondurant happy would go a long way toward keeping Lucas Brandt happy.

Kovac was waiting in the foyer on the first floor, staring in puzzlement at an abstract painting of a woman with three eyes and breasts growing out the sides of her head.

"Jesus Christ, that's uglier than my second wife's mother—and she could break a mirror from fifty feet away. You suppose they hang it there just to give their crazies an extra little tweak on the way in and out?"

"It's a Rorschach test," Quinn said. "They're looking to weed out the guys who think it's a woman with three eyes and breasts on the sides of her head."

Kovac frowned and stole a last look at the thing before they stepped outside.

"One phone call from Brandt and my sorry butt's in a sling," he groused as they descended the steps. "I can hear my lieutenant now—'What the hell were you thinking, Kovac?' Jesus, Brandt'll probably sic the chief on me. They're probably in the same fucking backgammon league. They probably get manicures together. Greer'll get up on a ladder, rip my head off, and shout down the hole—'What the hell were you thinking, Kovac? Thirty days without pay!' "

He shook his head. "What the hell was I thinking?"

"I don't know. What the hell were you thinking?"

"That I *hate* that guy, that's what."

"Really? I thought we were playing good cop-bad cop."

Kovac looked at him over the roof of the

Caprice. "I'm not that good an actor. Do I look like Harrison Ford?"

Quinn squinted. "Maybe if you lose the mustache..."

They slid into the car from their respective sides, Kovac's laugh dying as he shook his head. "I don't know what I'm laughing about. I know better than to go off like that. Brandt yanks my chain, that's all. I'm kicking myself because I didn't place him until I saw him. I just wasn't expecting..."

No excuse was a good excuse. He blew air between his lips and stared out the windshield through the naked fingerling branches of a dormant bush to the lake in the distance.

"You know him from a case?" Quinn asked.

"Yeah. Eight or nine years ago he testified for the defense in a murder case I worked. Carl Borchard, nineteen, killed his girlfriend after she tried to break up with him. Choked her. Brandt comes in with this sob story about how Borchard's mother abandoned him, and how this stress with his girlfriend pushed him over a line. He tells the jury how we all should pity Carl, 'cause he didn't mean it and he was so remorseful. How he wasn't really a killer. It was a crime of passion. He wasn't a danger to society. Blah, blah, blah. Boo-hoo-hoo."

"And you knew different?"

"Carl Borchard was a whiny, sociopathic little shit with a juvenile sheet full of stuff the prosecutors couldn't get admitted. He had a history of acting out against women. Brandt knew that as well as we did, but he wasn't on our payroll."

"Borchard got off."

"Manslaughter. First adult offense, reduced sentence, time served, et cetera, et cetera. The little creep barely had time to take a crap in prison. Then they send him to a halfway house. While he's living at this halfway house he rapes a woman in the next neighborhood and beats her head in with a claw hammer. Thank you, Dr. Brandt.

"You know what he had to say about it?" Kovac said with amazement. "He was in the *Star Tribune* saying he thought Carl had 'exhausted his victim pool' with the first murder, but, hey, shit happens. He went on to say he couldn't really be held accountable for this little blunder because he hadn't been able to spend all that much time with Borchard. Fucking amazing."

Quinn absorbed the information quietly. The feeling that he was getting too close to this case pressed in on him again. He felt the people in it crowding around him, standing too close for him to really see them. He wanted them back and away. He didn't want to know anything about Lucas Brandt, didn't want to have a personal impression of the man. He wanted what Brandt could give him from an arm's length. He wanted to go lock himself in the neat, paneled office the SAC had given him in the building on Washington Avenue downtown. But that wasn't the way things were going to work here.

194

"I know something else about your Dr. Brandt," he said as Kovac started the car and put it in gear.

"What's that?"

"He was standing in the background at the press conference yesterday."

"THERE HE IS." Kovac hit the freeze button on the remote control. The picture jerked and twitched as the VCR held the tape in place. To the side of the press mob, standing with a pack of suits, was Brandt. A muscle at the base of Kovac's diaphragm tightened like a fist. He punched the play button and watched the psychologist tip his head and say something to the man next to him. He froze the picture again.

"Who's that he's talking to?"

"Ahh..." Yurek tipped his head sideways for a better angle. "Kellerman, the public defender."

"Oh, yeah. Worm Boy. Call him. See if Brandt and him were together," Kovac ordered. "Find out if Brandt had any legit reason to be there."

Adler raised a brow. "You think he's a suspect?"

"I think he's an asshole."

"If that was against the law, the jails would be full of lawyers."

"He jerked me around this morning," Kovac complained. "Him and Bondurant are too cozy, and Bondurant's jerking us around too."

"He's the victim's father," Adler pointed out.

"He's the victim's *rich* father," Tippen added.

"He's the victim's rich, *powerful* father," Yurek, Mr. Public Relations, reminded all.

Kovac gave him a look. "He's part of a murder investigation. I've gotta run this investigation as tight as any other. That means we look at everybody. Family always comes under the microscope. I want to step on Brandt a little, let him know we're not just a pack of tame dogs Peter Bondurant can order around. If he can give us anything on Jillian Bondurant, I want it. And I also want to step on him because he's a fucking tick."

"This smells like trouble, Kojak," Yurek sang.

"It's a murder investigation, Charm. You want to consult Emily Post?"

"I want to come out of it with my career intact."

"Your career is investigating," Kovac returned. "Brandt had a connection to Jillian Bondurant."

"You got any reason other than not liking him to think this prick shrink would off two hookers and decapitate a patient?" Tippen asked.

"I'm not saying he's a suspect," he snapped. "He saw Jillian Bondurant Friday. He saw her every Friday. He knows everything we need to know about this vic. If he's withholding information on us, we have a right to squeeze him a little."

"And make him squeal privilege."

"He's already singing that song. Skate around it. Stay on the fringes. If we can so much as get him to mention the name of Jillian's boyfriend, that's something we didn't have before. As soon as we confirm the DB is Jillian, then there's no longer an expectation of privacy and we can lean on Brandt for details.

"Something else I don't like about this jerk," Kovac added, pacing beside the table, the wheels of his brain spinning. "I don't like that he's been associated with God knows how many criminals. I want a list of every violent offender he's ever testified for or against."

"I'll get it," Tippen offered. "My ex works in records for the felony courts. She hates my guts, but she'll hate this killer more. I'll look good by comparison."

"Man, that's sad, Tip." Adler shook his head. "You barely rank above the scumbags."

"Hey, that's a step up from when she filed the papers."

"And Bondurant," Kovac said, drawing another chorus of groans. "Bondurant won't talk to us, and I don't like that. He told Quinn he was worried about his privacy. Can't imagine why," he added with a sly grin, pulling the mini-cassette recorder out of his coat pocket.

The five members of the task force present crowded around to listen. Liska and Moss were still out doing victim background. The feds had returned to the FBI offices. Walsh was working through the list VICAP had provided of similar crimes committed in other parts

197

of the country. He would be calling agents in other Bureau field offices, and calling contacts he had in various law enforcement agencies through his affiliation with the FBI's National Academy program that offered training to law enforcement professionals outside the Bureau. Quinn had sequestered himself to work on Smokey Joe's profile.

The tape of Bondurant's conversation with Quinn played out. The detectives listened, barely breathing. Kovac tried to picture Bondurant, needing to see the man's face, needing the expressions that went with the mostly expressionless voice. He had gone over the conversation with Quinn, and had Quinn's impressions. But questioning someone via a third party was a lot like trying to have sex with someone who was in another room— a lot of frustration and not much satisfaction.

The tape played out. The machine shut itself off with a sharp click. Kovac looked from one team member to the next. Cop faces: stern with ingrained, guarded skepticism.

"That skinny white boy's hiding something," Adler said at last, sitting back in his chair.

"I don't know that it has anything to do with the murder," Kovac said. "But I'd say he's definitely holding something back on us about Friday night. I want to re-canvass the neighbors and talk to the housekeeper."

"She was gone that night," Elwood said.

"I don't care. She knew the girl. She knows her boss."

Yurek groaned and put his head in his hands.

"What's your problem, Charm?" Tippen asked. "All you have to do is tell the newsies we have no comment at this time."

"Yeah, on national television," he said. "The big dogs smelled this shit and came running. I've got network news people ringing my phone off the hook. Bondurant is news all by himself. Bondurant plus a decapitated, burned corpse that may or may not be his daughter is the kind of stuff that transcends Tom Brokaw, headlines *Dateline,* and sells tabloids by the truckload. Sniff too hard in Peter Bondurant's direction, get the press leaning that way, I'm telling you, he'll blow. We'll be hip-deep in lawsuits and suspensions."

"I'll work on Bondurant and Brandt," Kovac said, knowing he'd have to do a hell of a lot better job of it than he'd done that morning. "I'll take the heat, but I need people working them peripherally, talking to friends, acquaintances, and so forth. Chunk, you and Hamill checking around Paragon? Working the disgruntled-employee angle?"

"Got a meeting out there in thirty."

"Maybe we can talk to someone who knew the girl in France," Tippen suggested. "Maybe the feds can dig up someone over there. Let us in on some of her back story. The kid was screwed up for a reason. Maybe some friend over there knows if this reason has a name."

"Call Walsh and see what he can do. Ask him if there's any word yet on those medical records. Elwood, did you get anything back from Wisconsin on the DL our witness is running around with?"

"No wants, no warrants. I called information to get a phone number—she doesn't have one. I contacted the post office—they say she moved and left no forwarding address. Strike three."

"She give us a sketch yet?" Yurek asked.

"Kate Conlan brought her in this morning to work with Oscar," Kovac said, rising. "I'm gonna go see what's what right now. We'd better pray to God that girl has a Polaroid memory. A break on this thing now could save all our asses."

"I'll need copies ASAP for the press," Yurek said.

"I'll get it to you. What time are you set to play *America's Most Wanted*?"

"Five."

Kovac checked his watch. The day was running double time and they didn't have much to show for it yet. That was the hell of getting an investigation this size off the ground. Time was of the essence. Every cop knew that after the first forty-eight hours of an investigation, the odds of solving a murder dropped off sharply. But the amount of information that needed to be gathered, collated, interpreted, and acted upon at the start of a multiple murder investigation was staggering. And just one piece ignored could be the one piece that turned the tide.

His pager trilled. The readout gave his lieutenant's number.

"Everyone who can, meet back here at four," he said, grabbing his coat off the back of his chair. "If you're out, check in with me on the cell phone. I'm outta here."

"SHE DIDN'T SEEM very sure of herself, Sam," Oscar said, leading him to a tilt-top drawing table in a small office made smaller by a pack rat's clutter. Papers, books, magazines, filled all available space in precarious towers and piles. "I led her through it as gently as I could, but she was resistant at the core."

"Resistant as in lying or resistant as in scared?"

"Afraid. And as you well know, fear can precipitate prevarication."

"You've been into the thesaurus again, haven't you, Oscar?"

A beatific smile peeked through the copious facial hair. "Education is the wellspring of the soul."

"Yeah, well, you'll be drowning in it, Oscar," Kovac said, impatient, digging a lint-ridden Mylanta tablet out of his pants pocket. "So, let's see the masterpiece."

"I consider it a work in progress."

He peeled back the opaque protective sheet, revealing the pencil sketch Twin Cities residents had been promised by their top elected and appointed officials. The suspect wore a dark, puffed-up jacket—hiding his build— over a hooded sweatshirt, hood up, hiding the color of his hair. Aviator sunglasses hid the shape of his eyes. The nose was nondescript, the face of medium width. The mouth was partially obscured by a mustache.

Kovac's stomach did a slow roll. "It's the fucking Unabomber!" he snapped, wheeling on Oscar. "What the hell am I supposed to do with this?"

"Now, Sam, I told you it was a work in progress," Oscar said in that low, slow voice.

"He's wearing *sunglasses*! It was fucking midnight and she's got him wearing sunglasses!" Sam ranted. "Judas fucking priest! This could be anyone. This could be no one. This could be *me*, for godsake!"

"I'm hoping to work with Angie a little more," the artist said, unperturbed by Kovac's temper. "She doesn't believe she has the details in her memory, but I believe she does. She has only to release her fear and clarity will come. Eventually."

"I don't have *eventually*, Oscar! I've got a goddamn press conference at five o'clock!"

He blew out a breath and turned a circuit around the artist's small, cramped, cluttered workspace, looking around as if he wanted to find something to throw. Christ, he sounded like Sabin, wanting evidence on demand. He had been telling himself all day not to count on that lying, thieving little piece of baggage he had to call a witness, but beneath the cynicism, he'd been praying for a dead-on, got-you-by-the-balls-now composite. Twenty-two years on the job and the optimist in him still lived. Amazing.

"I'm working on a version without the mustache," Oscar said. "She seemed uncertain about the mustache."

"How can she be uncertain about a *mustache*! He either had one or he didn't! Fuck! Fuck, fuck, fuck!"

"I won't release it today, that's all," he said mostly to himself. "We'll hold off, get the girl back in here tomorrow, and try to get some better detail."

From the corner of his eye, he could see Oscar drop his head a little. He looked to be retreating into his beard. Kovac stopped his pacing and looked at him square.

"We can do that, can't we, Oscar?"

"I'll be pleased to work with Angie again tomorrow. I'd like nothing better than to help her unblock her memory flow. Confronting memory is the first step to neutralizing its negative power. As for the other, you'll have to take it up with Chief Greer. He was in here an hour ago to get a copy."

"SHE SAW HIS face for two minutes in the light of a burning corpse, Sam," Kate said, leading him into her office, not sure the small space would hold him. When he was wound, Kovac was a barely contained column of energy that required perpetual motion.

"She looked directly at the face of a murderer in bright light. Come on, Red. Wouldn't you think the details would be branded, so to speak, in her memory?"

203

Kate sat back against her desk, crossing her ankles, careful to keep her toes out of Kovac's way. "I think her memory might improve dramatically with the application of a little cash," she said dryly.

"What!"

"She got wind of Bondurant's reward and wants a chunk. Can you blame her, Sam? The kid's got nothing. She's got no one. She's been living on the street, doing God knows what to survive."

"Did you explain to her that rewards go out *on conviction*? We can't convict somebody we can't catch. We can't catch somebody we don't have a clue what the hell he looks like."

"I know. Hey, you don't have to preach to me. And—word of warning—don't preach to Angie either," Kate said. "She's on the fence, Sam. We could lose her. Figuratively and literally. You think life's a bitch now, imagine what'll happen if your only witness skips."

"What are you saying? Are you saying we should stick someone on her?"

"Unmarked, low-key, and well back. You set a uniform on the curb in front of the Phoenix, it's only going to make matters worse. She already thinks we're treating her like a criminal."

"Lovely," Kovac drawled. "And what else would her highness require?"

"Don't bust my chops," Kate ordered. "I'm on your side. And stop pacing, you'll make yourself dizzy. You're making *me* dizzy."

Kovac pulled in a deep breath and leaned

back against the wall, directly across from Kate.

"You knew what to expect from this girl, Sam. Why are you surprised by this? Or did you just want that composite to be a dead ringer for one of your exes?"

His mouth twisted with chagrin. He rubbed a hand across his face and wished for a cigarette. "I got a bad feeling about this deal, Kate," he admitted. "I guess I was hoping for the witness fairy to touch our little Miss Daisy with her wand. Or poke her with it. Or hold it to her head like a gun. I hoped that maybe the kid would be scared enough to tell the truth. Oscar tells me fear precipitates prevarication."

"He's been reading those pop psychology books again, hasn't he?"

"Or something." He heaved a sigh. "Bottom line: I need something to kick-start this investigation or I'll have to go digging in some nasty shitholes. I guess I was hoping this was it."

"Hold the sketch back a day. I'll bring her in again tomorrow. See if Oscar can apply his mystic powers and draw something out of her—no pun intended."

"I don't think I'll be able to hold it back. Big Chief Little Dick got his hands on the sketch before me. He'll want to run with it. He'll want to present it at the press conference himself.

"Goddamn brass," he grumbled. "They're worse than kids with a case like this. Everybody wants the credit. Everybody wants their

face on the news. They all have to look important—like they've got shit to do with the
investigation besides get in the way of the
real cops."

"That's what's really grating on you, Sam,"
Kate pointed out. "It's not the sketch, it's your
natural resistance to working under supervi-
sion."

He scowled at her. "You been reading
Oscar's books too?"

"I have a college degree in brain picking,"
she reminded him. "What's the worst that
happens if the sketch goes out and it isn't
totally accurate?"

"I don't know, Kate. This mope barbecues
women and cuts their heads off. What's the
worst that could happen?"

"He won't be offended by the sketch," Kate
said. "He's more likely to be amused, to think
he's outsmarted you again."

"Ahh, so then he'll feel more invincible
and be empowered to go out and whack
another one! Swell!"

"Don't be such a fatalist. You can use this
to your advantage. Ask Quinn. Besides, if
the sketch is even partially accurate, you
might get something off it. Maybe someone
out there will remember seeing a similar individual near a truck. Maybe they'll remember
a partial license plate, a dent in a fender, a guy
with a limp. You know as well as I do, luck plays
into an investigation like this in a big way."

"Yeah, well," Kovac said, reluctantly pushing
himself away from the wall. "We could use a

truckload. Soon. So where's the sunshine girl now?"

"I had someone take her back to the Phoenix. She's not happy about that."

"Tough."

"Ditto," Kate said. "She wants a hotel room or an apartment or something. I want her with people. Isolation isn't going to open her up. Plus, I'd like someone keeping an eye on her. Did you go through that backpack she carries around?"

"Liska checked it out. Angie was steamed, but, hey, she came running away from a headless corpse. We couldn't risk her going psycho and pulling a knife on us. The uniform picked her up should have done it at the scene, but he was all shook up thinking about Smokey Joe. Stupid rookie. He screws up that way with the wrong mutt, he'll get himself whacked."

"Did Nikki find anything?"

He pursed his lips and shook his head. "What are you thinking? Drugs?"

"I don't know. Maybe. Her behavior is all over the map. She's up, she's down, she's tough, she's on the verge of tears. I start to think something's off about her, then I stop and think: My God, look what she's been through. Maybe she's remarkably stable and sane, all things considered."

"Or maybe she needs a score," Kovac speculated, moving toward the door. "Maybe that's what she was doing in that park at midnight. I know some guys in narcotics. I'll reach out, see if maybe they know this kid. We got nothing else on her yet. Wisconsin had nothing."

"I talked to a Susan Frye in our juvenile division," Kate said. "She's been at this forever. She's got a great network. Rob is checking his contacts in Wisconsin. In the meantime, I need to get Angie some kind of perk, Sam. A show of appreciation. Can you kick her something out of petty cash as an informant?"

"I'll see what I can do."

Another duty to add to his long list. Poor guy, Kate thought. The lines in his face seemed deeper today. He had the weight of the city on those sturdy shoulders. His suit jacket hung limp on him, as if he had somehow drawn the starch out of it to supplement his draining energy.

"Listen, don't worry about it," she said as she pulled the door open. "I can weasel it out of your lieutenant myself. You've got better things to do."

Halfway out the door, he turned and gave her a lopsided smile. "What gave you that idea?"

"Just a hunch."

"Thanks. You're sure you're not too busy tackling armed gunmen?"

"Heard about that, did you?" Kate made a face, not comfortable with the attention yesterday's incident had gotten her. She'd turned down half a dozen requests for interviews and made too many trips to the ladies' room to dab makeup over the bruises.

"Wrong place, wrong time, that's all. The story of my life," she said dryly.

Kovac looked thoughtful, as if he were considering saying something profound, then shook his head a little. "You're a wonder, Red."

"Hardly. I've just got a guardian angel with a sick sense of humor. Go fight the fight, Sergeant. I'll take care of the witness."

12
CHAPTER

THE TRAFFIC annoys him. He takes 35W south out of downtown to avoid traffic lights and the tedious twists and turns of the alternate route. Stop-and-go traffic until he wants to abandon the car and walk down the shoulder, randomly pulling people out of their vehicles and beating their heads in with a tire iron. It amuses him that other motorists are likely entertaining the same fantasy. They have no idea that the man sitting in the dark sedan behind them, beside them, in front of them, could act on that fantasy without turning a hair.

He looks at the woman in the red Saturn beside him. She is pretty, with Nordic features and white-blond hair done in a voluminous, airy, tousled style that has been sprayed into place. She catches him looking, and he smiles and waves. She smiles back, then makes a gesture and a funny face at the traffic snarled ahead of them. He shrugs and grins, mouths "what can you do?"

He imagines that face drawn tight and pale with terror as he leans down over her with a knife. He can see her bare chest rise and fall in time with her shallow breathing. He can hear the tremor in her voice as she begs him for her life. He can hear her screams as he cuts her breasts.

Desire stirs deep in his groin.

"Probably the most crucial factor in the development of a serial rapist or killer is the role of fantasy."—John Douglas, Mindhunter.

His fantasies have never shocked him. Not in childhood, when he would think of what it might be like to watch a living thing die, what it would be like to close his hands around the throat of a cat or the kid down the block and hold the power of life and death literally within his grasp. Not in adolescence, when he would think of cutting the nipples from his mother's breasts, or cutting out her larynx and smashing it with a hammer, or cutting out her uterus and throwing it into the furnace.

He knows that for killers such as himself, these thoughts are a sustained part of the internal processing and cognitive operations. They are, in effect, natural for him. Natural, and, therefore, not deviant.

He exits on 36th and drives west on tree-lined side streets toward Lake Calhoun. The blonde is gone and the fantasy with her. He thinks again of the afternoon press briefing, both amused and frustrated. The police had a sketch—this amused him. He stood there in the crowd as Chief Greer held up the drawing that was supposed to be a rendition of him so accurate that people would recognize him at a glance on the street. And when the briefing had ended, all those reporters had walked right past him.

The frustration has its source in John Quinn. Quinn made no appearance at the briefing, and has made no official statement, which seems a deliberate slight. Quinn is too wrapped up in his deduction and speculation. He is probably focusing all his attention on the victims. Who they were and what they were, wondering why they were chosen.

"In a sense the victim shapes and molds the criminal...To know one we must be acquainted with the complementary partner."—Hans von Hentig.

Quinn believes this too. Quinn's textbook on sexual homicide is among many on his shelf. *Seductions of Crime* by Katz, *Inside the Criminal Mind* by Samenow, *Without Conscience* by Hare, *Sexual Homicide: Patterns and Motives* by Ressler, Burgess, and Douglas. He has studied all of them and more. A voyage of self-exploration.

He turns onto his block. Because of the way the lakes lie in this part of town, the streets immediately around them are often irregular. This one has a bend in it that gives the houses larger lots than usual. More privacy.

211

He parks the car on the concrete apron out-side the garage and gets out.

Night has inked out what meager daylight there had been earlier. The wind is blowing out of the west and bringing with it the scent of fresh dog shit. The smell hits his nostrils a split second before the sound of rapid-fire toy-dog barking.

Out of the darkness of the neighbor's yard darts Mrs. Vetter's bichon frise, a creature that looks like a collection of white pompoms sewn loosely together. The dog runs to within five feet of him, then stops and stands its ground, barking, snarling like a rabid squirrel.

The noise instantly sets off his temper. He hates the dog. He especially hates the dog now because it has triggered the return of his foul mood from the traffic jam. He wants to kick the dog as hard as he can. He can imagine the high-pitched yip, the animal's limp body as he picks it up by the throat and crushes its wind-pipe.

"Bitsy!" Mrs. Vetter shrieks from her front step. "Bitsy, come here!"

Yvonne Vetter is in her sixties, a widow, an unpleasant woman with a round, sour face and a shrill voice. He hates her in a deeply visceral way, and thinks of killing her every time he sees her, but something equally deep and funda-mental holds him back. He refuses to examine what that feeling is, and becomes angrier imagining what John Quinn would make of it.

"Bitsy! Come here!"

The dog snarls at him, then turns and runs

212

up and down the length of the garage, stopping to pee on the corners of the building.

"Bit-sy!!"

A pulse begins to throb in his head and warmth floods his brain and washes down through his body. If Yvonne Vetter were to cross the lawn now, he will kill her. He will grab her and smother her screams with the newspapers he holds. He will quickly pull her into the garage, smash her head against the wall to knock her out, then kill the dog first to stop its infernal barking. Then he will let loose his temper and kill Yvonne Vetter in a way that will satiate a vicious hunger buried deep within him.

She begins to descend the front steps of her house.

The muscles across his back and shoulders tighten. His pulse quickens.

"Bit-sy!! Come now!!"

His lungs fill. His fingers flex on the edge of the newspapers.

The dog barks at him one last time, then darts back to its mistress. Fifteen feet away, Vetter bends down and scoops the dog into her arms as if he were a child.

Opportunity dies like an unsung song.

"He's excited tonight," he says, smiling.

"He gets that way when he's inside too much. He doesn't like you either," Mrs. Vetter says defensively, and takes the dog back to her house.

"Fucking bitch," he whispers. The anger will vibrate within him for a long while, like a tuning fork still trembling long after it's been struck. He will play through the fantasy of killing Yvonne Vetter again and again and again.

He goes into the garage, where the Blazer and a red Saab sit, and enters the house through a side door, eager to read about the Cremator in the two newspapers. He will cut out all stories pertaining to the investigation and make photocopies of them, because newsprint is cheap and doesn't hold up over time. He has taped both the network evening news and the local evening news, and will watch for any mention of the Cremator.

The Cremator. The name amuses him. It sounds like something from a comic book. It conjures images of Nazi war criminals or B-movie monsters. The stuff of nightmares.

He is the stuff of nightmares.

And like the creatures of childhood nightmares, he goes to the basement. The basement is his personal space, his ideal sanctuary. The main room is outfitted with an amateur sound studio. Walls and ceiling of sound-absorbing acoustic tile. Flat carpet the color of slate. He likes the low ceiling, the lack of natural light, the sensation of being in the earth with thick concrete walls around him. His own safe world. Just like when he was a boy.

He goes down the hall and into the game room, holding the newspapers out in front of him to admire the headlines.

"Yes, I am famous," he says, smiling. "But don't feel bad. You'll be famous soon too. There's nothing quite like it."

He turns toward the pool table, holding the newspapers at an angle so that the naked woman bound spread-eagle on it can glance at the headlines if she wants to. She stares, instead, at him, her eyes glassy with terror and tears. The sounds she makes are not words, but the most basic vocalizations of that most basic emotion—fear.

The sounds touch him like electrical currents, energizing him. Her fear gives him control of her. Control is power. Power is the ultimate aphrodisiac.

"Soon you'll be a part of this headline," he says, running a finger beneath the bold black print on page one of the *Star Tribune*. "*Ashes to Ashes.*"

DAY SLIPPED INTO evening, into night. Quinn's only indicator was his watch, which he seldom checked. There were no windows in the office he'd been given, only walls, which he'd spent the day papering with notes, often with the telephone receiver sandwiched between ear and shoulder, consulting on the Blacksburg case, where the suspect seemed on the brink of confession. He should have been there. His need for control fostered the conceit that he could prevent all mistakes, even though he knew that wasn't true.

Kovac had offered him space at what the task force had unofficially dubbed the Loving Touch of Death offices. He had declined. He needed separation, isolation. He couldn't be there when a dozen cops were tossing theories and suspect names like a chopped salad. He already felt tainted as it was.

Now word was out that John Quinn had been brought on board the Cremator case. Kovac had called with the bad news after the press briefing. It was only a matter of hours before he would have to deal with the media himself.

Damn, he'd wanted more time. He had these next few hours. He should have settled in and lost himself, but he couldn't seem to. Exhaustion pulled at him. His ulcer was burning. He was hungry and knew he needed fuel to keep his brain running, but he didn't want to waste the time going out. There was too much information and the buzz of too much caffeine swarming in his head. And there was a familiar sense of restlessness vibrating deep within—the urgency that came with every on-site case, compounded this time by extenuating circumstances and intrusive, fragmented memories from the past. Compounded again by a feeling that had been creeping up on him more and more and more lately—fear. The fear that he wouldn't make a difference in the case fast enough. The fear that he would screw up. The fear that the fatigue pressing down on him would suddenly be too much. The fear that what he really wanted was to just walk away from it all.

Needing to move to escape the emotions, he began to pace back and forth in front of the wall of notes, taking in snatches of them at a glance. The faces of Bondurant and Brandt blew around inside his head like leaves.

Peter Bondurant was holding back more than he was giving them.

Lucas Brandt had a license to keep secrets.

Quinn wished he'd never met either of them. He should have argued harder against coming here so early in the investigation, he thought, rubbing at a knot in his right shoulder. The issue was control. If he walked onstage with his strategy mapped out, he had the upper hand.

That methodology applied to more than just this case. It was how he ran his whole life—from dealing with the bureaucracy on the job, to dealing with the Chinese people who ran the mailbox place where he kept a box, to buying his groceries. In any and all situations and relationships, control was key.

Kate slipped into the back of his mind, as if to taunt him. How many times over the years had he replayed what had happened between them, adjusting his own actions and reactions to get a different outcome? More times than he would admit. Control and strategy were his watchwords. He'd had neither where Kate was concerned. One minute they'd been acquaintances, then friends, then in over their heads. No time to think, too tangled up in the moment to have any perspective, drawn together by a need and a passion that was stronger than either of them. And then it was over, and she was gone, and...nothing. Nothing but regrets that he had let lie, sure that they both would eventually see it was for the best.

It *was* for the best. For Kate anyway. She had a life here. She had a new career, friends, a home. He should have had sense enough to back away from all that, leave well enough alone, but the temptation of opportunity lured him like a crooked finger and a seductive smile. And the force of all those regrets pushed him from behind.

He supposed five years was a long time to carry regrets, but he'd carried others longer. Cases not solved, trials lost, a child-killer who had slipped away. His marriage, his mother's death, his father's alcoholism. Maybe he never let anything go. Maybe that was why he felt so hollow inside: There was no room left for anything but the dried detritus of his past.

He swore under his breath, disgusted with himself. He was supposed to be delving into the mind of a criminal, not his own.

He didn't remember sitting back against the desk, had no idea how many minutes he'd lost. He rubbed his big hands over his face, licked his lips, and caught the phantom taste of scotch. An odd psychological quirk, and a need that would go unfulfilled. He didn't allow himself to drink. He didn't allow himself to smoke. He didn't allow himself much. If he added regret to that list, what would he have left?

He walked to the section of wall where he had taped up brief notes on the Cremator's victims, scrawled in his own hand in colored markers. All caps. Tight, with a hard right-hand slant. The kind of handwriting that made graphologists raise their brows and give him a wide berth.

Photographs of all three women were taped above his notes. A three-ring binder lay open on the desk, filled with page after page of neatly typed reports, maps, scale drawings of the crime scenes, crime scene photographs, autopsy protocols—his portable bible of the case. But he found it helpful to lay out some of the basic information in a more linear way, and thus the notes on the wall and the photographs of three smiling women—gone now from this world, their lives snuffed out like candles, their dignity torn violently from them.

Three white women. All between the ages of twenty-one and twenty-three. Height varied from five five to five nine. Body types ranged from large-boned Lila White to petite Fawn Pierce to average Jane Doe/Jillian Bondurant.

Two prostitutes and a college student. They had lived in different parts of town. The hookers worked two different neighborhoods as a rule, neither of which was frequented by Jillian Bondurant. Lila and Fawn may have crossed paths occasionally, but it was highly unlikely Jillian would have frequented any of the same bars or restaurants or stores.

He had considered the drug connection, but they had nothing to support it so far. Lila White had gotten straight after entering a county program more than a year ago. Fawn

Pierce had never been known to use, although she'd had a reputation for the occasional days-long bender on cheap vodka. And Jillian? No drugs had been found in her home, none in her system. She had no criminal record relating to drug use. As yet, no anecdotal stories of drug use.

"You think they'd like people to know why their daughters became whores and drug addicts?"

He could still hear the bitterness in Peter Bondurant's voice. Where had it come from?

Jillian was the piece that didn't fit in the puzzle of these crimes. She was the one that skewed the profile. There was a common type of killer who preyed on prostitutes. Prostitutes were high-risk victims, easy pickings. Their killers tended to be socially inadequate, under-employed white males who had a history of humiliating experiences with women and sought to get back at the gender by punishing what they considered to be the worst of the lot.

Unless Jillian had led a secret life as a hooker...Not beyond the realm, he supposed, but so far there were no indications Jillian had had a single boyfriend, let alone a list of johns.

"Boys didn't interest her. She didn't want temporary relationships. She'd been through so much...."

What had she been through? Her parents' divorce. Her mother's illness. A stepfather in a new country. What else? Something deeper? Darker? Something that pushed her into therapy with Lucas Brandt.

"...You should consider that the problems Jillian brought to me may have had nothing whatsoever to do with her death. Her killer may not have known anything at all about her."

"But I'll bet you a dollar he did, Dr. Brandt," he said softly, staring at the snapshot of the girl. He could feel it in his gut. Jillian was the key. Something in her life had put her in the crosshairs of this killer. And if they could find out what that something was, then they might have a hope in hell of catching the son of a bitch.

He went back to the desk and flipped through the binder pages to the section of photographs: eight-by-ten color prints, neatly labeled as to subject matter. The crime scenes: general shots, lay-of-the-land shots, body position from various angles, close-ups of the burned, defiled women. And from the ME's office: general and close-up shots of the victims before and after clean-up at the morgue, autopsy photographs, close-up shots of wounds. Wounds inflicted before death—indicative of a sexual sadist. Wounds inflicted after death—which were more fetishistic than sadistic, intrinsic to the killer's fantasies.

Sophisticated fantasies. Fantasies he'd been developing for a long, long time.

He paged slowly through the close-ups of the wounds, examining every mark the killer had left, lingering on the stab wounds to the victims' chests. Eight stab wounds clustered in a group, longer wounds alternating with shorter in a specific pattern.

221

Of all the gruesome aspects of the murders, this bothered him most. More than the burning. The burning seemed more for show, making a public statement. *Ashes to ashes.* A symbolic funeral, the end of his connection to the victim. These stab wounds meant something more personal, intimate. What?

A cacophony of voices filled Quinn's head: Bondurant's, Brandt's, the medical examiner's, Kovac's; cops and coroners and experts and agents from hundreds of past cases. All of them with an opinion or a question or an ax to grind. All of them so loud he couldn't hear himself think anymore. And the fatigue only seemed to magnify the noise until he wanted to beg someone to turn it off.

The Mighty Quinn. That was what they called him back in Quantico. If they could see him now...Feeling as if he might choke on the fear of missing something or turning the investigation in the wrong way.

The system was on overload, and he was the one at the switch—and there was the most frightening thought: that only he could make things change, and he wouldn't make things change because as awful as this was, the alternative scared him even more. Without the job, there was no John Quinn.

A fine trembling started deep within him and subtly worked its way out into his arms. He fought against it, hating it, tightening his biceps and triceps, trying to force the weakness back down inside him. Eyes squeezed shut, he dropped to the floor and began push-ups.

Ten, twenty, thirty, more, until his arms felt as if the skin would burst open, unable to contain the straining muscle mass, until the pain burned the noise out of his mind and all he could hear was the pounding of his own pulse. And then he forced himself to his feet, breathing hard, warm and damp with sweat.

He focused on the photograph before him, seeing not the torn flesh or the blood or the corpse; seeing only the pattern of the wound. X over X.

"Cross my heart," he murmured, tracing a fingertip over the lines. "Hope to die."

"**A SERIAL KILLER** stalks the streets of Minneapolis. Today, Minneapolis police released a composite sketch of the man who may have brutally slain three women, and *that* is our top story tonight..."

The women of the Phoenix House sat in, on, and around the mismatched assortment of chairs and couches in the living room, their attention on the broad-shouldered, square-jawed anchor of the Channel Eleven news. The camera cut to film footage of the afternoon press briefing, the chief of police holding up the sketch of the Cremator, then the screen was filled with the sketch itself.

Angie watched from the doorway, her attention on the women. A couple of them weren't much older than she was. Four were in their twenties. One was older, fat, and ugly. The fat one wore a sleeveless top because the furnace had gone haywire and the house was as hot and dry as a desert. Her upper arms were flabby and fish-belly white. Her stomach rested on her thighs when she sat down.

Angie knew the woman had been a hooker, but she couldn't imagine a man ever being hard up enough to pay to have sex with her. Men liked pretty girls, young girls. Didn't matter how old or ugly the man was, they all wanted pretty girls. That was Angie's experience. Maybe that was why Fat Arlene was there. Maybe she couldn't get a man to pay her, and the Phoenix was her retirement home.

A redhead who had the thin, pale, bruised look of an addict started to cry when photographs of the three murder victims came onscreen. The other women pretended not to notice. Toni Urskine, who ran the Phoenix, perched on the arm of the redhead's chair, leaned down, and touched her shoulder.

"It's okay," she said softly. "It's okay to cry. Fawn was your friend, Rita."

The redhead pulled her bony bare feet up onto the seat of her chair and buried her head against her knees, sobbing. "Why'd he have to kill her that way? She didn't hurt nobody!"

"There's no making sense of it," another one said. "It could have been any of us."

A fact that was clear to all of them, even the ones who tried to deny it.

Fat Arlene said, "You gotta be smart about who you go with. You gotta have a sense about it."

A black woman with ratty dreadlocks shot her

224

a mean glare. "Like you got to pick and choose. Who wanna tie your fat ass down? See all that fat jiggling like Jell-O while he cut you up."

Arlene's face went red and squeezed tight, eyes disappearing in the round mounds of cheeks and puffy brows. She looked like a chow chow Angie had seen once. "You can just shut your hole, you bony bitch!"

Looking angry, Toni Urskine left the crying redhead and moved toward the middle of the room, holding her hands up like a referee. "Hey! None of that! We've got to learn to respect and care for one another. Remember: group esteem, gender esteem, *self*-esteem."

Easy for her to say, Angie thought, slipping back from the door. Toni Urskine had never had to go down on some old pervert to get enough money for a meal. She was little miss do-gooder, in her casual-chic outfits from Dayton's and a hundred-dollar hairdo by Horst. She drove up to this crappy house in her Ford Explorer from some beautiful home out in Edina or Minnetonka. She didn't know what it did to a person inside to find out she was worth only twenty-five bucks.

"We *all* care about these murder victims," Urskine said passionately, dark eyes shining, her sharp-featured face aglow. "We *all* are angry that the police have done virtually nothing until now. It's an outrage. It's a slap in the face. It's the city of Minneapolis telling us the lives of women in desperate circumstances mean nothing. We need to be angry about that, not angry with each other."

The women listened, some intent, some halfheartedly, some pretending not to.

"I think what we need here is involvement. We need to be proactive," Urskine said. "We'll go down to city hall tomorrow. The press can hear our side of it. We'll get copies of the composite sketch and canvass..."

Angie backed away from the door and moved silently down the hall. She didn't like it when people started talking about the Cremator cases. The Phoenix women weren't supposed to know who she was or that she was involved in the case, but Angie always got the tense feeling that the other women would look at her and somehow figure out she was the mystery witness. She didn't want anyone to know.

She didn't want it to be true.

Sudden tears filled her eyes and she rubbed her hands against them. No show of emotion. If she showed what she felt, then someone would see a weakness in her, or a need, or the madness that sucked her into the Zone and made her cut herself. No one would understand that the blade severed the connection to insanity.

"Is everything all right?"

Startled, Angie jerked around and stared at the man standing in the open doorway to the basement. Late thirties, good-looking, dressed in tan chinos and a Ralph Lauren Polo shirt to work on the furnace: He had to be some relation to Toni Urskine. Sweat and dirt streaked his face. He worked a gray rag between hands dark with grime and something the color of blood.

He glanced down as Angie did and looked back up with a crooked smile. "The old furnace in this place," he said by way of explanation. "I keep it running with willpower and rubber bands.

"Greggory Urskine," he said, sticking out his hand.

"You cut yourself," Angie said, not accepting the gesture, her gaze still on the smear of blood that crossed his palm.

Urskine looked at it and rubbed the rag over it, chuckling in that nervous way people sometimes have when they are trying to make a good impression. Angie just stared at him. He looked a little like Kurt Russell, she thought: a wide jaw and small nose, tousled sandy hair. He wore glasses with silver wire rims. He had cut himself that morning shaving his upper lip.

"Aren't you hot in that jacket?" he asked.

Angie said nothing. She was sweating like a horse, but the sleeves of her sweater were too short and didn't cover all the scars on her arms. The jacket was a necessity. If she got any money out of Kate, she was going to buy herself some clothes. Maybe something brand new and not from the Goodwill or a thrift shop.

"I'm Toni's husband—and handyman," Urskine said. He narrowed his eyes. "I'm guessing you're Angie."

Angie just stared at him.

"I won't tell anyone," Urskine said in a

confidential tone. "Your secret's safe with me."

It seemed like he was making fun of her somehow. Angie decided she didn't like him, handsome or not. There was something about the eyes behind the expensive designer glasses that bothered her. Like he was looking down at her, like she was a bug or something. She wondered idly if he had ever paid a woman for sex. His wife seemed like the kind of woman who thought sex was dirty. Saving women from having to do it was Toni Urskine's mission in life.

"We're all very concerned about this case," he went on, looking serious. "The first victim—Lila White—was a resident here for a while. Toni took it hard. She loves this place. Loves the women. Works like a trooper for the cause."

Angie crossed her arms. "And what do you do?"

Again with the flashing smile, the nervous chuckle. "I'm an engineer at Honeywell. Currently on leave so I can help fix this place up before winter—and finally finish my master's thesis."

He laughed like that was some kind of big joke. He didn't ask Angie what she did, even though not all of the women in this place were hookers. He was looking at her stomach, at the navel ring and tattoos revealed as her too-small sweater crept up. She cocked a hip, flashing a little more skin, and wondered if he was thinking he might want her.

He glanced back up at her. "So, they've got a good chance of catching this guy, thanks to you," he said as a half-statement, half-question. "You actually saw him."

"No one's supposed to know that," Angie said bluntly. "I'm not supposed to talk about it."

End of conversation. She ignored the closing niceties, backed away from him, then headed up the stairs. She felt Greggory Urskine's eyes on her as she went.

"Uh, good night, then," he called as she disappeared into the darkness of the second story.

She went to the room she shared with a woman whose ex-boyfriend had held her down and cut all her hair off with a hunting knife because she refused to give him her AFDC check so he could buy crack. The woman's kids were in foster care now. The boyfriend had skipped to Wisconsin. The woman had been through drug rehab and come out of it with a need to confess. Therapy did that to some people. Angie had been too smart to let it happen to her.

Don't tell your secrets, Angel. They're all that make you special.

Special. She wanted to be special. She wanted not to be alone. It didn't matter that there were other people in this house. None of them were here *with* her. She didn't belong. She'd been dropped here like an unwanted puppy. Fucking cops. They wanted things from her, but they didn't want to give her anything back. They didn't give a shit about her. They didn't care about what she might want from them.

At least Kate was halfway honest, Angie thought as she paced the room. But she couldn't forget that Kate was still one of *them*. It was Kate Conlan's job to try to wedge open her defenses so the cops and the county attorney could get what they wanted. And that would be the end of it. She wasn't really a friend. Angie could count the only friends she'd ever had on one hand and have fingers left over.

She wanted one tonight. She wanted not to be stuck in this house. She wanted to belong somewhere.

She thought of the woman burning in the park, thought of where that woman had belonged, and wondered fancifully what would happen if she just took that woman's place. She would be a rich man's daughter. She would have a father and a home and money.

She'd had a father once: She had the scars to prove it. She'd had a home: She could still smell the sour grease in the kitchen, could still remember the big, dark closets with the doors that locked from the outside. She'd never had money.

She went to bed with her clothes on and waited until the house was quiet and her roommate was snoring. Then she slipped out from under the covers and out of the room, down the stairs, and out of the house through the back door.

The night was windy. Clouds rolled across the sky so fast, it looked almost like time-lapse photography. The streets were empty except for the occasional car rolling down one of the big cross streets going north and south. Angie headed west, jittery, skittish. The feeling that she was being watched constantly scratched at the back of her neck, but when she looked over her shoulder, there was no one.

The Zone was chasing her like a shadow. If she kept walking, if she had a purpose, focused on a goal, maybe it wouldn't catch her.

The houses along the way were dark. Tree limbs rattled in the wind. When she came to the lake, it was as black and shiny as an oil slick. She stuck to the dark side of the street and walked north. People in this neighborhood would call the cops if they saw someone out walking this late at night.

She recognized the house from the news reports—like something from England with a big iron fence around it. She turned and climbed the hill to the back side of the property, the big trees giving her cover. Hedges blocked the view of the house three seasons of the year, but their leaves were gone now, and she could look through the tangle of fine branches.

A light was on inside the house, in a room with fancy glass-paned doors that let out onto a patio. Angie stood at the fence, careful not to touch it, and gazed into Peter Bondurant's backyard. She looked past the swimming pool and the stone benches and the wrought iron tables and chairs that hadn't yet been taken into storage for the winter. She looked at the amber glow in the window and the figure of a man sitting at a desk, and wondered if he felt as alone as she did. She wondered if his money gave him comfort now.

PETER ROSE FROM the desk and moved around his office, restless, tense. He couldn't sleep, refused to take the pills his doctor had prescribed and had delivered to the house. The nightmare was alive in his mind: the orange brilliance of the flames, the smell. When he closed his eyes he could see it, feel the heat of it. He could see Jillian's face: the shock, the shame, the heartbreak. He could see her face floating free, the base of her throat ragged and bloody. If his mind was filled with images like these when he was awake, what would he see if he went to sleep?

Going to the French doors, he stared out at the night, black and cold, and imagined he felt eyes staring back. *Jillian.* He thought he could feel her presence. The weight of it pressed against his chest as if she had wrapped her arms around him. Even after death she wanted to touch him, cling to him; desperate for love, the meaning of it for her skewed and warped.

A strange, dark arousal flickered deep inside him, followed by disgust and shame and guilt. He turned away from the window with an animal roar and flung himself at his desk, sweeping everything from the tidy surface.

Pens, Rolodex, paperweights, files, appointment book. The telephone jingled a protest. The lamp hit the floor, the bulb bursting with an explosive *pop!,* casting the room into darkness.

The final bright flash of light remained in Peter's eyes, twin flares of orange that moved as he moved. Flames he couldn't escape. Emotion was a rock in his throat, lodged there, hard and jagged. He felt a pressure within his eyeballs, as if they might burst, and he wondered wildly if he might not still see the flames anyway.

A harsh, dry choking sound rasped from him as he stumbled in the dark to a floor lamp, tripping over the things he'd knocked from the desk. Calmer in the light, he began to pick up the mess. He put the things back one at a time, aligning them precisely. This was what he had to do: Put his life back together with seamless precision, smooth the tears in the surface and go on, just as he had when Sophie had taken Jillian and left him all those years ago.

He picked up the appointment book last and found it opened to Friday. *Jillian: dinner,* written in his own precise hand. It sounded so innocent, so simple. But nothing was ever simple or innocent with Jillie. No matter how hard she tried.

The phone rang, startling him from the dark memories.

"Peter Bondurant," he said as if this were normal business hours. In the back of his mind he was trying to remember if he'd been expecting a call from overseas.

"Daddy dearest," the voice sang softly, seductively. "I know all your secrets."

13

CHAPTER

"**WE'RE GOING** to look like asses if we have to release another composite," Sabin complained, prowling behind his desk. His lower lip jutted out like a sulky two-year-old's, an odd contrast to the sharp sophistication of his image. Ready to deal with the press at a moment's notice, he had decked himself out in a pewter-gray suit with a tie two shades darker and a French-blue shirt. Very dapper.

"I don't see how it reflects badly on your office, Ted," Kate said. "Chief Greer was the one who jumped the gun."

He frowned harder and gave her a meaningful look. "I know whose fault this is."

"You can't blame the witness," Kate said, knowing full well he meant to blame *her.*

"I'm told she's not been very cooperative," Edwyn Noble said with concern, wedging his way into the discussion. He sat in a visitor's chair, his body too long for it, the legs of his dark trousers hiking up above bony ankles and nylon socks.

Kate stared at him, half a dozen stinging remarks on the tip of her tongue, not the least of which was *"What the hell are you doing here?"* Of course, she knew what he was doing there. His presence skirted the bounds of propriety, but she had already run the argument through her head and knew what the outcome would be. The county attorney's office ran victim/witness services. Peter Bondurant was the immediate family of a victim—if the dead woman proved to be his daughter—and therefore entitled to be kept informed as to the disposition of the case. Edwyn Noble was Bondurant's envoy. Et cetera, et cetera.

She looked at Noble as if he were something she might scrape off her shoe. "Yes, well, there's always some of that going around."

The insinuation struck the bull's-eye. Noble sat up a little straighter in the too-small chair, his eyes going cold.

Rob Marshall moved between them as peacemaker, the bootlicker's grin stretching across his moon face. "What Kate means is that it's not unusual for a witness to such a brutal crime to become a little reluctant."

Sabin huffed. "She's not reluctant for the reward money."

"The reward will go out only upon conviction," Noble reminded them, as if it would take his client that long to scrape the cash together. As if Bondurant might be half hoping to get out of it altogether.

"This office does not buy witnesses," Sabin proclaimed. "I told you I wanted her dealt with, Kate."

He made her sound like a paid assassin. "I *am* dealing with her."

"Then why did she not spend Monday night in jail? I told Kovac to treat her like a suspect. Scare her a little."

"But you—" Kate began, confused.

Rob gave her a warning look. "We still have that option in our pocket, Ted. Trying Phoenix House first might soften her up, give the girl the impression that Kate is on her side. I'm sure that's what you had in mind, isn't it, Kate?"

She glared at her boss, openmouthed.

Sabin was pouting. "Now this sketch fiasco."

"It's not a fiasco. No one should've seen the sketch yesterday," Kate argued, turning away from Rob before she could go for his throat. "Ted, you pressure this kid, she'll walk. Get tough with her, she'll develop a real mean case of amnesia. I guarantee it. You and I both know you have nothing to hold her on with relation to the murder. You couldn't even get her arraigned. A judge would bounce it out of the courtroom like a Super Ball, and you'd be left with egg on your face and no witness."

He rubbed his chin as if he already felt the yoke drying. "She's a vagrant. That's against the law."

"Oh, yeah, that'll look good in the papers.

236

Teenage Murder Witness Charged for Homelessness. Next time you run for office, you can bill yourself as the Simon Legree candidate."

"My political life is not an issue here, Ms. Conlan," he snapped, suddenly stiff and steely-eyed. "Your handling of this witness is."

Rob looked at Kate with an expression that questioned her sanity. Kate looked to Edwyn Noble. *Not an issue. In a pig's eye.*

She could have pushed Sabin a little now and gotten herself reassigned. She could have confessed a total inability to deal with this witness and been out from under the burden that was Angie DiMarco. But the second Kate thought it, she saw herself leaving the girl at the mercy of the assembled wolves, and couldn't do it. The memory was too fresh of Angie standing in the ratty den at the Phoenix, sudden tears in her eyes, asking Kate why she couldn't go home with her.

She rose, discreetly smoothing the wrinkles from the front of her skirt. "I'm doing my best to get the truth out of this girl. I know that's everyone's goal. Give me a chance to work her my way, Ted. Please." She wasn't above giving him the hopeful, wide-eyed look if it would sway his mood. He didn't have to fall for it if he didn't want to. The word *mercenary* crawled through her mind, leaving a small trail of slime.

"She's not the kid next door," she went on. "She's had a tough life and it's made her a tough person, but I think she wants to do the right thing here. It won't do anyone any good to get impatient at this stage of the game. If you want corroboration of my opinion, ask Quinn. He knows as much about dealing with witnesses in this kind of case as I do," Kate said, thinking turnabout was fair play. John owed her one. At least.

Noble cleared his throat politely. "What about hypnosis? Will you try that?"

Kate shook her head. "She'll never go for it. Hypnosis requires trust. This kid hasn't got any. Oscar's as mystical as she's going to sit still for."

"I hate to play devil's advocate," the attorney said, unfolding himself from the chair, "but how are we to know the girl saw anything at all? It sounds to me as if she's the type to do anything for money. Perhaps the reward is her only goal."

"And she set her sights on that goal before she knew it would even exist?" Kate said. "If that's the case, then she's worth more than she ever was to this case because she'd have to be psychic. No reward was offered after the first two murders."

She glanced at her watch and swore under her breath. "I'm afraid you gentlemen will have to excuse me. I have to be at a hearing in a few minutes and my victim's probably already panicking because I'm not there."

Sabin had come around the desk to lean back against it with his arms crossed and his stern face on. Kate recognized the pose from the profile *Minnesota Monthly* had done on him a year earlier. Not that she discounted his power or his willingness to use it. Ted Sabin hadn't gotten where he was by being anybody's fool or pretty boy.

"I'll give you more time with this girl, Kate." He made it sound as if he were doing so grudgingly, even though the whole arrangement had been his idea. "But we need results, and we need them quickly. I thought you of all the advocates in your office would understand that."

"She's working with Oscar again this afternoon," she said, moving toward the door.

Sabin came away from his desk and walked with her, resting his hand between her shoulder blades. "You'll be through in court in time to be there with her?"

"Yes."

"Because I'm sure Rob can juggle something and have someone else take care of this hearing."

"No, sir. The hearing won't take long," she promised with a pained smile. "Besides, I wouldn't wish this particular client on any of my colleagues. They know where I live."

"Maybe we should have Agent Quinn sit in on this session with Oscar and the girl," he suggested.

The hand on her back had a knife in it suddenly.

"I don't see how that would be helpful."

"No, you were right, Kate," he argued. "This witness isn't ordinary. And as you said, Quinn has a great deal of experience. He might be able to pick up on something, suggest a strategy. I'll call him."

Kate stepped out the door and stood there as it closed behind her. "Me and my big mouth."

"Kate—" Rob Marshall began in a low voice. Kate wheeled on him as he slipped out into the hall.

"You weasel," she accused in a harsh whisper. It was all she could do to keep from grabbing him by the ears and shaking him. "You gave me the go-ahead to take Angie to the Phoenix. Now you stand in there and give Sabin the impression it was all *my* doing! I thought you'd cleared it with him. That's what I told Kovac. And I accused Kovac of being paranoid for not trusting it."

"I broached the subject of the Phoenix with him—"

"But he didn't go for it."

"He didn't say no."

"Well, he sure as hell didn't say yes."

"He had his mind on other things. I knew taking her there was how you would want to play it, Kate."

"Don't try to put this off on me. You took some initiative for a change. Can't you at least own up to it?"

He breathed heavily through his too-short nose and his face turned a dull red. "Kate, does it *ever* cross your mind that I'm your superior?"

She closed her mouth on the rejoinder that came to mind, and scraped together what respect she could. "I'm sorry. I'm angry."

"And I'm your boss. *I'm* in charge," he said. She could hear the frustration in his voice.

"I don't envy you that job," she said dryly. "I ought to really antagonize you. You could take me off this powder keg. But I don't want off it," she admitted. "Must be the Swedish masochist in me."

"You're exactly who I want with this witness, Kate," he said. He pushed his glasses up on his nose and smiled like a man with a toothache. "Now who's the masochist?"

"I'm sorry. I don't like being made to feel like a pawn, that's all."

"Focus on the outcome. We got what we wanted."

His relationship with Sabin was intact. Her apparent overstepping of boundaries would be written off to her well-known arrogance, Sabin would forgive her because he had the hots for her, and Rob came off looking like a diplomat, if not a leader. Once again the end justified the means. Nothing hurt but her pride.

"I'm not averse to conspiracy, you know," she said, still miffed. She'd had every intention of stealing Angie away from Sabin's clutches, and she would never in a million years have let Rob Marshall in on the plan. That was what was really grating on her—that Rob had one-upped her. She never wanted to think he was more clever than her or more shrewd or her superior in any way. A hell of an attitude to have toward her boss.

"Have you heard anything back from your friends in Wisconsin yet?" she asked.

"Nothing yet."

"It'd be nice to know who the hell this kid is. I feel like I'm working with a blindfold on."

"I've got the videotape of Angie's interviews," he said, setting his hands at his middle. "I thought it might be helpful to sit down together and go over it. Maybe we could bring Quinn into that too. I'd like to hear his opinion."

"Yeah, why not?" Kate said, resigning herself. "Let me know when you set it up. I have to get to court."

Some days it just seemed the better option to stay home and hit her thumb with a hammer. At least that was a pain from which she could easily recover. John Quinn was another matter altogether.

"I WAS AFRAID you weren't coming," David Willis said with no small amount of accusation. He rushed up to Kate as she made her way around the knots of lawyers in the hall outside the criminal courtrooms.

"I'm sorry I'm late, Mr. Willis. I was in a meeting with the county attorney."

"About *my* case?"

"No. Everything is ready to go for your case."

"I'm not going to have to testify, right?"

"Not today, Mr. Willis." Kate steered her client toward the courtroom. "This is just a hearing. The prosecutor, Mr. Merced, will be presenting just enough evidence to have the court bind Mr. Zubek over for trial."

"But he won't call me as a surprise witness or anything?" He looked half terrified, half hopeful at the prospect.

Somehow, Kate knew this was just how David Willis had looked in his high school yearbook back in the seventies: out-of-date crew cut and nerd glasses, pants that were an odd shade of green and an inch too high-waisted. People had probably assaulted him regularly all his life.

For the occasion of the hearing, he had worn the black horn-rimmed glasses that had been broken in the course of his assault. They were held together in two places by adhesive tape. His left wrist was encased in a molded plastic cast, and he wore a cervical collar like a thick turtleneck.

"Surprise witnesses happen only on *Matlock*," Kate said.

"Because I'm just not ready for that. I'm going to have to work myself up to that, you know."

"Yes, I think we're all aware of that, Mr. Willis." Because he had called every day for the last week to remind them: Kate, Ken Merced, Ken's secretary, the legal services receptionist.

"I won't be in any physical danger, will I? He'll be in handcuffs and leg irons, right?"

"You'll be perfectly safe."

"Because, you know, situational stress can push people over the edge. I've been reading up on it. I've been religiously attending the victims' group you set me up with, Ms. Conlan, and I've been reading everything I can get my hands on about the criminal mind, and the psychology of victims, and post-traumatic stress disorder—just the way you told me to do."

Kate often recommended her clients educate themselves as to what to expect of their own reactions and emotions following a crime. It gave them a sense of understanding and a small feeling of control. She didn't recommend it as an all-consuming hobby.

Knowing Willis would want to be close to the action, she chose the first row in the gallery behind the prosecution's table, where Ken Merced was going over some notes. Willis bumped into her as she stopped to indicate the row, then tripped over his own feet trying to move aside and gallantly motion Kate in ahead of him.

Kate shook her head as she stepped into the row and took a seat. Willis fumbled with the cheap briefcase he'd brought with him. Filled with news clippings about his case, Polaroids taken of him in the ER after the attack, brochures on victims' groups and therapists, and a hardcover copy of *Coping After the Crime*. He pulled out a yellow legal pad and prepared to take notes of the proceedings— as he had at every meeting Kate had had with him.

Merced turned to them with a pleasant poker face. "We're all set, Mr. Willis. This won't take long."

"You're certain you won't need me to testify?"

"Not today."

He gave a shuddering sigh. "Because I'm not ready for that."

"No." Merced turned back toward the table. "None of us are."

Kate sat back and tried to will the tension out of her jaw as Willis became engrossed in making his preliminary notes.

"You always were a secret soft touch."

The low whisper rumbled over her right shoulder, the breath caressing the delicate skin of her neck. Kate jerked around, scowling. Quinn leaned ahead on his chair, elbows braced on his knees, dark eyes gleaming, that little-boy-caught-with-his-hand-in-the-cookie-jar smile firmly and calculatingly in place.

"I need to talk to you," he murmured.

"You have my office number."

"I do," he admitted. "However, you seem not to want to answer my messages."

"I'm a very busy person."

"I can see that."

"Don't mock me," she snapped.

David Willis grabbed hold of her forearm and she turned back around. The side door had opened, and O. T. Zubek entered the courtroom with his lawyer, a deputy trailing after them. Zubek was a human fireplug, squat with thick limbs and a protruding belly. He wore a cheap navy-blue suit that showed a dusting of dandruff on the shoulders, and a baby-blue knit shirt underneath, untucked and too snug around the middle. He looked right at Willis and scowled, his face the doughy caricature of a cartoon tough guy with a blue-shadowed jaw.

Willis stared at him, bug-eyed for a second, then twisted toward Kate. "Did you see that? He threatened me! That was threatening eye contact. I perceived that as a threat. Why isn't he in handcuffs?"

"Try to stay calm, Mr. Willis, or the judge will have you removed from the courtroom."

"*I'm* not the criminal here!"

"Everyone knows that."

The judge entered from chambers and everyone rose, then sat again. The docket number and charges were read, the prosecution and defense attorneys stated their names for the record, and the probable-cause hearing was under way.

Merced called his first witness, a pear-shaped man who serviced Slurpee machines at 7-Eleven stores in the greater Twin Cities metropolitan area. He testified he had heard Willis arguing with Zubek about the condition of a delivery of Hostess Twinkies and assorted snack cakes in the store Willis managed, and that he had seen the two come tumbling down the chips aisle, Zubek striking Willis repeatedly.

"And did you hear who started this *alleged* argument?" the defense attorney questioned on cross-examination.

"No."

"So for all you know, Mr. Willis may have provoked the argument?"

"Objection. Calls for speculation."

"Withdrawn. And did you see who threw the first punch in this *so-called* attack?"

"No."

"Might it have been Mr. Willis?"

Willis trembled and twitched beside Kate. "I didn't!"

"Shhh!"

Merced sighed. "Your honor..."

The judge frowned at the defense attorney, who had come costumed as a bad used-car salesman. He looked seedy enough that he might have been Zubek's cousin. "Mr. Krupke, this is a hearing, not a trial. The court is more concerned with what the witnesses saw than with what they did not see."

"Not exactly the Richmond Ripper case, is it?" Quinn murmured in Kate's ear. She gave him the evil eye over her shoulder. The stiffness in her jaw began radiating down into her neck.

Merced's second witness corroborated the testimony of the Slurpee mechanic. Krupke went through the same cross, with Merced voicing the same objections, and the judge getting crankier and crankier. Willis fidgeted and recorded copious notes in tiny bold print that said frightening things about the inner workings of his mind. Merced entered into evidence the security surveillance tape showing much of the fight, then rested his case.

Krupke had no witnesses and put on no defense.

"We don't dispute that an altercation took place, your honor."

"Then why are you wasting my time with this hearing, Mr. Krupke?"

"We wanted to establish that events may not have taken place *exactly* as Mr. Willis claims."

"That's a lie!" Willis shouted.

The judge cracked his gavel. The bailiff frowned at Willis but didn't move from his post. Kate put a vise grip on her client's arm and whispered furiously, "Mr. Willis, be quiet!"

"I suggest you listen to your advocate, Mr. Willis," the judge said. "You'll have your turn to speak."

"Today?"

"No!" the judge snorted, turning his glare on Merced, who spread his hands and shrugged. He turned back to the defense. "Mr. Krupke, write me a check for two hundred dollars for wasting my time. If you had no intention of disputing the charges, you should have waived rights and asked for a trial date at the arraignment."

The date for the trial was set and the proceedings were over. Kate breathed a sigh of relief. Merced got up from the table and collected his papers. Kate leaned across the bar and whispered, "Can't you get this guy to cop, Ken? I'd rather gouge my eyes out than sit through a trial with this man."

"Christ, I'd pay Zubek to take a plea if it wouldn't get me disbarred."

Krupke asked someone to lend him a pen so he could write out the check for contempt of court. Willis looked around like he had just awakened from a nap and had no idea where he was.

"That's it?"

"That's it, Mr. Willis," Kate said, standing. "I told you it wouldn't take long."

"But—but—" He swung his blue-casted arm in the direction of Zubek. "They called me a liar! Don't I get to defend myself?"

Zubek leaned over the rail, sneering. "Everyone can see what a shitty job you do of that, Willis."

"We should leave now," Kate suggested, handing Willis his briefcase. The thing weighed a ton.

He fumbled with the case and his notepad and pen as she herded him toward the aisle. Kate was more concerned with what she was going to do about Quinn. He had already moved into the aisle and was backing toward the door, his gaze on her, trying to get her to look at him. Sabin must have called him the second she was out of the office.

"But I don't understand," Willis whined. "There should have been more. He hurt me! He hurt me and he called me a liar!"

Zubek twitched his shoulders like a boxer and made a Bluto face. "Weenie wuss."

Kate saw Quinn's reaction the second the war cry curdled up out of David Willis. She spun around as Willis launched himself at Zubek, swinging. The briefcase hit Zubek in the side of the head like a frying pan and knocked him backward across the defense table. The locks sprung and the contents exploded out of the briefcase.

Kate hurled herself at Willis as he drew his

arm back to swing again. She grabbed both his shoulders, and the two of them tumbled head-first over the bar and into a sea of table legs and chairs and scrambling people. Zubek was squealing like a stuck pig. The judge was shouting at the bailiff, the bailiff was shouting at Krupke, who was screaming at Willis and trying to kick him. His wingtip connected with Kate's thigh, and she swore and kicked back, nailing Willis.

It seemed to take forever for order to be restored and for Willis to be hauled off her. Kate sat up slowly, muttering a string of obscenities under her breath.

Quinn squatted down in front of her, reached out, and brushed a rope of red-gold hair back behind her ear. "You really ought to come back to the FBI, Kate. This job's going to be the death of you."

"DON'T YOU DARE be amused at me," Kate snapped, surveying the damage to herself and her clothes. Quinn leaned back against her desk, watching as she plucked at a hole in her stockings that was big enough to put her fist through. "This is my second pair of good tights this week. That's it: I'm giving up skirts."

"The men in the building will have to wear black armbands," Quinn said. He held his hands up in surrender as she shot him another deadly glare. "Hey, you always had a nice set of pegs on you, Kate. You can't argue."

"The subject is inappropriate and irrelevant."

He gave her innocence. "Political correctness prohibits one old friend from complimenting another?"

She straightened slowly in her chair, forgetting about the ruined tights. "Is that what we are?" she asked quietly. "Old friends?"

He sobered at that. He couldn't look her in the eye and be glib about the past that lay behind them and between them. The awkwardness was a palpable entity.

"That's not exactly the way we parted company," she said.

"No." He moved away from the desk, sticking his hands in his pants pockets, pretending an interest in the notices and cartoons she had tacked up on her bulletin board. "That was a long time ago."

Which meant what, she wondered. That it was all water under the bridge? While a part of her wanted to say yes, there was another part of her that held those bitter memories in a fist. For her, nothing was forgotten. The idea that it might be for him upset her in a way she wished weren't so. It made her feel weak, a word she never wanted associated with her.

Quinn looked at her out of the corner of his eye. "Five years is a long time to stay mad."

"I'm not mad at you."

He laughed. "The hell you're not. You won't return my phone calls. You don't want to have a conversation with me. Your back goes up every time you see me."

"I've seen you what—twice since you got

here? The first time you used me to get your way, and the second time you made fun of my job—"

"I did not make fun of your job," he protested. "I made fun of your client."

"Oh, that makes all the difference," she said with sarcasm, conveniently forgetting that everyone made fun of David Willis, including her. She stood, not wanting him looking down on her any more than their height difference allowed. "What I do here is important, John. Maybe not in the same way as what you do, but it *is* important."

"I'm not disagreeing with you, Kate."

"No? As I recall, when I decided to leave the Bureau, you told me I was throwing my life away."

The reminder struck a spark, and old frustration came alive in his dark eyes. "You threw away a solid career. You had what? Fourteen, fifteen years in? You were a tremendous asset to the BSU. You were a good agent, Kate, and—"

"And I'm a better advocate. I get to deal with people while they're still alive. I get to make a difference for them one-on-one, help them through a hard time, help them empower themselves, help them take steps to make a difference in their own lives. How is that not valuable?"

"I'm not against you being an advocate," Quinn argued. "I was against you leaving the Bureau. Those are two separate issues. You let Steven push you out—"

252

"I did not!"

"The hell you didn't! He wanted to punish you—"

"And I didn't let him."

"You cut and ran. You let him win."

"He didn't win," Kate returned. "His victory would have been in crushing the life out of my career one drop of blood at a time. I was supposed to stick around for that just to show him how tough I was? What was I supposed to do? Transfer and transfer until he ran out of cronies in his ol' boy network? Until I ended up at the resident agency in Gallup, New Mexico, with nothing to do but count the snakes and tarantulas crossing the road?"

"You could have fought him, Kate," he insisted. "I would have helped you."

She crossed her arms and arched a brow. "Oh, really? As I remember it, you didn't want much to do with me after your little run-in with the Office of Professional Responsibility."

"That had nothing to do with it," he said angrily. "The OPR never scared me. Steven and his petty little bureaucratic bullshit games didn't scare me. I was tied up. I was juggling maybe seventy-five cases including the Cleveland Cannibal—"

"Oh, I know all about it, John," she said caustically. "The Mighty Quinn, bearing the weight of the criminal world on your shoulders."

"What's that supposed to mean?" he demanded. "I've got a job and I do it."

And to hell with the rest of the world, thought

Kate, *including me.* But she didn't say it. What good would it do now? It wouldn't change history as she remembered it. And it wouldn't help to argue that he surely did give a damn what the OPR put in his file. There was no sense arguing that to Quinn the job was everything.

Long story short: She'd had an affair that had delivered the death blows to a marriage already battered beyond recognition. Her husband's retaliation had forced her out of her career. And Quinn had walked away from the wreck and lost himself in his first love— his work. When push had come to shove, he stepped back and let her fall. When she turned to go, he hadn't asked her not to.

In five years he hadn't called her once.

Not that she'd wanted him to.

The argument had drawn them closer together one step at a time. He was near enough now that she could smell the faint hint of a subtle aftershave. She could sense the tension in his body. And fragments of a thousand memories she'd locked away came rushing to the surface. The strength of his arms, the warmth of his body, the comfort he had offered that she had soaked up like a dry sponge.

Her mistake had been in needing. She didn't need him now.

She turned away from him and sat back on the desk, trying to convince herself that it wasn't a sign of anything that they'd fallen so readily into this argument.

"I've got a job to do too," she said, looking

pointedly at her watch. "I suppose that's why you showed up. Sabin called you?"

Quinn let out the air he'd held in his lungs. His shoulders dropped three inches. He hadn't expected the emotions to erupt so easily. It wasn't like him to let that happen. Nor was it like him to abandon a fight until he won. The relief he felt in doing so was strong enough to induce embarrassment.

He retreated a step. "He wants me to sit in with you and your witness when she comes back to work on the sketch."

"I don't care what he wants," Kate said stubbornly. "I won't have you there. This girl is hanging with me by a thread. Somebody whispers the letters *FBI* and she'll bolt."

"Then we won't mention those letters."

"She can smell a lie a mile off."

"She'll never have to know I'm there. I'll be a mouse in the corner."

Kate almost laughed. Yeah, who would notice Quinn? Six feet of dark, handsome masculinity in an Italian suit. Naw, a girl like Angie wouldn't notice him at all.

"I'd like to get a sense of this girl," he said. "What's your take on her? Is she a credible witness?"

"She's a foul-mouthed, lying, scheming little bitch," Kate said bluntly. "She's probably a runaway. She's maybe sixteen going on forty-two. She's had some hard knocks, she's alone, and she's scared spitless."

"The well-rounded American child," Quinn said dryly. "So, did she see Smokey Joe?"

Kate considered for a moment, weighing all that Angie was and was not. Whatever the girl hoped to gain in terms of a reward, whatever lies she may have told, seeing the face of evil was for real. Kate could feel the truth in that. The tension in the girl every time she had to retell the story was something virtually impossible to fake convincingly. "Yes. I believe she did."

Quinn nodded. "But she's holding back?"

"She's afraid of retaliation by the killer—and maybe by the cops too. She won't tell us what she was doing in that park at midnight."

"Guesses?"

"Maybe scoring drugs. Or she might have turned a trick somewhere nearby and was cutting across the park to get back to whatever alley she'd been sleeping in."

"But she doesn't have a record?"

"None that anyone's been able to find. We're flashing her picture around sex crimes, narcotics, and the juvie division. No bites yet."

"A woman of mystery."

"Pollyanna she ain't."

"Too bad you can't get her prints."

Kate made a face. "We'd have them now if I'd let Sabin get his way. He wanted Kovac to arrest her Monday and let her sit in jail overnight to put the fear of God in her."

"Might have worked."

"Over my dead body."

Quinn couldn't help but smile at the steel in her voice, the fire in her eyes. Clearly, she felt protective of her client, lying, scheming little bitch or not. Kovac had commented to him that while Kate was the consummate professional, she protected her victims and witnesses as if they were family. An interesting choice of words.

In five years she hadn't remarried. There was no snapshot of a boyfriend on the shelves above her desk. But inside a delicate silver filigree frame was a tiny photo of the daughter she had lost. Tucked back in the corner, away from the paperwork, away from the casual glance of visitors, almost hidden even from her own gaze, the cherubic face of the child whose death she carried on her conscience like a stone.

The pain of Emily's death had nearly crushed her. No-nonsense, unflappable Kate Conlan. Grief and guilt had struck her with the force of a Mack truck, shattering her, stunning her. She'd had no idea how to cope. Turning to her husband hadn't been an option because Steven Waterston had readily shoveled his own sense of guilt and blame onto Kate. And so she had turned to a friend....

"And if you tell Sabin it might have worked," she continued, "the dead body in question will be yours. I told him you'd back me up on this, John, and you'd damn well better. You owe me one."

"Yeah," he said softly, the old memories still too close to the surface. "At least."

14

CHAPTER

LOCATED in the Lowry Hill area, just south of the tangle of interstate highways that corralled downtown Minneapolis, D'Cup was the kind of coffeehouse funky enough for the artsy crowd and just clean enough for the patrons of the nearby Guthrie Theater and Walker Art Center. Liska walked in and breathed deep the rich aroma of exotic imported beans.

She and Moss had split the duties for the day, needing to cover as much ground as they could. Mother Mary, with her twenty-some years of maternal experience, had taken the unenviable task of talking with the families of the first two victims. She would open the old wounds as gently as possible. Liska had gladly taken the job of meeting with one of Jillian Bondurant's only known friends: Michele Fine.

Fine worked at D'Cup as a waitress and sometimes sang and played guitar on the small stage wedged into a corner near the front window. The three customers in the place sat at small tables near the window, absorbing the weak sunlight filtering in after three days of November gloom. Two older men—one tall and slender with a silver goatee,

one shorter and wider with a black beret—
sipped their espressos and argued the merits
of the National Endowment for the Arts. A
younger blond man with bug-eye gargoyle
sunglasses and a black turtleneck nursed a
grande something-or-other and worked a
newspaper crossword puzzle. A cigarette
smoldered in the ashtray beside his drink.
He had the thin, vaguely seedy look of a struggling actor.

Liska went to the counter, where a hunky
Italian-looking guy with a wavy black ponytail was pressing grounds into the fine cone-
shaped basket of an espresso machine. He
glanced up at her with eyes the color of dark
Godiva chocolate. She resisted the urge to
swoon. Barely. She wasn't as successful in
resisting the automatic counting of the weeks
since she'd had sex. Moss would have told her
mothers of nine- and eleven-year-old boys
weren't supposed to have sex.

"I'm looking for Michele."

He nodded, shoved the basket into place on
the machine, and cranked the handle around.
"Chell!"

Fine came through the archway that led
into a back room carrying a tray of clean
Fiestaware coffee cups the size of soup bowls.
She was tall and thin with a narrow, bony
face bearing several old scars that made Liska
think she must have been in a car accident a
long time ago. One curled down at one corner
of her wide mouth. Another rode the crest of
a high cheekbone like a short, flat worm. Her

dark hair had an unnatural maroon sheen, and she had slicked it back against her head and bound it at the nape of her neck. The length of it bushed out in a kinky mass fatter than a fox tail.

Liska flashed her ID discreetly. "Thanks for agreeing to meet with me, Michele. Can we sit down?"

Fine set the tray aside and pulled her purse out from under the counter. "You mind if I smoke?"

"No."

"I can't seem to stop," she said, her voice as rusty as an old gate hinge. She led the way to a table in the smoking section, as far away from the blond man as possible. "This whole business with Jillie...my nerves are raw."

Her hand was trembling slightly as she extracted a long, thin cigarette from a cheap green vinyl case. Puckered, discolored flesh warped the back of her right hand. Tattooed around the scar, an elegant, intricately drawn snake coiled around Fine's wrist, its head resting on the back of her hand, a small red apple in its mouth.

"Looks like that was a nasty burn," Liska said, pointing to the scar with her pen as she flipped open her pocket notebook.

Fine held her hand out, as if to admire it. "Grease fire," she said dispassionately. "When I was a kid."

She flicked her lighter and stared at the flame, frowning for a second. "It hurt like hell."

"I'll bet."

"So," she said, snapping out of the old memories. "What's the deal? No one will say for sure that Jillie's dead, but she is, isn't she? All the news reports talk about 'speculation' and 'likelihood,' but Peter Bondurant is involved and giving a reward. Why would he do that if it wasn't Jillie? Why won't anyone just *say* it's her?"

"I'm afraid I'm not at liberty to comment. How long have you known Jillian?"

"About a year. She comes in here every Friday, either before or after her session with her shrink. We got to know each other."

She took a deep pull on her cigarette and exhaled through teeth set wide apart. Her eyes were hazel, too narrow and too heavily lined with black, the lashes stubby and crusty with mascara. A mean look, Vanlees had called it. Nikki thought *tough* was a better word.

"And when was the last time you saw Jillian?"

"Friday. She stopped in on her way to see the psychic vampire."

"You don't approve of Dr. Brandt? Do you know him?"

She squinted through the haze of smoke. "I know he's a money-sucking leech who doesn't give a damn about helping anyone but himself. I kept telling her to dump him and get a woman therapist. He was the last thing she needed. All he was interested in was keeping his hand in Daddy's pocket."

"Do you know why she was seeing him?"

She looked just over Liska's shoulder and out

the window. "Depression. Unresolved stuff with her parents' divorce and her mom and her stepfather. The usual family shit, right?"

"Glad to say I wouldn't know. Did she tell you specifics?"

"No."

Lie, Nikki thought. "Did she ever do drugs that you know of?"

"Nothing serious."

"What's that mean?"

"A little weed once in a while when she was wired."

"Who'd she buy it from?"

Fine's expression tightened, the scars on her face seeming darker and shinier. "A friend."

Meaning herself, Liska figured. She spread her hands. "Hey, I'm not interested in busting anybody's ass over a little weed. I just want to know if Jillian could have had an enemy in that line."

"No. She hardly ever did it anyway. Not like when she lived in Europe. She was into everything there—sex, drugs, booze. But she kicked all that when she came here."

"Just like that? She comes over here and lives like a nun?"

Fine shrugged, tapping off her cigarette. "She tried to kill herself. I guess that changes a person."

"In France? She tried to kill herself?"

"That's what she told me. Her stepfather locked her up in a mental hospital for a while. Ironic, seeing as how she was going crazy because of him."

"How's that?"

"He was fucking her. She actually believed he was in love with her for a while. She wanted him to divorce her mother and marry her." She related the information in an almost offhand manner, as if that kind of behavior were the norm in her world. "She ended up taking a bunch of pills. Stepdaddy had her put away. When she got out, she came back here."

Liska scribbled the news in a personal short-hand no one but she could read, excitement making it all the more illegible. She'd hit the mother lode of dirt here. Kovac would love it. "Did her stepfather ever come here to see her?"

"No. The suicide thing freaked him out, I guess. Jillie said he never even came to see her in the loony bin." She sighed a cloud of smoke and stared off past the blond guy. "It's sad what passes for love, isn't it?"

"What kind of mood was she in Friday?"

The bony shoulders lifted and fell. "I don't know. Kind of wired, I guess. It was busy in here. We didn't have time to talk. I told her I'd call her Saturday."

"And did you?"

"Yeah. Got the machine. I left a message, but she never called back."

She stared out the window again, but without seeing anything in the street. Looking back to the weekend. Wondering if anything she could have done differently might have prevented a tragedy. Nikki had seen the expression many times. Tears washed across Michele

Fine's mean eyes and she pressed her wide, scarred mouth into a line.

"I just figured she stayed over at her dad's," she said, her throat tightening on the words. "I thought about trying to catch her Sunday, but then...I just didn't...."

"What'd you do Sunday?"

She wagged her head a little. "Nothing. Slept late. Walked around the lakes. Nothing."

She pressed her free hand over her mouth and squeezed her eyes shut, fighting for composure. Color flooded her pale face as she held her breath against the need to cry. Liska waited a moment.

The old guys were arguing now about performance art.

"How is pissing in a bottle full of crucifixes art?" Beret Man demanded.

The goatee spread his hands. "It makes a statement! Art makes a statement!"

The blond guy turned his paper over to the want ads and snuck a look at Michele. Liska gave him the cop glare and he went back to his reading.

"What about the rest of the weekend?" she asked, coming back to Fine. "What'd you do after work Friday night?"

"Why?" The suspicion was instantaneous, edged with affront and a little bit of panic.

"It's just routine. We need to establish where Jillian's family and friends were in case she might have tried to contact them."

"She didn't."

"You were home, then?"

"I went to a late movie, but I have a machine. She would have left a message."

"Did you ever stay over at Jillian's apartment?"

Fine sniffed, wiped her eyes and nose with her hand, and took another ragged puff on her cigarette. Her hand was shaking. "Yeah, sometimes. We wrote music together. Jillie won't perform, but she's good."

In and out of present tense when she talked about her friend. That was always a difficult transition for people to make after a death.

"We found some clothes in the dresser of the second bedroom that didn't look to be hers."

"That's my stuff. She's way the hell over by the river. Sometimes we'd sit up late working on a song and I'd just stay over."

"Do you have a key to her place?"

"No. Why would I? I didn't live there."

"What kind of housekeeper is she?"

"What difference does that make?"

"Neat? Sloppy?"

Fine fussed, impatient with what she didn't understand. "Sloppy. She left stuff everywhere—clothes, dishes, ashtrays. What difference does it make? She's dead."

She ducked her head then, and reddened and struggled as another wave of emotion hit on the heels of that final statement. "She's dead. He burned her. Oh, God." A pair of tears squeezed through her lashes and splashed on the paper place mat.

"We don't know for a fact that anything's happened to her, Michele."

Fine abandoned her cigarette in the ashtray and put her face in her hands. Not sobbing, but still struggling to choke the emotions back.

"Maybe she left town for a few days," Liska said. "We don't know. Do you?"

"No."

"Do you know of anyone who would want to hurt Jillian?"

She shook her head.

"She have a boyfriend? Ex-boyfriend? A guy who was interested in her?"

"No."

"How about yourself? Got a boyfriend?"

"No," she answered, looking down at the smoldering butt in the ashtray. "Why would I want one?"

"Jillian ever say anything about a man bothering her? Watching her, maybe? Hitting on her?"

Her laugh this time was bitter. "You know how men are. They all look. They all think they have a shot. Who pays any attention to the losers?"

She sniffed and pulled in a deep breath, then let it go slowly and reached for another cigarette. Her nails were bitten to the quick.

"What about her relationship with her father? They get along?"

Fine's mouth twisted. "She adores him. I don't know why."

"You don't like him?"

"Never met him. But he controls her, doesn't he? He owns the town house, pays for school, picks the therapist, pays for the therapist. Dinner every Friday. A car."

It sounded like a sweet deal to Liska. Maybe she could get Bondurant to adopt her. She let the subject drop. It was beginning to sound like if it had a penis, Michele didn't like it.

"Michele, do you know if Jillian had any distinguishing marks on her body: moles, scars, tattoos?"

Fine gave her a cross look. "How would I know that? We weren't lovers."

"Nothing obvious, then. No scar on her arm. No snake tattooed around her wrist."

"Not that I ever noticed."

"If you were to look around Jillian's apartment, would you know if things were missing? Like if she'd packed some clothes and gone somewhere?"

She shrugged. "I guess."

"Good. Let's see if we can take a ride."

WHILE MICHELE FINE squared an hour's absence with her boss, the Italian stallion, Liska stepped out of the coffeehouse, pulled her cell phone out of her pocket, and dialed Kovac.

The air was crisp, a stiff breeze blowing, as was common for November. Not a bad day. A paler imitation of the glorious weather of late September and early October that made Minnesota rival any state in the union for perfection. Her boys would be out on their bikes after school, trying to squeeze in every last wheelie they could before the snow flew and the sleds came out of storage. They were lucky that hadn't happened already.

"Moose Lodge," the gruff voice barked in her ear.

"Can I speak to Bullwinkle? I hear he's got a dick as long as my arm."

"Christ, Liska. Is that all you ever think about?"

"That and my bank balance. I can't get enough either way."

"You're preaching to the choir. What have you got for me?"

"Besides the hots? A question. When you went through Jillian's town house Monday, did you take a tape out of the answering machine?"

"It was digital. No messages."

"This friend of hers says she called Saturday and left a message. So who erased it?"

"Ooo, a mystery. I hate a mystery. Get anything else?"

"Oh, yeah." She looked through the window back into the coffee shop. "A tale to rival Shakespeare."

"SHE WAS PUTTING her life back together," Lila White's mother insisted. Her expression had the hard look of someone grown stubborn in the telling and retelling of a lie. A lie she wanted too badly to believe in and couldn't deep down in her heart.

Mary Moss felt a deep sadness for the woman.

The White family lived in the small farming

community of Glencoe, the kind of place where gossip was a common hobby and rumors cut like broken glass. Mr. White was a mechanic at a farm implement dealership. They lived on the edge of town in a neat rambler with a family of concrete deer in the front yard and a swingset out back. The swingset was for the grandchild they were raising: Lila's daughter, Kylie, a towheaded four-year-old blessedly immune to the facts of her mother's death. For now.

"She called us that Thursday night. She'd kicked the drugs, you know. It was the drugs that dragged her down." The features of Mrs. White's lumpy face puckered, as if the bitterness of her feelings left a taste in her mouth. "It's all the fault of that Ostertag boy. He's the one got her started on the drugs."

"Now, Jeannie," Mr. White said with the weariness of pointless repetition. He was a tall, rawboned man with eyes the color of washed-out denim. He had farmer's creases in his face from too many years of squinting under a bright sun.

"Don't Jeannie me," his wife snapped. "Everyone in town knows he peddles drugs, and his parents walk around pretending their shit don't stink. It makes me sick."

"Allan Ostertag?" Moss said, referring to her notes. "Your daughter went to high school with him?"

Mr. White sighed and nodded, enduring the process, waiting for it to be over so they could start the healing again and hope this was the last time the wounds would have to be reopened. His wife went on about the Ostertags. Moss waited patiently, knowing that Allan Ostertag was not and had never been a viable suspect in Lila White's murder, and was, therefore, irrelevant to her. He was not irrelevant to the Whites.

"Had she mentioned seeing anyone in particular last summer?" she asked when the rant ended. "A steady boyfriend? Someone who might have been a problem to her?"

"We've answered all these questions before," Jeannie White said impatiently. "It's like you people don't bother to write anything down. 'Course it didn't matter when it was just our girl dead," she said, the sarcasm as pointed as a needle. "We didn't see no task force on the news when it was just our Lila murdered. The police never cared—"

"That's not true, Mrs. White."

"They never cared when that drug dealer beat her up last fall neither. They never even bothered to have a trial. It's like our girl didn't count." The woman's eyes and throat filled with tears. "She wasn't important enough to anyone but us."

Moss offered apologies, knowing they wouldn't be accepted. No explanation could penetrate the hurt, the imagined insult, the anger, the pain. It didn't matter to the Whites that an individual murder was, by necessity, handled differently from a string of related murders. It mattered to them that the child they had loved had fallen down one of life's darker paths. It mattered to them she had died a prostitute. That was how she would be remembered by the world, when she was remembered at all. Victim number one, convicted prostitute and drug addict.

The Whites probably saw the headlines in their sleep. The hopes they had held for their daughter to turn her life around had died unfulfilled, and no one else in the world cared that Lila had wanted to become a counselor or that she had been a B student in high school or that she had often cried her heart out over not being able to raise her own child.

In the file folder on the passenger seat of Moss's car were snapshots of Lila and Kylie in the Whites' backyard. Smiling and laughing, and wearing party hats for Kylie's fourth birthday. Photos of mother and daughter splashing in a green plastic wading pool. Three weeks later someone had tortured the life from Lila White, desecrated her body and set it on fire like a pile of garbage.

Victim number one, convicted prostitute and drug addict.

Moss went through the reassurances in her own mind. The police couldn't form a task force for every homicide in the city. Lila White's murder had been investigated fully. Sam Kovac had caught the case, and Kovac's reputation was that he did his best for every victim, regardless of who or what they had been in life.

Still, she couldn't help but wonder—as Jeannie White had wondered aloud—how

271

differently things might have turned out if Jillian Bondurant had been victim number one.

THE LOCKS HAD been changed on Jillian Bondurant's town house at Edgewater and a new key delivered to the PD. Liska worked the shiny new key into the dead bolt and opened the door. She went to the bedrooms with Michele Fine and watched as Fine looked through the closets, pausing now and again to linger briefly over something that struck a memory for her.

"Jesus, it's eerie," she said, looking around. "Seeing the place so clean."

"Jillian didn't have a cleaning service?"

"No. Her old man tried to give her maid service as a present once. He's the most anal man on the planet. Jillie said no. She didn't want people going through her stuff.

"I don't see anything missing," she said finally.

As she stood at Jillian's dresser, her gaze drifted across the few objects there: a mahogany jewelry box, some scented candles in mismatched holders, a small porcelain figurine of an elegant woman in a flowing blue dress. She touched the figurine carefully, her expression wistful.

As Fine gathered her few clothing items from the guest bedroom, Liska walked down the steps and took in the main rooms at a glance, seeing the place differently from before she'd met Jillian's friend. It should have been a mess, but it wasn't. She'd never known a killer to offer maid services as part of the package, but someone had cleaned the place up. Not just wiped it down to get rid of prints. Cleaned it, folded and put away clothes, washed the dishes.

Her thoughts turned back to Michele Fine and Jillian as friends. They must have seemed an unlikely pair: a billionaire's daughter and a coffeehouse waitress. If there had been a ransom demand to Peter Bondurant, the relationship would have automatically fallen under scrutiny. Even without it, the suspicions flashed through Liska's mind out of habit.

Considered and dismissed. Michele Fine was cooperating fully. Nothing she had said or done seemed out of place. Her grief appeared genuine, and was colored with the shades of anger and relief and guilt Liska had encountered time and again in the people a murder victim left behind.

Still, she would run Michele Fine's name through the computer and see if anything kicked up.

She crossed the living room to the electronic piano. Jillian Bondurant had written music but was too shy to perform. That was the kind of detail that made her a real person in a way that knowing she was Peter Bondurant's daughter did not. The sheet music stacked neatly on the stand was classical. Another contradiction in Jillian's image. Liska lifted the padded seat and glanced through the collection there: folk, rock, alternative, new age—

"Hold it right there!"

Her first impulse was to go for her gun, but she held herself bent over at the piano stool, breathing through her mouth. Slowly, she turned her head and relief swept through her, her temper hot on its heels.

"It's me, Mr. Vanlees. Detective Liska," she said, straightening. "Put the gun down, please."

Vanlees stood just inside the doorway in his security guard's uniform, a Colt Python clutched in his hands. Liska wanted to pull the gun away from him and smack him in the head with it.

He blinked at her and lowered the weapon, a barely sheepish grin pulling at his mouth. "Oh, jeez, Detective, I'm sorry. I didn't know you were coming over. When I saw there was someone moving around over here, I thought the worst. You know, tabloid reporters have been coming around. I hear they'll steal anything that's not nailed down."

"You didn't recognize my car, then?" Liska said with a little too much edge.

"Uh, I guess I didn't. Sorry."

Like hell, she thought. Wanna-bes like Vanlees took note of everything about the cops they encountered in the real world. She would have bet he had her tag number written down somewhere. He sure as hell recognized the make and model. This little show had been about impressing her. Gil Vanlees: Man of Action.

On his toes. On the job. Ever diligent. *God help us all.*

Liska shook her head. "That's quite the gun you've got there, Gil," she said, moving toward him. "Don't suppose I've got to ask if you've got a permit for it?"

The eyes went a little cold and the smile sagged out of his face. He didn't like having her reprimand him. He didn't want to be reminded his uniform wasn't the real deal. He stuck the nose of the Python under his belt and eased the gun into place alongside his gut. "Yeah, I got a permit."

Liska forced a smile. "That's some piece of hardware. Not really a good idea to come up behind people with it, Gil. You never know what might happen. Reflexes a little too sharp that day and you blow somebody away. That'd be a bad deal all the way around, you know."

He wouldn't meet her eyes now, like a kid being scolded for getting into his father's tools.

"You say reporters have been nosing around here? No one's been in the house though, right?"

His attention shifted further away, and he frowned harder. Liska glanced over her shoulder. Michele Fine stood at the bottom of the steps with her messy pile of black clothing clutched to her. She looked offended by Vanlees's presence.

"Mr. Vanlees?" Liska prompted, turning back to him as Michele went into the kitchen. "No one's been in the house that you know of, right?"

"Right." He moved back a step toward the door, his hand resting on the butt of the Python. He kept his gaze on Michele, watching her as she dumped her clothes on the counter that divided kitchen and eating area. "I gotta go," he said glumly. "I was just keeping an eye out, that's all."

Liska followed him out onto the stoop. "Hey, Gil, I'm sorry if I snapped at you back there. You got the drop on me. Shook me up, you know."

He didn't bite this time. She had questioned his honor, impugned his status as a peer, bruised his ego. The rapport she had built two days ago teetered on its foundation. She had expected it to hold up better, and found its fragility telling. Another point to bring up with Quinn: Vanlees's self-image.

He barely looked at her, pouting. "Sure. No problem."

"I'm glad you're keeping an eye out," she said. "You heard about the community meeting tonight, right? You might want to drop by that if you get a chance."

Liska watched him walk away, wondering. From a distance Vanlees looked like a city cop in his blue-over-black uniform. It would be an easy thing for a guy in a uniform to get a woman to stop for him, talk to him. All three of Smokey Joe's victims had vanished with no report of a scream, no suspicious activity in the area. On the other hand, no one had mentioned seeing a uniform in the vicinity either.

"I'm ready."

She started a little at Michele Fine's announcement, and turned to find her standing in the doorway, her clothes crammed into a plastic bag from Rainbow Foods.

"Right. Great. I'll drive you back."

She locked up the house, Fine waiting for her at the bottom of the steps. Vanlees had disappeared down the winding path, but not from Liska's mind.

"You know that guy?" she asked as they settled into the car.

"Not personally," Fine said, hugging her Rainbow bag as if it were an infant. "Like I said before, who pays any attention to the losers?"

No one, Liska thought as she put the car in gear. And while no one was paying any attention to them, the losers were allowed to brood and fantasize and imagine getting back at all the women who didn't want them and would never love them.

15

CHAPTER

"SO, what do you think, John?" Sabin asked. "Is the girl holding back on us?"

They sat in a conference room in the county

attorney's offices: Quinn, Sabin, Kate, and Marshall. Quinn looked at Kate, sitting across from him with her jaw set and fire in her eyes, plainly telegraphing violence if he stepped on the wrong side of this argument. Just another minefield to cross. He kept his gaze on hers.

"Yes." The fire flared brighter. "Because she's afraid. She's probably feeling that the killer somehow knows what she's doing, as if he's watching her when she's talking with the police or describing him to your sketch artist. It's a common phenomenon. Isn't that right, Kate?"

"Yes." A banked fire in the eyes now. Reserving the right to burn him later. He liked it too much that she could still feel that strongly about him. Negative emotion was still emotion. Indifference was the thing to dread.

"A sense of omniscient evil," Marshall said, nodding wisely. "I've seen it time and again. It's fascinating. Even the most logical, sensible victims experience it."

He played with the VCR remote, running the tape back to the beginning of Angie DiMarco's initial interview, which had occurred within an hour of her being picked up. They had already gone through it. Freezing the tape at significant points, when Marshall and Sabin would then turn and stare at Quinn, waiting for a revelation like the disciples sitting at the feet of Christ.

"She's clearly terrified here," Marshall

said, repeating with authority what Quinn had said the first time they'd run through it. "You can see her shaking. You can hear it in her voice. You're absolutely right, John."

John. My buddy, my pal, my colleague. The familiarity rubbed Quinn the wrong way, even though it was something he purposely cultivated. He was tired of people pretending to know him, and even more tired of the people overly impressed with him. He wondered how impressed Rob Marshall would be to know he woke up in the middle of most nights, shaking and sick because he couldn't handle it anymore.

Marshall edged up the volume at a point where the girl lost her temper and shouted, voice quavering, "I don't *know* him! He set a fucking body on fire! He's some kind of fucking psycho!"

"She's not faking that," he pronounced quietly, squinting hard at the television screen, as if that would sharpen his myopic vision and allow him to see into the girl's mind.

Sabin looked displeased, as though he had been hoping for some excuse to put the girl on the rack. "Maybe she'd feel *safer* behind bars."

"Angie hasn't done anything wrong," Kate snapped. "She never had to admit she even saw this creep. She needs our help, not your threats."

Color starting creeping up from the county attorney's collar.

"We don't want an adversarial situation

here, Ted," Quinn said calmly. Mr. Laid Back. Mr. Coolheaded.

"The girl set herself up that way," Sabin argued. "I had a bad feeling about her the minute I set eyes on her. We should have called her bluff right off the bat. Let her know we're not screwing around here."

"I think you handled her perfectly," Quinn said. "A kid like Angie doesn't trust the system. You needed to give her a friend, and Kate was the ideal choice. She's genuine, she's blunt, she's not full of crap and phony sympathy. Let Kate handle her. You won't get anything out of her with threats. She expects threats; they'll just bounce off her."

"If she doesn't give us something we can use, there's nothing to handle," Sabin came back. "If she can't give us anything, then there's no point in wasting county resources on her."

"It's not a waste," Kate insisted.

"What do you think here, John?" Marshall asked, pointing to the screen with the remote. He had run the tape back again. "Her use of personal pronouns—*I don't know* him. He's *some kind of psycho.* Do you think it could be significant?"

Quinn blew out a breath, impatience creeping in on his temper. "What's she going to call the guy—it?"

One corner of Kate's mouth twitched.

Marshall sulked. "I've taken courses in psycholinguistics. The use of language can be very telling."

"I agree," Quinn offered, recovering diplomatically. "But there is such a thing as over-analyzing. I think the best thing you can do with this girl is step back and let Kate deal with her."

"Dammit, we need a break," Sabin said almost to himself. "She barely added anything to that sketch today. She stood right there and looked at the guy, and the picture she gives us could be anybody."

"It might be all her mind is allowing her to see," Kate said. "What do you want her to do, Ted? Make something up just so you believe she's trying harder?"

"I'm sure that's not what Mr. Sabin was suggesting, Kate," Marshall said with disapproval.

"I was being facetious to make a point, Rob."

"She's valuable to the investigation regardless," Quinn said. "We can use the threat of her. We can leak things to the press. Make it sound like she's told us more than she has. We can use her any number of ways. At this point she doesn't have to be a Girl Scout and she doesn't have to have total recall."

"My fear here is that she's lying about the whole thing," Sabin admitted, Edwyn Noble's skepticism having taken root.

Kate tried not to roll her eyes. "We've been over that. It doesn't make any sense. If all she wanted was money, she would have booked it out of that park Sunday night and never said a word until the reward was offered."

"And if the only thing on her mind was the

money," Quinn added, "then she'd be going out of her way to give us details. In my experience, greed outranks fear."

"What if she's involved in some way?" Marshall suggested. "To try to throw us off track or to get inside info—"

Kate glared at him. "Don't be absurd. If she was involved with this creep, then she'd be giving us a detailed sketch of a phantom to chase. And she isn't privy to any information the Cremator can't read in the paper."

Marshall looked down at the table. The rims of his ears turned hot pink.

"She's a scared, screwed-up kid," Kate said, rising. "And I have to get back to her before she sets my office on fire."

"Are we done here?" Marshall asked pointedly. "I guess we are. Kate has spoken."

She looked at him with undisguised dislike and walked out.

Sabin watched her go—his eyes on her ass, Quinn thought—and when she was out the door said, "Was she this headstrong at the Bureau?"

"At least," Quinn said, and followed her out.

"You're defecting too?" she said as he caught up with her. "You didn't want to stay and let Rob suck up to you? It's what he's best at."

He flashed her a grin. "You don't think much of your boss. Not that that's anything new."

"You don't think much of him either." Kate cast a precautionary glance back over her shoulder. "Rob Marshall is an obsequious, fussy little ass-kissing toad. But, in all fairness, he genuinely cares about the job we do and he tries to do it justice."

"Yes, well, he *is* trained in psycholinguistics."

"He's read your book."

Quinn raised his brows. "There are people who haven't?"

The reception area outside the secured boundaries of the major prosecution unit was vacant. The receptionist had slipped away from her post behind a sheet of bulletproof glass. Stacks of the new Yellow Pages had been left on the floor. The latest issue of *Truth & Justice* lay on the end table with half a dozen outdated news magazines.

Kate blew out a breath and turned to face him. "Thank you for backing me up."

Quinn winced. "Did it really hurt that much? God, Kate."

"I'm sorry. I'm not like you, John. I hate the game-playing that goes on in a case like this. I didn't want to have to ask for your help at all. But I suppose the least I could do is show some genuine gratitude."

"Not necessary. All I had to do was tell the truth. Sabin wanted a second opinion and he got it. You were right. That should make you happy," he said dryly.

"I don't need you to tell me I was right. And as for what would make me happy: nothing much to do with this case."

"Including my being here."

"I'm not having this conversation with you," she said flatly.

She walked out the door into the hall and took a left, going toward the atrium balcony. There wasn't another soul on the floor. Twenty-plus stories filled with people and not one of them convenient for a buffer. She knew Quinn was right behind her. And then he was beside her, his hand on her arm as if he still had some right to touch her.

"Kate, I'm sorry," he said softly. "I'm not trying to pick a fight. Really."

He was standing too close, the dark eyes too big, the lashes long and thick and pretty—an almost feminine feature in a face that was quintessentially rugged and male. The kind of face to make the average woman's heart skip. Kate felt something tighten in her chest as she drew a breath. The knuckle of his thumb pressed against the outer swell of her breast. They both became aware of the contact at the same instant.

"Kate, I—"

His pager went off and he swore under his breath and let go of her. Kate stepped away and leaned a hip against the balcony railing, crossing her arms over her chest and trying to ignore the feelings his touch had aroused. She watched him as he checked the display, swore again, and traded the pager for a slim cell phone from the pocket of his suit jacket.

The natural light that poured in through the south end of the atrium brought out the gray in his close-cropped hair. She wondered against her will if there was a woman back in Virginia worrying about his health and the level of stress he shouldered day in and day out.

"Goddammit, McCleary, can't you go two hours on this case without a fucking crisis?" he barked into the phone, then listened for a minute. "There's a lawyer involved. Shit...There's nothing you can do about it now. The interview is screwed...Back off and go over the evidence again. See if there's anything you can blow out of proportion. What about the tests on that pad of paper?...Well, he doesn't know you haven't got it. For godsake, use it!...No, I'm not coming down. I'm tied up here. Handle it."

Snapping the phone shut, he heaved a sigh and absently rubbed a hand against his stomach.

"I thought you'd be unit chief by now," Kate said.

"They offered. I declined. I'm no administrator."

But he was the natural leader for CASKU just the same. He was the resident expert the rest of the team would turn to. He was the control freak who believed no job could be handled as effectively without him being in charge of it. No, Quinn wouldn't relinquish his field duties for the unit chief's post. Instead, he would essentially do both jobs. The perfect answer for the man obsessed with his work and with his need to save humanity from its darker side.

"What kind of caseload are you carrying?" Kate asked.

He shrugged it off. "The usual."

Which was more than anyone else in the unit. More than any one person could humanly deal with, unless he had no other life. There had been times she had labeled his obsession ambition, and other times she had looked past the obvious and caught a glimpse of him standing at the edge of a deep, dark internal abyss. Dangerous thinking, because her instinctive response was to want to pull him back from that edge. His life was his own. She didn't even want him here.

"I have to get back to Angie," she said. "She won't be happy I abandoned her. I don't know why I care so much," she grumbled.

"You always liked a challenge," he said, offering her a hint of a smile.

"I ought to have my head examined."

"Can't help there, but how about dinner?"

Kate almost laughed, out of incredulity rather than humor. Just like that—*how about dinner?* Two minutes ago they'd been sniping at each other. Five years and a load of emotional baggage between them, and...*and what? He's over it and I'm not?*

"I don't think so. Thanks anyway."

"We'll talk about the case," he said, backpedaling. "I've got some ideas I'd like to bounce off you."

"That's not my job. I'm not with the BSU anymore," she said, moving toward the door into victim/witness services. The need to escape was so strong, it was embarrassing. "The BCA has an agent who's taken the behavioral analysis course and—"

286

"—is currently in Quantico for eight weeks at the National Academy."

"You can bring in another agent if you want. You've got all of CASKU to call on for backup, to say nothing of every expert and pioneer in the field. You don't need me."

With quick fingers she punched the code into the key panel beside the door.

"*You* were an expert in the field," he reminded her. "It's victim analysis—"

"Thanks for helping out with Sabin," she said as the lock relinquished its grip and she turned the knob. "I've got to get back to my office before my witness steals all my good pens."

ANGIE MOVED AROUND Kate's office, restless, curious, jumpy. Kate was pissed off about the sketch. She'd hardly said a word all the way back from the police department.

Guilt pricked Angie like so many tiny needles. Kate was trying to help her, but she had to look out for herself. The two didn't necessarily go together. How was she supposed to know what to do? How was she supposed to know what was right?

You're nothing but a fuckup! You never do anything right!

"I'm trying," she whispered.

Stupid little bitch. You never listen.

"I'm *trying.*"

Scared was what she was, but she would never speak the word, not even in her mind. The Voice would feed on her fear. The fear would feed on the Voice. She could feel both forces gaining strength inside her.

I'll give you something to be scared of.

She clamped her hands over her ears, as if she might be able to shut out the voice that echoed only in her mind. She rocked herself for a minute, eyes wide open, because if she closed them she would see things she didn't want to see again. Her past was like a bad movie playing over and over and over in her mind, always right there, ready to pull to the surface emotions better left buried deep. Hate and love, violent anger, violent need. Hate and love, hate and love, *hateandlove*—all one word for her. Feelings so intertwined they were inseparable, like the tangled limbs of two animals attacking each other.

The fear swelled a little larger. The Zone was zooming in.

You're afraid of everything, aren't you, crazy little bitch?

Trembling, she stared at the fliers tacked to Kate's bulletin board. She read the titles, trying to focus on something before the Zone could sweep in and suffocate her. *Community Resources for Crime Victims, Rape Crisis Center, The Phoenix: Women Rising to a New Beginning.* Then the titles blurred and she sat down, breathing just a little too hard.

What the hell was taking Kate so long? She'd left with no explanation, said nothing more than that she'd be back in a few minutes, which was—how many minutes ago? Angie looked around for a clock, found it, then couldn't remember what time it had been when Kate had left her. Hadn't she looked at the clock then? Why couldn't she remember?

Because you're stupid, that's why. Stupid and crazy.

She began to shiver. It felt like her throat was closing. There was no air in this stupid little room. The walls were pressing in on her. She tried to swallow as tears flooded her eyes. The Zone was zooming in. She could feel it coming, could feel the change in the air pressure around her. She wanted to run, but she couldn't outrun the Zone or the Voice.

So do something. Make it stop, Angel. You know how to make it stop.

Frantic, she shoved the sleeves of her jacket and sweater up and scratched a stubby thumbnail along the thin white lines of the scars, turning them pink. She wanted to get at the cut she'd opened yesterday, to make it bleed again, but she couldn't get her sleeve up that high and she didn't dare take her coat off for fear someone would come in and catch her. Kate had told her to wait there, that she would be back in a few minutes. The minutes were ticking by.

She'll know how crazy you are then, Angel.

The Zone was zooming in...

You know what to do.

But Kate was coming back.

Do it.

The shaking started.

Do it.

The Zone was zooming in...

Do it!

She didn't dare take the box cutter out of her backpack. How would she explain it? She could stick it in her pocket—

The panic was setting in. She could feel her mind begin to fracture just as her desperate gaze hit on the dish of paper clips on Kate's desk.

Without hesitation, she grabbed one and straightened it, testing the end with her fingertip. It wasn't as sharp as the razor. It would hurt more.

Coward. Do it!

"I hate you," she muttered, fighting the tears. "I hate you. I hate you."

Do it! Do it!

"Shut up! Shut up! Shut up!" she whispered, the pressure building in her head until she thought it would burst.

She dragged the piece of wire across an old scar on her wrist where the skin was as thin and white as paper. She cut parallel to a fine blue vein, and waited for her tear-blurred vision to fill with blood. Rich and red, a thin liquid line.

The pain was strong and sweet. The relief was immediate. The pressure lifted. She could breathe again. She could think.

She stared at the crimson ribbon for a moment, some lost part of her deep, deep inside wanting to cry. But the overwhelming sensation was relief. She set the paper clip aside and wiped the blood away with the bottom of her sweater. The line bloomed again, bringing an extra wave of calm.

She drew her thumb down along the cut, then looked at the way the blood had smeared into the whorls and between the ridges of the pad. Her fingerprint, her blood, her crime. She stared at it for a long time, then raised her thumb to her mouth and slowly licked it off. She felt a kind of release that was almost sexual. She had conquered the demon and consumed it. She drew her tongue along the cut, taking up the last few beads of red.

Still slightly weak-kneed and light-headed, she pulled her sleeve into place and got up from the chair to move around the office. She took in every detail and committed it to memory.

Kate's thick wool coat hung on a wall rack with a funky black crushed-velvet hat. Kate had cool taste in clothes for a woman her age. Angie wanted to try the hat on, but there was no mirror to look in to see it.

A small cartoon on the bulletin board showed a lawyer grilling a witness—a groundhog. *"So, Mr. Groundhog, you claim you saw your shadow that day. But isn't it true you have a drinking problem?"*

The desk drawers were locked. There was no purse in sight. She tried the file cabinet, thinking she might find her own file, but that too was locked.

As she fingered through the papers on the desk, she was struck by how she had been in such a state of panic just a few minutes ago and now she felt strong and in control, just as she had slipping out of and back into Phoenix House undetected. She hated that part of her that let the Zone take over. She hated how weak that part of her was. She knew she could be strong.

I make you strong, Angel. You need me. You love me. You hate me.

The fresh strength let her ignore the Voice.

She flipped through the Rolodex and stopped on the name *Conlan*. Frank and Ingrid in Las Vegas. Kate's parents, she guessed. Kate would have normal parents. A father who went to work in a suit. A mother who made pot roast and baked cookies. Not the kind of mother who did drugs and slept around. Not the kind of father who didn't give a shit about his kids, who left and left them at the mercy of the jerks their mother brought home. Kate Conlan's parents loved Kate like normal people loved their kids. Kate Conlan had never been locked in a closet or whipped with a wire hanger or forced to go down on her step-father.

Angie pulled the card from the Rolodex, tore it into tiny pieces, and stuffed the pieces into her jacket pocket.

A stack of mail sat unopened in the in basket. Another stack sat in the out basket. Angie picked the envelopes up and sorted through them. Three official pieces of correspondence in Hennepin County Government Center envelopes. One bright yellow envelope addressed by hand to someone named Maggie Hartman, the return address on a gold foil label in the upper left corner: Kate Conlan.

She memorized the address and put the envelopes back, her attention moving on to the collection of tiny angel statues she had spotted the first time she'd come into the office. They sat scattered atop the shelving unit on the desk. Each was different: glass, brass, silver, pewter, painted. None was more than an inch high. Angie singled out the one made of painted pottery. She had black hair and dots of turquoise on her dress. Gold edged her wings and circled her head in a halo.

Angie held the statue close and stared at its round face with black dots for eyes and a crooked little smile. She looked happy and innocent, simple and sweet.

Everything you're not, Angel.

Knowing better than to acknowledge the deep sadness that yawned inside her heart, Angie turned away from the desk, slipping the angel into her coat pocket just as the doorknob rattled. An instant later Kate came into the room.

"Where the hell have you been?" Angie demanded.

Kate looked at her, checking the instant retort before it could get to her tongue. "Damage control" was the most diplomatic thing she could say. "Sorry it took so long."

Instantly Angie's bravado faded. "I did the best I could!"

Kate doubted that was the truth, but there was nothing to gain in saying so. What she needed to do was figure out how to get the whole story out of this kid. She dropped into her chair, unlocked the desk, and took a bottle of Aleve out of the pencil drawer. She shook out two, downed them with cold coffee and a grimace, then paused to consider the possibility that her charming charge might poison her.

"Don't worry about the sketch," she said, rubbing at the tension in the back of her neck. The tendons stood out like steel rods. She swept her gaze discreetly across the desk. An automatic check that was second nature after she'd left a client alone in her office. One of her angels was missing.

Angie settled uneasily on the visitor's chair, leaning her arm on the desk. "What's going to happen?"

"Nothing. Sabin is frustrated. He needs something big and he was hoping you'd be it. He talked about cutting you loose, but I talked him out of it. For now. If he decides you're a scam artist just trying to collect reward money, he'll cut you loose and I won't be able to help you. If you go to a tabloid and try to give them something more than what you've given the cops, Sabin will throw your ass in jail, and no one will be able to help you.

"You're between a rock and a hard place here, Angie. And I know your first instinct is to pull everything inside you and shut the rest of the world out, but you have to remember one thing: That secret you're holding, you share it with one other person—and he'll kill you for it."

"I don't need you scaring me."

"God, I hope not. The man you saw tortures women, kills them, and sets their bodies on fire. I hope that scares you more than anything I could say."

"You don't know what scared is," Angie accused, her voice bitter with memories. She sprang up out of the chair and began to pace, chewing hard on a thumbnail.

"Then tell me. Tell me something, Angie. Anything I can toss Sabin and the cops to back them off. What were you doing in the park that night?"

"I told you."

"You were cutting through. From where? From what? If you'd been with someone, don't you realize he might have seen this guy too? He might have caught a glimpse of a car. He could, at the very least, confirm your side of things and at the most he could help us catch this monster."

"What do you think?" Angie demanded. "You think I'm a whore? You think I was there fucking some john for pocket money? I told you what I was doing there. So that means you think I'm a whore *and* a liar. Fuck you."

She was out the door that fast, with Kate right behind her.

"Hey! Don't give me that bullshit," Kate ordered, catching hold of the girl's arm, the thinness of it almost startling her.

Angie's expression held as much surprise as anger. This wasn't how it was supposed to go.

This wasn't how the umpteen social workers she'd seen in her young life would have reacted.

"What?" Kate demanded. "You thought I'd go contrite and apologize? 'Oh, gee, I offended Angie! She must never have done anything bad to stay alive on the streets!' " She feigned wide-eyed shock, one hand on her cheek, then dropped the act in a heartbeat. "You think I just rode in on the turnip wagon? I know what goes on in the big bad world, Angie. I know what women with no homes and no jobs are forced to do to survive.

"Yes, frankly, I *do* think you were in that park fucking some john for pocket money. And I know damn well you're a liar. You're a thief too. What I'm telling you is this: *I don't care.* I'm not judging you. I can't do anything about what happened to you before you came into my life, Angie. I can only help you with what's happening now and with what's going to happen. You're drowning in this thing and *I want to help you.* Can you get that through your thick head and quit fighting me?"

The silence was absolute for a second as they stood there in the hall of legal services, staring at each other—one angry, one wary. Then a phone rang in someone's office, and Kate became aware of Rob Marshall looking out his door down the hall. She kept her attention on Angie, and prayed to God Rob would keep his nose out of it. The bleakness in the girl's eyes was enough to break Kate's heart.

"Why would you care what happens to me?" Angie asked quietly.

"Because no one else does," Kate said simply.

Tears rose in the girl's dark blue eyes. The truth of what Kate had said was right there. No one had ever cared a damn about Angie DiMarco, and she didn't dare trust that someone would start now.

"All I have to gain is a congratulatory pat on the ass from Ted Sabin," Kate said, pulling a scrap of humor up through the thicker emotions. "Believe me, that's not my motivation."

Angie stared at her for another moment, weighing options, the weight of those options pressing down hard on her. A single tear rolled down her cheek. She drew a shallow, shaky breath.

"I don't like doing it," she whispered in a child's voice, her lower lip trembling.

Slowly and carefully, Kate put an arm around Angie's shoulders and drew the girl to her, the need to give comfort so strong, it frightened her. Someone had brought this child into the world, not wanting her for any reason other than to punish her for their mistakes. The injustice burned in Kate's chest. *This is why I don't do kids,* she thought. *They make me feel too much.*

The girl's body shuddered as she let go a fraction more of the emotion that was threatening to crush her. "I'm sorry," she whispered. "I'm so sorry."

"I know, kiddo," Kate murmured thickly as

she patted Angie's back. "I'm sorry too. Let's go sit down and talk about it. These damn heels. My feet are killing me."

16

CHAPTER

"YOU CAN'T BELIEVE some of the stuff coming in over the hotline," Gary Yurek said, carrying a thick file and a pad of paper to the table in the Loving Touch of Death war room. "They actually had a woman call in to say she thinks her neighbor is the Cremator because her *dog* doesn't like him!"

"What kind of dog?" Tippen called.

"American scumbag spaniel," Elwood said, pulling out a chair. "A hearty, cheerful breed known for digging up corpses and cavorting merrily with cadaver parts."

"Sounds like you, Elwood." Liska punched him in the arm as she passed.

"Hey, my hobbies are my own business."

"Any more sightings of Jillian Bondurant?" Hamill asked.

Yurek looked disgusted. "Yeah, a Jiffy Lube mechanic in Brooklyn Park whose every third word was *reward*."

Quinn took a seat at the table, his head throbbing, his mind trying to go in too many directions at once. Kate, Kate's witness. Bondurant. The profile he was struggling with. The Atlanta case. The Blacksburg case. The calls backing up on his voice mail about a dozen others. Kate. Kate...

His brain wanted a cup of coffee, but his stomach was saying no in strong and painful language. He fished a Tagamet out of his pocket and washed it down with diet Coke. Mary Moss handed him a packet of photographs.

"Lila White's parents gave them to me. I don't see how they'll help, but it was important to them. The pictures were taken just a few days before her murder."

"Progress reports!" Kovac called, shrugging out of his topcoat and juggling three files as he came to the head of the table. "Anything on the parks employees?"

"Found a convicted child-molester who lied about his record on his application," Tippen said. "Other than that, no red flags on the permanent staff. However, the parks department also gets work crews of misdemeanor offenders doing community service time. We're getting a list."

"Jillian's phone records don't show anything out of the ordinary," Elwood said. "Calls to her father, to her shrink, to this friend Tinks went to see. Nothing unusual in the last couple of weeks. I've requested the records from her cell phone service, but their computers were screwed up, so I don't have that yet."

"We've got a list of employees fired from Paragon in the last eighteen months," Adler said. "None of them stood out as being particularly vindictive toward Peter Bondurant. We ran their names through the system and came up with petty shit."

"One guy convicted of soliciting a prostitute," Hamill said. "But that was a one-time, bachelor-party situation. He's married now. Spent last weekend at his in-laws'."

"That could drive *me* to murder," Tippen quipped.

"One guy with a third-degree-assault charge. He attacked his manager when he got the news Paragon was giving him the ax," Adler said. "That was nine months ago. He's moved out of town. Lives in Cannon Falls now and works in Rochester."

"How far is that?" Quinn asked.

"Cannon Falls? Half an hour, forty-five minutes."

"An easy drive. He's not off the hook."

"Our Rochester field agent is checking him out," Hamill said.

"In general," Adler went on, "no one who works for Bondurant seems particularly fond of him, but no one had anything bad to say about him either—with one notable exception. Bondurant started Paragon back in the late seventies with a partner—Donald Thorton. He bought Thorton out in 'eighty-six."

"About the time of his divorce," Kovac said.

"Exactly the time of the divorce. He paid

Thorton top dollar—more than, according to some. Thorton developed serious problems with booze and gambling, and ran his Caddie into Lake Minnetonka in 'eighty-nine. Lake patrol fished him out before he drowned, but not before he sustained serious brain damage and a spinal cord injury. His wife blames Bondurant."

"How so?"

"She wouldn't say over the phone. She wants a face-to-face."

"I'll take it," Kovac said. "Anyone has something bad to say about Mr. Billionaire can be my friend."

Walsh raised one hand, covering his mouth with the other while he tried to cough up part of a lung. When he finally drew breath to speak, his face was purple. "I've been on the phone with the legal attaché's office in Paris," he said in a thin, strained voice. "They're checking out the stepfather—Serge LeBlanc—with Interpol and with the French authorities. But I'd say he's a dead end. Come all the way over here to off two hookers and then his stepdaughter? I don't think so."

"He could have hired it done," Tippen offered.

"No," Quinn said. "This is classic sadistic sexual homicide. The killer had his own agenda. He doesn't do it for money. He does it because he gets off on it."

Walsh pulled a nasty-looking handkerchief out of his pocket and stared into it, contemplating a sneeze. "LeBlanc is plenty pissed off about the inquiries, and not being too cooperative. He says he'll release Jillian's dental records—which will do us no good. He'll release any X rays she's ever had taken, but that's it. He won't let the whole file go."

Kovac's face lit up. "Why is that? What's he trying to hide?"

"Maybe the fact that he had sex with her, drove her to a suicide attempt, then had her committed," Liska offered, looking pleased to have scooped the boys. She filled them in on what she had learned from Michele Fine.

"I also asked Fine to stop in and get fingerprinted so we can eliminate her prints from the ones found in Jillian's apartment. And, by the way, somebody definitely cleaned the place up over the weekend. Fine says Jillian was a slob. The place is way too clean and the friend says there was no maid service."

"Maybe the killer was in her house that night," Adler speculated. "Didn't want to leave any trace."

"I can see he'd wipe the place for prints," Elwood said. "But tidy up? That doesn't make sense."

Quinn shook his head. "No. If he was there, he wouldn't have cleaned up. If anything, he would have made it worse as a sign of disrespect to his victim. He would have trashed the place, maybe urinated or defecated somewhere obvious."

"So, we got us another mystery," Kovac said. He turned to Liska again. "You ran Fine through the system?"

"No wants, no warrants, no record. No

boyfriend, she says, and I'd believe that. She says she and Jillian weren't lovers. There's a dope connection there somewhere. Small-time, I'd say."

"But it might be worth digging on," Moss said. "Lila White had connections too. One of them beat the snot out of her last fall."

"Willy Parrish," Kovac said. "He was a guest of the county at the time of White's murder. Had no connection to Fawn Pierce."

"I also checked the guy White's parents blame for hooking her on drugs in the first place," Moss said. "A Glencoe local named Allan Ostertag. No convictions. Strictly small-time. Works as a salesman at his father's car dealership. He can be accounted for all this last weekend."

"Jillian and Fine wrote music together," Quinn said, jotting himself a note. "What kind of music?"

"Folky alternative stuff," Liska said. "Man-hating female angst bullshit, I'd guess from my impression of Fine. She's a real trip. Alanis Morissette with PMS."

"So where's the music?" Quinn asked. "I'd like to see it."

"Super G-man and talent scout on the side," Tippen remarked snidely.

Quinn cut him a look. "Music is personal, intimate. It reveals a lot about the person who wrote it."

Liska's brow knitted as she thought. "I saw sheet music, like you'd buy in a store. I didn't see anything handwritten."

"See if the friend has copies," Kovac suggested.

"I will, but I think Vanlees is the direction we should be sniffing. The guy's got a screw loose, and he fits John's preliminary profile pretty well."

"Criminal background?" Quinn asked.

"Nothing serious. A slew of parking tickets and a couple of misdemeanors three or four years ago. Trespass charges and a DUI—all spread out over a period of eighteen months or so."

"Trespass?" The word raised a flag in Quinn's mind. "Was that the original charge or did he plead down from something else?"

"Final outcome."

"Dig deeper. A lot of Peeping Toms bargain down their first couple of offenses. They seem too pathetic to be worth charging out on a low-end sex crime. Check out the tickets too. Check the locations the tickets were issued in relation to the address of the trespass charges."

Tippen leaned toward Adler. "Yeah, we might have a serial weenie wagger on our hands."

"They all start somewhere, Tippen," Quinn said. "The Boston Strangler started out looking in windows, jerking off, and some asshole cop shrugged that off too."

The detective started to come up out of his chair. "Hey, fu—"

"Put 'em back in your pants, guys," Kovac ordered. "We got no time to get out the yardstick. Tinks, find out if this mutt did his community service in the parks."

304

"And find out what kind of car he's driving," Quinn added.

"Will do. I made a point of telling him about the meeting tonight. I'm betting he shows."

"Speaking of," Kovac said. "I want everyone there by seven-thirty. We'll have surveillance units from the BCA and from narcotics pulling plate numbers off the cars in the parking lot. Yurek will be our master of ceremonies. I want the rest of you in the crowd, and for God's sake, try not to look like cops."

"Except the cover boy," Tippen said, holding up a copy of the day's *Star Tribune* with the headline *FBI's Top Profiler on the Case*. "You might get two headlines in a row, Slick."

Quinn frowned, reining in his temper, fighting the urge to put his fist in Tippen's mouth. Christ, he knew better than to let jerks like Tippen yank his chain. He'd dealt with a hundred of them in the last year alone. "I don't want a headline. I'll say a few words, but I'll keep it brief and I'll keep it vague."

"Just like you have with us?"

"What do you want me to tell you, Tippen? That the killer will be wearing one red shoe?"

"It'd be something. What the hell have you given us so far for our tax dollars? An age range, the possible description of two vehicles the guy may or may not drive. That he slept with his mother and jacked off with porno magazines? Big deal."

"It will be if you get a suspect. And I don't believe I ever said anything about him sleeping with his mother."

"Tip reliving his childhood."

"Fuck you, Chunk."

"Maybe," Quinn said, watching the homely sheriff's detective just to see him twitch. "The UNSUB, that is. It's likely there was inappropriate sexual behavior both in the home in general and toward this man specifically when he was a child. His mother was probably promiscuous, possibly a prostitute. His father was a weak or absent figure. Discipline was inconsistent, swinging from nonexistent to extreme.

"He was a bright kid, but in trouble a lot at school. He couldn't relate to other kids. His mind was full of thoughts of domination and control of his peers. He was cruel to animals and to other children. He started fires, he stole things. He was a pathological liar at an early age.

"In high school he had trouble concentrating because of his addiction to his sexual fantasies, which were already becoming violent. He got into trouble with authority figures, maybe had run-ins with the police. His mother smoothed over the problems, rationalized for him, got him off the hook, thereby reinforcing a pattern where he was never held accountable for his destructive actions toward others. This empowered him and encouraged him to try even more extreme behavior. It also reinforced a lack of respect for his mother."

Tippen raised his hands. "And unless the guy sitting next to me tonight turns and says, 'Hi, my name is Harry. My mother had sex with me when I was a kid,' it's all just so much crap."

"I think *you're* full of crap, Tippen," Liska said. "When I'm digging up stuff on Vanlees, if I see any of these red flags, I can use them."

"The analysis is a tool," Quinn said. "You can make it work for you or you can leave it in the toolbox.

"When you're in the crowd tonight, watch for anyone who seems overstimulated—excited or nervous or too conscious of the people around them. Listen for anyone who seems to have too great a command of the facts of the case, anyone who seems unusually familiar with police work. Or you can take Detective Tippen's approach and wait for someone to tell you he fucked his mother."

"G, you know what you can do with that smart mouth?" Tippen said, rising again.

Kovac stepped between them. "Take yours over to Patrick's and stick a sandwich in it, Tippen. Go now, before you piss me off and I tell you not to come back."

A sour look twisted Tippen's face. "Oh, fuck this," he muttered, grabbing his coat and walking away.

Kovac looked askance at Quinn. A phone was ringing in one of the rooms down the hall. The rest of the task force began to disperse, everyone wanting to grab a bite or a drink before the big event.

"Being a good cop and being an asshole are not exclusive," Liska said, pulling on her coat.

"You talking about him or me?" Quinn said with chagrin.

"Hey, Sam!" Elwood called. "Come take a look at this."

"Tippen's a jerk, but he's a good detective," Liska said.

"It's all right." Quinn gave an absent smile as he slipped his trench coat on. "Skepticism makes for a good investigator."

"You think so?" She narrowed her eyes and looked at him sideways, then laughed and popped him on the arm. "Just a little cop humor. So, we've got some more background on Jillian and the two hookers. You want to sit down over dinner and go over it? Or maybe after the meeting tonight we could get a drink somewhere...."

"Hey, Tinks," Kovac barked as he strode back into the room with a fistful of fax paper. "No hitting on the fed."

Liska reddened. "Go bite yourself, Kojak."

"You'd pay money to see that."

"I'd throw pennies at your ugly butt."

He hooked a thumb in her direction as she walked away and gave Quinn a wry look. "She's crazy about me."

Liska flipped him off over her shoulder.

Kovac shrugged and turned to business. "You up for a ride, GQ? I need an extra hammer in my toolbox."

"What's the occasion?"

His eyes were as bright as a zealot's as he held up the fax. "Jillian Bondurant's cell phone records. She made two phone calls after midnight Saturday morning—*after* she left the old homestead. One to the head-shrinker and one to Daddy Dearest."

HE SAW THEM coming. Standing in the immaculate music room beside the baby grand piano that held a small gallery of framed photos of Jillian as a small child, he saw the car pull up at the gate. A dirt-brown domestic piece of junk. Kovac.

The intercom buzzed. Helen hadn't left yet. She was in the kitchen preparing his dinner. She would get the buzzer and she would let Kovac in because he was with the police, and like every older middle-class American woman in the country, she would not defy the police.

Not for the first time he thought he should have brought his personal assistant in from Paragon to guard his gates both figuratively and literally, but he didn't want another person that close to him now. Bad enough to have Edwyn Noble at his heels every time he turned around. He had purposely sent his media relations coordinator away from him to deal with the news and sensation seekers, who insisted on crowding his gate nevertheless.

Car doors. Quinn walked around from the passenger's side, an elegant figure, head up, shoulders square. Kovac, disheveled, hair sticking up in back, finished a cigarette and dropped it on the driveway. His trench coat flapped open in the wind.

Peter stared at the photographs for another minute. Jillian, too serious at the keyboard. Always something dark and turbulent and sad in her eyes. Her first recital. And her second, and third. Dressed up in frilly frocks that had never suited her—too innocent and prim, representative of the kind of carefree girlishness his daughter had never possessed.

He left the room as the doorbell sounded, shutting the door on that segment of his regret as voices sounded in the front hall.

"Is he in?" Quinn.

Helen: "I'll see if he's available. Have you had any new developments in the case?"

"We're working on some things." Kovac.

"Did you know Jillian very well?" Quinn.

"Oh, well—"

"You've been given instructions to reach me through my attorney," Peter said by way of greeting.

"Sorry about that, Mr. Bondurant," Kovac said, blatantly unrepentant. "John and I were just on our way over to the community meeting we've set up to try to help catch your daughter's killer, and we decided to swing by kinda spur-of-the-moment like to run some things by you. Hope it's not a bad time."

Bondurant leveled a heavy look at him, then turned to his housekeeper. "Thank you, Helen. If you're finished in the kitchen, why don't you head home?"

The housekeeper looked worried that she'd screwed up. Quinn watched Bondurant as the woman started back toward the kitchen.

The stress of the last few days was telling on him. He looked as if he hadn't eaten or slept. All dark circles and sunken cheeks and a pallor that was unique to people under tremendous pressure.

"I don't have anything useful to say to you," he declared, impatient. "My daughter is dead. I can't do anything to change that. I can't even bury her. I can't even make funeral arrangements. The medical examiner's office won't release the body."

"They can't release the body without a positive ID, Mr. Bondurant," Quinn said. "You don't want to bury a stranger by mistake, do you?"

"My daughter was a stranger to me," he said enigmatically, wearily.

"Really?" Kovac said, moving slowly around the foyer, like a shark circling. "Here I thought she might have been telling you all about who she really was when she called you that night—*after* she left here. After you said you never heard from her again."

Bondurant stared at him. No denial. No apology.

"What'd you think?" Kovac demanded. "Did you think I wouldn't find that out? Do you think I'm a moron? Do you think I've gotta have a fucking FBI shield in order to have a brain?"

"I didn't think it was relevant."

Kovac looked astounded. "Not relevant? Maybe she gave a clue where she was when she made the call. That would give us an area to

311

canvass for witnesses. Maybe there was a voice in the background, or a distinguishing sound. Maybe the call was interrupted."

"No on all counts."

"Why did she call?"

"To say good night."

"And is that the same reason she'd call her shrink in the middle of the night?"

No reaction. No surprise, no anger. "I wouldn't know why she called Lucas. Their relationship as doctor and patient was none of my business."

"She was your daughter," Kovac said, pacing fast, the frustration building. "Did you think it wasn't any of your business when her stepfather was fucking her?"

Direct hit. At last, Quinn thought, watching anger fill Peter Bondurant's thin face. "I've had all I want of you, Sergeant."

"Yeah? Do you suppose that's what LeBlanc said to Jillian that drove her to try to kill herself back in France?" Kovac taunted, reckless, skating on a thin edge.

"You bastard." Bondurant made no move toward him, but held himself rigid. Quinn could see him trembling.

"*I'm* a bastard?" Kovac laughed. "Your daughter's maybe dead and you don't bother to tell us jack shit about her, and *I'm* the bastard? That's rich. John, do you fucking believe this guy?"

Quinn gave the big sigh of disappointment. "We don't ask these questions lightly, Mr. Bondurant. We don't ask them to hurt you or your daughter's memory. We ask because we need the whole picture."

"I've told you," Bondurant said in a low, tight voice, the fury cold and hard in his eyes. "Jillian's past has nothing to do with this."

"I'm afraid it does. One way or another. Your daughter's past was a part of who she was—or who she *is*."

"Lucas told me you'd insist on that. It's ludicrous to think Jillian somehow brought this on herself. She was doing so well—"

"It's not your job to try to dissect this, Peter," Quinn said, shifting to the personal. *I'm your friend. You can tell me.* Giving him permission to let go of the control slowly and voluntarily. Quinn could see the logical part of Bondurant's mind arguing with the emotions he kept so firmly boxed. He was wound so tight that if Kovac pushed him hard enough and he snapped, it would be like suddenly loosing a high-tension wire—no control at all. Bondurant was smart enough to realize that and anal enough to dread the possibility.

"We're not saying it was Jillian's fault, Peter. She didn't ask for this to happen. She didn't deserve to have this happen."

A sheen of tears glazed Bondurant's eyes.

"I realize this is difficult for you," Quinn said softly. "When your wife left, she took your daughter to a man who abused her. I can imagine the kind of anger you must have felt when you found out."

"No, you can't." Bondurant turned away,

looking for some kind of escape but not willing to leave the hall.

"Jillian was an ocean away, in trouble, in pain. But everything was over by the time you found out, so what could you do? Nothing. I can imagine the frustration, the anger, the feeling of impotence. The guilt."

"I couldn't do anything," he murmured. He stood beside a marble-topped table, staring at a sculpture of ragged bronze lilies, seeing a past he would rather have kept locked away. "I didn't know. She didn't tell me until after she'd moved back here. I didn't know until it was too late."

With a trembling hand he touched one of the lilies and closed his eyes.

Quinn stood beside him, just encroaching on Bondurant's personal space. Near enough to invite confidence, to suggest support rather than intimidation. "It's not too late, Peter. You can still help. We have the same goal—finding and stopping Jillian's killer. What happened that night?"

He shook his head. Denying what? There was a sense of something—guilt? shame?—emanating from him almost like an odor. "Nothing," he said. "Nothing."

"You had dinner. She stayed till midnight. What happened that made her call Brandt? She must have been upset about something."

Still shaking his head. Denying what? Her emotional state, or just refusing to answer? Shaking off the questions as unacceptable because the answers would open a door he

314

didn't want to go through? The daughter who had come back to him after all those years had not come back the innocent child she had been. She had come back different, damaged. How would a father feel? Hurt, disappointed, ashamed. Guilty because he hadn't been there to prevent what had driven his daughter to try to end her own life. Guilty because of the shame he felt when he thought of her as damaged, as less than perfect. Emotions tangled and dark, tied in a knot that would take the skill of a surgeon to unravel. He thought of the photograph in Bondurant's office: Jillian, so unhappy in a dress meant for another kind of girl.

Kovac came up on Bondurant's right. "We're not out to hurt Jillian. Or you, Mr. Bondurant. We just want the truth."

Quinn held his breath, never taking his eyes off Bondurant. A moment passed. A decision was made. The scales tipped away from them. He could see it in Peter Bondurant's face as his hand slipped from the ragged bronze lily and he pulled everything inside him tight, and closed that inner door that had slipped ajar.

"No," Bondurant said, his face a vacant, bony mask as he reached for the receiver of the sleek black telephone that sat beside the sculpture. "You won't get the chance. I won't have my daughter's memory dragged through the mud. If I see one word in one paper about what happened to Jillian in France, I'll ruin you both."

Kovac blew out a breath and moved away

from the table. "I'm just trying to solve these murders, Mr. Bondurant. That's my only agenda here. I'm a simple guy with simple needs—like the truth. You could ruin me in a heartbeat. Hell, anything I ever had that was worth anything at all went to one ex-wife or the other. You can squash me like a bug. And you know what? I'll still want that truth, 'cause that's the way I am. It'll be easier on all of us if you give it to me sooner rather than later."

Bondurant just stared at him, stone-faced, and Kovac just shook his head and walked away.

Quinn didn't move for a moment, watching Bondurant, trying to measure, trying to read. They had been so close to drawing him out.…"You brought me here for a reason," he said softly, one-on-one, man-to-man. He pulled a business card from his pocket and laid it on the table. "Call me when you're ready."

Bondurant hit a direct dial button on the phone and waited.

"One last question," Quinn said. "Jillian liked to write music. Did you ever hear her perform? Ever see any of her stuff?"

"No. She didn't share that with me."

He looked away as someone answered on the other end of the line.

"This is Peter Bondurant. Put me through to Edwyn Noble."

HE STOOD IN the hall and waited for a long time after the rude rumble of Kovac's car had died

316

away. Just stood there in the silence, in the gloom. Time passed. He didn't know how much. And then he was walking down the hall to his office, his body and mind seemingly working independent of each other.

One floor lamp burned low in a corner of the room. He didn't turn on more. Night had crept up into the late afternoon and stolen the clear light that had fallen in through the French doors earlier in the day. The room had a gloomy cast to it that suited his mood.

He unlocked his desk, took a sheet of music from it, and went to stand by the window to read, as if the farther the words were away from the light, the less harsh their reality.

Love Child

I'm your love child
Little girl
Want you more than all the world
Take me to that place I know
Take me where you want to go
Got to make you love me
Only one way how
Daddy, won't you love me
Love me now
Daddy, I'm your love child
Take me now

—JB

17

CHAPTER

THE MEETING IS IN HIS HONOR, in a manner of speaking. He sits in the crowd, watching, listening, fascinated and amused. The people around him—he estimates 150, many of them with the media—have come here because they fear him or are fascinated by him. They have no idea the monster is sitting beside them, behind them, shaking his head as they comment on the frightening state of the world and the vicious mentality of the Cremator.

He believes some of them actually envy the Cremator his boldness, though they will never admit it. None of them have the nerve, the clarity of vision, to act on their fantasies and release the dark power within.

The meeting comes to order, the spokesman of the task force stating the alleged purpose of the meeting, which is a lie. The meeting is not to inform, or even to offer the community a show of action. The purpose of the meeting is Quinn's.

"More important in this ongoing cycle of murders, I told them, was to begin going proactive, using

police efforts and the media to try to lure the guy into a trap. For example, I suggested the police might set up a series of community meetings to 'discuss' the crimes. I was reasonably certain the killer would show up at one or more of these." — *John Douglas,* Mindhunter.

The purpose of the meeting is to trap him, and yet he sits here, cool and calm. Just another concerned citizen. Quinn is watching the crowd, looking for him, looking for something most people won't recognize: the face of evil.

"People expect evil to have an ugly face, a set of horns. Evil can be handsome. Evil can be ordinary. The ugliness is internal, a black, cancerous rot that consumes conscience and moral fiber and the controls that define civilized behavior, and leave an animal hiding behind the normal facade." —*John Quinn, in an interview with* People *magazine, January 1997.*

In his sharp tailored gray suit, Quinn is obviously a cut above the local stiffs. He has the bored, superior expression of a *GQ* model. This stirs anger—that Quinn has finally deigned to acknowledge him in public, and he looks as if he couldn't be less interested.

Because you think you know me, Quinn. You think I'm just another case. Nothing special.

But you don't know the Cremator. Evil's Angel.
And I know you so well.

He knows Quinn's record, his reputation, his theories, his methods. In the end, he will have Quinn's respect, which will mean more to Quinn than it does to him. His dark, true self is above the need for approval. Seeking approval is weak, reactive, induces vulnerability, invites ridicule and disappointment. Not acceptable. Not allowed on the dark side.

He recites his credo in his mind: *Domination. Manipulation. Control.*

Lights flash and camera motors whir as Quinn takes the podium. The woman sitting next to him begins to cough. He offers her a Life Saver and thinks about cutting her throat for disrupting his concentration.

He thinks about doing it here, now—grabbing a fistful of blond hair, pulling her head back, and in one quick motion slicing through her larynx and her jugular and her carotid—all the way back to her spine. The blood will flood out of her in a gushing wave, and he will melt back through the hysterical crowd and slip away. He smiles at the thought and thumbs off a piece of candy for himself. Cherry—his favorite.

Quinn assures the people the full services of the Bureau are at the disposal of the task force. He talks about the VICAP computers, NCIC and the NCAVC, ISU and CASKU. Reassurance through confusion. The average person can't decipher the alphabet soup of modern law enforcement agencies and services.

Most people don't know the difference between the police department and the sheriff's office. They know only that acronyms sound important and official. The people gathered here listen with rapt attention and sneak glances at the person sitting beside them.

Quinn gives away only the barest details of the profile he's building, experience allowing him to make a little information seem like the mother lode. He speaks of the common killer of prostitutes: an inadequate loser who hates women and chooses what he deems the worst of the lot to exact revenge for the sins of his mother. Quinn speculates this is not an entirely accurate profile of the Cremator, that this killer is special—highly intelligent, highly organized, clever—and it is going to take the diligence of not only the law enforcement community, but of the community itself to catch him.

Quinn is right about one thing—there is nothing common about the Cremator. He is superior rather than inadequate. He cares so little about the woman who spawned him, he could never be inspired to revenge against her memory.

And yet, in the back of his mind he hears her voice berating him, criticizing him, taunting him. And the anger, ever banked, begins to heat. Goddamn Quinn and his Freudian bullshit. He doesn't know anything about the power and euphoria in taking a life. He has never considered the exquisite music of pain and fear, or how that music elevates the musician. The killing has nothing to do with any feelings of inadequacy of his common self, and everything to do with power.

On one far side of the room, the contingent from the Phoenix House take up their chant: "Our lives matter too!"

Toni Urskine introduces herself and starts in. "Lila White and Fawn Pierce were forced by circumstance into prostitution. Are you saying they deserved what happened to them?"

"I would never suggest that," Quinn says. "It's simply a fact that prostitution is a high-risk profession compared to being an attorney or an elementary-school teacher."

"And so they're considered expendable? Lila White's murder didn't rate a task force. Lila White had been a resident of the Phoenix House at one time. No one from the Minneapolis Police Department has come to reinvestigate her death. The FBI didn't send anyone to Minneapolis for Fawn Pierce. One of our current residents was a close friend of Ms. Pierce. No one from the Minneapolis Police Department has *ever* interviewed her. But Peter Bondurant's daughter goes missing and suddenly we have network news coverage and community action meetings.

"Chief Greer, in view of these facts, can you honestly say the city of Minneapolis gives a damn about women in difficult circumstances?"

Greer steps up to the podium, looking stern and strong. "Mrs. Urskine, I assure you every *possible* measure was taken to solve the murders of the first two victims. We are *redoubling* our efforts to seek out and find this *monster*. And we *will not rest* until the monster is *caught!*"

"I want to point out that Chief Greer isn't using the term *monster* literally," Quinn says. "We're not looking for a raving lunatic, foaming at the mouth. For all appearances, he's an ordinary man. The monster is in his mind."

Monster. A word ordinary people misapply to creatures they don't understand. The shark is labeled a monster when in fact it is simply efficient and purposeful, pure in its thought and in its power. So, too, the Cremator. He is efficient and purposeful, pure in thought and in power. He doesn't waver in action. He doesn't question the compulsion. He gives himself over wholly to the needs of his Dark Self, and in that complete surrender rises above his common self.

"At this instant, when the victims were dying at their hands, many serial killers report an insight so intense that it is like an emotional quasar, blinding in its revelation of truth." —*Joel Norris,* Serial Killers.

"**SPECIAL AGENT QUINN,** what are your theories regarding the burning of the bodies?"

The question came from a reporter. The danger with these open community meetings was having them turn into press conferences,

323

and a press conference was the last thing Quinn wanted. He needed a controlled situation—for the purpose of the case, and for himself. He needed to give out just enough information, not too much. A little speculation, but nothing that could be construed by the killer as arrogance. He needed to condemn the killer, but be certain to weave into that condemnation a certain kind of respect.

A direct challenge could result in more bodies. Play it too soft and Smokey Joe might feel he needed to make a statement. More bodies. A wrong word, a careless inflection— another death. The weight of that responsibility pressed against his chest like a huge stone.

"Agent Quinn?"

The voice hit him like a prod, jarring him back to the moment. "The burning is this killer's signature," he answered, rubbing a hand against his forehead. He was hot. There wasn't enough air in the room. His head was pounding like a hammer against an anvil. The hole in his stomach lining was burning bigger. "Something he feels compelled to perform to satisfy some inner need. What that need might be, only he knows."

Pick a face, any face, he thought as he looked out at the crowd. After all the years and all the cases and all the killers, he sometimes thought he should have been able to recognize the compulsion to kill, to see it like an unholy aura, but it didn't work that way. People made much of the eyes of serial killers—the stark, flat emptiness that was like looking down a long, black tunnel where a soul should have been. But a killer like this one was smart and adaptable, and no one except his victims would see that look in his eyes until he stood for his mug shot.

Any face in the crowd could be the mask of a killer. One person in this group might listen to the descriptions of the crimes, smell the fear in this room, and feel elated, aroused. He had actually seen killers get erections as their monstrous exploits were related to a stunned and sickened jury.

The killer would be here with his own agenda. To gauge, to judge, to plan his next move. To enjoy the fuss being made over him. Maybe he would come forward as a concerned citizen. Maybe he would want the thrill of knowing he could stand within their grasp, then walk away. Or maybe he would choose his next victim from the women in this room.

Quinn's gaze went automatically to Kate as she slipped in the door at the back of the room. He scanned her face, careful not to linger, even though he wanted to. He wanted it too much, and she wanted nothing to do with him. He'd taken that hint once. He sure as hell should have been smart enough to take it now. He had a case to focus on.

"What about the religious overtones?"

"There may not be any as far as he's concerned. We can only speculate. He could be saying 'sinners burn in hell.' Or it could be a cleansing ceremony to save their souls. Or it could be that he deems burning the bodies the ultimate disrespect and degradation."

"Isn't it your job to narrow down the possibilities?" another reporter called out. Quinn almost looked for Tippen in the crowd.

"The profile isn't complete," he said. *Don't tell me my job. I know my job, asshole.*

"Is it true you were pulled off the Bennet child abduction in Virginia to work this case?"

"What about the South Beach gay murders?"

"I have a number of ongoing cases at any given time."

"But you're here because of Peter Bondurant," another stated. "Doesn't that reek of elitism?"

"I go where I'm sent," he said flatly. "My focus is on the case, not where the orders came from or why."

"Why hasn't Peter Bondurant been formally questioned?"

Chief Greer stepped up to the podium to put the official shut-down on that line of inquiry, to expound on Peter Bondurant's virtues in front of Edwyn Noble and the Paragon PR person who had attended on Bondurant's behalf.

Quinn stepped back beside Kovac and tried to breathe again. Kovac had his cop face on, the eyes hooded and flat, taking in far more than anyone in the audience would have imagined.

"You see Liska's mutt sitting next to her?"

he said under his breath. "He came in uniform, for chrissake."

"That would be handy for getting his victims to go with him," Quinn said. "He's got a petty record that might be something more."

"He's connected to Jillian Bondurant," Kovac said.

"Have Liska ask him in for a sit-down." Quinn wished for that rush of gut instinct that this might be the guy, but that sense had abandoned him, and he felt nothing. "Let it sound like a consultation. We're asking for his assistance, we want his take on things, his opinion as a trained observer. Like that."

"Kiss his wanna-be ass. Jeez." Kovac's mustache twitched with distaste. "You know, he's not far off that piece-of-shit drawing we've got."

"Neither are you. Get a Polaroid when he comes in. Build a photo array for the witness. Maybe she'll tag him."

Greer finished his talk with a final dramatic plea for the public's assistance in the case, and pointed out detectives Liska and Yurek as being available to take information tonight. As soon as he declared the meeting over, the reporters started in like a pack of yapping dogs. The crowd instantly became a moving mass of humanity, some drifting toward the door, some moving toward the end of the room, where Toni Urskine from the Phoenix House was trying to rally support for her cause.

Kate wedged her way to the front of the pack,

her attention on Kovac. As Kovac stepped toward her, Edwyn Noble moved in on Quinn like the specter of death, his wide mouth set in a hard line. Lucas Brandt stood beside him, hands in the pockets of his camel-hair topcoat.

"Agent Quinn, can we have a word in private?"

"Of course."

He led them away from the podium, away from the press, into the kitchen of the community center, where industrial-sized coffeepots lined the red Formica countertop, and a hand-lettered sign taped above the sink read PLEASE WASH YOUR CUPS!

"Peter was very upset by your visit this evening," Noble began.

Quinn raised his brows. "Yes, I know. I was there." He slipped his hands into his pockets and leaned back against the edge of the counter. Mr. Relaxation. All the time in the world. He gave a thin smile. "The two of you sat through this meeting to tell me that? Here I thought you were just another pair of concerned citizens."

"I'm here to represent Peter's interests," Noble said. "I think you should know he's talking about calling Bob Brewster. He's extremely displeased that you seem to be wasting valuable time—"

"Excuse me, Mr. Noble, but I know my job," Quinn said calmly. "Peter doesn't have to like the way I do it. I don't work for Peter. But if Peter is unhappy, then he can feel free to call the director. It won't change the fact that Jillian made two phone calls after she left his home that night, or that neither Peter nor you, Dr. Brandt, bothered to mention that to the police. Something was going on with Jillian Bondurant that night, and now she may be dead. Certain questions need to be answered one way or another."

The muscles in Brandt's square jaw flexed. "Jillian had problems. Peter loved his daughter. It would kill him to see her past and the difficulties she'd had splashed across the tabloids and paraded before America on the nightly news."

Quinn abruptly straightened away from the counter, putting himself into Brandt's space, frowning into his face. "I'm not in the business of selling cases to the media."

Noble spread his hands. The peacemaker, the diplomat. "Of course not. We're simply trying to be as discreet about this as possible. That's why we're talking to you rather than to the police. Peter and Lucas and I have discussed this, and we feel that you may be able to steer the rudder of the case, so to speak. That if we could satisfy you with regard to the calls Jillian made that night, the matter could be put to rest."

"What about your ethics?" Quinn asked, still looking at Brandt.

"A small sacrifice to the greater good."

His own, Quinn suspected.

"I'm listening."

Brandt took a breath, bracing himself for this

breach of his patient's trust. Somehow Quinn didn't think it bothered his conscience nearly as much as defying Peter Bondurant would bother him socially and financially.

"Jillian's stepfather had contacted her several times in the past few weeks, implying he wanted to mend their relationship. Jillian had very complicated, very mixed feelings toward him."

"Would she have wanted to resume some kind of relationship with him?" Quinn asked. "Her friend implied Jillian had been in love with him, that she wanted him to divorce her mother for her."

"Jillian was a very unhappy, confused girl when she was involved with Serge. Her mother had always been jealous of her, from Jillie's infancy. She was starving for love. I'm sure you know people will go to terrible lengths to get it—or, rather, to get what will pass for love for them."

"Yes. I've seen the result in crime scene photographs. Why was the stepfather never prosecuted?"

"No charges were ever brought. LeBlanc had brainwashed her," Noble said with disgust. "Jillian refused even to talk to the police."

"Peter had hoped that in moving back to Minnesota and getting therapy, she had put it all behind her," Brandt said.

"And had she?"

"Therapy is a long, ongoing process."

"And then LeBlanc started calling her again."

"Friday night she decided to tell Peter about it. Naturally, he was upset. He was frightened for Jillie. She'd been doing so well." Another strategically placed sigh. "Peter has difficulty expressing emotion. His concern came out as anger. They ended up arguing. Jillie was upset when she left. She called me from her car."

"Where was she?"

"In a parking lot somewhere. She didn't really say. I told her to go back to Peter and talk it through, but she was embarrassed and hurt, and in the end she just called him," Brandt said. "That's the whole story. It's as simple as that."

Quinn doubted him on both counts. What Lucas Brandt had just told him was by no means the whole story, and nothing about Jillian Bondurant's life or death would prove to be simple.

"And Peter couldn't have just told this story to Sergeant Kovac and me four hours ago when we were standing in his foyer."

Noble cast a nervous glance over his shoulder at the closed door on the other side of the room, as if he were waiting for the reporters to ram it down and storm in, microphones thrust before them like bayonets.

"It isn't easy for Peter to talk about these things, Agent Quinn. He's an intensely private man."

"I realize that, Mr. Noble," Quinn said, casually fishing a peppermint out of his pocket. He spoke as he unwrapped it. "The trouble with that is that this is a murder investigation. And in a murder investigation, there's no such thing as privacy." He set the wrapper on the counter and popped the candy in his mouth. "Not even if your name is Peter Bondurant and you have the ear of the director of the FBI—not as long as it's my case."

"Well," Edwyn Noble said, stepping back, his long face as cold and hard as marble. "It may not be your case much longer."

They left looking like spoiled children who would immediately run home and tell on him. They would tell Bondurant. Bondurant would call Brewster. Brewster might call and reprimand him, Quinn supposed. Or he might simply have the ASAC pull him off the case and send him on to another stack of bodies somewhere else. There was always another case. And another...and another...And what the hell else did he have to do with his life?

He watched as Noble and Brandt worked their way toward the exit, reporters dogging their heels.

"What was that about?" Kovac asked.

"Heading us off at the pass, I think."

"Kate says our wit came clean with her. Little Mary Sunshine says she was in the park that night earning a Jackson doing the hokey-pokey with some loser."

"This loser have a name?"

Kovac snorted. "Hubert Humphrey, he tells her. BOLO: republican asshole with a bad sense of humor."

"That narrows it down," Quinn said dryly.

The television crews were packing up lights and cameras. The last of the crowd was drifting out. The party was over, and with it went the adrenaline that had elevated his heart rate and tightened his nerves. He actually preferred the tension because it fended off the depression and the sense of being overwhelmed and exhausted and confused. He preferred action, because the alternative was to be alone in his hotel room with nothing but the fear to keep him company. The fear that he wasn't doing enough, that he was missing something; that despite the accumulated knowledge from a thousand or more cases, he had lost his feel for the job and was just stumbling around like a newly blinded man.

"Of course, she didn't get a license number," Kovac went on. "No address. No credit card receipt."

"Can she describe him?"

"Sure. He was about four inches long and made a sound like a meat grinder when he came."

"That'll be an interesting lineup."

"Yeah. Just another pathetic yuppie with an SUV and a wife who won't give him a blow job."

Quinn looked at him sharply. "A what?"

"A wife who—"

"The other part. He was driving what?"

"A sport utility vehi—" Kovac's eyes rounded and he threw down the cigarette he had been about to light. "Oh, Jesus."

∙ ∙ ∙ ∙

HE MOVES WITH the last of the crowd out of the doors of the community center, picking up bits and pieces of conversation about himself.

"I wish they would have talked more about the burning."

"I mean, the FBI guy says this killer looks and acts like anyone else, but how can that be? Setting bodies on fire? That's nuts. He's gotta be nuts."

"Or just smart. The fire destroys evidence."

"Yeah, but cutting someone's head off is nuts."

"Don't you think the fire is symbolic?" he asks. "I think maybe the guy has some kind of religious mania. You know: *ashes to ashes* and all that."

"Maybe."

"I'll bet when they catch him, the cops find out he had some kind of religious fanatic stepfather or something. A mortician, maybe," he says, thinking of the man who had been involved with his mother during much of his youth. The man who had believed he had been charged by God to redeem her through sexual subjugation and beatings.

"Sick bastard. Going around torturing and killing women because of his own inadequacies. Should have been drowned in a sack at birth."

"And these creeps always put everything off on their mothers. Like they have no minds of their own."

He wants to grab the two women saying these things. Grab them by their throats, scream his name in their purpling faces, and crush their windpipes with his bare hands. The anger is now a living flame, blue-centered and hot.

"I've read about that Quinn. He's brilliant. He caught that child-killer out in Colorado."

"He can interrogate me anytime he wants," the other woman says. "George Clooney's got nothing on him."

They laugh, and he wants to pull a claw hammer out of the air and smash their skulls in with it. He feels the heat of the fire in his chest. His head is throbbing. The need is a fever just beneath the surface of his skin.

Outside the community center, the parking lot is in a state of gridlock. He goes to the car and leans back against it, crossing his arms.

"No point trying!" he calls to one of the uniformed cops directing traffic.

"Might as well wait it out."

The idiot. Who in this picture is inadequate? Not the Cremator, but those who look for him and look at him and see a common man.

He watches others exit the building and come out onto the sidewalk. The yellow-white floodlight washes over them. Some are citizens. Some are cops assigned to the task force. Some he recognizes.

Quinn emerges from a side door toward the back of the building—a spot the media had chosen to ignore. He rushes out with no overcoat and stands just out of cover of the shadows in the doorwell, hands on hips, shoulders

335

square, his breath clouding the air as he looks around.

Looking for me, Agent Quinn? The inadequate loser with the mother complex? The mental monster. You're about to find out what a monster really is.

The Cremator has a plan. The Cremator will be a legend. The killer who broke John Quinn. The ultimate triumph for the ultimate killer over the ultimate hunter of his kind.

He slides behind the wheel of the car he has driven here, starts the motor, adjusts the heater, and curses the cold. He needs a warmer hunting ground. He backs the car out of the slot and follows a silver Toyota 4Runner out of the parking lot and into the street.

18

CHAPTER

KATE PILOTED THE 4RUNNER carefully into the narrow, ancient garage that sat just off the alley behind her house. During the winter months she regularly dreamed of an attached garage, but then spring would come and the backyard perennial beds would bloom and she would forget about the hassle of tromping through the snow, and the danger of walking in a dark alley in a city with a disturbing number of sex crimes.

The wind scrambled and scattered the dead leaves that lay in a drift along the side of the neighbor's garage. A little shiver snaked down Kate's back, and she paused to turn and stare back into the darkness behind her—just in case. But it was only her natural paranoia compounded by the knowledge that the meeting she had just attended had been staged for the sole purpose of baiting a serial killer.

Old feelings from her days in the BSU came rushing back. Memories of unspeakable crimes that were the topics of casual conversation around the water cooler. Serial murder had been such an ingrained part of her world, that kind of idle talk hadn't seemed strange to her until toward the end of her career—after Emily died. Death had then suddenly taken on a more personal quality, and she had lost the veneer of detachment that was necessary for people in law enforcement. Finally, she hadn't been able to stand it anymore.

She wondered how John still did...*if* he did. He'd looked pale tonight, gaunt and gray in the harsh lights. Back in the old days, his coping strategy had been overwork. He didn't have to deal with feelings if he was too busy to face them. That probably hadn't changed. And what did she care if it had or not?

She slid the key into the back-door dead bolt and paused again before turning it, the hair rising up on the back of her neck. Slowly, she turned, straining to see past the reach of the motion-detector light into the shadowed corners of the yard. It struck her then that she'd left her cell phone in the truck. In the truck, across the yard in the creepy garage.

Screw it. She could pick up any messages from the house phone. If there was a God, none of her clients would have a crisis tonight. And she could settle into a hot tub with a glass of her favorite coping method. This case might kill her, but at least she'd die clean and pleasantly numb.

No maniac rushed to push his way in the door behind her, and no maniac waited in the kitchen with a butcher knife. Thor ran in to complain loudly at the late dinner hour. Kate tossed her purse on the counter and clicked on the small television to catch the news. With one hand she unbuttoned her coat, with the other she reached into the fridge for the cat food and then the bottle of Sapphire.

The lead story on the ten o'clock news was the meeting. There was a clip of the crowd—Toni Urskine and her Phoenix women prominent in the shot—Chief Greer thumping the podium, and John looking grave as he spoke about the Bureau's role in the investigation.

Grave and handsome. The camera had always loved his face. He had aged hard, and even that looked good on him—the lines fanning out beside his eyes, the gray in his close-cropped hair. His physical, sexual appeal hit her on a basic level she couldn't block, and could only pretend to ignore.

Then it was back to the anchor, who rehashed the facts of the cases while photographs of Peter and Jillian Bondurant filled one corner of the screen. Reward and hotline information followed, and they were on to the next hot topic: beat cops warming themselves these chilly nights in the strip clubs downtown.

Kate left the news to Thor and wandered into the dining room, flipping on the old mission-style chandelier she had salvaged and rewired herself, thinking about the Bondurant connection and how Jillian did or didn't fit the victim profile.

"Damn you, John," she muttered.

"We'll talk about the case. I've got some ideas I'd like to bounce off you."

"It's not my job. I'm not with BSU anymore."

"You were an expert in the field..."

And he had access to every expert in the field. He didn't need her.

She hung her coat on the back of a chair and sat down at the oak table she'd refinished that first summer after she'd left the Bureau. She had been wound, wired, still reeling from Emily's death and the wreck of both her marriage and her relationship with Quinn. Life as she knew it had ended, and she had to start over again. Alone, except for the ghosts.

She'd never told anyone close to her about Quinn, not her sister or her parents. They didn't know her resignation from the Bureau had come under a cloud of scandal. She couldn't have adequately explained the connection she'd felt to Quinn as Steven had drifted away from her on a tide of grief and anger. Even severed, that connection had been too precious to share with people who wouldn't understand. And her parents wouldn't have understood any more than any of her colleagues back in Quantico had.

She'd had an affair, cheated on her husband. She was a villain. That was what people wanted to believe—the worst and most sordid. No one wanted to know how alone she'd felt, how in need of comfort and support she'd been. They didn't want to hear about the powerful pull of something far beyond physical attraction that had drawn her to John Quinn—and he to her. People preferred to believe the worst because it seemed less apt to touch their own lives.

And so Kate had kept her secret to herself—and the guilt and regret and heartache that were part and parcel of the deal. And she'd built that new life a block at a time, careful to give it a good foundation and balance. The job was eight-to-five most days. Clients came and went. She got to help them in specific ways, and then their lives moved on and out of hers. Her involvement was finite and manageable.

Even as she thought that, she saw Angie in her mind's eye, and took a long pull on the Sapphire. She remembered the girl's tears, the tough kid, the street kid, curled in on herself and crying like the child she would never admit she was. Scared and embarrassed and ashamed—and she would never admit that either.

Kate had kneeled at Angie's feet, maintaining contact with one hand—touching the girl's hand or her knee or stroking her head as she doubled over and tried to hide her face. And the whole time, the same loop of emotions, the same chain of thoughts, played through Kate's mind—that she was nobody's mother, that this connection she was making to this girl was more than Kate wanted and less than Angie needed.

But the stark truth was that Kate was all she had. The ball was in her court and there was no one else to dump it to. There wasn't another advocate in the office who would stand up to Ted Sabin. There weren't that many who would stand up to Angie.

The story the girl told was short and sad and sordid. She had got picked up on Lake Street and dumped out in the park, a disposable sex toy for a man who never even asked her name. He paid her twenty when the going rate was thirty-five, told her to call a cop when she complained, shoved her out of his vehicle, and drove away. He left her there in the middle of the night like an unwanted kitten.

The image of her standing there alone, disheveled, smelling of sex, with a crumpled twenty in her pocket stuck in Kate's mind. Abandoned. Alone. Her life stretching out in front of her like forty miles of bad road. She couldn't have been more than fifteen or sixteen. Not that much older than Emily would have been if she had lived.

The tears rose up in a sneak attack. Kate took another sip of the gin and tried to swallow the knot down with it. There was no time for crying and no point in it. Emily was gone and Angie was no substitute. She didn't even want a substitute. The sudden sense of emptiness could be dodged or numbed. She was an old hand at it. Put the pain back in its box. Keep those walls up high. God forbid anyone see over them...herself included.

The fatigue and the alcohol pulled at her as she got up and headed for the den. She had to check her messages. And she wanted to call the Phoenix to make one last connection with Angie for the night—to strengthen the connection that had been made that afternoon.

She refused to let herself think of the girl sitting alone in her room at the Phoenix, feeling vulnerable and afraid and disappointed in herself for reaching out. She refused to think that she should have tried harder to make that connection go deeper.

The entry hall was lit by a streetlight half a block away, the illumination coming soft and silver through a pair of sidelights Kate kept meaning to get rid of. It was a simple matter to break a sidelight and get into a house. That reminder unfailingly came at night just before she went upstairs to bed.

A lamp burned low in the library-cum-office, a room she had left much the way she remembered it from childhood, when her father had been a midlevel executive for Honeywell. Cluttered and masculine with a sturdy oak desk and a couple of hundred books lining the walls, it smelled of leather upholstery and the faintest memory of good cigars. The message light on the answering machine flickered like a flame, but the phone rang before she could hit the playback button.

"Kate Conlan."

"Kovac. Get your fanny to the Phoenix, Red. Our witness is missing. We'll meet you there."

"**I SHOULD HAVE** stayed," Kate said, pacing the ratty den of the Phoenix with her hands on her hips. "Goddammit, I should have stayed."

"You can't be with 'em twenty-four/seven, Red," Kovac said, lighting a cigarette.

"No," she muttered, turning a furious glare on the narcotics dick Kovac had borrowed to keep an eye on Angie while she was at the Phoenix—a grubby-looking skinny guy in an army jacket with the name Iverson stenciled over the pocket. "That was *your* job."

"Hey." He held up his hands to ward her off. "I was here, but I was told *you* didn't want me too close. She must have slipped out the back."

"Well, duh. Where did you think she would 'slip out'? By definition, that sorta rules out the front door, doesn't it?"

The narc tipped his head back and swaggered toward Kate, cocky and mean, an attitude that played well with dealers and hypes. "I didn't ask for this lame fucking job, and I

343

don't have to take a bunch of shit from a fucking social worker."

"Hey!" Quinn barked.

Kate stopped Iverson in his tracks with a look and closed the distance between them herself. "You lost the only witness we had, asshole. You don't want to answer to me? Fine. How about the chief? How about the county attorney? Why don't you tell the mayor how you lost the only witness to the burning of Peter Bondurant's daughter's body because you're a hot-shit narc and you think baby-sitting is beneath you?"

Iverson's face went purple to the rims of his ears. "Fuck this," he said, backing off. "I'm out of here."

Kovac let him walk out. The front door squeaked open and slammed shut, the sound reverberating in the cavernous hall.

"Every superior in the chain is gonna ream his ass," he said with a sigh. "He won't be able to sit down on the street sweeper they assign him to tomorrow."

Kate began to pace again. "Did she leave or was she taken?"

"Iverson said her stuff is gone from her room and there's no sign of forced entry at the back. There was another resident here the whole time. She told him she didn't see or hear anything. Quinn and I got here just ahead of you. We haven't looked for ourselves yet."

Kate shook her head at her own stupidity. "I'd actually made some progress with her. I should have stayed."

"What time did you drop her off?"

"I don't know. It must have been after eight. She told me about the john in the park late this afternoon, but then she was embarrassed and upset, and I didn't want to push it. I took her to City Center for something to eat, and let her do a little shopping."

"Lieutenant Fowler came up with some dough for her?"

Kate made a face and waved the question off. The money had come out of her own pocket, but it didn't matter. "Then I brought her back here."

Angie growing quieter and quieter the closer they got to the Phoenix. Slipping back inside the tough shell. *And I let her,* Kate thought.

"I dropped her off and went on to the meeting to tell you—oh, shit. I should have stayed."

"Who else was here when you let her off?"

"Gregg Urskine—but he was going to the meeting—and one other woman. I don't know who. I didn't see her. Gregg told me she was here. I didn't want Angie alone."

It was too easy to imagine Angie in this big old house, all but alone. If Smokey Joe had any way of knowing where she was...His three victims had vanished with no sign of a struggle. There and gone, simply, easily. And Angie DiMarco claimed she could identify him.

That fast, that easily, the girl was gone. One careless decision...

"I blew it, and now we've lost her."

Kate knew the emotions suddenly threatening

to swamp her were out of proportion, but she didn't seem able to pull them back. She felt vaguely ill, slightly dizzy. The aftertaste of gin was like metal in her mouth.

She felt Quinn come up behind her, knew it was he without looking. Her body was still attuned to his. There was a disconcerting thought: that the physical magnetism hadn't faded in all this time.

"It isn't your fault, Kate," he said softly.

He put a hand on her shoulder, his thumb unerringly finding the knot of tension in her trapezius and rubbing at it in an old, familiar way. Too familiar. Too comforting.

"It doesn't matter now," she said, turning away stiffly. "What matters is finding her. So let's start looking."

They went upstairs to the room Angie had been sharing with another Phoenix resident. The walls of the room were a nasty shade of yellow, the old woodwork dark with age and varnish. As it was all through the house, the furniture was mismatched and ill proportioned.

Angie's bed was a wad of unmade sheets. The shopping bag from their excursion to City Center lay in the midst of the mess, tissue tumbling out of it, the jeans and sweater she'd bought nowhere in sight. The dirty backpack was conspicuously absent, suggesting the girl had flown the coop of her own accord.

Sitting on the nightstand beside the cheap glass lamp was a tiny statue of an angel.

Kate picked it up and looked at it: an inch-high piece of pottery she'd bought for five bucks from a Navajo woman on the plaza in Santa Fe. She had slipped the old woman's five-year-old granddaughter an extra dollar for carefully wrapping the doll in tissue, her little brow furrowed as she concentrated on the importance of her task. Watching the little girl, she'd thought of Emily and, to her extreme embarrassment, had nearly started to cry.

"You know something about that?" Quinn asked softly, standing too close again.

"Sure. She stole it off my desk today." She touched the gold-painted halo on the angel's dark head. "I have a collection of guardian angels. Ironic, huh? I don't really believe in them. If there were such things as guardian angels, then you and I wouldn't have jobs, and I wouldn't have lost my daughter, and we wouldn't have kids living lives like Angie's.

"Stupid," she said, rubbing the angel's wings gently between her fingers. "I wish she'd taken this with her."

The statue slipped from her grasp and fell to the old rug beside the bed. Kate knelt down to get it, putting her left hand down on the floor for balance. Her heart thumped hard in her chest, and she sat back against her heels as she raised the same hand, turning it palm up.

"Oh, Jesus," she breathed, staring at the smear of blood.

Quinn swore, grabbing her hand, pulling it closer to the light.

Kate pulled away from him, twisting around,

crouching low and straining to see against the dark wood of the old floor. The angle had to be perfect. The light had to hit it just right...Iverson hadn't seen it because he hadn't been looking hard enough.

"No," she muttered, finding another droplet, then a smear where someone had tried to hastily clean up. *I should have stayed with her.*

The trail led to the hall. The hall led to the bathroom.

Panic fell like stone in Kate's stomach. "Oh, God, no."

I should have stayed with her.

She stumbled to her feet and down the hall, all senses magnified, the pounding of her heart like a jackhammer in her ears.

"Don't touch anything!" Kovac yelled, coming behind her.

Kate pulled up short of the bathroom door, which stood ajar, and allowed Kovac to bump it open with his shoulder. He pulled a ballpoint pen from his coat pocket and flipped on the light.

The room was awash in brain-bending hot pink, orange, and silver foil wallpaper from the seventies. The fixtures were older, the two-inch floor tiles long past being white. Dotted with blood. A fleck here. A smeared stain there.

Why didn't I stay with her?

"Come out in the hall, honey," Quinn said, setting his hands on Kate's shoulders as Kovac moved to pull back the shower curtain.

"No."

She held her ground, trembling, the breath held tight in her lungs. Quinn slipped an arm around her, ready to pull her out as Kovac drew the shower curtain back.

There was no body. Angie wasn't lying dead in the tub. Still Kate's stomach turned and a wave of cold washed over her. Quinn's arm tightened around her and she sagged back against him.

Blood streaked the tiled wall in pale smudges, like a faded fingerpainting. A thin line of water tinted rusty with diluted blood led from the center of the tub to the drain.

Kate pressed a hand across her mouth, smearing the blood on her palm across her chin.

"Shit," Kovac breathed, backing away from the tub.

He went to the plastic hamper beside the sink and opened it gingerly with the same pen he had used to turn on the light.

"Hey, Kojak," Elwood said, sticking his big head in the door. "What's up?"

"Call the crime scene guys." He pulled one towel and then another from the hamper, both of them wet and bloody. "Looks like we've got us a crime scene."

19

CHAPTER

TONI URSKINE ENTERED the front room still dressed to impress in slim black slacks and a cardinal-red blazer over a white blouse with an elaborate cravat. The fire of righteous indignation burned bright in her eyes.

"I don't appreciate those police cars out front. Could they at least turn their lights off? This is a neighborhood, Sergeant, and our neighbors are none too gracious about us being here as it is."

"I'm sorry for the disruption, Ms. Urskine," Kovac said dryly. "Abductions, murders, they're a big damn pain in the ass, I know."

A redhead with the thin, brittle look of a crack addict came into the room behind Toni Urskine, followed by Gregg Urskine, who looked like a model for Eddie Bauer in scuffed work boots, jeans, and a flannel shirt open at the throat to reveal a white T-shirt. He put a hand on the redhead's back and urged her forward.

"This is Rita Renner. Rita was here with Angie tonight after I left."

"I wasn't really with her," Renner said in a small voice. "I was watching TV. I saw her go upstairs. She was in the bathroom for a long

350

time—I could hear the water running. We're not supposed to take long showers."

"And what time did you notice the shower stopped running?"

"I didn't. I fell asleep on the couch. I didn't wake up until the news."

"And in the time you were awake, did you see or hear anyone else in the house—other than Angie?"

"Not after Gregg left."

"No doors opening, closing? No footsteps? No nothing?"

Renner shook her head, staring at her feet.

"She's already told you she didn't hear or see anything," Toni Urskine said impatiently.

Kovac ignored her. "Why didn't you go to the meeting with the others?"

Toni Urskine stiffened. "Is Rita under suspicion of something, Sergeant?"

"Just curious."

Nervous, Renner looked from one Urskine to the other, as if seeking some kind of invisible sign for permission to speak. "I don't like crowds," she said apologetically. "And, then, it's hard for me, you know. Because of Fawn."

"Rita and Fawn Pierce—or, as you call her, victim number two—were good friends." Toni put a supportive arm around Renner's bony shoulders. "Not that anyone in your investigation cares."

Kovac held back a scowl. "I'm sorry about the oversight. I'll have a detective come by tomorrow for an interview. My priority tonight is Angie DiMarco. We need to find her."

"You don't think this killer came in here and took her, do you?" Toni asked with sudden alarm.

"Don't be ridiculous," Gregg said, trying to smile away the edge in his voice. "No one broke in."

His wife turned on him with a venomous look. "I'm not ridiculous. Anyone could have come in here. I've been asking you for months to install new locks and seal off that old storm cellar door."

Urskine contained his embarrassment to a dull blush. "The storm cellar door is locked from the inside."

Kovac looked to Elwood. "Check it out."

"I'll show you," Urskine offered, starting for the door, eager to get away from his wife.

Kate held him up with a question. "Gregg, did Angie say anything to you before you left for the meeting?"

He gave the nervous laugh, and she thought what an annoying habit that was, on a par with the Rob Marshall bootlicker's grin.

"Angie never has anything to say to me. She avoids me like the plague."

"What time did you leave for the meeting?" Kovac asked.

Urskine's brows went up above the rims of his glasses. "Am *I* under suspicion of something?" he asked, pretending to be amused.

Toni glared at Kovac. "We're being punished, Gregg. Can't you see that? The police don't appreciate having attention called to their shortcomings."

Kovac gave her the cop eyes. "I'm just trying to get our time line straight, ma'am. That's all."

"I left not long after Kate," Gregg said. "I must have gotten to the meeting about—what, honey?—eight-thirty, quarter to nine?"

"Something like that," his wife said, pouting. "You were late."

"I was working on the furnace." A muscle flexed in Urskine's jaw, and he turned again to Elwood. "I'll show you that cellar door now."

"Are we free to go, Sergeant?" Toni Urskine asked. "It's been a very long evening."

"You're telling me," Kovac muttered, waving them off.

Kate followed them out of the room, but took a right to the front door, leaving Toni Urskine to rant to her captive audience of residents gathered in the living room.

OUR LIVES MATTER TOO. The banner stretched across the front porch of the Phoenix, the oilcloth crackling as the wind picked up.

"It's going to snow," she said, burying her hands in her coat pockets and hunching her shoulders, not against the weather, but against a cold that was internal. She wandered to the far end of the porch, almost out of reach of the yellow bug light that hadn't been changed at summer's end, away from the traffic that came and went through the front door.

If Toni Urskine was unhappy with two cruisers parked at the curb, she would be livid soon, Kate thought as the crime scene people parked their van on the front lawn. Uniforms had already begun KOD duty—knocking on doors in search of a neighbor who might have seen a strange car, or a man on foot, or a man carrying something, or a man and a young woman together—anything that might give them a time frame or a lead. Despite the late hour, the neighborhood homes were well lit, and the occasional figure could be seen at a window, pulling the drapes back to look out.

"Kate, we don't *know* what happened," Quinn said.

"Well, I think it's safe to say Angie didn't cut herself shaving her legs."

A tremor went through her as she saw the blood again in her mind. The blood on the floor, the blood-streaked tile, the bloody towels. She stiffened against the nauseating weakness seeping through her muscles.

Gotta be tough, Kate. Put those feelings in a box. Put the box in its proper cubicle. Keep the walls intact.

"Looks this way to me," she said around the knot in her throat. "He slips into the house through the back. Grabs her upstairs. There's a struggle, judging by the bloody handprints in the tub—I'm guessing they're Angie's. Maybe he kills her, or maybe he just starts the job—probably the first. And he lets her bleed out in the tub, otherwise there would have been more mess elsewhere. He wants to make it look like she just left, so he tries to clean up, but he's in a hurry and he does a poor job of it.

Still, even the poor job he did would have bought him some time if we hadn't come looking tonight."

"How did he know she was here?"

"I don't know. She felt like he was watching her. Maybe he was."

"And how does all this go down with no one hearing, no one seeing anything?"

"He'd already managed to grab, torture, and murder three women without anyone hearing or seeing a thing. Rita Renner was asleep on the first floor with the television going. It's a big house."

Quinn shook his head. "It doesn't feel right."

"Why not? Because you wanted him to be at the meeting?"

He sat back against the railing, shoulders hunched inside his trench coat. "He could still have been at the meeting. We're only a few blocks away, and the meeting was over half an hour before Kovac and I started over here. My question is, why would he risk it? The girl hadn't given the cops anything worthwhile—not a name, not a decent composite, she pulled nothing from the mug books. Why would he risk this?"

"To show us he can," Kate said. "What a nose-thumbing. The night of the meeting intended to draw him out, he slips into a house and takes the only witness to his crimes. A killer like this one, he'll have a hard-on the size of a Louisville Slugger over that. You know it."

Quinn looked over as one of the evidence guys carried a vacuum cleaner into the house.

"Why *did* you come here tonight?" Kate asked. "Kovac never said."

"When you told him about Angie and her john in the park Sunday night, you mentioned the guy was in an SUV. I think there's a good chance Smokey Joe is transporting his bodies to the parks in a truck of some kind. Something resembling a parks department vehicle. Possibly an SUV."

Kate felt her stomach turn. A chill pebbled her flesh from head to toe. "Oh, God, John. You don't think he was her customer?"

"It would be right on target. He hates women, particularly the sexually promiscuous variety. He's got a dead one in the back of his truck. He picks up another and takes her to his dumping grounds to have sex with her. This excites him. That excitement reminds him of the thrill and stimulation of the kill. At the same time he's mentally asserting domination and control over the woman he's with. The secret knowledge that he could do to his current partner what he did to his victim but chooses not to gives him a sense of control both over her and over his compulsion to kill."

"That decision not to kill bolsters his sense of power. And everything is building toward the burning ceremony—the completion of the cycle," Kate finished.

"Looks good on paper."

"Angie said the guy shoved her out of his truck and she watched him drive away. From where he left her, he would have had to have doubled around to that back lot in a hurry in order for her to have seen him burning that body."

Quinn moved his shoulders. "It's still just a theory."

A theory from a man who knew more about sexually sadistic killers than perhaps anyone else in the country. Kate stared out into the darkness, watching the cloud of her breath float-away.

"But if it was the same guy, why wouldn't she have told me? And why wouldn't she give us a better composite? She saw this john up close and personal."

"Those are questions only she can answer."

"And she can't answer them now," Kate said quietly. "It was so hard for her to tell me about it this afternoon. From the beginning of this mess, she'd talk so tough, give so much attitude, but when she finally told me about this john, it was like she was ashamed. She kept saying that she didn't like doing it, that she was so sorry. And she cried and cried."

Her own emotions threatened to rise up at the memory, just as they had that afternoon with Angie.

"You like this girl," Quinn declared.

She huffed a breath. "What's to like? She's a lying, thieving, foul-mouthed prostitute."

"And she needs you," he said simply.

"Yeah, well, look what that got her."

"This isn't your fault, Kate."

"I should have stayed with her."

"You couldn't have known this would happen."

"She was at a vulnerable point," she reasoned. "I should have stayed with her if for no other reason than to get something out of her. But I didn't because—"

She choked herself off, not wanting to admit it. Not here. Not to Quinn. He knew her too well—or once had. He knew every raw spot in her soul. He'd held her more times than she could count when she'd been so racked with the pain and guilt of Emily's death that the anguish was beyond sound. He had given her comfort and offered his strength and soothed her with his touch. She couldn't let him do that now, and she didn't want to find out that maybe he wouldn't try.

"She's not Emily, Kate."

Kate sucked in a breath as if he'd slapped her and turned sharply to glare at him. "I'm well aware of that. My daughter is dead."

"And you still blame yourself. After all this time."

"As far as I know, there's no statute of limitations on guilt."

"It wasn't your fault. And neither is this."

"Emily was my daughter, my responsibility. Angie is my client, my responsibility," she argued stubbornly.

"How many of your clients do you take home with you?" Quinn demanded, moving away from the railing, closer to her.

"None, but—"

"How many of your clients do you stay with around the clock?"

"None, but—"

"Then there's no reason for you to think you should have been with her."

"She needed me and I wasn't here."

"But anytime you get a chance to punish yourself, by God, you're right there," Quinn said, old anger of his own rising up sharp and pure. He could remember too well the frustration of trying to separate Kate from her sense of culpability in Emily's death. He could remember too well the need to shake her and hold her close at once, because that was exactly what he was feeling now.

She stood before him, fierce and angry and defensive. And beautiful. And vulnerable. He wanted to protect her from the pain she would inflict on herself. And she would fight him tooth and nail every step of the way.

"I'm taking responsibility—as if you don't know anything about that," she said bitterly, toe to toe with him. "The Mighty Quinn, curing the cancer of modern society. Single-handedly rooting out all evil. You carry the world around on your shoulders as if you were sole guardian, and you have the gall to stand there and criticize me? My God, you're amazing!"

Shaking her head, she started past him for the front steps.

"Where are you going?" He reached for her as if he still had some right to touch her. She stepped aside, giving him a look that could have frozen water at fifty paces.

"I'm going to do something. I'm not sitting

here biting my fingernails all night. On the slim chance Angie left here under her own power, the least I can do is help look for her."

Hands in her coat pockets, digging for her keys, she trotted down the steps and headed for her truck. Quinn glanced at the front door of the Phoenix. He was of no use here. And the sight of Kate walking away triggered his panic. Foolish thought. She didn't want him there, didn't want him, period. She was sure as hell better off without him. If he'd been a stronger man, he would have let it go at that.

But he wasn't feeling strong, and he wouldn't be here more than a few days, a week. Where was the harm in stealing a little time with her? Just to be near her. A fresh memory to put away with the old ones, to take out when the solace of his life threatened to swallow him whole.

"Kate!" he called, jogging after her. "Wait. I'm going with you."

She arched a brow imperiously. "Did I invite you?"

"Two pairs of eyes looking are better than one," he argued.

Kate told herself to say no. She didn't need him poking at old wounds. She did a mean enough job of that herself. Then she thought of the way he'd put his arms around her upstairs, ready to pull her away from the horror they hadn't found on the other side of that shower curtain, ready to hold her up if she needed it, giving her his own strength to lean against. She thought of how easily she'd let him do that, and knew she should say no.

He watched her, the dark eyes intent, the lines of his face serious, then he dredged up half a charming smile from somewhere, and she felt something clutch in her chest exactly as it had all those years before. "I promise not to be a jerk. And I'll let you drive."

She sighed and turned toward the 4Runner, punching the button on the keyless remote. "Well, I believe half of that."

THEY MADE THE rounds of the places on Lake Street where the nocturnal creatures passed the hours between dusk and dawn. Pool halls, bars, and all-night diners. A homeless shelter full of women with children. A Laundromat where a wino with a thick halo of filthy gray hair sat in one of the plastic bucket chairs and stared out the windows until the slightly more fortunate night clerk chased him back onto the street.

No one had seen Angie. Half of them barely glanced at the photograph. Kate refused to think about the lack of results. She hadn't expected results, she had expected to pass time. She couldn't decide which had to be more like penance: spending the night pounding the pavement in this rotten part of town or sitting home drinking gin until she couldn't see the bloodstains in her head anymore.

"I need a drink," she said as they walked into a place called Eight Ball's. The interior was obscured by a fog bank of cigarette smoke. The sharp clack of billiard balls colliding was underscored by Jonny Lang's blues wailing from the juke—"Lie to Me."

"You missed last call a while ago, gorgeous," the bartender said. He was the size of a minivan with a shaved head and a woolly Fu-Manchu mustache. "Name's Tiny Marvin. How 'bout something strong and black like me?"

Quinn flashed his ID and a no-nonsense G-man look.

"Damnation. It's Scully and Mulder," Tiny Marvin said, unimpressed, as he pulled a coffeepot off its warmer.

Kate planted her butt on a barstool. "Coffee's fine, thanks."

There were maybe a dozen serious players at the pool tables. A pair of hookers served as ornamentation, looking bored and impatient at the downtime. One caught an eyeful of Quinn and nudged the other, but neither made a move to get closer.

Tiny Marvin squinted at Quinn. "Hey, man, didn't I see you on TV? For real?"

"We're looking for a girl," Quinn said.

Kate slid the Polaroid across the bar, expecting Marvin to give it as little attention as every other bartender had. He picked it up with fingers as short and thick as Vienna sausages and squinted harder.

"Yeah, she been in here."

Kate sat up straighter. "Tonight?"

"Naw, Sunday night, around ten-thirty, eleven. Came in to warm up, she said. Jailbait.

I chased her skinny white ass outta here. I mean, consenting adults is one thing, man—you know what I mean? That child's trouble. I don't want no part of that shit."

"Did she leave with anybody?" Quinn asked.

"Not from here she didn't. She went back on the street and walked up and down for a while. Then I start feeling bad—like, what if she was my niece or something, and I found out some hard-ass threw her out on the street? Man, I'd bust his hard ass. So I go to tell her she can have a cup of coffee if she wants, but she's got a ride and they're going down the road."

"What kind of car?" Kate asked.

"Some kind of truck."

Her heart started to beat a little harder, and she looked to Quinn, but his attention was still on Tiny Marvin.

"Don't suppose you got the plates?"

"Hey, man, I ain't no neighborhood watch commander."

"It didn't bother you the guy was breaking the law," Kate said.

Tiny Marvin frowned at her. "Look, I take care of what goes on in here, Scully. Rest of the world ain't my problem. The girl was doing what hookers do. Wasn't none of my business."

"And if she'd been your niece?"

Quinn gave her a warning look and spoke again to the bartender. "Did you see the driver?"

"Didn't look. I just thought, man, what

about his sorry ass, picking up a kid like that. The world's a cold, sick place—you know what I'm saying?"

"Yeah," Kate muttered, picking up the snapshot of Angie from the bar, looking at the pretty, exotic face, the frowning mouth, the angry eyes that had seen too much. "I know exactly what you're saying."

She put the photo back in her purse, tossed a buck on the bar for the coffee she hadn't touched, and walked out. The snow had started in flurries, the clouds sending down a handful at a time on gusts of cold wind. The street was deserted, the sidewalks empty, the dingy storefronts dark except for the bail-bonds place across the street.

She leaned back against the building and wished the wind would blow away the feelings that were stacking up inside her. They'd about reached the back of her throat and she couldn't even begin to swallow them down.

She knew too much about the world to let its injustices and cruelties get to her too easily. Of course a bartender in a pool hall on Lake Street wouldn't be overly concerned about the life of a hooker, young or not. He saw it every day and never looked too closely. He had his own life to worry about.

It hit Kate hard only because she knew the next chapter to the story. The ride that had taken Angie DiMarco away from Eight Ball's had taken her to a crime scene, and the driver of that nondescript truck might have been a killer. Even if he'd been just another pathetic loser willing to pay for sex, he'd delivered her to a rendezvous with a fate that may just have gotten her killed.

Quinn came out of the pool hall, eyes narrowed against the cold and wind as he flipped up the collar of his trench coat.

"Kovac says: 'Good police work, Red.' If you ever want to give up the soft life, he'll put a word in for you."

"Yeah? Well, I've always wanted to work nights, weekends, and holidays up to my ass in dead bodies. Now's my big chance."

"He's sending a team out to talk to the bartender and whoever else they can find. If they can come up with somebody who remembers more about the vehicle, or saw the driver that night, they've got something to run with."

Kate pulled her coat closed up around her throat and stared across the empty street at the bail-bonds place. A red neon light glowed through the barred window: CHECK$ CA$HED HERE.

"Timing is everything," she said. "If Angie hadn't been standing on this street at the exact moment that truck pulled up, I'd be home in bed, and you'd be digging in someone else's boneyard."

She laughed at herself and shook her head, the wind catching a rope of hair and whipping it across her face. "As long as I've been around, I still shake my fist at chance. How stupid is that?"

"You always took the prize for stubborn." Quinn reached out automatically to brush her hair back, his fingertips grazing her cheek. "A cynic is a disappointed idealist, you know."

"Is that what happened to you?" she tossed back.

"I never saw life as ideal."

She knew that, of course. She knew about his life, about the abusive alcoholic father, and the grim years growing up in working-class Cincinnati. She was one of the few people he had allowed to see in that window.

"But that never saved you from disappointment," she said quietly.

"The only thing that can save you from disappointment is hopelessness. But if you don't have hope, then there's no point in living."

"And what's the difference between hope and desperation?" she asked, thinking of Angie, wondering if she dared hope.

"Time."

Which might have already run out for Angie DiMarco, and which had run out for the two of them years earlier. Kate felt disappointment sink down through her. She wanted to lay her head against Quinn's shoulder and feel his arms slip around her. Instead, she pushed away from the wall and started for the 4Runner parked down by the Laundromat. The homeless guy was looking in her back window as if considering it for his night's accommodations.

"I'll drop you off at your hotel," she said to Quinn.

"No. I'll ride home with you and call a cab. Tough as you are, I don't want you going home alone, Kate. It's not smart. Not tonight."

If she'd been feeling stronger, she might have argued just on principle, but she wasn't feeling strong, and the memory of phantom eyes watching her as she'd let herself in her back door just hours before was still too fresh.

"All right." She hit the remote lock. The alarm system on the truck beeped loudly, sending the homeless guy scuttling back into the doorwell of the Suds-O-Rama. "But don't try anything funny, or I'll sic my cat on you."

20

CHAPTER

"ANYTHING ON THE HOUSE-TO-HOUSE yet?" Kovac asked, lighting a cigarette.

Tippen hunched his bony shoulders. "A lot of people pissed off about having cops pounding on their doors in the middle of the night."

They stood on the front porch of the Phoenix, huddled under a jaundice-yellow bug light. The B of I van was still on the yard. The yard had been cordoned off to create a media-free zone.

The press had swooped in like a flock of vultures, suspiciously in sync. Kovac squinted through the smoke and the falling snow, staring out at the end of the sidewalk, where Toni Urskine was being interviewed in the eerie glow of portable lights.

"How much you wanna bet I pull the phone records for this dump tonight I find calls to WCCO, KSTP, and KARE?" he muttered.

"Raking publicity off crime and tragedy," Elwood said, pushing his goofy-looking felt hat down on his head. "It's the American way. All this media exposure, you can bet the donations will come rolling in."

"She even hints what's going on here is connected to our witness, I can just bend over and grab my ankles," Kovac groused. "The brass pricks will be lining up behind me."

"Better make nice with her, Sam," Liska suggested, bouncing up and down on the balls of her feet to keep warm. "Or I could loan you a tube of K-Y Jelly."

"Jeez, Tinks." Distaste rippled across Kovac's face. He turned to Elwood. "What've we got in the basement? What's the story with that cellar door?"

"Door's locked from the inside. We've got what looks like some bloodstains on the floor. Not a lot. Urskine says it's nothing, that he cut himself working on the furnace a few nights ago."

Kovac made a growling sound low in his throat and looked to Liska again. "What about your mutt, Vanlees?"

"Can't find him. I wanted to follow him from

the meeting, but between the crowd and the traffic getting out there, I lost him."

"He's not working tonight? He came to the meeting in his uniform."

"I'll bet he sleeps in that uniform," she said. "Ever ready to save the public from ticket scalpers and unruly basketball fans. He's got a cheap apartment over on Lyndale, but he's not in it. I finally talked to his soon-to-be ex-wife. She tells me he's house-sitting for someone. She doesn't know who and couldn't give a shit."

"Hey, he wants to be a cop, he might as well start out with one divorce under his belt," Tippen said.

"She give any indication he's into anything kinky?" Kovac asked.

"Oh, you'll love this," she said, eyes brightening. "I asked her about that misdemeanor trespass conviction eighteen months ago. Quinn was right. Ol' Gil had the hots for some woman his wife works with. He got caught trying to sneak a peek at her in her panties."

"And he's still working security?" Kovac said.

"He kept it quiet, pleaded down, no one paid attention. He claimed it was all a big misunderstanding anyway."

"Yeah," Tippen sneered. " 'It was all a big mistake, your honor. I was just driving along, minding my own business, when I was struck by an uncontrollable urge to play spank the monkey.' "

"I like this guy, Sam," Liska said. "His wife had nothing but disdain for him. She hinted their sex life was nonexistent when they were together. If that's true, he could be an even better fit to Quinn's profile. A lot of these guys are sexually inadequate with their partners."

"Is that the voice of experience?" Tippen dug.

"Well, I haven't been sleeping with you, so I guess not."

"Fuck you, Tinker Bell."

"What part of no don't you understand?"

"I'll put a car outside his apartment," Kovac said. "I want him downtown ASAP. See if you can't track down this house he's sitting. Somebody's gotta know where he is. Call his boss, call the wife again. Tonight. Get the names of his friends. Call them."

"I'll help with that," Moss said.

"Annoy everybody who knows him," Kovac said. "That'll get back to him and rattle him. Did you find out what he's driving?"

"A maroon GMC Jimmy."

Kovac felt like someone had punched him in the diaphragm. "A bartender on Lake Street spotted our witness Sunday night getting into a dark-colored truck or SUV. This was the john she did in the park before she came across victim number three."

"Did she name this john?" Adler asked.

"No."

"Would Vanlees have had any way of knowing the girl was staying here?" Moss asked.

Liska shook her head. "I don't see how, unless he somehow managed to tail her here from downtown. Seems unlikely."

"Who all *did* know the witness was here?" Adler asked.

"Us, Sabin, the vic/wit people, the brass cupcake out there"—Kovac hooked a thumb in Toni Urskine's direction— "and the husband. The mayor, Bondurant's people—"

"And a partridge in a pear tree," Elwood finished.

"One of the other victims had a connection to this place," Moss pointed out.

"And when she turned up croaked back when, we interviewed everybody at the house, checked records, alibis, known associates, yadda, yadda, yadda," Kovac said. "I remember the body was found on a Friday. She'd been out of here six months or more. I make it over here on Sunday to see if she was still tight with anyone. The Urskines are gone to some cabin up north, so I can't talk to them, right? Monday morning, eight o'clock, Toni Urskine's on the horn to the lieutenant, demanding he ream me a new one because I hadn't called her yet."

"Now we get to do it all again for a fresh batch of hookers." Tippen groaned. "Like we need more fucking paperwork to do."

"Hey, that's why they pay you slave wages and treat you like dirt," Kovac said.

"Here I thought it was something personal."

"Okay. Who wants to hit Lake Street?" Kovac asked. "See if you can find anyone who might have seen the DiMarco girl get in that truck Sunday night? If you can get a plate number, I'll kiss you full on the mouth."

"That ain't no incentive, Kojak," Adler said.

"Let Tippen do it," Liska said. "He might find a girlfriend."

"Send Charm," Tippen said. "The hookers will pay *him*."

"The two of you," Kovac said, pointing to Yurek and Tippen both. "You're the perfect pair."

"God's Gift and the Mercy Fuck," Liska snickered.

Tippen jerked the end of the scarf around her throat. "You'll get it one of these days, Liska."

"Not if I stay more than three inches away from you."

"Hit the bricks," Kovac ordered. "Time's a-wastin' and this case is starting to cook. No pun intended. Let's get this dirtbag before he lights someone else's fire."

"THAT'S A HELL of a cat," Quinn remarked, regarding Thor as Thor regarded him from the front hall table. "But I think I could take him."

The cat had to be twenty pounds. Fantastic tufts of hair sprouted from his ears. His whiskers looked a foot long. He tucked his chin back into a great ruff of fur and made a sound like "hmmm" deep in his throat. He raised his hind leg up behind his ear in a yoga move and licked his butt.

Quinn made a face. "Guess I know what he thinks of me."

"Don't take it personally," Kate said. "Thor is above the petty considerations of mere humans."

She hung her coat in the hall closet and nearly reached for a second empty hanger, but stopped herself.

"Thanks for your help tonight," she said, closing the door and leaning back against it. "I was less than gracious about the offer, but I know it's not your job to investigate."

"Or yours."

"True, but I needed to do something proactive. You know I can't bear to just sit back and let things happen. What about you? It wasn't your job to go to the Phoenix with Kovac."

"This case has been anything but normal."

"Because of Peter Bondurant. I know." She stroked a hand over Thor. The cat gave her a look of affront, hopped down, and trotted away, belly hanging low to the ground.

"Money changes all the rules," Kate said. "There's not a politician in the Cities who wouldn't bend over backward to kiss Peter Bondurant's ass, then tell him it smells like a rose. Because he's got money and they want him to keep it here. Because of that his attorney can sit in on meetings with Sabin, and he can have the ear of the mayor, and of the director of the FBI, no less. I'll bet Lila White's parents couldn't get past Director Brewster's secretary. If it would even occur to them to try."

"Now you're sounding like Toni Urskine, saying there's no equal justice under the law."

"It's a lovely ideal we both know doesn't hold water in the real world. Money can and does buy justice—and injustice—every day.

"Still, I guess I can't blame Bondurant. What parent wouldn't do everything in their power to get their child back?" she said, her expression somber. "I would have made a deal with the devil himself when Em got sick. In fact, I believe I tried," she confessed, forcing a lopsided smile. "No takers. Shook my faith in evil."

Her pain was still a palpable thing, and Quinn wanted to pull her into his arms and invite her to divide it between the two of them, like old times.

"Bondurant's money didn't stop his daughter's death either," he said. "If that body is Jillian's. He's convinced it is."

"Why would he want to believe that?" Kate asked, bewildered by the notion. She had been so violently resistant to the news of Emily's death that even after a nurse had taken her into the room to see her daughter's body, to touch the cold little hand, to feel for herself there was no pulse, no breath, she had insisted it wasn't true.

"What an odd man," she said. "I was surprised to see him at the meeting tonight. He's been keeping such a low profile."

The offhand remark hit Quinn like an invisible fist. "You saw Bondurant at the meeting? Are you sure?"

"Sure looked like him to me," Kate said. "I saw him on my way out. I thought it was strange he wasn't with his camp, but it was clear he didn't want any attention. He was dressed down like one of the common folk in a parka and a crumpled-looking hat, trying to look anonymous, slipping out the back with the rest of the crowd."

Quinn frowned. "I can't get a handle on him. I'd say he's being uncooperative, but he's the one who brought me in, then he turns around and refuses to answer questions. He's one contradiction after another.

"Christ, I can't believe I didn't see him there."

"You weren't looking for him," Kate said reasonably. "You were looking for a killer."

And did I miss him too? Quinn wondered, rubbing harder at the sudden searing pain in his gut. What else had he missed? Some subtle sign: a look, a squint, the hint of a smile. And if he'd seen it, would Angie DiMarco be in bed at the Phoenix right now? Logically, he thought no. But catching a killer like this one required something more than logic. It required instinct, and it seemed that he was feeling around in the dark through a blanket for his these days.

"I can't shake the feeling that his daughter is the key to this whole thing," he said. "If she's the third vic. Smokey Joe deviated from the pattern with that one. Why? With the first two, he burned the bodies but didn't try to make them unrecognizable in any other way. With number three he obliterates her fingertips and the soles of her feet. He takes her head. He makes it as difficult as possible to identify her."

"But he left her driver's license."

"Why do both?"

"Maybe the first as part of the torture," Kate suggested. "As part of the depersonalization. He reduced her to no one. He doesn't care if we know who she is after she's dead, so he leaves the DL as if to say 'Hey, look who I killed.' But maybe he wanted this victim to feel like nobody in those last few moments of her life, let her die thinking no one would be able to identify her or take care of her body or mourn her."

"Maybe," Quinn said. "And maybe this extreme depersonalization is the deviation in his pattern because he knew Jillian. If, for instance, we can develop this security guard who lived at Jillian's town house complex, we might speculate he killed the two prostitutes for practice, projecting his feelings for Jillian onto them. But that didn't satisfy his need, so he does Jillian, goes overboard, keeps her head because he wants to own her.

"Or maybe the killer takes the head because that body *isn't* Jillian Bondurant and he wants us to believe it is. But that's definitely her DL, and if the body isn't her, then how'd Smokey Joe get it?" he asked. "We know this is no kidnapping. It's been days with no call, no ransom demand—at least that we know of. Bondurant won't allow a tap on his phone—another odd bit of behavior on his part."

"And if Jillian is alive," Kate said, "then where is she and how is she tied to all this?"

"I don't know. And there doesn't seem to be anyone who knew Jillian willing or able to tell us. This case gives me a bad feeling, Kate."

"The kind you should see a doctor for?" she asked with a pointed look to the hand he was rubbing against his stomach. "You keep doing that."

He killed the gesture. "It's nothing."

Kate shook her head. "You've probably got a hole in your stomach lining big enough to drive a Buick through. But God forbid you admit it. Think what that would do to the Quinn mystique. It would bring you down to the level of Superman with his weakness for kryptonite. How embarrassing."

She wanted to ask if he had talked to anyone in Psych Services, but she knew it would be a waste of breath. Every other agent in Investigative Support could line up at the shrink's door and no one would bat an eye. Stress disorders were the norm in the unit. Everyone understood. They saw too much, got too deep into the heads of victims and killers in case after horrific case. They saw the worst the world had to offer every day, and made life-and-death decisions based on an inexact science: their own knowledge of human behavior. But John Quinn would never admit to bending beneath the strain of that. Vulnerability did not become a legend well.

"Bullets don't really bounce off you, John," she said quietly.

He smiled as if she had amused him in some small, endearing way, but he wouldn't meet her eyes. "It's nothing."

"Fine." If he wasn't taking care of himself, that was his problem—or the problem of some faceless woman back in Virginia, not hers. "I'm having that drink now. You want something before you go? Maalox? Mylanta? A roll of Tums to chew on for the cab ride?"

She headed for the kitchen, kicking herself for giving him the opportunity to linger, then rationalized it was payback. She owed him for tonight. Besides, he looked like he could do with a drink.

Of course, she knew he wouldn't allow himself one. He was too conscious of the alcoholism that ran rampant both in his family and in his profession. As much as he may have needed to douse the frustration and the tension the job induced, the risk of drowning was too high.

"Great house," he said, following her to the kitchen.

"I bought it from my parents when they lost their minds and moved to Las Vegas."

"So you really did come home."

From the shattered mess that had been her life in Virginia to a house with warm memories and a sense of security. The house would have substituted its comfort for the comfort of her family—whom he doubted she had ever told the whole story. When everything had broken in Quantico, she'd been embarrassed and ashamed. It still hurt him to think of it.

What they'd had together had been a connection deeper than any other he'd ever known, but not deep enough or strong enough to survive the stress of discovery and disapproval and Kate's predisposition to guilt.

He watched her now as she moved around the kitchen, getting a cup from the cupboard and a box of herbal teabags, her long hair falling down her back in a wave of red-gold. He wanted to stroke a hand over it, rest that hand at the small of her back.

He had always seen her femininity, her vulnerability. He doubted many people looked at Kate and thought she might need protecting. Her strength and tenacity were what others noted. But just behind that wall was a woman not always so certain as she seemed.

"How are you, Kate?"

"Hmm? What?" She turned toward him from the microwave, her brow knit in confusion. "I'm tired. I'm upset. I've lost a witness—"

Stepping close, Quinn put a finger to her lips. "I don't mean with the case. It's been five years. How are you, really?"

Kate's heart thumped hard against her sternum. Answers log-jammed in her throat. Five years. The first was remembered as a pain so sharp, it stole her breath. The second had been like trying to relearn how to walk and talk after a stroke. Then came the third and the fourth and another after that. In that time she'd built a career, made a home for herself, done some traveling, settled into a nice, safe rut.

But the answers that rushed to mind were other words.

How are you? Empty. Alone. Walled off.

"Let's not play that game," she said softly. "If you'd really wanted to know, it wouldn't have taken you five years to ask."

She heard the regret in those words and wished them back. What was the point now, when all they would have was a few days. Better to pretend there'd been no fire at all than to poke at the ash and stir up the dust of memories. The timer went off on the microwave, and she turned her back to him and busied herself making a cup of tea.

"You told me that was what you wanted," he said. "You wanted out. You wanted a clean break. You wanted to leave, to start over. What was I supposed to do, Kate?"

Ask me not to go. Go with me. The answers were right there, as fresh as yesterday and just as futile. By the time she'd left Virginia, the anger and the pain had taken them past the point of his asking her not to go. And she knew without having to ask that he would never have left Investigative Support to go with her. The job was who John Quinn was. He was bound to it in a way he would never be bound to a woman. And, God, how it still hurt to think that.

"What were you supposed to do? Nothing," she whispered. "You did it well."

Quinn moved in close behind her, wanting to touch her, as if that might magically erase the time and the trouble that had passed between them. He wanted to tell her the phone worked both ways, but he knew she would never have backed away from her pride or the insecurity it covered. A part of him had been relieved that she had never called, because he would then have had to face himself in life's big mirror and finally answer the question of whether or not there was enough left in him to build a lasting relationship. His fear of the answer had kept him running from that question for a long, long time.

And now he stood here, an inch away from the better part of his past, knowing he should let it lie. If he hadn't had enough to give a relationship five years ago, he sure as hell didn't have any more now.

He raised a hand to touch her hair, his memory of its texture meeting the silk of reality. He let his hand rest on her shoulder, his thumb finding the familiar knot of tension there.

"Do you regret it, Kate? Not the way it ended, but *us*."

Kate squeezed her eyes shut. She had a truckload of regret she had to move out of her way every day in order to get on with her life. But she had never been able to find it in her to regret turning to him. She regretted she had wished for more. She regretted he hadn't had more to give. But she couldn't think of a single touch, a single kiss, a single night in his arms, and regret a second of it. He had given her love and understanding, passion and compassion, tenderness and comfort when she had needed so badly, when she had hurt so much, when she had felt so alone. How could she regret that?

"No," she said, turning and holding the steaming mug of tea between them. "Here. It's good for what ails you."

He took the cup and set it aside.

"I don't regret us," he said. "There were times when I thought I should, but I didn't, and I don't."

His fingertips touched her cheek and slid back into her hair, and he leaned down and touched his mouth to hers. Need, sharp and bitter and sweet, instantly sprang up inside her. Her lips moved against his out of memory and longing. A perfect fit. The perfect balance of pressure and passion. Their tongues tangled, seeking, searching, tasting, touching, deepening the kiss and the emotions it evoked. Her heart beat hard against the wall of her chest and his. She was instantly aware of a tenderness in her breasts, a longing for the touch of his hand, his mouth, a need for a connection beyond this simple act. His arms tightened around her. She could feel him hard against her belly as he pressed against her.

He would be here a matter of days, her fading logic reminded her. He had come for a case, not because he needed her or missed her or wanted to resolve what they had walked away from. All of that was incidental.

"No," she said softly as he raised his head. "I don't regret it. But that doesn't mean I'll go through it again, John. I'm not here for your convenience."

"You think that's what I expect?" he asked, hurt. "You think I expect you to go to bed with me because you're handy and you know what I like? I thought you knew me better than that, Kate. His voice dropped low and rough, and skimmed across her heart like a callused hand. "My God, you're the only person who ever knew me."

"Well, at least I thought I did," Kate murmured. "It seemed at the end there we didn't know each other very well at all."

He sighed and stepped back.

"Let's just call ourselves old friends and leave it at that, huh?" she said around the knot in her throat. "You didn't come here for me, John. You would have done that years ago if it was what you wanted. I'll go call you that cab."

21

CHAPTER

THE HOUSE WAS DARK. The neighborhood was dark. People living on Lake of the Isles kept civilized hours. In Kovac's neighborhood there was always a light on somewhere—people coming in late, going to work early, watching infomercials.

Kovac parked on the street at the edge of Bondurant's property and made a complete circuit of the place on foot through the fresh snow. Fresh, *wet* snow. Heavy and sticky, it clung to his pant legs and worked down into his shoes, but he ignored it, his attention on the mansion that seemed to loom even larger in the dark than in the light. Security lights marked entrances on the back side. There were no lights visible in the house. If Peter Bondurant was watching TV, learning how to get buns of steel, he was in some windowless room in the heart of his home.

Some home. It looked like something out of medieval England, like someplace that would have a torture chamber in the basement. For all he knew, it *did* have.

Christ, wouldn't that be just his luck? He'd have to be the one to tell the world billionaire Peter Big Deal Bondurant was a homicidal lunatic. The mayor would have his throat cut and dispose of his body in the footings of the new jail. The bigwigs wanted a killer caught, all right. And this killer would preferably be a bug-eyed, drooling ex-con from Wisconsin.

Circling back around to his car, he kicked the snow off his legs and feet, slid in behind the wheel, and started the engine, setting the anemic heater to full blast. The bones in his feet and ankles and shins had absorbed the cold into their marrow, and it was now making its way up his legs like mercury in a thermometer.

He dug his cell phone out from under a pile of junk on the seat and dialed Bondurant's home number. Quinn had called to tell him Kate had spotted Bondurant in the back at the meeting, hiding out among the common folk. The guy was a twitch. He was holding out on them about that last night with Jillian, and God knew what else.

The phone rang.

It burned his ass that Bondurant got special treatment, was privy to information, didn't have to come downtown to make a statement. It was wrong. They should have been able to rattle his cage same as anyone else's.

On the fifth ring the answering machine picked up and an emotionless voice gave instructions. Kovac left his name and number, and a request for a return call.

He put the car in gear, rolled up to the intercom panel at the security gate, and hit the buzzer. No one responded. He sat there for another five minutes, leaning on the buzzer again and again, well schooled in how to be an asshole to get someone's attention. No one ever responded.

A prowl car from a private security company came by and a weightlifter in a spiffy uniform asked to see his ID. Then he was alone again, left to stare up at Peter Bondurant's house and wonder what secrets hid inside.

Some people didn't answer their phones when they rang after midnight. Not the parents of missing children. Maybe Peter Bondurant never answered his gate buzzer, and was, even at that moment, cowering in his bed, waiting for a mob of the desperate poor to burst in and loot his house. But he hadn't been the one to call in the security car. Routine driveby, the weightlifter had said.

Kovac stared at the house and let seventeen years of experience tell him there was no one in. Peter Bondurant was not at home in the dead of this night when their witness had gone missing. Peter Bondurant, who demanded answers but refused to give any. Peter Bondurant, who had fought with his daughter the night she disappeared, then lied about it. Peter Bondurant, who had the power to crush a cop's career like an empty beer can.

I'm probably a moron for sitting here, he thought. Vanlees was their hot ticket. Vanlees looked to fit Quinn's profile. He had a history. He'd known Jillian, had access to her town house. He even drove the right kind of vehicle.

But there was still something off about Peter Bondurant. He could feel it like hives just under his skin, and come hell or high water, he was going to find out what.

He sighed, shifted his weight to a new uncomfortable position, and settled in, lighting a cigarette. What the hell did he need with a pension anyway?

THE CORPSES FLOATED above him like logs. Naked, rotting bodies. Torn, hacked apart, riddled with holes. Decomposing flesh shredded away from the wounds. Fish food. Eels swam in and out of the bodies through the gaping holes.

Quinn looked up at the bodies from below, trying to identify each one by name in the dim blue watery light. He was out of oxygen. His lungs were burning. But he couldn't go to the surface until he had identified every body and named the killer that went with each.

The bodies bobbed and shifted position. Decaying limbs fell away from torsos and sank toward him. Below him, a bed of lush green weeds caught at his feet like the tentacles of a squid.

He needed to think hard. Names. Dates. Facts. But he couldn't remember all the names. He didn't know all the killers. Random facts raced through his head. The bodies seemed to be multiplying, kept drifting and bobbing. He was running out of air.

He couldn't breathe, couldn't think.

He struck out with his arms, trying to grab hold of anything that might help pull him up. But the hands he caught hold of were cold and dead, and held him under. The bodies and his responsibility to them held him under. He had to think hard. He could solve the puzzles if only the pieces would stop moving, if only his thoughts would stop racing, if only he could breathe.

The bodies shifted again above him, and he could see Kate's face on the other side of the surface, looking down at him. Then the bodies shifted again and she was gone.

Just as it felt as if his lungs were starting to

bleed, he gave one last hard kick and broke the surface of the water and the dream, gasping for air, coming up off the bed. Sweat drenched his body, ran off the end of his nose and down the valley of his spine.

He staggered away from the bed, his legs weak beneath him, and fell into the chair by the writing desk, shaking now as the air chilled him. Naked, shaking, sweating, sick, the taste of bile and blood bitter in his mouth.

He sat doubled over the wastebasket, his focus not entirely on the writhing fire in his belly. As ever, there was the sound of that inner voice that always found him wanting, and never hesitated to kick him when he was down. It told him he didn't have time for this shit. He had cases to work, people depending on him; if he lost his focus and fucked up, people could die. If he fucked up bad enough, if anyone found out what a mess his head was, that he'd lost his nerve and his edge, he'd be out of a job. And if he didn't have the job, he didn't have anything, because it wasn't just what he did, it was all he was, all he had.

The dream was nothing new, nothing to shake over, nothing to waste his energy on. He had any number of variations on that one. They were all stupidly simple to interpret, and he always felt vaguely embarrassed for having them at all. He didn't have time for it.

He could hear exactly what Kate would have to say about that. She would give him the sharp side of her tongue and another lecture on Superman, then try to make him drink herbal tea. She would try to mask her concern and her maternal instincts with the wise-ass sarcasm that seemed so much safer and more familiar and more in character with the image others had of her. She would pretend he didn't know her better.

And then she'd call him a cab and shove him out of her house.

"Let's just call ourselves old friends and leave it at that, huh? You didn't come here for me, John. You would have done that years ago if it was what you wanted."

That was what she thought, that he hadn't come because he didn't want her. Maybe that was what she wanted to think. She was the one who had walked away. It justified her action to believe there'd been no reason to stay.

Still feeling weak, he went to the window that looked out on a wedge of downtown Minneapolis and an empty street filling with snow.

What he wanted. He wasn't sure what that even was anymore. He didn't allow himself to want outside the scope of the job. A lead, a piece of evidence, a fresh insight to help pry open a killer's head. He could want those things. But what was the point in wanting what couldn't be had?

The point was whether or not to allow himself hope.

"The only thing that can save you from disappointment is hopelessness. But if you don't have hope, then there's no point in living."

His own words. His own voice. His own

wisdom. Coming right back around to bite him in the ass.

He didn't ask the point of his life. He lived to work and he worked to live. He was as simple and pathetic as that. That was the Quinn machine of perpetual function. The trouble was he could feel the wheels coming loose. What would happen when one came off altogether?

Closing his eyes, he saw the corpses again, and felt the panic wash down through him, a cold, internal acid rain. He could hear his unit chief demanding answers, explanations, prodding for results. *"The director chewed my tail for half an hour. Bondurant isn't the guy to piss off, John. What the hell's wrong with you?"*

Tears burned his eyes as the answer called up from the hollow in the center of his chest: *I've lost it.* His edge, his nerve, his instincts. He felt it all torn asunder and scattered to too many parts of the country. He didn't have the time to go hunting for the pieces. He could only pretend he was intact and hope not too many people caught on.

"Are you getting anywhere with this? Have they developed a suspect? You know what they're looking for, don't you? It's pretty straightforward, isn't it?"

Sure it was. If you looked at the murders of two prostitutes and ignored the fact that Peter Bondurant's daughter may or may not have been the third victim. If you pretended Peter Bondurant's behavior was normal. If you didn't have a hundred unanswered questions about the enigma that was Jillian Bondurant. If this was simply about the murder of prostitutes, he could have pulled a profile out of a textbook and never left Quantico.

But if this were simply about the murders of two prostitutes, no one would ever have called his office.

Giving up on the notion of sleep, he brushed his teeth, took a shower, pulled on sweat pants and his academy sweatshirt. He sat down at the desk with the murder book and a bottle of antacid, drinking straight out of the bottle as he browsed through the reports.

Wedged in between pages was the packet of photographs Mary Moss had gotten from Lila White's parents. Pictures of Lila White alive and happy, and laughing at her little girl's birthday party. Her lifestyle had aged her beyond her years, but he could easily see the pretty girl she had once been before the drugs and the disillusioned dreams. Her daughter was a doll with blond pigtails and a pixie's face. One shot captured mother and daughter in bathing suits in a plastic wading pool, Lila on her knees with the little girl hugged close in front of her, both of them smiling the same crooked smile.

It had to break her parents' hearts to look at this, Quinn thought. In the baby's face they would see their daughter as she had been when her world was simple and sunny and full of wonderful possibility. And in Lila's face they would see the lines of hard lessons learned, disappointment, and failure. And the hope for something better. Hope that had been rewarded with a brutal death not long after these photographs had been taken.

Quinn sighed as he held the picture under the lamplight, committing Lila White's image to memory: the style of her hair, the crooked smile, the slight bump in the bridge of her nose, the curve where her shoulder met her neck. She would join the others who haunted his sleep.

As he went to set the picture aside, something caught his eye and he pulled it back. Half obscured by the strap of her swimming suit was a small tattoo on her upper right chest. Quinn found his magnifying glass and held the snapshot under the light again for closer scrutiny.

A flower. A lily, he thought.

With one hand he flipped through the murder book to the White autopsy photos. There were about a third of the photos of the victim believed to be Jillian Bondurant. Still, he found what he was looking for: a shot showing a section of flesh missing from Lila White's upper right chest—and no tattoo in sight.

KATE SAT CURLED into the corner of the old green leather sofa in her study, another glass of Sapphire on the table beside her. She'd lost count of its number. Didn't care. It took the sharp corners off the pain that assaulted her on several different fronts. That was all that mattered tonight.

How had her life taken such a sudden left

turn? Things had been going so smoothly, then BAM! Ninety degrees hard to port, and everything fell out of the neat little cubicles into a jumbled mess that came up to her chin. She hated the feeling that she didn't have control. She hated the idea of her past rear-ending her. She'd been doing so well. Focus forward, concentrate on what was ahead of her for the day, for the week. She tried not to think too much about the past. She tried never to think about Quinn. She never *ever* allowed the memory of his mouth on hers.

She lifted a hand and touched her lips, thinking she still felt the heat of him there. She took another drink, thinking she could still taste him.

She had more important things to think about. Whether or not Angie was still alive. Whether or not they had a hope in hell of getting her back. She'd made the dreaded call to Rob Marshall to inform him of the situation. He had the unenviable task of passing the news on to the county attorney. Sabin would spend the rest of the night contemplating methods of torture. Tomorrow Kate figured she would be burned at the stake.

But a confrontation with Ted Sabin was the least of her worries. Nothing he could do to her could punish her more than she would punish herself.

Every time she closed her eyes she saw the blood.

I should have stayed with her. If I'd been there for her, she would still be alive.

And every time she thought that, Angie's face

morphed into Emily's, and the pain bit deeper and held on harder. Quinn had accused her of being a martyr, but martyrs suffered without sin, and she took full blame. For Emily. For Angie.

If she'd just gone into the house with the girl...If she'd just pressed a little harder to get a little closer...But she'd pulled back because a part of her didn't want to get that close or care that much. Christ, this was why she didn't do kids: They needed too much and she was too afraid of the potential for pain to give it.

"And I thought I was doing so well."

She rose from the couch just to see if she could still stand without aid, and went to the massive old oak desk that had been her father's. She picked up the phone and dialed the number for her voice mail, feeling the lump form in her throat before she punched the code to retrieve the messages. She'd listened three times already. She skipped through messages from David Willis and her cooking instructor to hit the one she wanted.

10:05 P.M., the mechanical voice announced. A long silence followed the tone.

10:08 P.M. Another long silence.

10:10 P.M. Another long silence.

She had left the cell phone in the truck. Hadn't wanted to go back out to get it because she was spooked. Any callers could leave a message. She'd check her voice mail later, she remembered thinking.

If those calls had come from Angie...

But there was no way of knowing, and nothing to do but wonder and wait.

THE CALL CAME into Hennepin County 911 dispatch at 3:49 A.M. A car fire. Kovac listened with one ear out of habit. He was cold to the bone. His feet felt like blocks of ice. Snow blew in the window he had kept cracked open to prevent carbon monoxide poisoning. Maybe he should set *this* car on fire. The heat could thaw his blood out, and the powers that ruled the motor pool could move him up to something better—like a Hyundai with a hamster wheel under the hood.

And then came the address, and adrenaline instantly burned off the chill.

They'd sure as hell drawn Smokey Joe out with the meeting, all right. He gunned the engine and rocked the car away from the curb and onto the street half a block down from Peter Bondurant's empty house.

Their killer had just lit up his fourth victim...in the parking lot of the community center where the meeting had been held.

22

CHAPTER

KATE RAN OUT THE BACK DOOR with her coat half on, half off. She had managed to pull on a pair of snow boots, but the heavy soles were little help as she hit the ice on the steps. An involuntary shriek raked her throat as she tumbled down into the yard, where what looked to be half a foot of wet snow cushioned her landing. She didn't even allow herself to catch her breath, but kept her legs moving and pushed herself upright.

Kovac had called on his way to the community center where the meeting had been held. A car fire in the parking lot. Reports of someone in the vehicle.

Angie.

No one knew at this point, of course, but the thought that it could be Angie burned in Kate's mind as she ran for the garage, fumbling in her pocket for her keys.

Quinn had given her an earful of his opinion on her garage. Terrible location. Poorly lit. Left her vulnerable. All of which was true, but she didn't have time to think about it. Anyone wanting to mug her or rape her would just have to wait.

God help her if she got pulled over en route,

she thought as she hit the light switch. She probably had no business getting behind the wheel of a vehicle at all, but she wasn't waiting for a ride. No one was on the streets this time of night anyway. It wasn't five minutes to that community center.

She was halfway to the 4Runner before she realized the garage light hadn't come on.

The realization held her up a step, a fraction of a second in which time all her senses sharpened and her heart gave an exaggerated thump. She hit the key for the remote lock, and the truck's interior lit up. *Keep moving,* she thought. If she kept moving, she wasn't allowing an opportunity for anyone to stop her. A ridiculous notion, but she grabbed on to it, yanked the door of the truck open, and hauled herself up into the driver's seat.

In a quick succession of moves, she locked the doors, started the engine, punched on the four-wheel drive, and put the truck in gear. It rocked back into the snow, pulling to the left. The exterior mirror missed disaster by a fraction of an inch. The back bumper kissed the neighbor's privacy fence, then she was rolling forward, the engine revving loudly. She pulled the wheel too hard as she hit the street and skidded sideways, just whispering past the front end of a black Lexus parked on the street.

Stupid to rush, she thought, fighting the sense of desperation, trying to lighten her foot on the accelerator. Whoever it was in that burning car would not be going anywhere, but still the urgency burned in her veins, in her gut. If there was any chance of discounting her fear—and thereby absolving herself of one stone of guilt—she wanted to grab it.

The street in front of the community center was clogged with emergency vehicles, red, white, and blue lights rolling like so many carnival rides. Mixed in among them were the omnipresent news vans, spilling reporters and cameramen and equipment. The house-to-house canvass had already begun, rousing neighbors from their beds. Overhead, a state patrol chopper cruised above the rooftops, spotlight washing down on lawns and shining in windows, flashing briefly over a pair of K-9 dogs and their officers.

If Smokey Joe had driven the car to the lot to set it ablaze, then it followed that he had left on foot. There was a good chance he lived in or near this neighborhood. Not five minutes from Kate's, though she didn't let herself think about that now.

She slid the 4Runner in behind the KMSP van, slammed it into park, and abandoned it sitting cockeyed to the curb. Despite the hour, some of the neighbors had come out of their homes to get the scoop and to further clutter the periphery of the scene. One of them could have been the killer, come back to recharge his batteries watching the resulting chaos his act had touched off. There was no way of knowing, and Kate had set her priority elsewhere. She dodged through the gathering throng, bumping shoulders, pushing, shoving.

Her eyes were on the emergency personnel

working inside a circle of uniformed cops some distance away from the burned-out car. The paramedics swarmed around the victim, snapping off rapid-fire medicalese.

One of the uniforms caught Kate by the arm as she tried to pass, and held her back.

"Sorry, ma'am. Authorized personnel only."

"I'm with victim services. I've got ID."

"This one ain't gonna need you. He's toast."

"He?"

The cop shrugged. "It. Who can tell?"

Kate's stomach double-clutched. *Oh, Jesus, Angie.* "Where's Kovac?"

"He's busy, ma'am. If you'll just step over to the side—"

"Don't 'little lady' me," Kate snapped. "I've got cause to be here."

"I can vouch for her, Officer," Quinn said, holding up his ID. "Better let her go before you lose a hand."

The cop scowled at the order and at the FBI ID, but relinquished his hold. Kate bolted for the paramedics. Four steps closer, then Quinn caught her from behind and pulled her up short, holding tight as she fought to twist away from him.

"Let me go!"

"Let's find out what Kovac knows. If this is Smokey Joe, then there should be an ID around here somewhere."

"No. I have to see!"

"It's going to be bad, Kate."

"I know that. I've seen it before. God, what *haven't* I seen?"

Nothing. She'd spent years poring over photographs of unspeakable horror. She knew every evil thing one human being could do to another. Still, there was nothing quite like the stark, raw reality of an actual crime scene. Photographs never captured the sounds, the electricity in the air, the smell of death.

The smell of burnt flesh was horrific, and it hit her in the face like a club, the sensation it caused something akin to pain. Her stomach, already rolling on anxiety and half a tank of gin, pitched its contents up the back of her throat, and she nearly turned and vomited. It felt as if her knees turned to water. She couldn't understand why she didn't fall, then realized Quinn had hold of her again, his arms wrapped around her from behind. She sank back against him and made a mental note to chide herself for it later.

Of the hundreds of victims she'd seen, none had potentially been someone she'd known.

Hideously charred and half melted, the body lay on one side, limbs bent and fused into a sitting position. The heat of the fire had to have been incredible. The hair was gone, the nose was gone; the lips were twisted and burned away, revealing the teeth in a macabre grimace. The sternum was exposed, white bone shining where the thin layer of flesh had been seared away. The uniform had been right: At a glance there was no determining gender, except that the scraps of fabric that clung to the back of the body might have once been women's clothing—a piece of pink sweater, a swatch of skirt.

A burly paramedic with soot on his face looked up and shook his head. "This one's for the bonepicker. She was long gone before we got here."

Kate's head swam. She kept trying to think of what to do, how to know if it was Angie. The ideas seemed to bend and elongate and swoop through her brain.

Dental records were out of the question. They didn't know who the hell Angie DiMarco was or where she had come from. There were no parents who could give them dental records or medical records that might have pointed out old bone fractures to look for when the body was X-rayed. There were no personal effects to pick through.

Earrings. Angie wore earrings.

The ears of the corpse had been burned down to charred nubs.

Rings. She had half a dozen, at least.

The hands of the corpse were black and curled like monkey's paws. It looked as if there were fingers missing.

A shudder went through Kate that had nothing to do with the cold. Quinn drew her away a step at a time.

"I don't know," she mumbled, still staring at the body. The toes were pointed like a gymnast's, a result of tendons constricting. "I don't know."

She was shaking so badly, Quinn could feel it through her heavy wool coat. He pulled her out of the traffic flow and pushed her hair from her face, tipping her head back so that she had to look up. Her face was ashen beneath the sodium vapor lights of the parking lot. She stared up at him, her eyes glassy with shock and dread. He wanted nothing more at that moment than to pull her close and hold her tight.

"Are you all right, honey?" he asked gently. "Do you need to sit down?"

She shook her head, looking away from him to the ambulance crew, to the fire engines, to the glare of lights around the television people. "I—no—um—oh, God," she stammered, her breath coming too hard and too fast. Her eyes found his again and her mouth trembled. "Oh, God, John, what if it's her?"

"If it's her, you didn't put her there, Kate," he said firmly.

"Rotten kid," she muttered, fighting tears. "This is why I don't do kids. Nothing but trouble."

He watched her fight, knowing she wasn't half as tough as she pretended to be, knowing she had no one in her life to turn to and lean against. Knowing she probably wouldn't have chosen him for the job now. Knowing all those things, he whispered, "Hey, come here," and drew her close.

She offered no resistance—strong, independent Kate. Her head found his shoulder and she fitted against him like his missing half. Familiar, comfortable, perfect. The noise and commotion of the crime scene seemed to recede into the distant background. He stroked a hand over her hair and kissed her temple, and felt complete for the first time in five years.

"I'm here for you, sweetheart," he whispered. "I've got you."

"Is it her?" Rob Marshall scuttled toward them on his too-short legs. He was bundled into a fat down parka that appeared to be creeping up around his ears; a stocking cap sat tight on his round head.

At the sound of his voice, Kate stiffened, straightened, moved a step away from Quinn. He could almost see her reining in the emotions and hastily reconstructing the wall around them.

"We don't know," she said, her voice husky. She cleared her throat and swiped a gloved finger beneath one eye. "The body is unrecognizable. No one's found an ID yet that we know of."

Rob looked past her to the paramedics. "I can't believe this is happening. You think this is her, don't you? You think this is your witness."

Your witness, Kate noted. He was already distancing himself from the disaster, the same way he'd distanced himself from the decision to take Angie to the Phoenix in the first place. The miserable toad.

"How did this happen?" he demanded. "I thought you were watching out for her, Kate."

"I'm sorry. I told you on the phone I was sorry. I should have stayed with her." The admission grated now because it was a concession to her boss, and she automatically wanted to disagree with him.

"We chose you for this case for a reason."

"I'm well aware of that."

"Your background, the strength of your personality. For once I thought your stubbornness would actually work to my benefit—"

"You know, I'm blaming myself enough for both of us, Rob," she said. "So you can just get off my back, thank you very much."

"Sabin is furious. I don't know how I'll placate him."

The witness was hers to lose, the peace was his to make. Kate could already hear him whining and wheedling to Sabin, taking her name in vain every chance he got.

"I'm sure you'll be fine," she snapped, too angry for prudence. "Just get down on your knees and pucker up like you always do."

Rob's whole being quaked in a spasm from his feet up, the fury erupting from his mouth. "How dare you speak that way to me! How dare you! You've lost the witness. Maybe gotten her killed—"

"We don't know that," Quinn intervened.

"—and still you have the gall to talk to me that way! You've never shown me an ounce of respect. Even now. Even after *this*. I can't believe you! You fucking bitch!"

"Back off," Quinn ordered. He stepped between them and knocked Rob in the sternum hard with the heel of his hand. Rob stumbled backward, lost his footing in the snow, and landed on his butt.

"Why don't you go take a look at what Kate's just seen," Quinn said, not bothering to offer a hand up. "Get a fresh perspective as to what's important here right now."

Rob scrambled to his feet, muttering, jerked around and stomped toward the ambulance, dusting the snow off his jacket with quick, angry movements.

"Dammit, John, *I* wanted to knock him on his ass," Kate said.

"Then I probably just saved your job for you."

The sudden possibility that her career might indeed be in danger struck Kate belatedly. God, why *wouldn't* Rob fire her? He was right: She'd never given him more than the barest requirement of respect. Never mind that he hadn't earned it. He was her boss.

She watched him as he stood near the ambulance with a mittened hand over his mouth. The crew was preparing to put the body in a bag. When he came back, his face looked both waxy and flushed.

"That's—that's—horrific," he said, breathing heavily through his mouth. He pulled off his glasses and wiped his face with a mitten. "Incredible." He swallowed a couple of times and shifted his weight from one foot to the other. "That smell..."

"Maybe you should sit down," Kate suggested.

Rob partially unzipped his coat and tugged down on the bottom. His gaze was still on the ambulance. "Incredible...horrible..."

The search helicopter swept near, blades pounding the air like the wings of a giant hummingbird.

"He's challenging us, isn't he? The Cremator," he said, looking to Quinn. "Taking the girl. Doing this here, where the meeting was held."

"Yes. He wants to make us look like fools while he makes himself look invincible."

"I'd say he's doing a damn good job of it," Rob said, staring across the way as the paramedics loaded the corpse into the ambulance.

"Anybody can look like a genius if they have all the answers ahead of time," Quinn said. "He'll screw up eventually. They all do. The trick is to get it to happen sooner rather than later. And to get him by the balls the instant he stumbles."

"I'd like to be around to see that happen." Rob wiped his face again and adjusted the parka. "I'll go call Sabin," he said to Kate. "While we still work for him."

Kate said nothing. Her silence had nothing to do with the county attorney or the suddenly precarious disposition of her job.

"Let's go find Kovac," she said to Quinn. "See if they've found the driver's license yet."

KOVAC STOOD ARGUING jurisdiction with an African American woman in a dark parka with ARSON printed across the back. The car, smallish and red, was the centerpiece in a ring of portable lights. The fire had gutted it

406

and blown out the windshield. The driver's door hung open, twisted by the tools the rescue squad had used to wrench it free. The interior was a mess of ash, melted plastic, and dripping foam fire retardant. The driver's seat had been eaten away, the flames leaving nothing but a carcass of distorted springs.

"It's an arson, Sergeant," the woman insisted. "It's up to *my* office to determine the cause."

"It's a homicide, and I could give a shit about the cause of the fire," Kovac returned. "I want B of I in that car to get whatever evidence your people haven't already fucked up."

"On behalf of the Minneapolis Fire Department, I apologize for trying to put out a fire and save a life. Maybe we'll get that straight before someone sets *your* car on fire."

"Marcell, I should be so lucky someone sets that piece of crap on fire."

As crime scenes went, this one was a disaster, Kate knew. Called to a fire, the firefighters didn't worry about trampling the scene. Their job was saving lives, not finding out who might have taken one. And so they ruined car doors and sprayed foam over any trace evidence that might have survived inside.

"The thing's already burned to a crisp," Kovac said to the arson investigator. "What's *your* hurry? Me, I got a flame-throwing fruit-loop running around killing women."

"Maybe this was an accident," Marcell shot back. "Maybe this has nothing to do with your killer and you're standing here arguing with me and wasting our time for nothing."

"Sam, we got the plates back." Elwood waded toward him through the snow. He waited until he was near enough for confidentiality, even though there was no hope of keeping this news under wraps for long. "It's a 'ninety-eight Saab registered to Jillian Bondurant."

The arson investigator saluted Kovac and stepped out of his way. "As pissing contests go, Sergeant, you just wrote your name in the snow."

THE B OF I Team swarmed over the burned-out Saab like vultures cleaning an elephant carcass. Kate sat behind the wheel of Kovac's car and watched, feeling numb and exhausted. The body—whoever she was—had been transported to HCMC. Someone else's corpse had just been knocked to number two on Maggie Stone's itinerary for the day that would soon be dawning.

Quinn opened the passenger door and climbed in on a cold breath of air. Snow clung to his dark head like dandruff. He rubbed a gloved hand over it.

"It's pretty clear the fire was set on the driver's side," he said. "It burned hottest and longest there. The dashboard and steering wheel are melted. Our two best bets for fingerprints gone."

"He's escalating," Kate said.

"Yes."

"Changing his MO."

"To make a point."

"He's building toward something."

"Yes. And I'd give everything I have to know what and when."

"And why."

Quinn shook his head. "I don't care why anymore. There are no valid reasons. There are only excuses. You know all the contributing factors as well as I do, but you also know not all kids with abusive parents grow up to abuse, and not all kids with emotionally distant mothers grow up to kill. At some point in time a choice is made, and once it's made, I don't care why, I just want the bastards off the planet."

"And you've appointed yourself responsible for catching them all."

"It's a shit job, but what else have I got going for me?" He flashed the famous Quinn smile, worn around the edges now, running on too little sleep and too much stress.

"You don't need to be here now," Kate said, feeling the fatigue and the pressure in every muscle of her body. "They'll fill you in at the morning briefing. You look like you could use a couple hours' sleep."

"Sleep? I gave that up. It was taking the edge off my paranoia."

"Careful with that, John. They'll pull you out of CASKU and stick you in *The X-Files.*"

"I am better-looking than David Duchovny."

"Far and away."

Funny, she thought, how they fell back

into the old patterns of teasing, even now, even after all that had gone on tonight. But then, it was familiar and comforting.

"You don't need to be here either, Kate," he said, going serious.

"Yes, I do. I'm the closest thing Angie DiMarco has to someone who cares about her. If that body turns out to be hers, the least I can do is miss a little sleep to hear the news."

She expected another lecture from Quinn on her lack of culpability, but he didn't say anything.

"Do you think there's any chance that body is Jillian Bondurant?" she asked. "That she wasn't victim number three, and she did this to herself?"

"No. Self-immolation is rare, and when it does happen, the person usually wants an audience. Why would Jillian come here in the dead of night? What's her connection to this place? Nothing. We'll know for certain if it's Jillian after the autopsy, seeing as we can compare dental records this time, but I'd say the chances this is her and the fire was self-inflicted are nil."

Kate turned up the corners of her mouth in a pseudo-smile. "Yeah, I know all that. I was just hoping that corpse might be someone I wasn't responsible for."

"I'm the one who called the meeting, Kate. Smokey Joe did this to say 'Fuck you, Quinn.' Now I get to wonder what set him off. Should I have been harder on him? Should I have tried to pretend I feel sympathy for him? Should I have stroked his ego and made him out as a genius? What did I do? What *didn't* I do? Why didn't I know better? If he was at the meeting, if he was sitting right there in front of me, why didn't I see him?"

"Guess your super X-ray vision that allows you to see what evil lurks in the hearts of men is on the fritz."

"Along with your ability to foresee the future."

This time the smile was genuine, if sad. "We're a pair."

"Used to be."

Kate stared at him, seeing the man she'd known and loved, and the man the intervening years had turned him into. He looked tired, haunted. She wondered if he saw the same in her. It was humbling to admit that he ought to. She'd fooled herself into believing she was fine. But that was all it had been: an act, a ruse. She had fully realized that truth an hour ago as she stood in the warm shelter of his arms. It had been like suddenly having back a crucial part of herself she had spent years refusing to acknowledge was missing.

"I loved you, Kate," he said softly, his dark gaze holding hers. "Whatever else you think of me, and of the way things came apart, I loved you. You can doubt everything else about me. God knows, I do. But don't doubt that."

Something fluttered inside Kate. She refused to name it. It couldn't be hope. She didn't want to hope for anything with regard to John

Quinn. She preferred annoyance, indignation, a dash of anger. But none of that was what she really felt, and she knew it, and he would know it as well. He'd always been able to read the slightest shadow that crossed her mind.

"Damn you, John," she muttered.

Whatever else she might have said was lost as Kovac's face appeared suddenly at Quinn's window. Kate started and swore, then lowered the window from the control panel on the driver's door.

"Hey, kids, no making out," he quipped. "It's after curfew."

"We're trying to save ourselves from hypothermia," Quinn said. "I have a toaster that gives off more warmth than this heater."

"Did you find the DL?" Kate asked.

"No, but we found this." He held up a microcassette tape inside a clear plastic case. "It was on the ground about fifteen feet from the car. It's a pure damn miracle one of the firemen didn't squash it.

"It's probably some reporter's notes from the meeting," he said. "But you never know. Every once in a blue moon we find evidence there is a God. I've got a player somewhere on the seat there."

"Yeah, that and the Holy Grail," Kate muttered as she dug through the junk on the seat: reports, magazines, burger wrappers. "Are you living in this car, Sam? There are shelters for people like you, you know."

She came up with the player and handed it

to Quinn. He popped the cassette out and carefully inserted the one Kovac handed him on the end of a ballpoint pen.

What came from the tiny speaker ran through Kate like a spike. A woman's screams, thick with desperation, interspersed with breathless, broken pleas for mercy that would never be delivered. The cries of someone enduring torture and begging for death.

Not proof there was a God, Kate thought. Proof there wasn't.

23

CHAPTER

ELATION. ECSTASY. AROUSAL. These are the things he feels in his triumph, stirred into the darker emotions of anger and hatred and frustration that burn constantly inside him.

Manipulation. Domination. Control. His power extends beyond his victims, he reminds himself. He exercises the same forces over the police and over Quinn.

Elation. Ecstasy. Arousal.

Never mind the rest. Focus on the win.

The intensity is overwhelming. He is shaking, sweating, flushed with excitement as he drives toward the house. He can smell himself. The odor is peculiar to this kind of excitement—strong, musky, almost sexual. He wants to wipe his armpits with his hands and rub the sweat and the scent all over his face, into his nostrils, lick it from his fingers.

He wants to strip and have the woman in his fantasies lick it all from his body. From his chest and his belly and his back. In his fantasy she ends up on her knees before him, licking his balls. His erection is huge and straining and he shoves it into her mouth and fucks her mouth, slapping her every time she gags on him. He comes in her face, then forces her down on her hands and knees and penetrates her anally. His hands around her throat, he rapes her viciously, choking her between screams.

The images excite him, arouse him. His penis is stiff and throbbing. He needs release. He needs to hear the sounds that are as sharp and beautiful as finely honed blades. He needs to hear the screams, that raw, pure quality of sound that is terror, and to pretend the screams come from the woman in his mind. He needs to hear the building crescendo as a life reaches its limit. The fading energy absorbed greedily by death.

He digs a hand into his coat pocket for the tape and finds nothing.

A wave of panic sweeps over him. He pulls to the curb and searches all pockets, checks the seat beside him, checks the floor, checks the cassette player. The tape is gone.

Anger burns through him. Huge and violent.

A wall of rage. Cursing, he slams the car into gear and pulls back onto the street. He's made a mistake. Unacceptable. He knows it won't be fatal. Even if the police find the tape, even if they are able to lift a fingerprint from it, they won't find him. His prints are in no criminal database. He hasn't been arrested since his juvenile days. But the very *idea* of a mistake infuriates him because he knows it will give the task force and John Quinn encouragement, when he wants only to crush them.

His triumph is now diminished. His celebration ruined. His erection has gone soft, his cock shriveling to a pathetic nub. In the back of his mind he can hear the sneering voice, the disdain as the fantasy woman gets up and walks away from him, bored and disinterested.

He pulls into the driveway, hitting the remote control for the garage door. The anger is a snake writhing inside him, oozing poison. The sound of toy-dog barking follows him into the garage. That goddamn mutt from next door. His night ruined, now this.

He gets out of the car and goes to the trash bin. The garage door is descending. The bichon makes eye contact with him, yapping incessantly, bouncing backward toward the lowering door. He pulls a dropcloth out of the garbage and turns toward the dog, already imagining scooping the dog up, then swinging the makeshift bag hard against the concrete wall again and again and again.

"Come on, Bitsy, you rotten little shit,"

he murmurs in a sweet tone. "Why don't you like me? What have I ever done to you?"

The dog growls, a sound as ferocious as an electric pencil sharpener, and holds her ground, glancing back toward the door now less than a foot from sealing her fate.

"Do you know I've killed little rat dogs like you before?" he asks, smiling, stepping closer, bending down. "Do you think I smell like evil?"

He reaches a hand toward the dog. "That's because I am," he murmurs as the dog lunges toward him, teeth bared.

The grinding of the garage door mechanism stops.

The dropcloth falls, muffling the yip of surprise.

24

CHAPTER

KATE WAS STILL SHAKING when they reached her house. Quinn had insisted on seeing her home for the second time that night, and she hadn't argued. The memory of the screams echoed in her head. She heard them, faint but constant, as she slipped wordlessly from the truck

416

and left the garage, as she fumbled with the keys for the back door, as she passed through the kitchen to the hall and turned the thermostat up.

Quinn was behind her like a shadow the whole time. She expected him to say something about the burnt-out light in the garage, but if he did, she didn't hear him. She could hear only the whoosh of her pulse in her ears, the magnified rattle of keys, Thor meowing, the refrigerator humming...and beneath all that, the screams.

"I'm so cold," she said, going into the study, where the desk lamp still burned and a chenille throw lay in a heap on the old sofa. She glanced at the answering machine—no blinking light—and thought of the hang-up calls that had come to her cell phone at 10:05, 10:08, 10:10.

A half-empty glass of Sapphire and tonic sat on the blotter, the ice long melted. Kate picked it up with a shaking hand and took a swallow. The tonic had gone flat, but she didn't notice, didn't taste anything at all. Quinn took the glass from her hand and set it aside, then turned her gently by the shoulders to face him.

"Aren't you cold?" she prattled on. "It takes forever for the furnace to heat this place. I should probably have it replaced—it's old as Moses—but I never think of it until the weather turns.

"Maybe I should start a fire," she suggested, and immediately felt the blood drain from her face. "Oh, God, I can't believe I said that. All I can smell is smoke and that horrible—Jesus, what an awful—"

She swallowed hard and looked at the glass that was now out of easy reach.

Quinn laid a hand against her cheek and turned her face toward him. "Hush," he said softly.

"But—"

"Hush."

As carefully as if she were made of spun glass, he folded his arms around her and drew her close against him. Another invitation to lean on him, to let go. She knew she shouldn't. If she let go for even a second now, she would be lost. She needed to keep moving, keep talking, *do something*. If she let go, if she went still, if she didn't occupy herself with some mindless, meaningless task, the tide of despair would sweep over her, and then where would she be?

Without defense in the arms of a man she still loved but couldn't have.

The full import of that answer was heavy enough to strain what little strength she had left, ironically tempting her further to take the support Quinn offered for now.

She had never stopped loving him. She had just put it away in a lockbox in her secret heart, never to be taken out again. Maybe hoping it would wither and die, but it had only gone dormant.

Another chill washed over her, and she let her head find the hollow of his shoulder. With her ear pressed against his chest, she could hear his heart beat, and she remembered all the other times, long ago, when he had held her and comforted her, and she had pretended what they had in a stolen moment might last forever.

God, she wanted to pretend that now. She wanted to pretend they hadn't just come from a crime scene, and her witness wasn't missing, and that Quinn had come here for her instead of the job he had always put first.

How unfair that she felt so safe with him, that contentment seemed so close, that looking at her life from the vantage point of his arms, she could suddenly see all the holes, the missing pieces, the faded colors, the dulled senses. How unfair to realize all that, when she had decided it was better not to need anyone, and certainly best not to need him.

She felt his lips brush her temple, her cheek. Against the weaker part of her will, she turned her face up and let his lips find hers. Warm, firm, a perfect match, a perfect fit. The feeling that flooded her was equal parts pain and pleasure, bitter and sweet. The kiss was tender, careful, gentle—asking, not taking. And when Quinn raised his head an inch, the question and the caution were in his eyes, as if her every want and misgiving had passed to him through the kiss.

"I need to sit down," Kate murmured, stepping back. His arms fell away from her and the chill swept back around her like an invisible stole. She grabbed the glass off the desk as she went to the couch and wedged herself into a corner, pulling the chenille throw into her lap.

"I can't do this," she said softly, more to herself than to him. "It's too hard. It's too cruel. I don't want that kind of mess to clean up when you go back to Quantico." She sipped at the gin and shook her head. "I wish you hadn't come, John."

Quinn sat down beside her, forearms on his thighs. "Is that what you really wish, Kate?"

Tears clung to her lashes. "No. But what does it matter now? What I wish has never had any bearing on reality."

She finished the drink, set the glass aside, and rubbed her hands over her face.

"I wished Emily would live, and she didn't. I wished Steven wouldn't blame me, but he did. I wished—"

She held short on that. What was she supposed to say? That she'd wished Quinn had loved her more? That they had married and had children and lived in Montana, raising horses and making love every night? Fantasies that should have belonged to someone more naive. Christ, she felt like a fool for even having such thoughts and stowing them away in a dusty corner of her mind. She sure as hell wasn't going to share them and risk looking more pathetic.

"I've wished a lot of things. And wishing never made them so," she said. "And now I'll wish to close my eyes and not see blood, to close my ears and not hear screams, to close out this nightmare and go to sleep. And I might as well wish for the moon."

Quinn laid a hand on her shoulder, his thumb finding the knot of tension in the muscle and rubbing at it. "I'd give you the moon, Kate," he said. An old, familiar line they had passed back and forth between them like a secret keepsake. "And unhook the stars and take them down, and give them to you for a necklace."

Emotions stung her eyes, burning away the last of her resolve to hold strong. She was too tired and it hurt too much—all of it: the case, the memories, the dreams that had died. She buried her face in her hands.

Quinn put his arms around her, guided her head to his shoulder once more.

"It's all right," he whispered.

"No, it isn't."

"Let me hold you, Kate."

She couldn't bring herself to say no. She couldn't bear the idea of pulling away, of being alone. She'd been alone too long. She wanted his comfort. She wanted his strength, the warmth of his body. Being in his arms, she felt a sense of being where she belonged for the first time in a long time.

"I never stopped loving you," he whispered.

Kate tightened her arms around him, but didn't trust herself to look at him.

"Then why did you let me go?" she asked, the pain just beneath the surface of her voice. "And why did you stay away?"

"I thought it was what you wanted, what you needed. I thought it was best for you. You didn't exactly beg for my attention at the end."

"You were tied up with the OPR because of me—"

"Because of Steven, not because of you."

"Semantics. Steven wanted to punish you because of me, because of *us*."

"And you wanted to hide because of us."

She didn't try to deny it. What they'd had in their secret love had been so special: the kind of magic most people wished for and never found, the kind of magic neither of them had ever known before. But when the secrecy had finally been broken, no one had seen that magic. Under the harsh light of public scrutiny, their love had become an affair, something tawdry and cheap. No one had understood; no one had tried; no one had wanted to. No one had seen her pain, her need. She wasn't a woman drowning in grief, shut out by a husband who had turned distant and bitter. She was a slut who had cheated on her grieving husband while their daughter was barely cold in the ground.

She couldn't say her own sense of guilt hadn't reflected back some of those same feelings, even though she knew better. It had never been in her to lie, to cheat. She'd been raised on a combination of Catholic guilt and Swedish self-reproof. And the wave of self-condemnation from Emily's death and her own sense of breached morality had come up over her head, and she hadn't been able to surface—especially not when the one person she would have reached to for help had backed away, wrestling with anger and pain of his own.

The memory of that turmoil pushed her now to her feet again, restless, not liking the emotions that came with the memories.

"You might have come after me," she said. "But between the OPR and the job, suddenly you were never there.

"I thought you loved the job more than me," she admitted in a whisper, then offered Quinn a twisted half-smile. "I thought maybe you finally figured out I was more trouble than I was worth."

"Oh, Kate..." He stepped close, tipped her head back, and looked in her eyes. His were as dark as the night, shining and intense.

Hers brimmed with the uncertainty that had always touched him most deeply—the uncertainty that lay buried beneath layers of polish and stubborn strength. An uncertainty he recognized perhaps as being akin to his own, the thing he hid and feared in himself.

"I let you go because I thought that was what you wanted. And I buried myself in work because it was the only thing that dulled the hurt.

"I've given everything I ever was to this job," he said. "I don't know if there's anything left of me worth having. But I know I've never loved it—or anything, or anyone—the way I loved you, Kate."

Kate said nothing. Quinn was aware of time slipping by, of a tear sliding down her cheek. He thought of how they'd come apart, and all the time they'd lost, and knew it was more complicated than a simple lack of communication. The feelings, the fears, the pride, and the pain that had wedged between them had all been genuine. So sharp and true that neither of them had ever found the nerve to face them down. It had been easier to just let go—and that had been the hardest thing he'd ever done in his life.

"We're a pair," he whispered, echoing what she'd said in Kovac's car. "What did you feel, Kate? Did you stop needing me? Did you stop loving me? Did you—"

She pressed trembling fingers to his lips, shaking her head. "Never," she said, so softly the word was little more than a thought. "Never."

She had hated him. She had resented him. She had blamed him and tried to forget him. But she had never stopped loving him. And what a terrifying truth that was—that in five years the need had never died, that she'd never felt anything close to it. Now it rose within her like an awakening flame burning through the exhaustion and the fear and everything else.

She leaned up to meet his lips with hers. She tasted his mouth and the salt of her own tears. His arms went around her and crushed her to him, bending her backward, fitting her body against his.

"Oh, God, Kate, I've needed you," he confessed, his mouth brushing the shell of her ear. "I've missed you so."

Kate kissed his cheek, ran a hand over the short-cropped hair. "I've never needed anyone the way I needed you...need you..."

He caught the distinction, and stood back

to look at her for a moment. He didn't ask if she was sure. Afraid she might answer, Kate supposed. And so was she. There was no certainty in her. There was no logic, no thought of anything beyond the moment, and the tangle of raw feelings, and the need to lose herself with Quinn...only with him.

She led him upstairs by the hand. He stopped her three times to kiss her, touch her, bury his face in her hair. In her bedroom they helped each other undress. Tangled hands, impatient fingers. His shirt on the back of a chair, her skirt in a puddle on the floor. Never losing contact with each other. A caress. A kiss. An anxious embrace.

For Kate, Quinn's touch was a memory overlapping real time. The feel of his hand on her skin was imprinted on her mind and in her heart. It drew to the surface the desire she had known only with him. Instantly, in a warm rush and a sweet ache. As if they'd been apart five days instead of five years.

Her breath caught at the feel of his mouth on her breast, and shuddered from her as his hand slipped between her legs, and his fingers found her wet and hot. Her hips arched automatically to the angle they'd found so many times before, so very long ago.

Her hands traveled over his body. Familiar territory. Ridges and planes of muscle and bone. Smooth, hot skin. The valley of his spine. His erection straining against her, as hard as marble, as soft as velvet. His thick, muscular thigh urging her legs farther apart.

She guided him into her, felt the absolute thrill of him filling her perfectly, the same as she had felt every single time they'd ever made love. The sensation, the wonder of it, had never dulled, only sharpened. For him as well as for her. She could see it in his eyes as he looked down at her in the lamplight: the intense pleasure, the heat, the surprise, the hint of desperation that came from knowing this magic happened only with each other.

The last made her want to cry. He was the one, the only one. The man she'd married, whose child she'd borne, had never come close to making her feel what John Quinn made her feel with his mere presence in the room.

She held him tighter, moved against him stronger, dug her fingernails into his back. He kissed her deeply, possessively, with his tongue, with his teeth. He moved into her with building force, then pulled himself back, gentled, eased them both away from the edge.

Time lost all meaning. There were no seconds, only breaths and murmured words; no minutes, just the ebb and flow of pleasure. And when the end finally came, it was with an explosion of emotion running head-on from each extreme of the spectrum. And then came an odd mix of peace and tension, contentment and completion and wariness, until exhaustion overrode all else, and they fell asleep in each other's arms.

25

CHAPTER

"LISTEN UP!"

Kovac leaned heavily on the end of the table in the Loving Touch of Death war room. He had been home long enough to fall asleep on a kitchen chair while waiting for the coffee to brew. He hadn't showered or shaved, and imagined he looked like a bum in the same limp, wrinkled suit he'd worn the day before. He hadn't had time to even change his shirt.

Everyone on the team was showing similar signs of wear. Dark circles under bloodshot eyes. Deep frown lines etched into pale faces.

The room stank of cigarettes, sweat, and bitter coffee over the original aromas of mice and mildew. A portable radio on the counter tuned to WCCO competed with a ten-inch television tuned to KSTP, both on to catch the latest reports the media had to offer. Photos from the car fire and of victim number four had been hastily pinned to one of the boards, so fresh from the developing trays, they were curling in on themselves.

"The media is going nuts with the stuff from last night," Kovac said. "Smokey Joe lights up a vic practically under our noses, and we look like we've been sitting around picking our toenails. I've already had the chief and Lieutenant Fowler on me like a couple of trick riders this morning. Long story short: If we can't make something happen fast, we'll all be on jail duty doing body cavity searches."

"That'd be the closest thing to sex Tip's had in years," Adler said.

Tippen fired a paper clip at him from a rubber-band slingshot. "Very funny. Let me start with you, Chunk. Mind if I use a crowbar?"

Kovac ignored them. "We managed to keep word of that cassette tape away from them."

"Thank God none of them found it," Walsh said, contemplating the state of his handkerchief. "They'd be playing it on every station in town."

Kovac hadn't been able to get the sound of those screams out of his head. The idea of that tape playing into every house in the Twin Cities was enough to make his stomach roll.

"The tape is at the BCA lab," he said. "Some techno-geek is going over it, trying to pick up background noise and the like. We'll see what he has to say later. Tinks, did you find Vanlees?"

Liska shook her head. "No go. It seems the only close friend he's got is whoever he's house-sitting for. And he sure won't be making any new ones soon. Mary and I managed to piss off everyone he knows, calling up in the middle of the night. One guy said Vanlees was bragging on this house though. He thought it sounded like it might be Uptown or thereabouts. Near a lake."

"I've got a car sitting on his Lyndale apartment," Kovac said. "Another one at the Target Center, and one at the Edgewater town houses. And every cop in town is looking for his truck."

"We've got no probable cause to arrest him," Yurek pointed out.

"You won't need it," Quinn said, walking into the middle of the conversation. Flecks of snow melted in his hair. He shrugged out of his trench coat and tossed it on the counter. "It's not an arrest. We're asking for his assistance. If this guy is Smokey Joe, then he's feeling cocky and smug. He made us look like idiots last night. The idea of the cops asking him for help will have enormous appeal to his ego."

"We don't want to lose the guy on a technicality, that's all," Yurek pointed out.

"The first person to screw up that way, I will personally shoot in the kneecaps," Kovac promised.

"So, G," Tippen said, eyes narrowed. "You think this guy is it?"

"He fits the picture pretty well. We'll get him in here and have a chat, then I'd recommend a bumper-lock surveillance. Make him sweat, see what we can get him to do. If we can rattle him, get him to spook, doors will open. If things fall right, we'll end up with cause for a search warrant."

"I'll head over to the Edgewater," Liska said. "I'd like to be on hand, try to put him at ease, get his guard down."

"How did he seem at the meeting last night?" Quinn asked.

"Fascinated, a little excited, full of theories."

"Do we know where he was Sunday night?"

"The ever-popular home alone."

"I want to be there when you get him in the box," Quinn said. "Not in the room, but watching."

"You don't want to question him?"

"Not right off the bat. We'll have you in there, and someone he's never seen before. Probably Sam. I'll come in later."

"Beep me as soon as you've got him," Kovac said as a phone rang in the background. Elwood got up to answer it. "Tip, Charm, did you find anybody who saw the DiMarco girl get in a truck Sunday night?"

"No," Tippen said. "And the going rate for that answer is ten bucks. Unless you're Charm. In which case, you can get that answer and a blow job for a smile."

Yurek gave him a dirty look. "Like it's some kind of treat to get the clap for free."

"It is for Tip," Liska pointed out.

"Charm! Telephone!" Elwood called.

"Stay on it," Kovac ordered. "Get some fliers printed off with the girl's picture and a picture of a GMC Jimmy. Ask Lieutenant Fowler about a reward. Chances are someone just hanging out in that area at that time of night will be willing to turn in his mother for a couple hundred bucks."

"Will do."

"Someone diplomatic has to go to the

Phoenix and talk again to this hooker that knew the second vic," Kovac went on.

"I'll do it," Moss offered.

"Ask her if Fawn Pierce had a tattoo," Quinn said, forcing himself to sit ahead. He rubbed at a knot in the back of his neck. "Lila White had a tattoo exactly where that chunk of flesh was missing from her chest. Smokey Joe may be an art lover. Or an artist."

"Where'd you get that?" Tippen asked, skeptical, as if maybe Quinn had just pulled it down out of the sky.

"I did something no one else bothered to do: I looked," he said bluntly. "I looked at the photographs Lila White's parents gave Agent Moss. They were taken days before her death. If it turns out Fawn Pierce had a tattoo removed by the killer, you'll need to find where both women got them done and check out the parlors and everyone associated with them."

"Do we know if Jillian Bondurant had any tattoos?" Hamill asked.

"Her father says none he knew of."

"Her friend, Michele Fine, claims not to know of any either," Liska said. "And I think she'd know. She's a walking scratch pad herself."

"Did she ever come in to get printed?" Kovac asked, digging through a messy stack of notes.

"I haven't had time to check."

A cell phone rang, and Quinn swore and got up from the table, digging in the pocket of his suit coat.

Adler pointed at the television, where scenes from the car fire filled the screen. "Hey, there's Kojak!"

The sun guns washed Kovac's skin out to the color of parchment. He frowned heavily at the cameras and shut down the questions with a stiff rendition of "The investigation is sensitive and ongoing. We have no comment at this time."

"You need to lose that mustache, Sam," Liska said. "You look like Mr. Peabody from Rocky and Bullwinkle."

"Any mutilation on the latest vic?" Tippen called from the coffeepot.

"Autopsy's scheduled for eight," Kovac said, checking his watch. Seven-forty. He turned to Moss. "Rob Marshall from legal services will meet you at the Phoenix. That's the brass making public nice-nice with the Urskines after the Bitch Queen of the North kicked up that stink last night.

"Personally, don't care how offended they are. I want someone to have a heart-to-heart with Vampira's mate at the station later today. Mary, ask him to come in, and be vague when they demand to know why. Routine procedure, like that. And ask if they have a credit card receipt or canceled check from the cabin they were in the weekend Lila White was killed.

"Gregg Urskine was one of the last people to see our witness last night. The first vic was a guest of theirs. The second was a friend of one of their current hookers. That's too many close calls for me," Kovac declared.

432

"Toni Urskine will be on the phone to every news outlet in the metro," Yurek cautioned.

"If we're polite, that only makes her look bad," Kovac said. "We're being thorough, leaving no stone unturned. That's what Toni Urskine wanted."

"Did we get anything from the meeting last night?" Hamill asked.

"Nothing of use to us from the cars," Elwood said. "Just the videotape."

Kovac checked his watch again. "I'll look at it later. Doc'll be sharpening her knives. You with me, GQ?"

Quinn held up a hand in acknowledgment and signed off on his call. They grabbed their coats and went out the back way.

The snow had covered the filth of the alley—including Kovac's car—camouflaging tire hazards like broken Thunderbird and Colt 45 malt liquor bottles, which covered the ground in these downtown alleys like dead leaves. Kovac pulled a brush out from under a pile of junk in the backseat and swept off the windshields, the hood, and the taillights.

"You got back to your hotel all right last night?" he asked as they slid into their seats and he turned the engine over. "'Cause I sure could've taken you. It's not that much out of my way."

"No. I was fine. It was fine," Quinn said, not looking at him. He could feel Kovac's gaze on him. "Kate was so upset over that tape, I wanted to make sure she was all right."

"Uh-huh. Was she? All right?"

"No. She thinks that body was her witness, that those screams were the screams of her witness being tortured. She blames herself."

"Well, it's probably a good thing you saw her home, then. What'd you do? Catch a cab downtown?"

"Yeah," he lied, the morning scene playing through his mind.

Waking up and looking at Kate across the pillow in the faint light, touching her, watching those incredible clear gray eyes open, seeing the uncertainty there. He would rather have been able to say making love had solved all their problems, but that wasn't true. It had given them some solace, reconnected their souls, and complicated everything. But, God, it had been like returning to heaven after years in purgatory.

Now what? The unspoken question had hung between them awkwardly as they'd cleaned up, gotten dressed, grabbed bagels, and hustled out the door. There had been no morning afterglow touching, kissing, lingering passion. There had been no time to talk, not that he could have gotten Kate to. Her first tendency when feeling cornered was to retreat within herself, shut the door, and stew. God knew he wasn't much better.

She'd dropped him off at the Radisson. He'd shaved too hastily, thrown on a fresh suit, and run out the door, late.

"I tried to call you this morning," Kovac said, putting the car in reverse but keeping his foot on the brake. "You didn't answer."

"Must have been in the shower." Quinn stayed poker-faced. "Did you leave a message? I didn't take time to check."

"Just wanted to see how Kate was doing."

"Then why didn't you call her?" Quinn asked, his temper tightening. He looked at Kovac and turned the conversation around on a dime. "You know, if you'd shown this much interest in the White murder back when, we may not be here right now."

Kovac flushed. More with guilt than anger, Quinn thought, though the cop played the latter. "I did that case by the numbers."

"You took the express lane, Sam. How else do you explain missing that tattoo?"

"We asked. I'm sure we did. We must have," Kovac said, certain, then less so, then not at all. He craned his neck and looked out the back window as he let his foot off the brake. "Maybe we didn't ask the right person. Maybe no one had noticed the goddamn thing."

"Her parents are a couple of square pegs from a farming town. You think they wouldn't have noticed their daughter had a calla lily tattooed on her chest? You think none of her regular johns noticed it?"

Kovac gunned the engine, rocked the car out of its spot too fast, then hit the brakes too hard. The Caprice slid on the slick wet snow and the back bumper met the corner of a trash Dumpster with a nasty thud.

"Shit!"

Quinn winced, then relaxed, his attention still on Kovac. "You never checked the

Urskines' alibi when Lila White was killed."

"I didn't make them produce the receipt. What motive did they have to kill the woman? None. Besides, Toni Urskine was kicking up such a stink that we weren't trying hard enough..."

"I read the reports," Quinn said. "You worked the case hard for a week, then less and less and less. Same thing with Fawn Pierce."

Kovac cracked the window open, lit a cigarette, and blew the first lungful outside. The Caprice still sat cockeyed, ass up against the Dumpster. Liska came out of the building and pointed at him, shaking her head, then climbed into her car.

"You've seen enough of these cases to know how it works," he said. "A hooker buys it, the department is about as concerned as if someone had run over a stray dog. Tag 'em, bag 'em, give 'em the no-frills investigation. If the case isn't solved fast, it gets pushed to the back burner to make way for the taxpaying citizens getting murdered by jealous husbands and crack-crazed carjackers.

"I did what I could while I could," he said, staring out the windshield at the falling snow.

"I believe you, Sam." Though Quinn thought Kovac did not entirely believe himself. The regret was etched in the lines of his weathered face. "It's just too bad for those other three victims that it wasn't enough."

•   •   •

"**HOW LONG HAD** you known Fawn Pierce?" Mary Moss asked.

In the den of the Phoenix House, she sat down at one end of a pea-green couch, silently inviting Rita Renner to take the other end, creating a certain sense of intimacy. A spring poked her in the butt.

"About two years," Renner said, so softly Mary reached out to the small tape recorder on the coffee table and pushed it closer. "We met downtown and we just got to be friends."

"You worked the same territory?"

She glanced up at Toni Urskine, who sat on the arm of the couch, a hand resting reassuringly on Renner's shoulder. Then she looked to Rob Marshall, who hovered on the other side of the coffee table, looking impatient to be somewhere else. His left leg was jiggling like an idling motor.

"Yeah," she said. "We worked around the strip clubs and the Target Center."

Her voice sounded as if it were coming from another dimension. So quiet and mousy, dressed in old jeans and a flannel shirt, she hardly looked the picture of a woman strutting her stuff for the horny sleazeballs that trolled the seedier streets of Minneapolis, looking to pay for sex. But then, this was the "reformed" Rita Renner, not the woman who had been arrested for possession and found to keep her crack pipe in her vagina. What a difference sobriety had made.

"Did she have any enemies? Did you ever see anybody hassle her on the street?"

Renner looked confused. "Every night. That's the way men are," she said, glancing under her lashes at Rob. "She got raped once, you know. People don't think you can rape a hooker, but you can. The cops caught the guy and he went away, but not for raping Fawn. He did some woman accountant in a parking ramp downtown. That's what he went away for. They didn't even want Fawn to testify. Like it didn't matter what he done to her."

"Testimony about other possible crimes committed by a defendant isn't admissible in court, Ms. Renner," Rob said. "That seems unfair, doesn't it?"

"It sucks."

"Someone should have explained that to Ms. Pierce. Do you know if she ever met with anyone from victim/witness services?"

"Yeah. She said it was a bunch of shit. She was supposed to go back a few times, but she never did. All they wanted to do was rehash it all."

"Restating the events is crucial to the healing process," Rob stated. He smiled in a way that seemed awkward and made his little pig eyes disappear. "I highly recommend it to all my clients. In fact, I recommend they tape record themselves talking about their experience over a period of time, so they can actually hear the changes in their emotions and attitudes as they heal. It can be very cathartic."

Renner just stared at him, her head a little to one side, like a small bird contemplating something new and strange.

Mary stifled a sigh of impatience. Having someone not in law enforcement "helping" with an interview was about as helpful as an extra pinkie finger. "Do you know of anyone in particular who might have wanted to hurt Fawn?"

"She said some guy had been calling her. Bugging her."

"When was this?"

"Couple days before she died."

"Did this guy have a name?"

"I don't remember. I was pretty strung out at the time. One of her johns, I guess. Can't you check the phone records?"

"It would work only if *she* called *him*."

Renner frowned. "It's not in a computer somewhere?"

"If you knew the guy's name, we could check *his* phone records."

"I don't know." Tears came to her eyes and she looked up at Toni Urskine, who patted her shoulder again. "Fawn called him the Toad. I remember that."

"Unfortunately, I don't think that'll be the name he uses with the phone company," Rob Marshall said.

Toni Urskine gave him a pointed look. "There's no need to get snide. Rita is doing the best she can."

Rob scrambled to recover. "Of course she is. I didn't mean to imply otherwise," he said with a nervous smile, which he turned to Rita Renner. "Can you recall any conversation you had with Fawn about this...Toad? If you could replay a conversation in your mind, it might come to you."

"I don't know!" Renner whined, twisting one shirttail around her hand. "I was on the rock then. And—and—why would I remember anyway? It wasn't like she was scared of him or anything."

"That's okay, Rita. It might come to you later," Moss said. "Can you tell me if Fawn had any tattoos?"

Renner looked at her, confused again by the sudden change of direction. "Sure, a couple. Why?"

"Can you tell me where they were on her body?"

"She had a rose on her ankle, and a shamrock on her stomach, and a pair of lips with a tongue sticking out on her butt. Why?"

Moss was saved from finding the noncommittal lie, as Gregg Urskine chose that moment to enter the room with a coffee tray. Picking up her tape recorder from the table, she rose and smiled apologetically.

"I'm afraid I can't stay. Thank you for the thought."

"You don't want to warm up before you go back out into the cold, Detective?" Urskine asked, looking pleasant and vacuous.

"No time, but thanks."

"I suppose there's extra pressure today," Toni Urskine said with a hint of malicious pleasure. "With everything that happened last night, the task force is looking exceptionally inept."

"We're doing everything we can," Moss

said. "In fact, Sergeant Kovac asked me to have you stop by the station later today, Mr. Urskine, with a copy of your receipt for the inn you were staying at the weekend Lila White was murdered."

Toni Urskine shot off the couch, her face flaming. "What! That's outrageous!"

"It's a formality," Moss assured. "We're just crossing all our T's and dotting all our I's."

"It's harassment, that's what."

"A simple request. Of course, you're under no obligation to comply at this time. Sergeant Kovac didn't see the need for a warrant, considering how strongly you both feel about the thoroughness of the investigation."

Gregg Urskine gave a nervous laugh, his attention on Toni. "It's okay, honey. I'm sure I can find the receipt. It's not a problem."

"It's an outrage!" Toni snapped. "I'm calling our attorney. We've been nothing but conscientious citizens in all of this, and *this* is how we're treated! You can leave now, Ms. Moss. Mr. Marshall," she added, including Rob as an afterthought.

"I think what we have here is a simple communication problem," Rob said with the nervous grin. "If my office can in any way facilitate—"

"Get out."

Gregg Urskine reached out. "Now, Toni—"

"Get out!" she shrieked, batting his hand away without even looking.

"We're only trying to do the best job for the victims, Mrs. Urskine," Moss said quietly. "I thought that was what you wanted. Or is that only when the cameras are rolling?"

"HAVE YOU HAD a chance to talk to your friend in Milwaukee?" Kate asked. "You faxed her the picture, right?"

"Yes, on the second. No, on the first," Susan Frye answered.

Kate thanked God she had chosen to call rather than walk to the woman's office. Her frustration and impatience would have shown, she knew. Stress had shredded the veneer of manners, leaving all the emotional nerve endings exposed and raw. At this point, she thought, one wrong answer might drive her over the edge, and she'd wind up like the guy with the gun in the atrium.

"She's been tied up with a trial," Frye said. "I'll call and leave her a message."

"Today." Kate realized too late the word had come out as an order rather than as a question. "Please, Susan? I'm in a world of hurt with this kid. I don't know what Rob was thinking. He should have assigned her to someone on your side of the fence. I don't do kids. I don't know how. And now she's gone—"

"I heard she might be dead," Frye said bluntly. "Don't they think she's the victim from last night?"

"We haven't heard for certain." Kate mouthed the word *bitch* after. Some friend, swinging for the low blow. "Even if it's true, we have to know who the kid is—was—so we can try to contact her family."

"I'll guarantee you right now, Kate: You won't find any who could give a damn or she never would have ended up in this mess. Poor kid would have been better off aborted in the first trimester."

The callousness of that statement struck Kate hard as she thanked Susan Frye for her dubious assistance and hung up the phone. It made her wonder what exactly had brought Angie DiMarco into the world—chance? fate? love? the desire for a check from Aid to Families with Dependent Children? Had her life gone wrong from conception, or had the mistakes come later, like tarnish slowly growing on silver that had been minted shiny and bright?

Her gaze went to the little picture of Emily in the pocket of her overhead cupboard. A beautiful small life, luminous with the promise of the future. She wondered if Angie had ever looked that innocent, or if her eyes had always held the weary bitterness of a bleak existence.

"Poor kid would have been better off aborted in the first trimester."

But Angie DiMarco was living out her sad life, while Emily's had been taken.

Kate bolted out of her chair and began to pace the tiny space that was her office. If she didn't lose her mind by the end of the day, it was going to be a miracle.

She had fully expected a command to Sabin's office first thing, or, at the very least, an order to Rob's office for a formal dressing-down for the things she'd said in the parking lot the previous night. No such call had come...yet. And so she had tried to fend off thoughts of Angie being dead by taking proactive measures to find out about the girl's life. But every time she so much as slowed down her thought process, she heard the screams from the tape.

And every time she tried to think of something else entirely, she thought of Quinn.

Not wanting Quinn in her mind, she sat down again, grabbed the telephone receiver, and dialed another number. She had other clients to think of. At least she did until Rob fired her.

She called David Willis and got a very long, overly detailed explanation of how to leave a message on his machine. She tried her rape victim at home with similar results, then tried her at work and was told by the manager of the adult bookstore that Melanie Hessler had been fired.

"As of when?" Kate demanded.

"As of today. She's had too many absences."

"She's suffering from post-traumatic stress," Kate pointed out. "Because of a crime committed against her on *your* property, I might add."

"That wasn't *our* fault."

"Post-traumatic stress has been ruled a disability by the courts, and therefore falls under the Americans with Disabilities Act." She sank her teeth into the sense of injustice, almost glad for the chance to tear into someone. "If you discriminate against Melanie on the basis of this disability, she can sue you out of existence."

"Listen, lady," the manager said, "maybe

you ought to talk to Melanie about this before you go around threatening people, 'cause I don't think she's all that bent out of shape about it. I haven't heard boo from her all week."

"I thought you said you fired her."

"I did. I left it on her machine."

"You *fired* her on her answering machine? What kind of rotten coward are you?"

"The kind that's hanging up on you, bitch," he said, slamming down the receiver.

Kate hung up absently, trying to think when she had last spoken to Melanie Hessler. A week ago at most, she thought. BC—before the Cremator case. There hadn't been time to call her since. Angie had taken up all her time. It seemed too long now that she thought of it. Melanie's calls had become more frequent as the trial drew closer and her nerves wound tighter and tighter.

"I haven't heard boo from her all week."

Kate supposed she might have gone out of town, but Melanie would have let her know. She checked in as if Kate were her parole officer. This felt wrong. The court, in its infinite wisdom, had seen fit to release Melanie's attackers on bail, but the cops had been good about keeping tabs on them, with the detective in charge of the case staying on top of the situation.

I'm just spooked about everything because of Angie, Kate thought. There was probably no cause for alarm. Still, she followed her instincts, picked up the phone again, and dialed the detective in sex crimes.

He'd heard nothing from their victim either, but knew that one of her perps had been picked up over the weekend for assaulting a former girlfriend. Kate explained what she knew and asked him to drop by Melanie Hessler's house, just to check.

"I'll head over that way after lunch."

"Thanks, Bernie. You're a peach. I'm probably just being paranoid, but..."

"Just because you're paranoid doesn't mean life's not out to get you."

"True. And my luck isn't exactly on high tide here."

"Hang in there, Kate. Things can always get worse."

Cop humor. She couldn't quite appreciate it today.

She tried to turn her attention to a stack of paperwork, but turned away from it and pulled Angie's file instead, hoping she might see something in it that would prompt an idea for some kind of action. Sitting in this office, waiting, was going to make her brain explode.

The file was woefully thin. More questions than answers. Could the girl have left the Phoenix herself? If so, where had the blood come from? She flashed on the scene in the bathroom: the bloody handprint on the tile, the diluted blood trickling down the tub drain, the bloody towels in the hamper. More blood than any reasonable explanation could account for.

But if Smokey Joe had come for her, how had he found her, and how was it Rita Renner had heard nothing—no doors, no struggle, no nothing?

More questions than answers.

The phone rang, and Kate picked it up, half hoping, half dreading to hear Kovac on the other end of the line with news of the autopsy on victim number four.

"Kate Conlan."

The polished voice of a secretary delivered unwelcome news of another variety. "Ms. Conlan? Mr. Sabin would like to see you in his office now."

26

CHAPTER

"SO IS THIS SEARGEANT KOVAC coming or what?"

Liska checked her watch as she walked back into the interview room. It was almost noon and the room was uncomfortably hot. Vanlees had been waiting almost an hour, and he wasn't liking it.

"He's on his way. He should be here any-time now. I called him the minute you said you'd come talk, Gil. He really wants to get your take on things regarding Jillian. But, you know, he's over at that autopsy—the

447

woman that got lit up last night. That's why he's running late. It won't be much longer."

She'd given him that line at least three times, and he was clearly tired of hearing it.

"Yeah, well, you know I want to help, but I got other things to do," he said. He sat across the table from her wearing work clothes—navy pants and shirt. Like a janitor might wear, Liska thought. Or like a cop uniform with no embellishments. "I've got to work this afternoon—"

"Oh, you're squared with that." She waved off his concern. "I called your boss and cleared it. Didn't want you getting into trouble for being a good citizen."

He looked as if he didn't like that idea much either. He shifted on his chair. His gaze went to the mirror on the wall behind Liska. "You know we have one of those at the Target Center, back in the offices. Anybody on the other side?"

Liska blinked innocence. "Why would there be anybody on the other side? It's not like you're under arrest. You're here to help us."

Vanlees stared at the glass.

Liska turned and stared at it too, wondering how she must look to Quinn. Like some worn-out barfly in a smoky lounge, no doubt. If the bags under her eyes got any bigger, she was going to need a luggage cart to carry them. The middle of a serial murder investigation was not the time to want to impress anyone with her fresh good looks.

"So you heard about the fourth victim," she

said, turning back to Vanlees. "That's some balls this guy has, lighting her up in that parking lot, huh?"

"Yeah, like he's trying to send a message or something."

"Arrogant. That's what Quinn says. Smokey Joe's flipping us off."

Vanlees frowned. "Smokey Joe? I thought you called him the Cremator."

"That's what the press calls him. To us, he's Smokey Joe." She leaned across the table to suggest intimacy. "Don't tell anyone I told you that. It's supposed to be just an inside cop thing—you know?"

Vanlees nodded, hip to the ways of the cop world. Cool with the inside secrets. Mr. Professional.

"SHE'S GOOD," Quinn said, watching through the glass. He and Kovac had been standing there twenty minutes, biding their time, watching, waiting, letting Gil Vanlees's nerves work on him.

"Yeah. No one ever suspects Tinker Bell will work them over." Kovac sniffed at the lapel of his suit and made a face. "Jesus, I stink. Eau de autopsy with a hint of smoke. So what do you think of this mutt?"

"He's twitchy. I think we can scare him a little here, then ride his tail from the second he leaves. See what he does. If he spooks hard enough, you might get a search warrant out of it," Quinn said, his eyes never leaving

Vanlees. "He fits in a lot of ways, but he's not the sharpest knife in the drawer, is he?"

"Maybe he just plays it stupid so people expect less of him. I've seen that more than once."

Quinn made a noncommittal sound. As a rule, the type of killer they were looking for went out of his way to show off what brains he had. That vanity was a common downfall. Invariably, they were not as smart as they wanted to believe, and screwed up trying to show off to the cops.

"Let him know you know about the window peeping," Quinn said. "Press on that nerve. He won't like it. He won't want cops thinking he's a pervert. And if he's held to the usual pattern, if he's looked in windows, he's maybe tried fetish burglaries. These guys work their way up. Fish in that pond a little.

"Keep him off balance," he suggested. "Let him think you might do something crazy, that you're fighting with yourself to keep control. The case and the brilliance of this killer are pushing you to the edge. Suggest it, don't admit it. Put all your acting skills to use."

Kovac jerked his tie loose and mussed his hair. "Acting? You'll want to give me the fucking Oscar."

"DO THEY KNOW yet who the vic is?" Vanlees asked.

The *vic*.

"I heard they found her ID during the

autopsy," Liska said. "Kovac wouldn't tell me about it, except to say it made him sick. He said he wants to find this sick son of a bitch and stick something in him."

"It was *in her body*?" Vanlees said with a mix of horror and fascination. "I read about a case like that once."

"You read true crime?"

"Some," he admitted cautiously. "It gives me insights."

Into what? Nikki wondered. "Yeah, me too. So what was the guy's story?"

"His mother was a prostitute, and because of that he hated prostitutes, and so he killed them. And he always stuck something in their—" He caught himself and blushed. "Well, you know..."

Liska didn't blink. "Vagina?"

Vanlees looked away and shifted on his chair again. "It's really hot in here."

He picked up a glass, but it was empty and so was the plastic pitcher on the table.

"What do you suppose the killer gets out of that?" Liska asked, watching him closely. "Sticking things in a woman's vagina. You think it makes him feel tough? Powerful? What?

"Is it disrespect on an adult level?" she posed. "It always strikes me as something a snotty brat little boy would do—if he knew what a vagina was. Like sticking beans up his nose, or wanting to poke the eyes out of a dead cat in the road. It seems juvenile somehow, but on this job I see where grown men do it all the time. What's your take on that, Gil?"

He frowned. A single bead of sweat skimmed down the side of his face. "I don't have one."

"Well, you must, all the studying and true crime reading you've done. Put yourself in the killer's place. Why would you want to stick some foreign object up a woman's vagina? Because you couldn't do the job with your dick? Is that it?"

Vanlees had turned pink. He wouldn't look at her. "Shouldn't Kovac be here by now?"

"Any minute."

"I gotta use the men's room," he mumbled. "Maybe I should go do that."

The door swung open and Kovac walked in—hair mussed, tie jerked loose, rumpled suit hanging on him like a wet sack. He scowled at Liska, then turned it on Vanlees.

"This is him?"

Liska nodded. "Gil Vanlees, Sergeant Kovac."

Vanlees started to offer his hand. Kovac stared at it as if it were covered with shit.

"I got four women hacked up like Halloween pumpkins and burned to a crisp. I'm in no mood to fuck around. Where were you last night between the hours of ten and two A.M.?"

Vanlees looked as if he'd been hit in the face. "What—?"

"Sam," Liska said with annoyance. "Mr. Vanlees came in to give us some insight on—"

"I want his insight on last night between ten and two. Where were you?"

"Home."

"Home where? I understand your wife threw you out for wagging your willy at a friend of hers."

"That was a misunderstanding—"

"Between you and your johnson, or between you and this broad whose windows you were looking in?"

"It wasn't like that."

"It never is. Tell me: How much time did you spend looking in Jillian Bondurant's windows?"

His face was crimson now. "I didn't—"

"Oh, come on. She was kind of a hot little ticket, wasn't she? Curvy. Exotic. Dressed a little provocatively—those filmy little dresses and combat boots and dog collars and shit like that. A guy might want a piece of that—especially if the home fires went out, you know what I'm saying?"

"I don't like what you're saying." Vanlees looked to Liska. "Do I need a lawyer? Should I have a lawyer here?"

"Jesus, Sam," Liska said, disgusted. She turned to Vanlees. "I'm sorry, Gil."

"Don't apologize for me!" Kovac snapped.

Vanlees looked warily from one to the other. "What is this? Good cop–bad cop? I'm not stupid. I don't need to take this shit."

He started to get out of his chair. Kovac lunged toward him, wild-eyed, pointing at him with one hand and slamming the other on the tabletop. "Sit! Please!"

Vanlees dropped back into the chair, his face washing white. Making an obvious show to control himself, Kovac pulled himself back one step and then another, lifting his hands and lowering his head, breathing heavily through his mouth.

"Please," he said more quietly. "Please. Sit. I'm sorry. I'm sorry."

He paced for a minute between the table and the door, watching Vanlees out of the corner of his eye. Vanlees was looking at him the way he might look at a wild gorilla had he found himself accidentally locked in the pen with one at the Como Park Zoo.

"Do I need a lawyer?" he asked Liska again.

"Why would you need a lawyer, Gil? You haven't done anything wrong that I know of. You're not under arrest. But if you think you need one..."

He looked between the two detectives, trying to figure out if this was some kind of trick.

"I'm sorry," Kovac said as he pulled a chair out at the end of the table and sat down. Shaking his head, he fished a cigarette out of his shirt pocket, lit it, and took a long drag.

"I've had about three hours of sleep all week," he said on a breath of smoke. "I've just come from one of the worst autopsies I've seen in years." He shook his head and stared at the table. "What was done to this woman—"

He let the silence drag, smoking his cigarette as if they were all in the break room taking their fifteen minutes away from the desk. Finally, he stubbed it out on the sole of his shoe and dropped the butt in an empty coffee cup. He rubbed his hands over his face and combed his mustache with his thumbs.

"Where is it you're living now, Gil?" he asked.

"On Lyndale—"

"No. I mean this friend you're house-sitting for. Where is that?"

"Over by Lake Harriet."

"We'll need an address. Give it to Nikki here before you go. How long you been doing that—house-sitting?"

"Off and on. The guy travels a lot."

"What's he do?"

"He imports electronics and sells them over the Internet. Computers and stereos, and stuff like that."

"So why don't you just bunk in with him all the time and dump the apartment?"

"He's got a girlfriend. She lives with him."

"She there now?"

"No. She travels with him."

"So, how about you, Gil? You seeing anybody?"

"No."

"No? You been separated for a while. A man has needs."

Liska made a sound of disgust. "Like you think a woman doesn't?"

Kovac gave her a perturbed look. "Tinks, your needs are common knowledge. Would you pretend for a minute you're not liberated and go get us some more water? It's hotter than hell in here."

"I don't mind the heat," she said. "But the way you smell could turn the stomach of a sewer rat. Jeez, Sam."

"Just get the water."

He shrugged out of his suit jacket and let it fall inside out over the back of his chair as Liska left grumbling. Vanlees watched her go, unhappy.

"Sorry about the stink," Kovac said. "You ever wanted to know what a charred dead body smells like, now's your chance. Breathe deep."

Vanlees just looked at him.

"So, you never answered my question, Gil. Do you pay for it? You like hookers? You see a lot of them around where you work. Pay them enough, you can do what you like. Some of them will even let you knock 'em around a little, if you're into that. Tie them down, stuff like that."

"Detective Liska said you wanted to talk to me about Ms. Bondurant," Vanlees said stiffly. "I don't know anything about those other murders."

Kovac paused, rolling up his shirtsleeves and gave him the cop stare. "But you know something about Jillian's murder?"

"No! That's not what I meant."

"What *do* you know about Jillian, Gil?"

"Just how she was around the Edgewater, that's all. My take on her. Like that."

Kovac nodded and sat back. "So how was she? She ever come on to you?"

"No! She mostly kept her head down, didn't talk much."

"She didn't talk to anyone or she didn't talk to you? Maybe she didn't like the way you watched her, Gil," he said, poking once again at the sore spot.

Sweat beaded on Vanlees's forehead. "I didn't watch her."

"Did you flirt with her? Come on to her?"

"No."

"You had a key to her place. You ever go in there when she wasn't around?"

"No!" The denial did not come with eye contact.

Kovac went for another of Quinn's hunches. "Ever dig through her panty drawer, maybe take a souvenir?"

"No!" Vanlees shoved his chair back from the table and got to his feet. "I don't like this. I came in here to help you. You shouldn't treat me like this."

"So help me, Gil," Kovac said with a nonchalant shrug. "Give me something I can use. You ever see a boyfriend hanging around her place?"

"No. Just that friend of hers—Michele. And her father. He came over sometimes. He owns her place, you know."

"Yeah, I suppose. The guy's as rich as Rockefeller. You ever think maybe this deal with Jillian was a kidnapping? Someone wanting to tap in to the father lode, so to speak? You ever see any suspicious characters hanging around, scoping out the place?"

"No."

"And you've been hanging around enough to notice, isn't that right?"

"I work there."

"Not exactly, but what the hay—saying so gives you just cause to be there, check out the various apartments, maybe do a little lingerie shopping."

Purple in the face, Vanlees declared, "I'm leaving now."

"But we've barely started," Kovac protested.

The door swung open again and Liska came in with the water. Quinn held the door and came in behind her. In contrast to Kovac, he looked crisp and fresh except for the dark circles under his eyes and the lines etched deep beside them. His face was a hard, emotionless mask. He took a paper cup from Liska, filled it with water, and drank it down slowly before he said a word. Vanlees's gaze was on him the whole time.

"Mr. Vanlees, John Quinn, FBI," he said, holding out his hand.

Vanlees was quick to accept the gesture. His hand was wide and clammy with stubby fingers. "I've read about you. It's an honor to meet you."

He took his seat again as Quinn went to the chair directly across from him. Quinn slipped his dark suit jacket off and hung it neatly on the back of the chair. He smoothed his gray silk tie as he sat down.

"You know a little about me, do you, Mr. Vanlees?"

"Yeah. Some."

"Then you probably have some idea how my mind works," Quinn said. "You probably know what conclusion I might draw looking at the history of a man who wanted to be a cop but couldn't cut it, a man with a history of window peeping and fetish burglary—"

Vanlees's face dropped. "I'm not—I didn't—"

Liska picked up the Polaroid camera sitting on the table and quickly took his picture.

Vanlees jumped as the flash went off. "Hey!"

"A man whose wife has evicted him and criticizes his sexual abilities," Quinn went on.

"What? She said what?" Vanlees sputtered. His expression now was a mix of torment and embarrassment and disbelief. A man caught awake in a nightmare. He came out of the chair once more to pace. Circles of sweat ringed the armpits of his dark shirt. "I can't believe this!"

"You knew Jillian Bondurant," Quinn went on without emotion. "You were watching her."

He denied it again, shaking his head, his eyes on the floor as he paced. "I didn't. I don't care what that bitch told you."

"What bitch is that?" Quinn asked calmly.

Vanlees stopped and looked at him. "That friend of hers. She said something about me, didn't she?"

"That friend whose name you didn't know?" Liska asked. She stood between Quinn and Kovac, looking tough. "You told me you didn't know her. But you said her name not five minutes ago, Gil. Michele. Michele Fine. Why would you lie to me about knowing her?"

"I didn't. I don't know her. Her name just slipped my mind, that's all."

"And if you'd lie to me about a little thing

like that," Liska said, "I've got to wonder what else you'd lie about."

Vanlees glared at them, red in the face, tears in his eyes, mouth quivering with temper. "Fuck you people. You've got nothing on me. I'm leaving. I came here to help you and you treat me like a common criminal. Fuck you!"

"Don't sell yourself short, Mr. Vanlees," Quinn said. "If you're the man we're looking for, there's nothing common about you."

Vanlees said nothing. No one stopped him from throwing open the door. He stormed out, his steps hurried as he made for the men's room down the hall.

Kovac leaned against the doorjamb, watching. "Touchy guy."

"Almost like he has something to feel guilty about." Liska looked up at Quinn. "What do you think?"

Quinn watched Vanlees bull the men's room door open with his shoulder, already reaching for his fly with his other hand. He adjusted the knot in his tie and stroked a hand down the strip of silk. "I think I'll go freshen up."

The stench in the men's room was hot and fresh. Vanlees was not at the urinals. One pair of thick-soled black work shoes showed beneath the stalls. Quinn went to the sinks, turned on a faucet, filled his cupped hands, and rinsed his face. The toilet flushed and a moment later Vanlees emerged, sweaty and pale. He froze in his tracks at the sight of Quinn.

"Everything all right, Mr. Vanlees?" Quinn

asked without real concern as he dried his hands on a paper towel.

"You're harassing me," he accused.

Quinn raised his brows. "I'm drying my hands."

"You followed me in here."

"Just making sure you're all right, Gil." *My buddy, my pal.* "I know you're upset. I don't blame you. But I want you to realize this isn't personal. I'm not after *you* personally. I'm after a killer. I have to do what I have to do to make that happen. You understand that, don't you? What I'm after is the truth, justice, nothing more, nothing less."

"I didn't hurt Jillian," Vanlees said defensively. "I wouldn't."

Quinn weighed the statements carefully. He never expected a serial killer to admit to anything. Many of them spoke of their crimes in the third person, even after they had been proven guilty beyond any doubt. And many referred to the side of themselves that was capable of committing murder as a separate entity. The evil twin syndrome, he called it. It enabled those with some small scrap of conscience to rationalize, to push the guilt away from themselves and onto their dark side.

The Gil Vanlees standing before him wouldn't kill anyone. But what about his dark side?

"Do you know someone who would hurt Jillian, Gil?" he asked.

Vanlees frowned at his feet. "No."

"Well, in case you think of someone." Quinn held out a business card.

Vanlees took it reluctantly and looked at the front and the back, as if searching for some tiny homing device embedded in the paper.

"We need to stop this killer, Gil," Quinn said, giving him a long, level stare. "He's a bad, bad guy, and I'll do whatever I have to do to put him away. Whoever he is."

"Good," Vanlees murmured. "I hope you do."

He slipped the card into his breast pocket and left the men's room without washing his hands. Quinn frowned and turned back to the sink, staring at himself hard in the mirror, as if he might be able to see some sign in his own visage, some secret sure knowledge that Gil Vanlees was the one.

The pieces were there. If they all fit together right...If the cops could come up with just one piece of evidence...

Kovac came in a moment later and reeled backward at the lingering smell. "Jeez! What'd that guy eat for breakfast—roadkill?"

"Nerves," Quinn said.

"Wait'll he figures out there's a cop on his tail every time he turns around."

"Let's hope he bolts. If you can get in his truck, you might hit pay dirt. Or maybe he's just another pathetic loser who's a couple of clicks to the right of killing anybody. And the real Smokey Joe is sitting home right now, jerking off as he listens to one of his torture tapes."

"Speaking of, the techno-geek at the BCA called," Kovac said. "He thinks we'll want to come listen to that tape from last night now that he's played with it."

"Could he pull out the killer's voice?"

"*Killers,* plural," Kovac said soberly. "He thinks there's two of them. And get this. He thinks one is a woman."

KATE WALKED INTO Sabin's office, thinking it had been just a matter of days since the meeting that had brought her into this case. In some ways it seemed like a year. In that span of days, her life had changed. And it wasn't over yet. Not by a long shot.

Sabin and Rob rose from their chairs. Sabin looking tired and dour. Rob sprang up. His small eyes seemed too bright in his pumpkin head, and he looked as if he had a temperature. The fever of self-righteous indignation.

"So where's the guy with the black hood and the ax?" Kate asked, stopping behind the chair intended for her.

Sabin frowned as if she'd just spoiled his opening line.

Rob looked to him. "See? That's exactly what I'm talking about!"

"Kate, this is hardly the time for cracking jokes," Sabin said.

"Was I joking? I've managed to lose the only witness in the biggest murder investigation the Cities have seen in years. You're not giving me the ax? After last night, I'm surprised Rob isn't holding it himself."

"Don't think I wouldn't like to be," Rob said.

"You're entirely too flip, Kate. I've had it with your attitude toward me. You have no respect."

She turned to Sabin, discounting her boss without saying a word. "But...?"

"But I'm intervening, Kate," Sabin said, taking his seat. "This is a highly charged situation. Tempers are running high all around."

"But she *always* treats me like this!"

"Stop whining, Rob," Sabin ordered. "She's also the best advocate you've got. You know it. You suggested her for this assignment for very specific reasons."

"Need I remind you, we no longer have a witness?"

Sabin glared at him. "No, you don't need to remind me."

"Angie was my responsibility," Kate said. "No one is more sorry about this than I am. If I could do anything— If I could go back to yesterday and do something differently—"

"You delivered the girl to the Phoenix last night yourself. Isn't that right?" Sabin said in his prosecutor's voice.

"Yes."

"And the house was supposedly under surveillance by the police. Isn't that right?"

"Yes."

"Then I blame this nightmare on them. Whatever became of the girl—whether she was taken or left on her own—is their fault, not yours."

Kate glanced at her watch, thinking the autopsy was long over by now. If there had been

464

any definitive proof the body in the car last night was Angie's, Sabin would know.

"I want you to remain available to the case, Kate—"

"Do we know—" she began, her heart rate picking up as she struggled to phrase the question, as if the answer would depend on how she put it. "The victim in the car—have you heard one way or the other?"

Rob gave her a nasty look. "Oh, didn't one of your police buddies call you from the morgue?"

"I'm sure they're a little busy today."

"The victim's driver's license was found during the autopsy." He drew a breath to deliver the news fast and hard, then seemed to think better of it. At that hesitation, Kate felt her nerves tighten. "Maybe you should sit down, Kate," he said, overly solicitous.

"No." Already chills were racing up and down her body, raising goose bumps in the wake. Her fingers tightened on the back of the chair. "Why?"

Rob no longer looked smug or angry. His expression had gone carefully blank. "The victim was Melanie Hessler. Your client."

27

CHAPTER

"I'M SORRY," Rob said.

His voice sounded far away. Kate felt all the blood drain from her head. Her legs gave way beneath her. She went down on one knee, still holding on to the back of the chair, and scrambled to stand again just as quickly. Emotions swirled through her like a cyclone— shock, horror, embarrassment, confusion. Sabin came around from behind his desk to take her arm as Rob stood staring, flatfooted and awkward, four feet away.

"Are you all right?" Sabin asked.

Kate sank down on the chair, for once not minding when he put his hand on her knee. He knelt beside her, looking at her with concern.

"Kate?"

"Um—no," she said. She felt dizzy and weak and ill, and suddenly nothing seemed quite real. "I—ah—I don't understand."

"I'm sorry, Kate," Rob said again, coming forward suddenly, looking as if it had just occurred to him that he should do something now that it was too late. "I know you were very protective of her."

"I just tried to call her," Kate said weakly.

466

"I should have called her Monday, but suddenly there was Angie, and everything just got away from me."

Images of Melanie Hessler played through her mind in a montage. An ordinary, almost shy woman with a slight build and a bad home perm. Working in an adult bookstore embarrassed her, but she needed the job until she could scrape together enough money to go back to school. A divorce had left her with no cash and no skills. The attack she had suffered months ago had left her fragile—damaged emotionally, psychologically, physically. She had become chronically fearful, skittish, waiting for her attackers to come after her again—a common fear among rape victims. Only it wasn't the men who had raped her Melanie had to fear, as it turned out.

"Oh, Jesus," Kate said, putting her head in her hands.

She closed her eyes and saw the body, charred and horrible, disfigured, twisted, shrunken, stinking, violated, mutilated. Kate had held Melanie's hand and comforted her as she had related the awful details of her rape, the deep sense of shame and embarrassment she had felt, the confusion that such a terrible thing should have happened to her.

Melanie Hessler, who had been so frightened of being hurt again. Tortured, brutalized, burned beyond recognition.

And in the back of her mind, Kate could hear the store manager's voice: *I haven't heard boo from her all week.*

When had the son of a bitch taken her? How long had he kept her alive? How long had she begged for death, all the while wondering what kind of God could make her suffer that way?

"Dammit." Kate let the anger well up, trying to draw strength from it. "Goddammit."

Rob's voice came to her again through the maze of her thoughts. "Kate, you know it would help you to talk about what you're feeling now. Let it out. You knew Melanie. You'd helped her through so much. To think of her the way you saw her last night—"

"Why?" she demanded of no one in particular. "Why would he choose her? I don't understand how this happened."

"It probably had to do with her working in that adult bookstore," Rob offered.

Rob knew the case as well as she did. He had sat in on several meetings with Melanie, had gone over the tapes of those meetings with Kate, and suggested a support group for Melanie.

Tapes.

"Oh, God," Kate whispered, her strength draining again in a rush. "That tape. Oh, my God." She doubled over, putting her head in her hands.

"What tape?" Rob asked.

The screams of pain, of fear, of torment and anguish. The screams of a woman she had known, a woman who had trusted her and looked to her for support and protection within the justice system.

"Kate?"

"Excuse me," she mumbled, pushing unsteadily to her feet. "I have to go be sick."

The dizziness tilted her one way and then another, and she grabbed what solid objects she could as she went. The ladies' room seemed a mile away. The faces she encountered en route were blurred and distorted, the voices warped and muted and slurred.

One of her clients was dead. One was missing. She was the only common link between them.

Crouching beside a toilet, holding her hair back with one hand, she lost what little she'd eaten, her stomach trying to reject not only the food, but the images and ideas she had just been force-fed in Ted Sabin's office, and the thoughts that were now seeping like poison through her brain. *Her client, her responsibility. She was the only link...*

When the spasms stopped, she sank down on the floor of the stall, feeling weak and clammy, not caring where she was, not feeling the cold of the floor through her slacks. The tremors that shook her body came not from the cold, but from shock and from a heavy black sense of foreboding that swept over her soul like a storm cloud.

One of her clients was dead. Tortured, murdered, burned. One was missing, a hastily wiped trail of blood left behind.

She was the only common link between them.

She had to be logical, think straight. It was coincidence, certainly. How could it be anything else? Rob was right: Smokey Joe had chosen Melanie because of her connection to the adult bookstore that happened to be in the same part of town frequented by hookers like the first two victims. And Angie had already been connected to the killer when Kate had been assigned the case.

Still that black cloud hovered, pressing down on her. A strange instinctive reaction she couldn't shake.

Too much stress. Too little sleep. Too much bad luck. She leaned her head back against the wall and tried to force her brain to move past the images from the crime scenes last night.

Do something.

The directive that had gotten her through every crisis she'd ever faced. *Don't just sit there. Do something.* Action countered help-lessness, regardless of outcome. She had to move, go, think, *do something.*

The first thing she wanted to do was call Quinn, an instinctive urge she immediately defied. Just because they'd spent a night together didn't mean she could lean on him. There had been no guarantee of a future in those few hours. She didn't know that she even wanted to hope for a future with him. They had too much of a past.

At any rate, this wasn't the time to think about it. Now that she knew Angie hadn't been the victim in the car, there was still some hope the girl was alive. There had to be something she could do to help find her.

She hauled herself up off the floor, flushed the john, and left the stall. A woman in a prissy, snot-green suit stood at one of the sinks, redoing her already perfect makeup, tubes and jars spread out on the counter. Kate gave her a wan smile and moved two sinks down to wash her hands and face.

Making a cup of her hand, she rinsed her mouth out. She looked at herself in the mirror, the makeup woman just in the fringe of her peripheral vision. She looked like hell— bruised up, beat up, dragged down, pale. She looked exactly the way she felt.

"This job will be the death of you, Kate," she muttered to her reflection.

Brandishing a mascara wand, Makeup Woman paused to frown at her.

Kate flashed her a lunatic smile. "Well, I guess they can't start that competency hearing without me," she said brightly, and walked out.

Rob waited for her in the hall, looking embarrassed to be within proximity of a women's toilet. He pulled a handkerchief out of his hip pocket and dabbed at his forehead. Kate scowled at him.

"What?" she demanded. "Now that Sabin's out of earshot, you're going to tell me how Melanie Hessler's death is somehow my fault? If I'd turned her case over to you on Monday, that would have somehow prevented her from falling into the hands of this sick son of a bitch?"

He faked a look of affront. "No! Why would you say such a thing?"

"Because maybe that's what I'm thinking," she admitted, going to the railing overlooking the atrium. "I think nobody can do my job as well as I can. But I didn't do my job, and now Melanie's dead."

"Why would you think you could have prevented what happened?" He stared at her with a mix of bemusement and resentment. "You think you're Wonder Woman or something? You think everything is about you?"

"No. I just know that I should have called her and I neglected to do so. If I had, at least someone would have known and cared she was missing. She didn't have anyone else."

"And so she was your responsibility," he said. "Like Angie."

"The buck has to stop somewhere."

"With you. Kathryn the Great," he said with a hint of bitter sarcasm.

Kate lifted her chin and gave him the imperious glare. "You were quick enough to dump the blame on me last night," she pointed out. "I don't get you, Rob. You tell me I'm just the person you want for this case, then you turn around and whine about the way I work it. You want to blame me for what's gone wrong, but you don't want me to accept that blame.

"What's your problem?" she asked. "Does my taking responsibility somehow screw up your strategy with Sabin? If I'm willing to take the blame, you can't be contrite and obsequious on my behalf. Is that it?"

The muscles of his wide jaw worked and something nasty flashed in his small eyes.

"You'll live to regret the way you treat me, Kate. Maybe not today. Maybe not tomorrow. But one day—"

"You can't fire me today, Rob," she said. "Sabin won't let you. And I'm in no mood to play your little posturing games. If you have a point for being here right now, please get to it. I have a job to do—at least for the next few hours."

His eyes narrowed to slits and he moved his weight from foot to foot. His face grew darker. She'd pushed too hard, crossed a line she might not be able to get back over with a simple apology and a promise to behave, but she wasn't about to back down from him now.

"The police want you to go over Melanie's interview tapes to see if she mentioned something that might be pertinent to this case," he said stiffly. "I thought it would be too much for you, considering," he went on with the affected tone of the wounded martyr. "I was going to offer to help."

"*Was?* Does that mean the offer has been rescinded because you've decided I'm an ungrateful bitch after all?"

He gave her an unpleasant smile, his eyes disappearing behind the lenses of his glasses. "No. I won't let your attitude interfere with my job. We'll listen to the tapes together. You listen for things that seem out of place to you because you knew her. I'll listen objectively from a linguistics angle. Meet me in my office in five minutes."

Kate watched him waddle off, thinking that she hated him almost as much as she was going to hate doing this job.

"Why can't I just stick an ice pick in my forehead?" she muttered to herself, and fell in step after him.

"THIS TAPE IS a copy," the BCA tech explained.

Kovac, Quinn, Liska, and a skinny guy Kovac called Ears—crowded together around a bank of black-faced electronics equipment studded with an amazing array of knobs and levers and lights and gauges.

"The quality of the sound is much better than you'd ever get off a microcassette recorder," Ears said. "In fact, I'd say the killer actually had a mike clipped to the victim, or stationed very close to her. That would account for the distortion in the screams. It would also explain why the other voices are so indistinct."

"You're sure there are two voices?" Quinn asked, the ramifications of that possibility filling his brain.

"Yes. Here, listen."

The tech punched a button and adjusted a knob. A scream filled the small room, all four people tensing against it as if it were a physical assault.

Quinn fought to focus not on the emotions within the scream, but on the individual components of sound, trying to eliminate the human factor and his own human reaction to it. Reliving their crimes was a crucial component of a serial killer's life cycle—fantasy, violent fantasy, facilitators to murder, murder, fantasy, violent fantasy, and on and on, around and around.

Cheap technology made it as easy as the flick of a switch and the focus of a lens for them to play back something more perfect than a memory. Cheap technology combined with the killer's egotistic need had also made for a lot of damning evidence in recent years. The trick for cops and prosecutors was to stomach hearing and seeing it. Bad enough to see the aftermath of crimes like these. Having to watch or listen to them in progress could take a horrible toll.

Quinn had watched or listened to one after another, after another, after another...

Ears turned one knob down and pushed two small levers up. "Coming up here. I've isolated and muted the victim's voice and pulled out the others. Listen close."

No one so much as took a breath. The screams faded into the background and a man's voice, soft and indistinct, said, "...Turn...do it..." followed by white noise, followed by an even less distinct voice that said, "...Want to...of me..."

"That's as good as it gets," Ears said, punching buttons, running the tape back. "I can make it louder, but the voices won't be any more distinguishable. They were too far away from the mike. But by the readings I'm seeing, I'd say the first one is a man and the second one is a woman."

Quinn thought of the stab wounds to each victim's chest, the distinct pattern: long wound, short wound, long wound, short wound...*Cross my heart, hope to die*...A pact, a pledge, a covenant. Two knives—the light flashing off one and then the other as they descended in a macabre rhythm.

Those wounds made sense now. He should have thought of it himself: two knives, two killers. It wasn't as if he hadn't seen it happen before. But he sure as hell didn't want to have to see it again, he realized as resistance rose like panic up through his chest.

Murder didn't get any darker or more twisted than when the killers were a couple. The dynamics of that kind of relationship epitomized the sickest extremes of human behavior. The obsessions and compulsions, the fears and sadistic fantasies of two equally disturbed people tangled like a pair of vipers trying to devour each other.

"Will you play with the tape some more, Ears?" Kovac asked. "See if you can't pull out a few more words from one or both of them? I'd like to know what they're talking about."

The tech shrugged. "I'll try, but I'm not making any promises."

"Do what you can. The career you save could be mine."

"Then you'll owe me *two* cases of beer I'll never see in this lifetime."

"Crack this for me, I'll send you a lifetime supply of Pig's Eye."

Quinn led the way back into the hall, already

trying to sort through the tangle in his head in order to take his attention away from the tight feeling in his throat. Concentrate on the problem at hand, not the problem inside. Try not to think that just when he was beginning to feel they were making some progress, the number of killers multiplied, like something in a nightmare.

Kovac brought up the rear, shutting the door behind him.

"There's a wrinkle we didn't need," he complained. "Bad enough looking for one psycho. Now I get to tell the bosses we're looking for two of them."

"Don't tell them," Quinn said. "Not right away. I need to think about this."

He put his back to the wall as if he intended to stand right there until the answer came to him.

"What's it do to the profile if he's got a partner?" Liska asked.

"What's it do to the profile if he's got a partner and his partner is a woman?" Quinn asked back.

"Complicates the hell out of my life," Kovac said.

The hall was dark with a low ceiling and not much traffic this time of day. Two women in lab coats walked past, engrossed in a conversation about office politics. Quinn waited until they were out of earshot.

"Are they equal partners, or is the woman what we call a 'willing victim'? Is she participating because she likes it, or because she feels she has to for one reason or another—she's afraid of him, he controls her, whatever." He turned to Liska. "Does Gil Vanlees have a girlfriend?"

"Not that I've heard about. I asked his wife, his boss, coworkers. Nothing."

"Did you ask the wife about Jillian Bondurant? Whether she knew Jillian, whether she thought her husband knew her a little too well?"

"She said he liked to look at anything with tits. She didn't single out Jillian."

"What are you thinking?" Kovac asked.

"I'm thinking it's bothered me all along that we've never gotten a positive ID on the third victim. Why the decapitation? The extra mutilation of the feet? Now using Jillian's car to burn the fourth victim. Why so much emphasis on Jillian?" Quinn asked. "We know she was an unhappy, troubled girl. What more permanent escape from an unhappy life than death—real or symbolic."

"You think that could be Jillian's voice on the tape," Liska said. "You think she could be Vanlees's partner?"

"I've said all along the key to this thing is Jillian Bondurant. She's the piece that doesn't fit. It just never hit me until now that maybe she isn't just the key. Maybe she's a killer."

"Jesus," Kovac said. "Well, it was a decent career while it lasted. Maybe I can take over Vanlees's job, chasing groupies away from the stage door at the Target Center."

He glanced at his watch and tapped its

face. "I gotta go. I've got a date with the wife of Peter Bondurant's ex-partner. Maybe I'll find out something about Jillian there."

"I want to talk to this friend of hers— Michele Fine. See if she has copies of the music she wrote with Jillian. We could get some insights to her state of mind, maybe even to her fantasy life through her lyrics. I also want to find out what Fine's take on Vanlees is."

"She doesn't have one," Liska said. "I asked her the day we were at the apartment and we saw him. She said, 'Who ever notices the losers?' "

"But predators recognize their own kind," Quinn said. He turned to Kovac. "Who's on Vanlees?"

"Tippen and Hamill."

"Perfect. Have them go ask him if this friend whose house he's staying at imports recording equipment, video cameras, stuff like that."

Kovac nodded. "Will do."

"There are a couple of possibilities to consider other than Vanlees," Quinn pointed out. "If the relationship between Smokey Joe and his partner is about control, domination, power, then we have to look at Jillian's life and ask ourselves what men have held that kind of sway over her. I can name two that we know of."

"Lucas Brandt and Daddy Dearest," Kovac said with a grim look. "Great. We may finally be on to something, and it's that the daughter of the most powerful man in the state is a sicko freak murderer—and maybe she gets it from Dad. I just get all the luck."

Liska patted his arm as they started down the hall. "You know what they say, Sam: You can't pick your relatives or your serial killers."

"I've got a better one," Quinn said as the myriad ugly possibilities for the close of this case flashed through his head. "It ain't over till it's over."

28

CHAPTER

D'CUP WAS MOSTLY EMPTY, with the same pair of old geezers in beret and goatee arguing about pornography today, and a different struggling artist contemplating his mediocrity by the window with a three-dollar *latte* at hand.

Michele Fine had called in sick. Liska gleaned this information from the Italian stallion behind the bar and made a mental note to start a daily cappuccino habit. Never mind D'Cup was miles out of the way to anything in her life. That was actually part of the allure.

"Did you know her friend at all?" Quinn asked. "Jillian Bondurant?"

The Roman god pursed his full lips and shook his head. "Not really. I mean, she came in here a lot, but she wasn't very sociable. Very internal, if you know what I mean. She and Chell were tight. That's about all I know besides what I've read in the papers."

"Did you ever see her in here with anyone else?" Quinn tried.

"Michele or Jillian Bondurant?"

"Jillian."

"Can't say that I did."

"What about Michele? She have a boyfriend?"

He didn't seem to like that question, like maybe they were getting too personal and he was thinking he should take a stand for the Fourth Amendment. Liska pulled out the Polaroid of Vanlees and held it out.

"You ever see either one of them with this guy? Or the guy in here alone?"

Studly squinted at the photo the way people do in an effort to improve both their memory and their vision. "Nah. He doesn't look familiar."

"What about their music?" Quinn asked. "Michele said they performed here sometimes."

"Chell sings and plays the guitar on open-mike nights. I know they wrote some stuff together, but I couldn't tell you who contributed what. Jillian never performed. She was a spectator. She liked to watch other people."

"What kind of music?" Quinn asked.

"The edgy feminist folk thing. Lots of anger, lots of angst, kind of dark."

"Dark in what way?"

"Bad relationships, twisted relationships, lots of emotional pain."

He said it as if he were saying "the usual," with a certain air of boredom. A commentary on modern life.

Quinn thanked him. Liska ordered a mocha to go and tipped him a buck. Quinn smiled a little as he held the door.

"Hey," Liska said. "It never hurts to be kind."

"I didn't say anything."

"You didn't have to."

The snow was still coming down. The street in front of the coffeehouse was a mess. Lanes invisible, drivers had adopted a survival-of-the-fittest mentality. As they watched, a purple Neon nearly lost its life to an MTC bus.

"You're pretty good at this cop stuff," Liska said, digging the car keys out of her coat pocket. "You should consider giving up the glamour of CASKU and the FBI for the relative ignominy of the Minneapolis homicide unit. You get to be hassled by the brass, abused by the press, and ride around in a piece-of-shit car like this one."

"All that and I'd get to live in this weather too?" Quinn turned up his collar against the wind and snow. "How can I resist an offer like that?"

"Oh, all right," Liska said with resignation as she climbed behind the wheel. "I'll throw in all the sex you want. But you have to promise to want a lot."

Quinn chuckled and looked out the back window at the traffic. "Tinks, you're something."

Michele Fine's apartment was less than a mile away, in a slightly seedy neighborhood full of sagging old duplexes and square, ugly apartment buildings that housed an inordinate number of parolees and petty criminals on probation, according to Liska.

"Vanlees's apartment on Lyndale is just a few blocks south of here," she said as they picked their way up the sidewalk, stepping in the rut others had stomped into the wet snow. "Don't you just love a coincidence like that?"

"But they seemed not to know each other when you were at the apartment?"

She thought back to the scene, furrowing her brow. "Not more than in passing. They didn't speak. Do you really think she might have caught him looking in Jillian's windows?"

"That was a shot in the dark, but it sure got a rise out of your boy. The thing I'm wondering is, if she caught him doing something like that, why wouldn't she have told you about it?"

"Good question." Liska tried the building's security door, finding it unlocked. "Let's go get an answer."

The elevator smelled of bad Chinese takeout. They rode up to the fourth floor with an emaciated hype who huddled into one corner, trying to look inconspicuous and eye Quinn's expensive trench coat at the same time. Quinn gave him a flat stare and watched the sweat instantly bead on the man's pasty forehead. When the doors opened, the hype hung back in the elevator and rode it back down.

"You must be something at a poker table," Liska said.

"No time for it."

She arched a brow, blue eyes shining invitingly. "Better watch out. All work and no play makes John a dull boy."

Quinn ducked her gaze, mustering a sheepish smile. "I'd put you to sleep, Tinks."

"Well, I doubt that, but if you need to prove it scientifically..."

She stopped in front of Fine's door and looked at him. "I'm just giving you a hard time, you know. The sad truth is, you strike me as a man who has someone on his mind."

Quinn rang the bell and stared at the door. "Yeah. A killer." Though for the first time in a very long time, his thoughts were not entirely on his work.

As if Liska had given him permission, he flashed on Kate. Wondered how she was doing, what she was thinking. He wondered if she had yet gotten his message that the victim in the car had not been her witness. He hated the idea of her blaming herself for what had happened, and he hated even more the idea of her boss blaming her. It made his protective instincts rise up, made him want to do something more violent to Rob Marshall than knock him on his ass. He wondered if Kate would be amused or annoyed to know that.

He rang the bell again.

"Who is it?" a voice demanded from inside the apartment.

Liska stood in view of the peephole. "Sergeant Liska, Michele. I need to ask you a couple more questions about Jillian."

"I'm sick."

"It'll only take a minute. It's very important. There's been another murder, you know."

The door opened a crack, and Fine peered out at them from the other side of the safety chain. The wedge of space framed the scarred portion of her narrow, angular face. "That's got nothing to do with me. I can't help you."

She saw Quinn then, and her gaze hardened with suspicion. "Who's he?"

"John Quinn, FBI," Quinn said. "I'd like to talk with you a little about Jillian, Ms. Fine. I'm trying to get a better idea of who she was. I understand you and she were close friends."

The seconds ticked past as she stared at him, sizing him up in a way that seemed odd for a waitress in a trendy coffee bar. It was more the look of someone who had seen too much of the streets. As she raised her hand to undo the safety chain, he caught a glimpse of the snake tattooed around her wrist.

She opened the door and stepped back reluctantly.

"You haven't heard from her since Friday?" Quinn asked.

Fine gave him a look of suspicion and dislike. "How could I hear from her?" she asked bitterly, her eyes filling. "She's dead. Why would you ask me something like that?"

"Because I'm not as certain about it as you seem to be."

"What the hell are you talking about?" she demanded, looking frustrated and confused. "It's all over the news. Her father is offering a reward. What kind of game are you trying to play?"

Quinn let her hang as he looked around the room. The apartment was vintage seventies—original, not retro—and he figured nothing had been changed or dusted since. The woven drapes looked ready to rot off their hooks. The couch and matching chair in the small living room were square, brown and orange plaid, and worn nubby. Dog-eared travel magazines lay on the cheap coffee table like abandoned dreams beside an ashtray brimming with butts. Everything had been permeated by the smell of cigarette and pot smoke.

"I don't need you trying to fuck with my mind," Fine said. "I'm sick. I'm sick about Jillian. She was my friend—" Her voice broke and she looked away, her mouth tightening in a way that emphasized the scar hooking down from the one corner. "I'm—I'm just sick. So, whatever you want, ask for it and get the hell out of my life."

She plucked up her smoke and sidestepped away, hugging her free arm across her middle. She was an unhealthy kind of thin, Quinn thought, pale and bony. Maybe she really was sick. She wore a huge, ratty black cardigan sweater, and beneath it a grimy white T-shirt, so small it looked as if it had been intended for a child. Her legs looked as skinny as pegs in worn black leggings. Her feet were bare on the filthy carpet.

"So, what have you got?" Liska asked.

"Huh?"

"You said you were sick. What have you got?"

"Uhhh...the flu," she said absently, looking at the television, where a grotesquely obese woman appeared to be telling Jerry Springer all about her relationships with the pock-marked dwarf and the black transsexual sitting on either side of her. Fine picked a fleck of tobacco off her tongue and flicked it in the direction of the screen. "Stomach flu."

"You know what I hear is good for nausea?" Liska said, deadpan. "Marijuana. They're using it for chemotherapy patients. Of course, it's otherwise illegal..."

The threat was subtle. Maybe just enough to weigh in their favor if Fine found herself struggling with the idea of cooperation.

Fine stared at her with flat eyes.

"The other day—when we ran into the care-taker at Jillian's place," Liska said. "You didn't have much to say about him."

"What's to say?"

"How well did Jillian know him? Were they friends?"

"No. She knew him enough to call him by name." She went to the postage-stamp-sized dining table, sat down, and propped herself against it as if she didn't have enough strength to sit up on her own. "He had his eye on her."

"In what way?"

Fine looked at Quinn. "In the way men do."

"Did Jillian ever say he was hitting on her, watching her, anything like that?" Liska asked.

"You think he killed her."

"What do you think, Michele?" Quinn asked. "What's your take on the guy?"

"He's a loser."

"Did you ever have any kind of run-in with him?"

She lifted a shoulder as thin as a bird's wing. "Maybe I told him to fuck off once or twice."

"Why?"

"Because he was staring at us. Like maybe he was picturing us naked together. Fat bastard."

"And what did Jillian say about it?"

Another shrug. "She said once if that was the biggest thrill of his life, let him stare."

"She never said anything to you about him bothering her."

"No."

"She ever mention anything to you about feeling like she was being watched or followed, anything like that?"

"No. Even though she was."

Liska looked at her sharply. "How's that?"

"Her father and that Nazi shrink of hers watched her like hawks. Her father had a key to her apartment. Sometimes we'd get to her place and he'd be waiting for her inside. Talk about invasion of privacy."

"Did it bother Jillian when he did that?"

Michele Fine's mouth twisted in a strange little bitter smile, and she looked at the ashtray as she stubbed out her cigarette. "No. She was Daddy's girl, after all."

"What's that mean?"

"Nothing. She just let him pull her strings, that's all."

"She told you about her relationship with her stepfather. Did she ever say anything to you about her relationship with her father?"

"We didn't talk about him. She knew what I thought about him trying to control her. The subject was out of bounds. Why?" she asked matter-of-factly. "Do you think he was trying to fuck her too?"

"I don't know," Quinn said. "What do you think?"

"I think I never met a man who wouldn't take a piece of ass if he got the chance," she said, deliberately brazen, her gaze sliding down Quinn's body to his groin. He let her look, waited her out. Finally her eyes returned to his. "If he was, she never said it in so many words."

Quinn helped himself to the chair at the end of the small table, sitting down and settling in as if he meant to stay for supper. He looked again around the apartment, noting that there was very little in the way of ornamentation, nothing homey, nothing personal. No photos. The only thing that appeared to be well taken care of was the small stack of stereo and recording equipment in the far corner of the living room. A guitar was propped nearby.

"I understand you and Jillian wrote music together," he said. "What was Jillian's part of that?"

Fine lit another cigarette and blew smoke at the cheap chandelier. Quinn's gaze caught again on the snake tattooed around her wrist, twisting around the scars that had been seared into the flesh there long ago. The serpent from the Garden of Eden, a small red apple in its mouth.

"Sometimes lyrics," she said, smoke drifting through the gap between her front teeth. "Sometimes music. Whatever she felt like. Whatever I felt like."

"Have you published anything?"

"Not yet."

"What did she like to write about?"

"Life. People. Relationships."

"Bad relationships?"

"Is there another kind?"

"Did she keep copies of the stuff you'd written?"

"Sure."

"Where?" Liska asked.

"In her apartment. In the piano bench and the bookcase."

"I didn't find anything there the other day."

"Well, that's where it was," Fine said defensively, blowing another stream of smoke.

"Do you have any copies I could look at?" Quinn asked. "I'd like to read her lyrics, see what they have to say about her."

"Poetry is a window to the soul," Fine said

in an odd, dreamy tone. Her gaze drifted away again, and Quinn wondered just what she was on and why. Had the alleged murder of Jillian Bondurant pushed her over some mental edge? It seemed she had been Jillian's only friend. Perhaps Jillian had been hers. And now there was no one—no friend, no writing partner, nothing but this crappy apartment and a dead-end job.

"That's what I'm counting on," he said.

She looked right at him then, homely and slightly exotic, greasy dark hair scraped back from her face, vaguely familiar—as every face in the world seemed to be to him after so many cases. Her small eyes seemed suddenly very clear as she said, "But does it reflect who we are or what we want?"

She got up and went across the room to a set of shelves made from cinder blocks and wood planks, and came back sorting through a file folder. Quinn rose and reached out for it, and Fine twisted away, giving him a look from beneath her lashes that was almost coquettish.

"It's the window to my soul too, Mr. Fed. Maybe I don't want you peeking."

She held out half a dozen pieces of sheet music. Her fingernails had been bitten to the quick. Then she hugged the folder to her belly, an action that emphasized her small breasts beneath the tight T-shirt. She wasn't wearing a bra.

Liska put her briefcase on the table, popped it open, and produced a fingerprint kit. "We still need your prints, Michele. So we can eliminate them from all the prints taken in Jillian's town house. I knew you hadn't made it in to do that, busy as you are and all."

Fine stared at the ink pad and print card, wary and unhappy.

"It'll take only a minute," Liska said. "Have a seat."

Fine fell down on her chair and offered her hand reluctantly.

"When was the last time you heard from Jillian?" Quinn asked.

"I saw her Friday before her session with the mind fucker," Michele said as Liska rolled her thumb across the ink pad and pressed it to a card.

"She didn't call you Friday night?"

"No."

"She didn't come to see you?"

"No."

"Where were you around midnight, one o'clock?"

"In bed. Naked and alone." She looked up at him from under her lashes. Sultry.

"Seems odd, don't you think?" Quinn asked. "She'd had a fight with her father. She was upset enough to run out of his house. But she didn't try to contact her best friend."

"Well, Agent Quinn," she said, the voice of sad experience. "I learned a long time ago, you can never really know what's in another person's heart. And sometimes that's just as well."

• • •

KOVAC JAMMED THE Caprice into a Police Vehicles Only slot on the Fifth Street side of City Hall and abandoned it. Swearing a blue streak, he tried to run through the plow-made snowdrift covering the curb, sinking to his knee in one spot. Stumbling, staggering, he got over the hump and hurried up the steps and into the building. Breathing like a bellows. Heart working too hard to pump blood and adrenaline through arteries that probably looked like the inside of bad plumbing pipes.

Christ, he was going to have to get himself in shape if he wanted to survive another case like this one. Then again, his career wasn't likely to survive this one.

The hall was full of angry women who turned on him in a tide as he tried to negotiate his way to the criminal investigative division. It wasn't until he was swamped in the middle of them that he saw the protest signs bobbing above their heads: OUR LIVES MATTER TOO! JUSTICE: A PHOENIX RISING.

Their voices came at him in a barrage, like two dozen shotguns going off at once.

"Police harassment!"

"Only the Urskines want true justice!"

"Why don't you find the *real* killer!"

"That's what I'm trying to do, sister," Kovac snapped at the woman blocking his path with a bitter scowl and a belly the size of a beer keg. "So why don't you move the wide load and let me get on with it?"

That was when he noticed the media. Flashes went off left and right. *Shit.*

Kovac kept moving. The only rule of survival in a situation like this: Shut your mouth and keep moving.

"Sergeant Kovac, is it true you ordered Gregg Urskine's arrest?"

"No one is under arrest!" he shouted, forging through the mob.

"Kovac, has he confessed?"

"Was Melanie Hessler your mystery witness?"

Leak in the ME's office, he thought, shaking his head. That was what was wrong with this country—people would sell their mothers for the right money, and never think twice about the consequences to anyone else.

"No comment," he barked, and pushed his way past the last of them.

He negotiated the clutter of boxes and file cabinets into homicide, hanging a right at Lieutenant Fowler's makeshift office. Toni Urskine's voice raked over his nerve endings like a serrated knife on raw meat.

"...And you can rest assured every station, every paper, every reporter who will listen to me, will hear about it! This is an absolute outrage! *We* have been victimized by these crimes. *We* have lost friends. *We* have suffered. And this is how we're treated by the Minneapolis Police Department after we've bent over backward to cooperate!"

Kovac ducked through the door into the offices. Yurek jumped up from his desk, telephone receiver stuck to the side of his face, and made wild eye contact with Kovac, holding up a hand to keep him in the general vicinity. Kovac held up for five seconds, motor running, the excitement he had brought with him into the building like currents of energy humming through his arms, his legs, his veins and arteries. He bounced up and down on the balls of his feet like a boy who had to pee.

"I've got places to go and people to rake over the coals, Charm."

Yurek nodded and said into the phone, "I'm sorry, ma'am. I have to go now. I have an emergency situation here. I'm sorry. Yes, someone will get back to you. I'm sorry, ma'am."

He came around his desk, shaking his head. "These people are driving me batshit. There's a woman insisting her neighbor is the Cremator, and not only has he brutally murdered four women, she thinks he killed *and ate* her dog."

"I got time for this shit like I got time for root canal," Kovac snapped. "Is Quinn here?"

"He just got back. He's watching Urskine's interview," Yurek said, falling in step beside Kovac, heading for the interview rooms. "I just got a call from upstairs—"

"And the woman with the dead poodle is the mayor? That's how frigging weird this case is."

"No, before the dog lady. You're wanted in the mayor's office. They tried to get you on your cell phone."

"Dead battery. And you didn't see me. The battle-ax can wait. I've got a big damn fish to fry. I've got Jonah's goddamn whale."

Worry creased Yurek's perfect brow. "What do you mean, 'big fish'? Where've you been?"

Kovac didn't answer, his mind already on the confrontation ahead. Quinn stood near the one-way glass, looking dead on his feet as he stared through to the next room, where Gregg Urskine sat across the table from Elwood.

"We paid cash. I couldn't find the receipt," Urskine said, exasperated, fighting to keep that pleasant yuppie smile hanging on his face. "Do you keep all your receipts, Sergeant? Could you find a receipt for something you did months ago?"

"Yes, I could. I keep a simple but efficient home filing system," Elwood said conversationally. "You never know when you might need a record of something. For tax purposes, for an alibi—"

"I don't need an alibi."

"I know someone who does," Kovac said, snagging Quinn's attention. "You want to take another ride?"

"What's up?"

"I just talked to Mrs. Donald Thorton, Peter Bondurant's ex-partner. You want to know how the emotionally unstable Sophie Bondurant got custody of Jillian in the divorce? You'll love this," he promised sarcastically.

"I'm almost afraid to ask."

"She threatened to expose him to the court and to the media. For molesting Jillian."

29
CHAPTER

"**OH, GOD,**" Yurek groaned with dread.

Kovac wheeled on him. "What now? You want me to pretend I don't know Bondurant was molesting his daughter?"

"*Allegedly* molesting—"

"You think I don't know I've just stepped in it up to my ass?"

"I think you'd better hear what the mayor wants."

"I could give a rat's—"

"She wants you in her office to give Mr. Bondurant a personal briefing on the status of the case. They're up there waiting for you now."

The room fell silent for a heartbeat, then Elwood's calm voice came over the speaker again from the interview room next door. "Have you ever paid for sex, Mr. Urskine?"

"No!"

"No offense intended. It's just that working around all those women who've sold their bodies professionally might give rise to a certain curiosity. So to speak."

Urskine shoved his chair back from the table. "That's it. I'm leaving. If you want to speak to me again, you can do it through my attorney."

"All right," Kovac said to Quinn, nerves and anticipation knotting in his stomach. "Let's go give the mayor and Mr. Bondurant the big update. I'll fill you in on the way."

"I'M SURE YOU can understand Peter's need for closure in this matter," Edwyn Noble said to Chief Greer. "Do we have any kind of time frame as to when the body may be released?"

"Not *specifically*." Greer stood near the head of the mayor's conference table, feet slightly spread, hands clasped before him, like a soldier at ease, or a bouncer with an attitude. "I have a call in to Sergeant Kovac. I understand he's waiting to hear from the FBI lab on some tests. *Possibly* after those are completed, which could be *any* day—"

"I want to bury my daughter, Chief Greer." Bondurant's voice was tight. He didn't look at the chief, but seemed to be staring into a dimension only he could see. He had ignored the offer of a seat, and moved restlessly around the conference room. "The thought of her body sitting in some refrigerated locker like so much meat...I want her back."

"Peter darling, we understand," Grace Noble said. "We feel your pain. And I can assure you, the task force is doing everything possible to solve this—"

"Really? Your lead detective has spent more time harassing me than he's spent pursuing any suspects."

"Sergeant Kovac can be a bit gruff," Greer

said. "But his record in homicide speaks for itself."

"At the risk of sounding glib, Chief Greer," Edwyn Noble said, "Sergeant Kovac's record notwithstanding, what has he done for us lately? We have another victim. The killer seems to be thumbing his nose, not only at the task force, but at the city. Does Sergeant Kovac even have a viable suspect at this point?"

"Lieutenant Fowler tells me someone was questioned earlier today."

"Who? A legitimate suspect?"

Greer frowned. "I'm not at liberty—"

"She was *my daughter*!" Peter shouted, the rage in his voice reverberating off the walls. He turned away from the stares of the others and put his hands over his face.

The mayor pressed a hand to her ample bosom, as if the sight was causing her chest pains.

"If someone has been brought in," Noble said, the voice of reason, "then it will be only a matter of hours before the press reveals that information. That isn't a comment on the security of your force, per se, Chief. It's simply impossible to eliminate all leaks in a case of this magnitude."

Greer looked from Bondurant's lawyer to Bondurant's lawyer's wife—his boss. Unhappy and unable to see any escape routes, he sighed heavily. "The caretaker from Ms. Bondurant's town house complex."

The intercom buzzed, and Grace Noble

answered it from the phone on the side table. "Mayor Noble, Sergeant Kovac and Special Agent Quinn are here to see you."

"Send them in, Cynthia."

Kovac was through the door almost before the mayor finished her sentence, his eyes finding Peter Bondurant like a pair of heat-seeking missiles. Bondurant looked thinner than he had the day before, his color worse. He met Kovac's gaze with an expression of stony dislike.

"Sergeant Kovac, Agent Quinn, thank you for joining us," the mayor said. "Let's all have seats and talk."

"I'm not going into particulars of the case," Kovac stated stubbornly. Neither would he sit down and be a still target for Bondurant or Edwyn Noble.

No one sat.

"We understand you have a suspect," Edwyn Noble said.

Kovac gave him the eagle eye, then turned it on Dick Greer and thought *cocksucker*.

"No arrests have been made," Kovac said. "We're still pursuing all avenues. I've just been down an interesting one myself."

"Does Mr. Vanlees have an alibi for the night my daughter went missing?" Bondurant asked sharply. He looked at Kovac as he paced back and forth along the table, passing within a foot of him.

"Do *you* have an alibi for the night your daughter went missing, Mr. Bondurant?"

"Kovac!" the chief barked.

"With all due respect, Chief, I'm not in

500

the habit of giving up my cases to anybody."

"Mr. Bondurant is the father of a victim. There are extenuating circumstances."

"Yeah, a few billion of them," Kovac muttered.

"Sergeant!"

"Sergeant Kovac believes I should be punished for my wealth, Chief," Bondurant said, still pacing, staring at the floor now. "He perhaps believes I deserved to lose my daughter so I could know what real suffering is."

"After what I heard today, I believe you never deserved to have a daughter at all," Kovac said, eliciting a gasp from the mayor. "You sure as hell deserved to lose her, but not in the way she's lost now. That is to say if she's dead at all—and we're nowhere near ready to say that she is."

"Sergeant Kovac, I hope you have a very good explanation for this behavior." Greer moved toward him aggressively, drawing his weight lifter's shoulders up.

Kovac stepped away from him. His full attention was on Peter Bondurant. And Peter Bondurant's attention was on him. He stopped his pacing, an instinctive wariness in the narrowed eyes, like an animal sensing danger.

"I had a long talk today with Cheryl Thorton," Kovac said, and watched what color Peter Bondurant had leech away. "She had some very interesting things to say about your divorce from Jillian's mother."

Edwyn Noble looked startled. "I fail to see what relevance—"

"Oh, I think it could be very relevant." Kovac still stared hard at Bondurant.

Bondurant said, "Cheryl is a bitter, vindictive woman."

"You think so? After she's kept her mouth shut all this time? I'd say you're an ungrateful son of a bitch—"

"Kovac, that's enough!" Greer shouted.

"Hardly," Kovac said. "You want to kiss the ass of a child-molester, Chief, that's your business. I won't do it. I don't give a shit how rich he is."

"Oh!" Grace Noble exclaimed, pressing her hand to her chest again.

"Maybe we should take this downstairs," Quinn suggested mildly.

"Fine by me," Kovac said. "We've got an interview room all warmed up."

Bondurant had begun to tremble visibly. "I *never* abused Jillian."

"Maybe you think you didn't." Kovac circled slowly around him, moving away from Greer, keeping Bondurant's eyes on him and putting his back to his lawyer. "A lot of pedophiles convince themselves they're doing the kid a favor. Some even confuse fucking little kids with love. Is that what you made yourself believe?"

"You son of a bitch!"

Bondurant launched himself, grabbing Kovac by the lapels and running him backward across the room. They crashed into a side table and sent a pair of brass candlesticks flying like bowling pins.

Kovac held back the urge to roll Bondurant over and pound the shit out of him. After what he'd heard today, he dearly wanted to, and maybe he could have if they'd crossed paths in a dark alley. But men like Peter Bondurant didn't frequent dark alleys, and rough justice never touched them.

Bondurant got in one good swing, glancing his knuckles off the corner of Kovac's mouth. Then Quinn grabbed him by the back of the collar and pulled him away. Greer rushed in between them like a referee, arms spread wide, eyes rolling white in his dark face.

"Sergeant Kovac, I think *you* should step *outside*," he said loudly.

Kovac straightened his tie and jacket. He wiped a smear of blood away from the corner of his mouth, and a smirk twisted his lips as he looked at Peter Bondurant.

"Ask him where he was last night at two o'clock in the morning," he said. "While someone was setting his daughter's car on fire with a mutilated dead woman inside it."

"I won't even dignify that with a comment," Bondurant said, fussing with his glasses.

"Jesus, you're just the cat's ass, aren't you?" Kovac said. "You get away with child abuse. You get away with assaulting an officer. You're into this case like a bad infection. You think you might get away with murder if you want to?"

"*Kovac!*" Greer screamed.

Kovac looked to Quinn, shook his head, and walked out.

Bondurant jerked out of Quinn's hold. "I want him off the case! I want him off the force!"

"Because he's doing his job?" Quinn asked calmly. "It's his job to investigate. He can't help what he finds, Peter. You're killing the messenger."

"He's not investigating the case!" he shouted, pacing again, gesturing wildly. "He's investigating *me*. He's harassing me. I've lost my daughter, for God's sake!"

Edwyn Noble tried to take hold of his arm as he passed. Bondurant twisted away. "Peter, calm down. Kovac will be dealt with."

"I think we should deal with what Sergeant Kovac found, don't you?" Quinn said to the lawyer.

"It's nonsense," Noble snapped. "There's nothing to the allegation whatsoever."

"Really? Sophie Bondurant was an emotionally unstable woman. Why would the courts award her custody of Jillian? More to the point, why wouldn't you fight her, Peter?" Quinn asked, trying to establish eye contact with Bondurant.

Bondurant kept moving, highly agitated, sweating now, pale in the way that made Quinn think he might be ill.

"Cheryl Thorton says the reason you didn't fight was that Sophie threatened to expose you for molesting Jillian."

"I *never* hurt Jillian. I wouldn't."

"Cheryl has always blamed Peter for her husband's accident," Noble said bitterly. "She didn't want Donald to sell out of Paragon. She punished him for it too. Drove him to drink. She's the one who caused the accident—indirectly—but she blames Peter."

"And this bitter, vindictive woman never said anything until now about this alleged abuse?" Quinn said. "That would be hard to imagine if not for the generous monthly payments Peter sends to the convalescent home where Donald Thorton is spending the last of his life."

"Some people would call that generosity," Noble said.

"And some people would call it blackmail. Some people would say Peter was buying Cheryl Thorton's silence."

"They'd be wrong," Noble stated unequivocally. "Donald and Peter were friends, partners. Why shouldn't he see to it the man's needs are taken care of?"

"He took very good care of him in the buyout of Paragon—which, coincidentally, went on about the same time as the divorce," Quinn continued. "The deal might have been considered overly generous on Peter's part."

"What was he supposed to do?" Noble demanded. "Try to steal the company from the man who'd helped him build it?"

Bondurant, Quinn noticed, had stopped talking, and now confined his pacing to the corner by the window. Retreating. His head was down and he kept touching his hand to his forehead as if feeling for a fever. Quinn moved casually toward him, neatly cutting his pacing area in half. Subtly crowding his space.

"Why didn't you fight Sophie for custody, Peter?" he asked softly, an intimate question between friends. He kept his own head down, his hands in his pants pockets.

"I was taking over the business. I couldn't handle a child too."

"And so you left her to Sophie? A woman in and out of mental institutions."

"It wasn't like that. It wasn't as if she was insane. Sophie had problems. We all have problems."

"Not the kind that make us kill ourselves."

Tears filled the man's eyes. He raised a hand as if to shade his eyes from Quinn's scrutiny.

"What did you and Jillian argue about that night, Peter?"

He shook his head a little, moving now in a tight, short line. Pacing three steps, turning, pacing three steps, turning...

"She'd gotten a call from her stepfather," Quinn said. "You were angry."

"We've been over this," Edwyn Noble said impatiently, clearly wanting to get between Quinn and his client. Quinn turned a shoulder, blocking him out.

"Why do you keep insisting Jillian is dead, Peter? I don't know that she is. I think she may not be. Why would you say that she is? What did you fight about that night?"

"Why are you doing this to me?" Bondurant whispered in a tortured voice. His prim, tight-lipped mouth was quivering.

"Because we need to know the truth, Peter,

and I think you're holding back pieces of the puzzle. If you want the truth—as you say you do—then you have to give those pieces to me. Do you understand? We need to see the whole picture."

Quinn held his breath. Bondurant was on the edge. He could feel it, see it. He tried to will him over it.

Bondurant stared out the window at the snow, still now, looking numb. "All I wanted was for us to be father and daughter—"

"That's enough, Peter." Noble stepped in front of Quinn and took his client by the arm. "We're leaving."

He glared at Quinn. "I thought we understood each other."

"Oh, I understand you perfectly, Mr. Noble," Quinn said. "That doesn't mean I'm interested in playing on your team. I'm interested in two things only: the truth, and justice. I don't know that you want either."

Noble said nothing. He led Bondurant from the room like a caretaker with a sedated patient.

Quinn looked to the mayor, who had finally taken a seat herself. She looked partly stunned and partly reflective, as if trying to sort through old memories for any that might have implicated Peter Bondurant in something she would never have suspected. Chief Greer looked like a man in the early stages of diverticulitis.

"That's the thing about digging holes," Quinn said. "There are no assurances you'll find what you want—or want what you find."

BY FIVE O'CLOCK every news agency native to and camped in the Twin Cities had the name of Gil Vanlees. The same media that would plaster that name in print and fill television screens with bad photographs of the man would point fingers at the police department for leaking information.

Quinn had no doubt where the leak had sprung, and it pissed him off. Bondurant's people having the kind of access they had tainted the case. And in the light of Kovac's revelation that afternoon, Bondurant's meddling took on an even darker quality.

No one had leaked *that* story to the press. Not even the allegedly bitter, vindictive Cheryl Thorton, whose brain-damaged husband was supported by Peter Bondurant. He wondered exactly how much money it took to hold a grudge like that at bay for a decade.

What had gone on in the lives of Jillian and her mother and father in that pivotal time of the divorce? he wondered in his windowless room at the FBI offices. From the start, Bondurant had struck him as a man with secrets. Secrets about the present. Secrets about the past. Secrets as dark as incest?

How else would Sophie Bondurant have gotten custody of Jillian? Unstable as she was. Powerful as Peter was.

He flipped through the casebook to the crime scene photos of the third murder. Certain aspects of the murder gave the impression the killer and victim may have known each other.

508

The decapitation when none of the other victims had been decapitated, the extreme depersonalization. Both suggested a kind of rage that was personal. But what of the latest theory that the killer worked with a partner, a woman? That didn't fit Peter Bondurant. And what of the thought that perhaps the woman involved was Jillian Bondurant herself?

A history of sexual abuse would fit the profile of a woman involved in this type of crime. She would have a skewed view of male-female relationships, of sexual relationships. Her partner was likely older, some twisted suggestion of a father figure, the dominant partner.

Quinn thought of Jillian, of the photograph in Bondurant's office. Emotionally troubled, with low self-esteem, a girl unhappily pretending to be something she wasn't in order to please. To what lengths might she go to find the approval she craved?

He thought of her involvement with her stepfather—supposedly consensual, but these things never really are. Children need love and can be easily manipulated by that need. And if Jillian had escaped an abusive relationship with her father, only to be coerced into another by her stepfather, that would have reinforced every warped idea she had of relationships with men.

If Peter had abused her.

If Jillian wasn't a dead victim, but a willing victim.

If Gil Vanlees was her partner in this sickness.

If Gil Vanlees was a killer at all.

509

If if if if...

Vanlees seemed a perfect fit—except he didn't strike Quinn as having the brainpower to outsmart the cops for this long, or the balls to play the kind of taunting game this killer played. Not the Gil Vanlees he'd seen in that interview room today. But he knew from experience people could have more than one side, and that a dark side that was capable of killing the way the Cremator killed was capable of anything, including disguising itself very, very well.

He pictured Gil Vanlees in his mind and waited for that twist in his gut that told him this was the guy. But the feeling didn't come. He couldn't remember the last time it had. Not even after the fact, after a killer had been caught and fit his profile point by point. That sense of knowing didn't come anymore. The arrogance of certainty had abandoned him. Dread had taken its place.

He flipped farther into the murder book, to the fresh photographs from Melanie Hessler's autopsy. As with the third victim, the wounds inflicted both before and after death had been brutal, unspeakably cruel, worse than with the first two victims. As he looked at the photographs he could hear the echo of the tape recording in his head. Scream after scream after scream.

The screams ran into one another and into the cacophony that filled his nightmares, growing louder and louder. The sound swelled and expanded in his brain until he felt as if his head would burst and the contents run out in a sickly gray ooze. And all the while he stared at the autopsy photographs, at the charred, mutilated thing that had once been a woman, and he thought of the kind of rage it took to do that to another person. The kind of poisonous, black emotions kept under tight control until the pressure became too much. And he thought of Peter Bondurant and Gil Vanlees and a thousand nameless faces walking the streets of these cities just waiting for that main line of hate to blow and push them over the edge.

Any of them could have been this killer. The necessary components resided in a great many people, and needed only the proper catalyst to set them off. The task force was putting its money on Vanlees, based on circumstance and the profile. But all they had was logic and a hunch. No physical evidence. Could Gil Vanlees have been that careful, that clever? They had no witness to put him with any of the victims. Their witness was gone. They had no obvious connection between all four victims or anything tying Vanlees to any victim other than Jillian—if Jillian was a victim.

If this. If that.

Quinn dug a Tagamet out of his pants pocket and washed it down with diet Coke. The case was crowding in on him; he couldn't get perspective. The players were too close around him, their ideas, their emotions, bleeding into the cold facts that were all he needed for his analysis.

The professional in him still wished for the

distance of his office in Quantico. But if he had stayed in Quantico, then he and Kate would have remained in the past tense.

On impulse, he grabbed up the telephone receiver and dialed her office number. On the fourth ring her machine picked up. He left his number again, hung up, picked up again, and dialed her home line with the same result. It was seven now. Where the hell was she?

Instantly he flashed on the decrepit garage in the dark alley behind her house and muttered a curse. Then he reminded himself—as Kate herself would surely do—that she had gotten along just fine without him for the past five years.

He could have used her expertise tonight, to say nothing of a long, slow kiss and a warm embrace. He turned back to the casebook and flipped to the victimologies, looking for the one thing he felt he'd missed that would tie it all together and point the finger.

The notes on Melanie Hessler were in his own hand, sketchy, too brief. Kovac had set Moss to the task of gathering the information on the latest of the Cremator's victims, but she had yet to bring him anything. He knew she'd worked in an adult bookstore—which, in the killer's mind, likely put her into the same category as the two hookers. She'd been attacked in the alley behind the store just months before, but the two men who had raped her had solid alibis and were not considered suspects in her death.

It was sad to think how each of these women

had been victimized repeatedly in their brief lives. Lila White and Fawn Pierce in a profession and a lifestyle that specialized in abuse and degradation. White had been assaulted by her drug dealer just last summer. Pierce had been hospitalized three times in two years, the victim of her pimp once, once a mugging victim, and once a rape victim.

Jillian Bondurant's victimization had taken place behind the closed doors of her home. If Jillian was a victim.

He turned back to the photographs of victim number three once again and stared at the stab wounds to her chest. The signature. Long wound, short wound, long wound, short wound, like the arms of a star or the petals of a gruesome flower. *I love you, I love you not. Cross my heart, hope to die.*

He thought of the faint voices on the tape.

"...Turn...do it..."

"...Want to...of me..."

Too easily he could picture the killers standing on either side of their victim's warm, lifeless body, each with a knife, taking turns punching their signature into the woman's chest, sealing the pact of their partnership.

It should have horrified him to think it, but it wasn't the worst thing he'd ever seen. Not by a long way. Mostly it left him numb.

That made him shudder.

A man and a woman. He scrolled through the possibilities, considering people known to be attached to the victims in some way. Gil Vanlees, Bondurant, Lucas Brandt. The Urskines—

possibilities there. The hooker who had been at the Phoenix last night when the DiMarco girl had disappeared—and claimed not to have seen or heard a thing, who had also known the second victim. Michele Fine, Jillian's only friend. Strange and shaky. Scarred—physically and emotionally. A woman with a long, dark story behind her, no doubt—and no good alibi for the night Jillian went missing.

He reached for the sheet music Fine had handed over to him and wondered about Jillian's compositions she'd kept to herself.

Outsider

Outside
On the dark side
Alone
Looking in
On a whim
Want a home

Outsider
In my blood
In my bones
Can't have
What I want
Doomed to roam
All alone
On the outside

Let me in
Want a friend
Need a lover

514

Be with me
Be my boy
Be my father

Outsider
In my blood
In my bones

Can't have
What I want
Doomed to roam
All alone
On the outside

Knuckles cracked against the door, and Kovac stuck his head in without waiting for an invitation.

"Can you smell it?" he asked, letting himself in. He leaned back against Quinn's wall of notes, suit rumpled, lip swollen where Peter Bondurant had popped him, tie askew. "Cooked goose, burned ass, toast."

"You're out," Quinn said.

"Give the man a cigar. I'm off the task force. They'll name my successor at a press conference sometime tomorrow."

"At least Bondurant didn't get you thrown off the force altogether," Quinn said. "You played bad cop a little too hard this time, Sam."

"Bad cop," Kovac said with disgust. "That was me, and I meant every word of it. I'm fed up to my back teeth with Peter Bondurant, and

515

his money and his power and his people. What Cheryl Thorton told me pushed me over the edge. I just kept thinking about the dead women nobody cared about, and Bondurant playing with the case like it was his own personal live game of Clue. I kept thinking about his daughter and how she should have had such a great life, but instead—dead or alive—she's fucked up forever, thanks to him."

"*If* he molested her. We don't know what Cheryl Thorton said is true."

"Bondurant pays her husband's medical bills. Why would she say something that rotten against the man if it wasn't true?"

"Did she give any indication she thinks Peter killed Jillian?"

"She wouldn't go that far."

Quinn held out the sheet of music. "Make what you want of that. It could say you're on a hot trail."

Kovac scowled as he read the lyrics of the song. "Jesus."

Quinn spread his hands. "Could be sexual or not. Might refer to her father or her step-father or not mean anything at all. I want to talk more with her friend Michele. See if she has an interpretation—if she'll give it to me."

Kovac turned and looked at the photographs Quinn had taped up. The victims when they were alive and smiling. "There's nothing I hate more than a child-molester. That's why I don't work sex crimes—even if they do get better hours. If I ever worked sex crimes, I'd be in the tank so fast, I'd get whiplash. I'd get my hands on some son of a bitch who raped his own kid, and I'd just fucking kill him. Get 'em out of the gene pool, you know what I'm saying?"

"Yeah, I do."

"I don't know how a man can look at his own daughter and think, 'Hey, I gotta have me some of that.'"

He shook his head and dug a cigarette out of the pack in the breast pocket of his limp white shirt. The FBI offices were nonsmoking, but Quinn said nothing.

"I've got a daughter, you know," Kovac said, exhaling his first lungful. "Well, you *don't* know. Hardly anyone knows. From my first marriage, which lasted about a minute and a half after I joined the force. Gina. She's sixteen now. I never see her. Her mother remarried with embarrassing haste and moved to Seattle. Some other guy got to be her dad."

He moved his shoulders and looked at the pictures again. "Not so different from Bondurant, huh?" he said, his mouth twisting. The shoulders sagged on a long sigh. "Christ, I hate irony."

Quinn could see the regret in his eyes. He'd seen it many times in many faces across the country. The job took a toll, and the people who were willing to pay it didn't get nearly enough in return.

"What're you going to do about the case?" he asked.

Kovac looked surprised by the question. "Work the damn task force, that's what. I don't care what Little Dick says. It's my case, I'm lead. They can *name* whoever they want."

"Your lieutenant won't reassign you?"

"Fowler's on my side. He put me on the support team on the QT. I'm supposed to keep my head down and my mouth shut."

"How long has he known you?"

"Long enough to know better."

Quinn found a weary laugh. "Sam, you're something."

"Yeah, I am. Just don't ask too many people what." Kovac grinned, then it faded away. He dropped the last of his cigarette into an empty diet Coke can. "It's no ego trip, you know. I don't need my name in the paper. I don't care what goes in my jacket. I've never looked for a promotion, and I sure as hell don't expect to ever see another.

"I want this scumbag," he said with steel in his voice. "I should've wanted him this bad when Lila White was killed, but I didn't. Not that I didn't care about her, but you were right: I went through the motions. I didn't hang in, didn't dig hard enough. When it didn't wrap up fast, I let it slide 'cause the brass was on my case and she was a hooker and hookers get whacked every once in a while. Hazard of the profession. Now we're up to four. I want Smokey Joe's ass on a platter before the body count goes up again."

Quinn listened as Kovac said his piece, and nodded at the end of it. This was a good cop standing in front of him. A good man. And this case would break his career more easily than it would make it—even if he solved the mystery. But especially if the answer to the question turned out to be Peter Bondurant.

"What's the latest on Vanlees?" he asked.

"Tippen's riding his tail like a cat on a mouse. They pulled him over on Hennepin to ask about his buddy, the electronics dealer. Tip says the guy about shit his pants."

"What about the electronics?"

"Adler checked out the guy's Web page. He specializes in computers and related gizmos, but if it plugs into a wall, he can get it for you. So there's nothing to say that he isn't up to his ears in recording equipment. I wish we could get a search warrant for his house, but there isn't a judge in the state who'd give us one based on what we've got on this mutt—which is nothing."

"That bothers me," Quinn admitted, tapping a pen against the file on Vanlees. "I don't think Gil's the brightest bulb in the chandelier. He's a good fit to the profile on a lot of points, but Smokey Joe is smart and he's bold, and Vanlees seems to be neither—which also makes him a perfect fall guy."

Kovac fell into a chair as if the weight of this latest concern made the burden all suddenly too much for him. "Vanlees is connected to Jillian, *and* to Peter. I don't like that. I keep having this nightmare that Bondurant is Smokey Joe, and that no one will listen to me and no one else will look at him, and the son of a bitch will get away with it.

"I try to dig on him a little and he damn near gets me fired. I don't like it." He pulled out another cigarette and just ran his fingers over it, as if he hoped that alone might calm him. "And then I think, 'Sam, you're an idiot. Bondurant brought in Quinn.' Why would he do that if he was the killer?"

"For the challenge," Quinn said without hesitation. "Or to get himself caught. I'd go with the first in this case. He'd get off on knowing I'm here and unable to spot him. Outsmarting the cops is big with this killer. But if Bondurant is Smokey Joe, then who's his accomplice?"

"Jillian," Kovac offered. "And this whole thing with her murder is a sham."

Quinn shook his head. "I don't think so. Bondurant believes his daughter is dead. Believes it more strongly than we do. That's no act."

"So we're back to Vanlees."

"Or the Urskines. Or someone we haven't even considered."

Kovac scowled at him. "Some help you are."

"That's why they pay me the big bucks."

"My tax dollars at work," he said with disgust. He hung the cigarette on his lip for a second, then took it away. "The Urskines. How twisted would that be? They whack two of their hookers, then do a couple of citizens in order to make a political point."

"And to push suspicion away from themselves," Quinn said. "No one considers the person trying to draw attention."

"But to snatch the witness staying in their house? That's titanium balls." Kovac tipped his head, considering. "I bet Toni Urskine can grow hair on hers."

Quinn went to his wall of notes and scanned them, not really reading the words, just seeing a jumble of letters and facts that tangled in his mind with the theories and the faces and the names.

"Any word on Angie DiMarco?" he asked.

Kovac shook his head. "No one's seen her. No one's heard from her. We're flashing her picture on television, asking people to call the hotline if they've seen her. Personally, I'm afraid finding someone else in that car last night was just postponing the inevitable. But, hey," he said, dragging himself up out of his chair, "I am, as my second wife used to call me, the infernal pessimist."

He yawned hugely and consulted his watch.

"Well, GQ, I'm calling it. I can't remember the last time I slept in a bed. That's my goal for the night—if I don't pass out in the shower. How about you? I can give you a ride back to your hotel."

"What for? Sleep? I gave that up. It was cutting into my anxiety attacks," Quinn said, ducking his gaze. "Thanks anyway, Sam, but I think I'll stick to it awhile yet. There's something here I'm just not seeing." He gestured to the open casebook. "Maybe if I stare at it all a little longer..."

Kovac watched him for a few moments without saying anything, then nodded. "Suit

yourself. See you in the morning. You want
me to pick you up?"

"No. Thanks."

"Uh-huh. Well, good night." He started
through the door, then looked back in. "Say
hello to Kate for me. If you happen to talk to
her."

Quinn said nothing. He did nothing for a
full five minutes after Kovac left, just stood
there thinking Kovac had a hell of an eye. Then
he went to the phone and dialed Kate's
number.

30

CHAPTER

"KATE, IT'S ME. Uh—John. Um, I'm at the
office. Give me a call if you get the chance.
I'd like to go over some points in these victimologies with you. Get your take. Thanks."

Kate stared at the phone as the line went dead
and the message light began to flash. A part
of her felt guilty for not picking up. A part of
her felt relieved. At the core she ached at the
lost opportunity to touch him in some way. A
bad sign, but there it was.

She was exhausted, stressed out, overwhelmed, feeling as low as she had in years...and she wanted John Quinn's arms around her. She hadn't taken his call precisely for that reason. She was afraid.

What a rotten, unwelcome feeling it was.

The office was silent. She and Rob were the only ones left in their section. Rob sequestered in his office down the hall, no doubt writing a long and virulent report to file in her personnel jacket. On the other side of the reception area, in the county attorney's offices, there were any number of assistant prosecutors at work preparing for court, strategizing and researching and writing briefs and motions. But for the most part the building was empty. For all intents and purposes, she was alone.

Her nerves were raw from spending hours listening to the voice of her dead client confessing her fears of being hurt, her fears of being raped, of being killed, of dying alone, and Kate's own voice reassuring her, promising to look out for her, to get her help, fostering a false security that had ultimately failed Melanie Hessler in the worst possible way.

Rob had insisted on playing the tapes over and over, stopping and rewinding in sections, asking Kate the same questions over and over. As if any of it would make any difference at all. The cops didn't want to hear about the subtle nuances of Melanie's speech. All they wanted to know was if Melanie had expressed a fear of anyone in particular in the last few weeks of her life.

He'd been punishing her, Kate knew.

Finally, he'd hit the nerve one time too many. Kate stood, leaned across the table, and pressed stop.

"You've made your point. You've had your revenge. Enough is enough," she said quietly.

"I don't know what you're talking about." He said it almost as a taunt, without a speck of sincerity. He wouldn't look directly at her.

"I like this office, Rob. I like most of the people I work with. But I'm damn good at what I do, and I can get another job in a heartbeat. I won't take you trying to manipulate me and punish me.

"Now you'll excuse me," she went on. "Because I've just had the third worst twenty-four hours of my life and I feel like I'm on the verge of a psychotic break. I'm going home. Call if you don't want me to come back."

He hadn't said a word as she walked out. At least she hadn't heard him for the pulse roaring in her ears. God knew she probably deserved to have him fire her, but there simply wasn't any tact left in her. All pretense of manners and social bullshit had been scraped away, leaving nothing but raw emotion.

She felt it flooding through her still, as if some vital artery had ruptured inside her. She felt as if she might choke on it, drown in it.

And all she wanted was to find Quinn and fall into his arms.

She'd worked so hard to put her life back together, piece by piece on a new foundation, and now that foundation was shifting. No. Worse—she'd discovered it was built directly over the fault line of her past, just covering up. Not new, not stronger, just a lie she'd told herself every day for the last five years: that she didn't need John Quinn to feel complete.

Tears welled in her eyes, and despair yawned through her, leaving her aching and empty and alone and afraid. And God, she was so tired. But she choked the tears back and put one foot in front of the other. Go home, regroup, have a drink, try to sleep. Tomorrow was another day.

She pulled her coat on, scooped up her file on Angie, grabbed her mail and her messages and the faxes that had piled up in the tray during the day, and dumped it all into her briefcase. She reached to turn the desk lamp off, but her hand strayed to the shelves, and she plucked out the little framed photo of Emily.

Sweet, smiling little cherub in a sunny yellow dress. The future bright before her. Or so anyone with ordinary human arrogance would have thought. Kate wondered if tucked away somewhere in someone's old shoe box there might be a similar photograph of Angie DiMarco...or Melanie Hessler...Lila White, Fawn Pierce, Jillian Bondurant.

Life didn't come with any guarantee. There'd never been a promise made that couldn't be broken. She knew that firsthand. She'd made too many with the best of intentions, then watched them crack and come apart.

"I'm sorry, Em," she whispered. She pressed the picture to her lips for a good-night kiss, then tucked the frame back into its hiding place, where the cleaning woman would find it and dig it back out.

She let herself out of the office and locked the door behind her. A vacuum cleaner was running in the office across from hers. Down the hall, Rob Marshall's door was closed. He might still have been there, plotting how to screw her out of her severance pay. Or he might have gone home to—to what? She didn't even know if he had a girlfriend—or a boyfriend, for that matter. Thursday could have been his bowling league night for all she knew about him. He didn't have any close personal friends within the department. Kate had never socialized with him outside the obligatory office Christmas party. She wondered now if he had someone to go home to and complain to about that bitch from the office.

The snow had finally stopped, she noticed as she took the skyway to the Fourth Street ramp. Six inches total, she'd heard someone say. The street below was a mess that city crews would clear away overnight, though this time of year they might decide to leave it and hope for a couple of warm days to save the city some money for the storms that were sure to come in the next few months.

She pulled her keys out and folded them into her fist, the longest, sharpest one protruding between her index and middle fingers—a habit she'd developed living in the D.C. suburbs. The ramp was well lit, but not busy this time of night, and it always made her edgy walking around in it alone. More so tonight, after all that had gone on. Between the murders and the lack of sleep, her paranoia was running high. A shadow falling between cars, the scrape of a footstep, the sudden thump of a door—her nerves twisted tight every time. The 4Runner seemed a mile away.

Then she was in it, doors locked, motor running, heading home, one layer of tension peeling away. She tried to focus on letting the knots out of her shoulders. Pajamas, a drink, and bed. She'd drag her briefcase there with her and sit propped up by pillows on the sheets still rumpled from lovemaking.

Maybe she would change the sheets.

The enterprising guy from down the block kept a blade on the front of his pickup five months a year and supplemented his income plowing driveways. He had plowed the alley. Kate would write him a check and leave it in his mailbox tomorrow.

She drove into the garage, remembering too late the burned-out light. Swearing under her breath, she dug the big flashlight out of her glove compartment, then climbed down from the truck, juggling too much stuff.

The smell hit her nose just a second before her foot hit the soft, squishy pile.

"Oh, shit!" Literally. "Shit!"

"Kate?"

The voice came from toward the house. Quinn's voice.

"I'm in here!" she called back, fumbling with

the briefcase and the flashlight and her purse.

"What's wrong? I heard you swearing," he said, coming in.

"I just stepped in a pile of shit."

"What—Jesus, I smell it. That must have been some dog."

The flashlight clicked on and she shined it down at the mess. "It couldn't have been a dog. The door was shut. Gross!"

"That looks human," Quinn said. "Where's your shovel?"

Kate flashed the beam of light at the wall. "Right there. My God, you think someone came into my garage and did this?"

"You have a more viable theory?" he asked.

"I just can't imagine why anyone would do that."

"It's a sign of disrespect."

"I know that. I mean, why to me? Who do I know who would do something that strange, that primitive?"

"Who've you pissed off lately?"

"My boss. But somehow I can't envision him squatting in my garage. Nor would I want to." She limped outside with him, stepping only with the toe of her soiled boot, trying not to smear more feces on her garage floor.

"Do your clients know where you live?"

"If any of them do, it's not because I gave them the information. They have my office number—which forwards to my house machine after hours—and they have my cell phone number for emergencies. That's it. My home number is unlisted, not that that would necessarily stop anyone from finding me. It isn't that hard to do if you know how."

Quinn dumped the mess between the garage and the neighbor's privacy fence. He cleaned the shovel off in a snowbank while Kate tried to do the same with her boot.

"This is just the exclamation point at the end of my day," she grumbled as they went back into the garage to put the shovel away. She shone the light around to see if anything was missing. Nothing seemed to be.

"Have you had any odd things happen lately?"

She laughed without humor. "What about my life lately *isn't* odd?"

"I mean vandalism, hang-up calls, strange mail, anything like that?"

"No," she said, then automatically thought of the three hang-up calls last night. God, was it just last night? She'd attributed them to Angie. That made the most sense to her. The idea of a stalker had never occurred. It still didn't seem a possibility.

"I think you should park on the street," Quinn said. "This might have been some transient going through the neighborhood, or it might have been some kid playing a joke, but you can't be too careful, Kate."

"I know. I will—starting tomorrow. How long have you been here?" Kate asked as they started for the house.

"Not long enough to have to do *that*."

"That's not what I meant."

"I just got here. I tried calling you at the

office. I tried calling here. I went to the office—you were gone. So I took a cab. Did you get my messages?"

"Yes, but it was late and I was tired. It's been a rotten, rotten day, and I just wanted out of there."

She let them in the back door and Thor greeted them with an indignant meow. Kate left her boots in the entry, dropped her briefcase on a kitchen chair, and went directly to the fridge to pull out the cat food.

"You weren't avoiding me?" Quinn said, shrugging out of his coat.

"Maybe. A little."

"I was worried about you, Kate."

She set the dish down on the floor, stroked a hand over the cat, and straightened with her back to Quinn. Just that one little sentence brought the volatile emotions swirling once more to the surface, brought tears to her eyes. She wouldn't let him see them if she could help it. She would choke them back down if she could. He was inviting her to need him. She wanted to so badly.

"I'm sorry," she said. "I'm not used to anyone caring—"

Christ, what a poor choice of words. She wasn't used to anyone caring about her anymore. The truth, but it made her sound pathetic and wretched. It made her think of Melanie Hessler—missing for a week without anyone caring enough to find out why.

"She was my client," she said. "Melanie Hessler. Victim number four. I managed to lose two in one night. How's that for a record?"

"Oh, Kate." He came up behind her and slipped his arms around her, folding his warmth and his strength around her. "Why didn't you call me?"

Because I'm afraid of needing you. Because I'm afraid of loving you.

"Nothing you could do about it," she said.

Quinn turned her in his arms and brushed her hair back from her face, but he didn't try to make her look at him. "I could have done this," he murmured. "I could have come and put my arms around you and held you for a while."

"I don't know that that would have been such a good idea," she said quietly.

"Why not?"

"Because. You're here to work a case. You've got more important things to do."

"Kate, I love you."

"Just like that."

"You know it's not 'just like that.'"

She stepped away from him, instantly missing the contact. "I know that we went five years without a word, a note, nothing. And now in a day and a half we're in love again. And in a week you'll go. And then what?" she said, moving restlessly, hands on her hips. "What am I thinking?"

"Apparently, nothing good."

Kate could see that she'd hurt him, which hadn't been her intent at all. She cursed herself for being so clumsy with such fragile feelings, but she was out of practice, and she was so afraid, and fear made her awkward.

"I'm thinking about every time in those five years that I wanted to pick up the phone but didn't," Quinn said. "But I'm here now."

"By chance. Can't you see how that scares me, John? If not for this case, would you ever have come? Would you ever have called?"

"Would you?"

"No," she said without hesitation, then softer and softer, shaking her head. "No...no...I've had enough pain to last me a lifetime. I wouldn't have gone looking for it. I don't want any more. I'd rather not feel anything at all. And you make me feel *so much,*" she said, her throat tightening. "Too much. And I don't trust it all not to just disappear."

"No. No." He caught hold of her by the arms and held her in front of him. "Look at me, Kate."

She wouldn't, didn't dare, wanted to be anywhere but right there in front of him on the brink of tears.

"Kate, look at me. It doesn't matter what we would have done. It matters that we're here now. It matters that we feel exactly what we felt back then. It matters that making love to you this morning was the most natural, perfect thing in the world—as if we'd never been apart. That's what matters. Not the rest of it.

"I love you. I do," he murmured. "That's what matters. Do you love me?"

She nodded, head down, as if she were ashamed to admit it. "I always did."

Tears slipped down her cheeks. Quinn caught them with his thumbs and brushed them away.

"That's what matters," he whispered. "Anything else we can work around.

"My life has been so empty since you left, Kate. I tried to fill the hole with work, but the work just ate away more of me, and the hole just got bigger and bigger, and I kept digging like crazy, trying to backfill. Lately, I've been feeling like there's nothing left. I blamed the job, thought I'd given away so many pieces of myself to it that I don't know who I am anymore. But I know exactly who I am when I'm with you, Kate. That's what's been missing all this time—the part of me I gave to you."

Kate stared at him, knowing he meant what he said. Quinn might have been a chameleon when it came to the job, changing colors at will to get the result he wanted, but he had never been less than honest with her in their relationship—at least until the end of it, when both of them had pulled the armor tight around bruised hearts. And she knew what it cost him to open himself up that way. Vulnerability was not something John Quinn did well. It was something Kate tried never to do at all herself. But she felt it now inside her, pushing hard at the gate.

"Have you noticed how our timing really sucks?" she said, winning a smile from him. He knew her well enough to realize she was trying to back them both away from this edge. A little joke to slacken the tension. A subtle sign that she wasn't ready, didn't have the strength to deal with it all just then.

"Oh, I don't know," he said, easing his arms around her. "I think right now you need to be held, and I need my arms around you. So that's working out pretty well."

"Yeah, I guess." She let herself put her head on his shoulder. *Resigned* was the word that came to mind, but she didn't fight it. She was too tired to fight, and she did indeed need to be held. She didn't get many opportunities these days. Her own fault, she knew. She told herself she was too busy to date, that she didn't need the complication of a man in her life right now, when the truth was that there was only one man for her. She didn't want any other.

"Kiss me," he whispered.

Kate raised her head and invited his mouth to settle on hers, parted her lips, and invited the intimacy of his tongue on hers. As with every kiss they had ever shared, she felt a glowing warmth, a sense of excitement, but also a sense of contentment deep within her soul. She felt as if she had been unconsciously holding her breath, waiting for this, and could now relax and breathe again. A sense of rightness, of completeness.

"I need you, Kate," Quinn whispered, dragging his mouth across her cheek to her ear.

"Yes," she whispered, the need pounding inside her like waves against rock. The need speaking above the fear that this would all end in heartache in a day or a week.

He kissed her again, deeper, harder, hotter, letting the reins out on the hunger racing through him. She could feel it in his muscles, in the heat of him; she could taste it in his mouth. His tongue thrust against hers even as he dropped one hand down her back and pulled her hips tight against his, letting her feel just how much he wanted her. She groaned deep in her throat, as much at the stunning depth of the need as at the feel of him hard against her.

Breaking the kiss, he leaned back from her and stared at her, his eyes hard and bright and dark, his lips slightly parted. He was breathing hard.

"My God, I need you."

Kate took his hand and led him to the hall. At the foot of the stairs, Quinn pulled her to him again for another kiss, still hotter and deeper, more urgent. He pressed her back against the wall. His hands caught the bottom of her black sweater and pulled it up between them, exposing her skin to the air, to his touch, giving him access to her breasts. She gasped as he pulled the cup of her bra aside and filled his hand with her. It didn't matter where they were. It didn't matter that anyone going by could have glimpsed them through the sidelights at her front door. That fast her desire for him outstripped all sense. There was only need, primal and fierce.

She gasped again as his mouth found her nipple. She cradled his head and arched into the contact. She lifted her hips away from the wall as he shoved her snug knit skirt up and stripped down her black tights. Suddenly there was no case, no past, nothing but the need and feel of his fingers exploring her, stroking her, finding her most sensitve flesh, sliding into her.

"John. Oh, God, John," she breathed, her fingers digging into his shoulders. "I need you. I need you now."

He straightened and kissed her quick and hard, twice, then looked up the stairs and back at her, then over his shoulder at the open door to her study, where the desk lamp cast an amber glow that just reached the old leather couch.

In the next moment they were beside the couch, Quinn stripping her sweater over her head, Kate impatiently pulling at his tie. In a few rough moves their clothes were off and abandoned on the floor. They sank down, tangled together on the couch, breath catching at the coldness of the leather. And then the sensation was forgotten, gone, burned away by the heat of their bodies and the heat of their passion.

Kate wrapped her long legs around him, took him into her body in one smooth stroke. He filled her perfectly, completely, physically and deep within her soul. They moved together like dancers, each body exquisitely comple-menting the other, the passion building like a powerful piece of music, building to a tremendous crescendo.

Then they were over the peak and free-falling, holding each other tight, murmuring words of comfort and assurance Kate already feared wouldn't hold up to the pressures of reality. But she didn't try to dispel the myth or break the promise of "everything will be all right." She knew they both wanted to believe it, and they could in those few quiet moments before the real world came back to them.

She knew that John needed to give that promise. He had always had a strong compulsion to protect her. That had always touched her deeply—that he could see the vulnerabilities in her when no one else, not even her husband, could. They had always recognized the secret needs in each other, had always seen each other's secret heart, as if they had always been meant for each other.

"I haven't made out on this couch since I was seventeen," she said softly, looking into his eyes in the glow of the lamplight. They lay on their sides, pressed close together, almost nose to nose.

Quinn smiled like a shark. "What was the guy's name—so I can go and kill him."

"My caveman."

"I am with you. I always was."

Kate didn't comment, though she instantly called to mind the ugly scene of Steven confronting her and John in his office. Steven choosing the weapons he used best: cruel words and threats. Quinn taking it and taking it until Steven turned on her. A broken nose and some dental work later, her husband had taken the war to a new playing field and done his best to ruin both their careers.

Quinn caught a finger beneath her chin and brought her head up so he could look into her eyes. He knew exactly what she was remembering. She could see it in his face, in the lowered line of his brow. "Don't," he warned.

"I know. The present is screwed up enough. Why dredge up the past?"

He stroked his hand down her cheek and kissed her softly, as if the gesture would seal off the door to those memories. "I love you. Now. Right now. In the present—even if it is screwed up."

Kate burrowed her head under his chin and kissed the hollow at the base of his throat. There was that part of her that wanted to ask what they were going to do about it, but she kept her mouth shut for once. It didn't matter tonight.

"I'm sorry about your client," Quinn said. "Kovac says she worked in an adult bookstore. That's probably the connection for Smokey Joe."

"Probably, but it spooked me," Kate admitted, absently stroking a hand down his bare back—all lean muscle and hard bone, too thin. He wasn't taking care of himself. "A week ago I didn't have anything to do with this case. Today I've lost two clients to it."

"You can't blame yourself for this one, Kate."

"Of course I can. I'm me."

"Where there's a will there's a way."

"I don't *want* to," she protested. "I just wish I'd called Melanie on Monday, like I usually do. If I hadn't been so preoccupied with Angie, I would have been concerned that I hadn't heard from her. She'd become emotionally dependent on me. I seemed to be her sole support network.

"I know this sounds odd, but I wish I had at least worried about her. The thought of her being caught in a nightmare like that with no one waiting for her, wondering about her, concerned for her...It's too sad."

Quinn hugged her close and kissed her hair, thinking she had a heart as soft as butter behind the armor. It was all the more precious to him because she tried so hard to hide it from everyone. He had seen it all along, from the first time he'd ever met her.

"You couldn't have prevented this from happening," he said. "But you may be able to help her now."

"In what way? By reliving my every conversation with her? Trying to pick out clues to a crime she couldn't have known would be committed against her? That's how I spent my afternoon. I would rather have spent the day poking myself in the eye with a needle."

"You didn't get anything off the tapes."

"Anxiety and depression, culminating with a row with Rob Marshall that could have me reading want ads soon."

"You're pushing your luck there, Kate."

"I know, but I can't seem to help it. He knows just how to punch my buttons. What do you have for me to do? Could I stretch it into a new career?"

"It's your old career. I brought you copies of the victimologies. I keep having the feeling that I'm looking right at the key we need and not seeing it. I need fresh eyes."

"You have all of CASKU and Behavioral Sciences at your disposal. Why me?"

"Because you need to," he said simply. "I know you, Kate. You need to do something, and you're as qualified as anyone in the Bureau. I've forwarded everything to Quantico, but you're right here, and I trust you. Will you take a look?"

"All right," she answered, for exactly the reason he'd said: because she needed to. She'd lost Angie. She'd lost Melanie Hessler. If there was something she could do to try to balance that out, she would.

"Let me put some clothes on." She pulled the chenille throw around her as she sat up.

Quinn scowled. "I knew there'd be a downside."

Kate gave him a wry smile, then went to her desk, where the light was blinking on the answering machine. She was a vision in the amber glow of the desk lamp, her hair flame red, the curve of her back a sculptor's dream. It made him ache just to look at her. How incredibly lucky he was to get a second chance.

A petulant voice whined from the machine, "Kate, it's David Willis. I *need* to speak with you. Call me tonight. You *know* I'm not home during the day. I feel like you're deliberately avoiding me. *Now*—when my confidence level is *so* low. I *need* you—"

Kate hit the button to forward to the next message. "If they were all like him, I'd get a job at Wal-Mart."

The next message was from the leader of a businesswoman's group, asking her to speak at a meeting.

Then next a long silence.

Kate met Quinn's sober stare with one of her own. "I had a couple of those last night. I thought they might be Angie. I wanted to believe it might be."

Or it might be whoever had Angie, Quinn thought. Smokey Joe. "We need to put a trap on your phone, Kate. If he's got Angie, he's got your number."

He could see that hadn't occurred to her. He saw the flash of surprise followed by annoyance with herself for having missed it. But of course Kate wouldn't think of herself as a possible victim. She was strong, in control, in charge. But not invulnerable.

Quinn got up from the couch and went to her, still naked, and put his arms around her.

"God, what a nightmare," she whispered. "Do you think she could still be alive?"

"She could be," he said, because he knew Kate needed to hear it. But he also knew that she was as aware of the odds and the horrible possibilities as he was. She knew as well as he did Angie DiMarco might still be alive, and that they might have been kinder hoping she was not.

• • •

I am dead
My need alive
Keeps me going
Keeps me hoping
Will he want me?
Will he take me?
Will he hurt me?
Will he love me?

The words cut at him. The music clawed at his senses. He played the tape anyway. Letting it hurt, needing to feel.

Peter sat in his office, the only light coming in through the window, just enough to turn black to charcoal, gray to ash. The anxiety, the guilt, the longing, the pain, the need, the emotions he could seldom grasp and never express, were trapped inside him, the pressure building until he thought his body would simply explode and there would be nothing left of him except fragments of tissue and hair stuck to the walls and the ceiling and the glass of the photographs of him with the people he had deemed important in his life in the last decade.

He wondered if any part of him would touch the pictures of Jillie crowded down into one small corner of the display. Out of the way, not calling any attention. Subtle shame—of her, of his failure, his mistakes.

"...We need to know the truth, Peter, and I think

you're holding back pieces of the puzzle....We need to see the whole picture."

Dark pieces of a disturbing picture he didn't want anyone to see.

The surge of shame and rage was like acid in his veins.

> *I am dead*
> *My need alive*
> *Keeps me going*
> *Keeps me hoping*
> *Will he want me?*
> *Will he take me?*
> *Will he hurt me?*
> *Will he love me?*

The sound of the phone was like a razor slicing along his nerves. He grabbed the receiver with a trembling hand.

"Hello?"

"Da-ddy, Da-ddy, Da-ddy," the voice sang like a siren. "Come see me. Come give me what I want. You know what I want. I want it now."

He swallowed hard at the bile in his throat. "If I do, will you leave me alone?"

"Daddy, don't you love me?"

"Please," he whispered. "I'll give you what you want."

"Then you won't want me anymore. You won't like what I have in store. But you'll come anyway. You'll come for me. Say you'll come."

"Yes," he breathed.

He was crying as he hung up, tears scalding his eyelids, burning his cheeks, blurring his vision. He opened the lower right-hand drawer of his desk, took out a matte black Glock nine-millimeter semiautomatic, and slipped it gently into the black duffel bag at his feet. He left the room, the duffel bag hanging heavy in his hand. Then he left the house and drove out into the night.

31

CHAPTER

"WHAT'S YOUR DREAM JOB?" Elwood asked.

"Technical consultant to a cop movie, set in Hawaii and starring Mel Gibson," Liska said without hesitation. "Turn the motor on. I'm cold." She shivered and burrowed her hands down into her coat pockets.

They sat in an employee lot near the Target Center, watching Gil Vanlees's truck by the white glow of the security light. Like the vultures they were often compared to, reporters circled the block around the building and sat in the many small parking lots scattered around it, waiting. They had been on Vanlees like ticks as soon as his name had been leaked in connection with Jillian Bondurant's murder.

Vanlees had yet to leave the building. Groupies lingering after the Dave Matthews Band concert required his full attention. Word from detectives inside the Target Center was that management had kept him behind the scenes—afraid of a lawsuit from Vanlees if they dismissed him based on suspicion alone, afraid of lawsuits from the public if they let him work as usual and something went awry. Press passes had been handed from music critics to crime reporters, who had roamed the halls, looking for him.

The radio crackled. "Coming your way, Elwood."

"Roger." Elwood hung up the handset and chewed thoughtfully on his snack. The whole car smelled of peanut butter. "Mel Gibson is married and has six children."

"Not in my fantasy he doesn't. Here he comes."

Vanlees came lumbering through the gate. Half a dozen reporters swarmed after him like a cloud of gnats. Elwood ran the window down to catch their voices.

"Mr. Vanlees, John Quinn has pegged you as a suspect in the Cremator murders. What do you have to say about that?"

"Did you murder Jillian Bondurant?"

"What did you do with her head? Did you have sex with it?"

Elwood sighed heavily. "It's enough to put you off the First Amendment."

"Assholes," Liska complained. "They're

worse than assholes. They're the bacteria that gather in assholes."

Vanlees had no comment for the reporters. He kept moving, having quickly learned that rule of survival. When he was directly in front of their car, Elwood cranked the key and started the engine. Vanlees bolted sideways and hurried on toward his truck.

"A nervous, antisocial individual," Elwood said, putting the last of his sandwich in a plastic evidence bag as Vanlees fumbled with his keys at the door of his truck.

"The guy's a twitch," Nikki said. "*My* twitch. Do you think I'll get anything out of it if we nail him for these murders?"

"No."

"Be brutally honest, why don't you? I don't want to hold any false expectations."

Vanlees gunned his engine and pulled out of his slot, scattering the reporters. Elwood eased in behind him, then turned the headlights on bright for an instant.

"A commendation would look good on my résumé when I send it off to Mel Gibson's people."

"The credit will go to Quinn," Elwood said. "The media is enamored of mind hunters."

"And he looks great on television."

"He could be the next Mel Gibson."

"Better—he's not losing his hair."

They sat behind Vanlees as he waited to pull onto First Avenue, and rolled out right behind him, causing an oncoming car to hit the brakes and the horn.

546

"Think Quinn would hire me as a technical adviser when he goes Hollywood?" Liska asked.

"It seems to me advising isn't your true goal," Elwood observed.

"True. I'd rather have a participatory role, but I don't think that'll happen. I think he's haunted. Doesn't he seem haunted to you?"

"Driven."

"Driven *and* haunted. Double whammy."

"Very romantic."

"If you're Jane Eyre." Liska shook her head. "I don't have time for driven *or* haunted. I'm thirty-two. I've got kids. I need Ward Cleaver."

"He's dead."

"My luck."

They stayed on the truck's tail, negotiating the maze of streets going toward Lyndale. Elwood checked the rearview, grumbling.

"We look like a funeral procession. There must be nine loads of newsies behind us."

"They'll get everything on videotape. Put away the nightsticks and saps."

"Police work just isn't the fun it used to be."

"Watch him in here," Liska said as they came to the worst of the confusing tangle of streets. "We might get him on a traffic violation. I break nine laws every time I drive through here."

Gil Vanlees didn't break any. He kept his speed a fraction under the limit, driving as if he were carrying a payload of eggs in crystal cups. Elwood stayed on the truck's tail, riding Vanlees's bumper a little too close, violating his space, goading him.

"What do you think, Tinks? Is he the guy, or is this the Olympic Park bombing all over again?"

"He fits the profile. He's hiding *something*."

"Doesn't make him a killer. Everybody's hiding something."

"I would have liked a chance to find out what, without a pack of reporters at our heels. He'd be an idiot to try anything now."

"They might not be at our heels long," Elwood said, checking the rearview again. "Look at this son of a bitch."

An older Mustang hatchback came up alongside them on the left, two men in the front seat, their focus on Vanlees's pickup.

"That's balls," Liska said.

"They probably think we're the competition."

The Mustang sped up, passing them, coming even with Vanlees, the passenger's window rolling down.

"Son of a bitch!" Elwood yelled.

Vanlees sped up. The car stayed with him.

Liska grabbed the handset and radioed their position, calling for backup and reporting the tag number on the Mustang. Elwood grabbed the dash light off the seat, slapped it onto the bracket, and turned it on. Ahead of them, the passenger in the car was leaning out the window with a telephoto lens.

Vanlees gunned ahead. The car raced even with him.

The flash was brilliant, blinding.

Vanlees's truck swerved into the Mustang, knocking it ass end into the next lane, directly into the path of an oncoming cab. There was no time for even the screech of tires, no time for brakes, just the horrific sound of tons of metal colliding. The photographer was thrown as the cars hit. He tumbled across the street like a rag doll that had been flung out a window. A ball of flame rolled through the Mustang.

Liska saw it all in slow motion—the crash, the fire, Vanlees's truck ahead of them swerving to the curb, one wheel jumping up, the front bumper taking out a parking meter. And then time snapped back to real speed, and Elwood swung the Lumina past the truck and dove into the curb at an angle, cutting off the escape route. He slammed the car into park and was out the door. Liska clutched the handset in a trembling fist and called for ambulances and a fire truck.

Some of the cars that had been tailing them pulled to the side. Several raced past, making Elwood dodge them as he ran for the burning wreck. Liska shoved her door open and went for Vanlees as he tumbled out of his pickup. She could smell the whiskey on him two feet away.

"I didn't do it!" he shouted, sobbing.

Camera flashes went off like strobes, illuminating his face in stark white light. Blood ran from his nose and his mouth where his face had evidently met with the steering wheel. He threw his arms up to block the glare and spoil the shots. "Goddammit, leave me alone!"

"I don't think so, Gil," Liska said, reaching

for his arm. "Up against the truck. You're under arrest."

"NOW I KNOW how they break spies with sleep deprivation," Kovac said, striding toward Gil Vanlees's truck, which was still hung up on the curb. "I'm ready to transfer to records so I can get some sleep."

Liska scowled at him. "Come crying to me when you have a nine-year-old look up at you with big teary blue eyes and ask why you didn't come to his Thanksgiving pageant at school when he was playing a Pilgrim and everything."

"Jesus, Tinks," he growled, hanging a cigarette on his lip. The apology was in his eyes. "We shouldn't be allowed to breed."

"Tell it to my ovaries. What the hell are you doing here anyway?" she asked, turning him away from the reporters. "Trying to get yourself fired altogether? You're supposed to lie low."

"I'm bringing you coffee." The picture of innocence, he handed her a steaming foam cup. "Just trying to support the first team."

Even as he said it, his gaze was roaming to Vanlees's truck.

The truck was surrounded by uniformed cops and the crime scene team setting up to do their thing. Portable lights illuminated it from all angles, giving the scene the feel of a photo shoot for a Chevy ad. The totaled cars sitting in the middle of the street were being dealt with by tow trucks.

Reporters hung around the perimeter of the scene, backed off by the uniforms, their interest in the accident made all the more keen by their own involvement in the drama.

"Any word on your replacement?" Liska asked.

Kovac lit a cigarette and shook his head. "I put in a word for you with Fowler."

She looked surprised. "Wow, thanks, Sam. You think they'll listen?"

"Not a chance. My money's on Yurek because they can scare him. So what's the latest here?"

"Vanlees is at HCMC getting looked at before we haul his sorry ass downtown. I think he broke his nose. Other than him, we've got one dead, one critical, one in good condition." Liska leaned back against the car she and Elwood had been riding in. "The driver of the Mustang is toast. The cabbie broke both ankles and cracked his head, but he'll be okay. The photographer is in surgery. They think his brain is bleeding. I wouldn't be too optimistic. Then again, I wouldn't have said he had a brain, doing what he was doing."

"Do we know who these guys are—were?"

"Kevin Pardee and Michael Morin. Freelancers looking to score with an exclusive photo. Life and death in the age of tabloid news. Now they're the headline."

"How'd Vanlees get behind the wheel if he was drunk enough you could smell it on him?"

"You'd have to ask the reporters that. They

were the ones crowded around him as he left the building. All our people had to watch him from a distance or spark a lawsuit for harassment."

"Ask the reporters," Sam grumbled. "They'll be the first ones to raise questions about *our* negligence. Scumsuckers. How's Elwood?"

"Burned his hands pretty bad trying to get Morin out of the car. He's at the hospital. Singed his eyebrows off too. Looks pretty damn goofy."

"He looked goofy to start with."

"Vanlees registered .08 on the Breathalyzer. Lucky for us. I was able to impound the truck. Gotta inventory everything in it," she said with a shrug, blinking false innocence. "Can't know what we might find."

"Let's hope for a bloody knife under the seat," Kovac said. "He looks like he'd be that stupid, don't you think? Christ, it's cold. And it's not even Thanksgiving."

"Bingo!" called one of the crime scene team.

Kovac jumped away from the car. "What? What'd you get? Tell me it's got blood on it."

The criminalist stepped back from the driver's door. "The economy self-gratification kit," she said, turning around, holding up a copy of *Hustler* and one very disgusting pair of black silk women's panties.

"The pervert's version of the smoking gun," Kovac said. "Bag it. We may just have the key to unlock this mutt's head."

"WHAT'S THE WORD on getting a warrant to search Vanlees's place?" Quinn asked, shrugging out of his trench coat. He wore the same suit he'd had on the night before, Kovac noticed. Heavily creased.

Kovac shook his head. "Based on what we've got, not a chance in hell. Not even with Peter Bondurant's name attached to the case. We went over every inch of that truck and didn't come up with anything that would tie him directly to any of the murder victims. We might get lucky with the panties—a few weeks from now when the DNA tests come back. We can't even run the tests now. The underpants are just part of the inventory of his stuff at this point. We don't know who they belonged to. We can't say he stole them. And whacking off ain't a crime."

"You hear that, Tippen?" Liska said. "You're in the clear."

"I heard those were your panties, Tinks."

"Tinks wears panties?" Adler said.

"Very funny."

They stood in a conference room at the PD, the task force minus Elwood, who had refused to go home and was now sitting with Vanlees in an interview room down the hall.

"Why couldn't he be dumb enough to keep a bloody knife under the seat?" Adler asked. "He looks like he'd be that stupid."

"Yeah," Quinn agreed. "That bothers me.

We're not exactly dealing with a brainiac here—unless he's got multiple personalities and one of the alters keeps the brain to himself. What do we know about his background, other than his more recent escapades?"

"I'm checking it," Walsh said. His voice was almost gone, choked off by his cold and his pack-a-day habit.

"Nikki and I have both talked with his wife," Moss said. "Should I see if she'll come down?"

"Please," Quinn said.

"She's gotta know if her husband's this kind of a sick pervert," Tippen said.

Quinn shook his head. "Not necessarily. It sounds like she's the dominant partner in that relationship. He's likely kept his hobby a secret from her, partly out of fear, partly as an act of defiance. But if he's got a female partner—and we think he has—then who is she? The wife is clean?"

"The wife is clean. Jillian?" Liska ventured.

"Possibly. Has the wife given any indication she thought he might have a girlfriend?"

"No."

Quinn checked his watch. He wanted Vanlees waiting just long enough to get nervous. "You get anything back on Michele Fine's prints?"

"Nothing in Minnesota."

"Has Vanlees called a lawyer?"

"Not yet," Liska said. "He's got his logic going. He says he's not calling a lawyer because an innocent man doesn't need one."

Tippen snorted. "Christ, how'd he ever find his way out of St. Cloud?"

"Dumb luck. I told him we weren't charging him right off on the accident. I told him we needed to sit down and sort through what happened before we could determine negligence, but that we had to hold him on the DUI. He can't decide if he should be relieved or pissed."

"Let's go to it before he makes up his mind," Quinn said. "Sam—you, Tinks, and me. We work him like before."

"I wouldn't if I were you, Sam," Yurek cautioned. "Fowler, Little Dick, Sabin, and that assistant prosecutor Logan—they're all there to observe."

"Fuck me," Kovac said with abject disgust.

Liska arched a brow. "Will you respect me afterward?"

"Do I respect you now?"

She kicked him in the shin.

"Charm," he said to Yurek through his teeth. "If you were me, I wouldn't be in this mess."

GREER, SABIN, LOGAN, and Fowler stood in the hall outside the interview room, waiting. At the sight of Kovac, Fowler got an expression as if he were having angina. Greer's eyes bugged out.

"What are you doing here, Sergeant?" he demanded. "You've officially been removed from the task force."

555

"My request, Chief," Quinn said smoothly. "We've already established a certain way of dealing with Mr. Vanlees. I don't want to change anything at this point. I need him to trust me."

Greer and Sabin looked sulky; Logan, impatient. Fowler pulled a roll of Tums out of his pocket and thumbed one off.

Quinn dismissed the topic before anyone could think to defy him. He held the door for Liska and Kovac, and followed them in.

Gil Vanlees looked like a giant raccoon. Both eyes had blackened in the hours since the accident. He had a split lip and a wide strip of adhesive tape across his nose. He stood at one end of the room with his hands on his hips, looking pissed and nervous.

Elwood sat in a chair with his back against the wall. Both hands were bandaged. His face was seared red. Without eyebrows his expression seemed one of perpetual unpleasant surprise.

"I hear you had a little accident, Gil," Kovac said, falling into a chair at the table.

Vanlees pointed a finger at him. "I'm gonna sue. You people harassed me, you let the press harass me—"

"You got behind the wheel of a truck with a snootful," Kovac said, lighting a cigarette. "Did I buy it for you? Did I pour it down your throat?

"Your people let me get behind that wheel," Vanlees began with all the sanctimonious indignation of a master at rationalization.

He shot a quick, nervous glance at Elwood.

Kovac made a face. "Next thing you're gonna tell me it's my fault you killed Jillian Bondurant and those other women."

Vanlees reddened, his eyes teared. He made a sound like a man straining on the toilet. "I *didn't*." He turned on Liska then. "You told me this was about the accident. You're such a lying little cunt!"

"Hey!" Kovac barked. "Sergeant Liska's doing you a favor. You killed someone last night, you fucking drunk."

"That wasn't my fault! That son of a bitch shot a flash off in my face! I couldn't see!"

"That's what Sergeant Liska says. She was there. She's your witness. You want to call her a cunt again? I was her, I'd feed you your dick for dinner, you sorry sack of shit."

Vanlees looked at Liska, contrite.

"Liska says you're innocent as a vestal virgin," Kovac went on, "and that you don't want a lawyer. Is that right?"

"I haven't done anything wrong," he said, sulking.

Kovac shook his head. "Wow. You've got a broad definition of reality there, Gil. We've got you dead to rights on the DUI—which is wrong by law. I know you were looking in Jillian Bondurant's windows. That would be considered wrong."

Vanlees sat down, chair turned sideways to the table, presenting his back to Kovac and to the people on the other side of the one-way glass. He rested his forearms on his thighs and looked at the floor. He looked prepared to sit there all night without saying another word.

Quinn studied him. In his experience it wasn't the innocent man who refused counsel, it was the man with something on his conscience he wanted to unload.

"So, were those Jillian's panties we pulled out from under your driver's seat, Gil?" Kovac asked bluntly.

Vanlees kept his head down. "No."

"Lila White's? Fawn Pierce's? Melanie Hessler's?"

"No. No. No."

"You know, I wouldn't have guessed it looking at you, but you're a complex individual, Gil," Kovac said. "Multilayered—like an onion. And every layer I peel away smells worse than the last. You look like an average Joe. Peel one layer back and—oh!—your wife's leaving you! Well, that's not so unusual. I'm a two-time loser myself. Peel another layer back and—jeez!—she's leaving you because you're a window peeper! No, wait, you're not just a window peeper. You're a weenie wagger! You're just one big, bad progessive joke. You're a drunk. You're a drunk who drives. You're a drunk who drives and gets somebody killed."

Vanlees hung his head lower. Quinn could see the man's swollen mouth quivering.

"I didn't mean to. I couldn't see," Vanlees said in a thick voice. "They won't leave me alone. That's *your* fault. I didn't do any-thing."

"They want to know what happened to Jillian," Kovac said. "I want to know what happened to her too. I think there was something more going on between you than what you're telling us, Gil. I think you had the hots for her. I think you were watching her. I think you stole those panties out of her dresser so you could whack off with them and fantasize about her, and I'm gonna prove it. We already know the panties are her size, her brand," he bluffed. "It's just a matter of time before we get the DNA match. A few weeks. You'd better get used to those reporters, 'cause they're gonna be on you like flies on roadkill."

Vanlees was crying now. Silently. Tears dripping onto the backs of his hands. He was trembling with the effort to hold them back.

Quinn looked to Kovac. "Sergeant, I'd like to have a few moments alone with Mr. Vanlees."

"Oh, sure, like I got nothing better to do," Kovac complained, getting up. "I know where this is going, Quinn. You G-men want it all to yourself. Fuck that. His ass is mine."

"I just want a few words with Mr. Vanlees."

"Uh-huh. You don't like the way I talk to this piece of cheese. You're sitting there thinking I should go easy on him on account of his prostitute mother used to beat his bare ass with a wire hanger or some such psychobabble bullshit. Fine. I'll see you in the headlines, I'm sure."

Quinn said nothing until the cops had gone

out, and then he said nothing for a long time. He took a Tagamet and washed it down with water from the plastic pitcher on the table. Casually, he turned his chair perpendicular to Vanlees's, leaned ahead, rested his forearms on his thighs, and sat there some more, until Vanlees glanced up at him.

"More of that good cop-bad cop shit," Vanlees said, pouting. "You think I'm a dumb shit."

"I think you watch too much TV," Quinn said. "This is the real world, Gil. Sergeant Kovac and I don't have identical agendas here.

"I'm not interested in headlines, Gil. I've had plenty. You know that. I get them automatically. You know all I'm interested in, right? You know about me. You've read about me."

Vanlees said nothing.

"The truth and justice. That's it. And I don't care what the truth turns out to be. It's not personal with me. With Kovac, everything is personal. He's got you in his crosshairs. All I want to know is the truth, Gil. I want to know your truth. I get the feeling you've got something heavy on your chest, and maybe you want to get it off, but you don't trust Kovac."

"I don't trust you either."

"Sure you do. You know about me. I've been nothing but up front with you, Gil, and I think you appreciate that on some level."

"You think I killed Jillian."

"I think you fit the profile in a lot of respects. I admit that. Moreover, if you look at the situation objectively, you'll agree with me. You've studied this stuff. You know what we look for. You know some of your pieces fit the puzzle. But that doesn't mean I believe you killed her. I don't necessarily believe Jillian is dead."

"What?" Vanlees looked at him as if he thought Quinn might have lost his mind.

"I think there's a lot more to Jillian than first meets the eye. And I think you may have something to say about that. Do you, Gil?"

Vanlees looked at the floor again. Quinn could feel the pressure building in him as he weighed the pros and cons of answering truthfully.

"If you were watching her, Gil," Quinn said very softly, "you're not going to get in trouble for that. That's not the focus here. The police will gladly let that go in trade for something they can use."

Vanlees seemed to consider that, never thinking, Quinn was sure, that the "something" they were looking for could in turn be used against him. He was thinking of Jillian, of how he might cast some odd light on her and away from himself, because that was what people tended to do when they found themselves in big trouble—blame the other guy. Criminals regularly blamed their victims for the crimes committed against them.

"You were attracted to her, right?" Quinn said. "That's not a crime. She was a pretty girl. Why shouldn't you look?"

"I'm married," he mumbled.

"You're married, you're not dead. Looking is free. So you looked. I don't have a problem with that."

"She was...different," Vanlees said, still staring at the floor but seeing Jillian Bondurant, Quinn thought. "Kind of...exotic."

"You told Kovac she didn't come on to you, but that's not exactly true, is it?" Quinn ventured, still speaking softly, an intimate chat between acquaintances. "She was aware of you, wasn't she, Gil?"

"She never said anything, but she'd look at me in a certain way," he admitted.

"Like she wanted you." A statement, not a question, as if it came as no surprise.

Vanlees shied away from that. "I don't know. Like she wanted me to know she was looking, that's all."

"Kind of mixed signals."

"Yeah. Mixed signals."

"Did anything come of it?"

Vanlees hesitated, struggled. Quinn waited, held his breath.

"I just want the truth, Gil. If you're innocent, it won't hurt you. It's just between us. Man to man."

The silence stretched.

"I—I know it was wrong," Vanlees murmured at last. "I didn't really mean to do it. But I was checking the yards one night, making the rounds—"

"When was this?"

"This summer. And...I was there..."

"At Jillian's house."

He nodded. "She was playing the piano, wearing a silky robe that wanted to fall off her shoulder. I could see her bra strap."

"So you watched her for a while," Quinn said, as if it was only natural, any man would do it, no harm.

"Then she slipped the robe off and stood up and stretched."

Vanlees was seeing it all in his mind. His respiration rate had picked up, and a fine sheen of sweat misted his face. "She started moving her body, like a dance. Slow and very...erotic."

"Did she know you were there?"

"I didn't think so. But then she came to the window and pulled the cups of her bra down so I could see her tits, and she pressed them right to the glass and rubbed against it," he said in a near whisper, ashamed, thrilled. "She—she licked the window with her tongue."

"Jesus, that must have been very arousing for you."

Vanlees blinked, embarrassed, looked away. This would be where parts of the story would go missing. He wouldn't tell about getting an erection or taking his penis out and masturbating while he watched her. Then again, he didn't have to. Quinn knew his history, knew the patterns of behavior, had seen it over and over in the years of studying criminal sexual behavior. He wasn't learning anything new here about Gil Vanlees. But if the story was true, he was learning something very significant about Jillian Bondurant.

"What'd she do then?" he asked softly.

Vanlees shifted on his chair, physically uncomfortable. "She—she pulled her panties down and she...touched herself between her legs."

"She masturbated in front of you?"

His face flushed. "Then she opened the window and I got scared and ran. But later I went back, and she had dropped her panties out the window."

"And those are the panties the police found in your truck. They *are* Jillian's."

He nodded, bringing one hand up to his forehead as if to try to hide his face. Quinn watched him, trying to gauge him. Truth or a tale to cover his ass for having the underwear of a possible murder victim in his possession?

"When was this?" he asked again.

"Back this summer. July."

"Did anything like that ever happen again?"

"No."

"Did she ever say anything about it to you?"

"No. She almost never talked to me at all."

"Mixed signals," Quinn said again. "Did that make you mad, Gil? That she would strip in front of you, masturbate in front of you, then pretend like nothing happened. Pretend like she hardly knew you, like you weren't good enough for her. Did that piss you off?"

"I didn't do anything to her," he whispered.

"She was a tease. If a woman did that to me—got me hard and hot for her, then turned it off—I'd be pissed. I'd want to fuck her good, make her pay attention. Didn't you want to do that, Gil?"

"But I never did."

"But you wanted to have sex with her, didn't you? Didn't some part of you want to teach her a lesson? That dark side we all have, where we hold grudges and plan revenge. Don't you have a dark side, Gil? I do."

He waited again, the tension coiled tight inside him.

Vanlees looked bleak, defeated, as if the full import of all that had happened tonight had finally sunk in.

"Kovac is going to try to hang that murder on me," he said. "Because those panties are Jillian's. Because of what I just told you. Even when she was the bad one, not me. That's what's going to happen, isn't it?"

"You make a good suspect, Gil. You see that, don't you?"

He nodded slowly, thinking.

"Her father was there, at the town house," he mumbled. "Sunday morning. Early. Before dawn. I saw him coming out. Monday his lawyer gave me five hundred dollars not to say anything."

Quinn absorbed the information in silence, weighing it, gauging it. Gil Vanlees was ass deep in alligators. He might say anything. He might say he'd seen a stranger, a vagrant, a one-armed man near Jillian's apartment. He chose to say he'd seen Peter Bondurant, and that Peter Bondurant had paid him to shut up.

"Early Sunday morning," Quinn said.

Vanlees nodded. No eye contact.

"Before dawn."

"Yes."

"What were you doing around there at that hour, Gil? Where were you that you saw him—and that he saw you?"

Vanlees shook his head this time—at the question or at something playing through his own mind. He seemed to have aged ten years in the last ten minutes. There was something pathetic about him sitting there in his security guard's uniform, the wanna-be cop playing pretend. The best he could do.

He spoke in a small, soft voice. "I want to call a lawyer now."

32

CHAPTER

KATE SAT ON THE OLD LEATHER COUCH in her study, curled into one corner, warding off the old house's morning chill with black leggings, thick wool socks, and a baggy old sweatshirt she hadn't worn in years. Quinn had given it to her back when. The name of the gym he frequented was stitched across the front. That she'd kept it all this time should have told her something, but then, she'd always been selectively deaf.

She had pulled it out of her closet after Quinn had gone to meet with the task force, freshening it in the clothes drier for a few minutes, and putting it on while it was still warm, pretending it was his warmth. A poor substitute for the feel of his arms around her. Still, it made her feel closer to him somehow. And after a night in his arms, the need for that was strong.

God, what an inconvenient time to rediscover love. But given their professions and their lives, what choice did they have? They were both too aware that life held no guarantees. Too aware that they had already given up too much time they could never get back because of fear and pride and pain.

Kate imagined she could look down from the height of another dimension and see the two of them as that time had passed. Her time spent focusing myopically on the minutiae of building a "normal" life for herself with a job and hobbies and people she saw socially at the requisite functions and holidays. Nothing deeper. Going through the motions, pretending not to mind the numbness in her soul. Figuring it was preferable to the alternative. Quinn's time poured into the job, the job, the job. Taking on more responsibility to fill the void, until the weight of it threatened to crush him. Crowding his brain with cases and facts until he couldn't keep them straight. Giving away pieces of himself and masking others until he couldn't remember what was genuine. Exhausting the well of strength that had once seemed almost bottomless. Wearing his confidence in his abilities and his judgment as threadbare as the lining of his stomach.

Both of them denying themselves the one thing they had needed most to heal after all that had happened: each other.

Sad, what people could do to themselves, and to each other, Kate thought, her gaze skimming across the pages of the victimologies she had spread out on the coffee table. Four more lives fucked up and ruined before they had ever met the Cremator. Five with Angie. Ruined because they needed love and couldn't find anything but a twisted, cheap replica. Because they wanted things out of their reach. Because it seemed easier to settle for less than work for more. Because they believed they didn't deserve anything better. Because the people around them who should have, didn't believe they deserved better either. Because they were women, and women are automatic targets in American society.

All of those reasons made a victim.

Everyone was a victim of something. The difference in people was what they did about it—succumb or rise above and move beyond. The women whose pictures lay before her would not be given that choice again.

Kate leaned over the coffee table, skimming her gaze across the reports. She had called the office to say she was taking some personal time. She'd been told Rob was out as well, and that office speculation was that they had beaten each other up and didn't want anyone to see the bruises. Kate said it was more likely Rob was still working on his written complaint to put in her personnel file.

At least she was free of him for the day. Which would have been a sweet deal if not for the photographs she had to look at of burned and mutilated women, and if not for all the emotions and depressing realities that those photographs evoked.

Everyone was a victim of something.

This group presented a depressing laundry list. Prostitution, drugs, alcohol, assault, rape, incest—if what Kovac had been told about Jillian Bondurant was true. Victims of crime, victims of their upbringing.

From a distance, Jillian Bondurant would have seemed to have been the anomaly because she wasn't a prostitute or in any sex-associated profession, but from the standpoint of her psychological profile, she wasn't all that far removed from Lila White or Fawn Pierce. Confused and conflicted feelings about sex and about men. Low self-esteem. Emotionally needy. Outwardly, she would seem not to have had as hard a life as a streetwalking prostitute because she wasn't as vulnerable to the same kind of crime and open violence. But there was nothing easy about suffering in silence, covering up pain and damage to save face for the family.

Quinn said there was considerable doubt that Jillian was dead at all, but that didn't mean she wasn't a victim. If she was Smokey Joe's accomplice, she was just a victim of another sort. The Cremator himself had been a victim once. Victimization as a child was one of many components that went into making a serial killer.

Everyone was a victim of something.

Kate turned to her own notes about Angie. Spare. Mostly hunches, things she had learned in her years of studying people to see what shaped their minds and their personalities. Abuse had shaped Angie DiMarco. Likely from a very early age. She expected the worst of people, dared them to show it to her, to prove her right. And that had undoubtedly happened again and again, because the kind of people who lived in Angie's world tended to live down to expectations. Angie included.

She expected people to dislike her, to distrust her, to cheat her, to use her, and made certain that they did. This case had been no exception. Sabin and the police had wanted nothing more than to use her, and Kate had been their tool. Angie's disappearance was an inconvenience to them, not a tragedy. If not for her status as a witness, no one on earth would have posted a reward or flashed her photograph on television asking "Have you seen this girl?" Even then, the police were not putting forth a tremendous search effort to find her. The energies of the task force were all dedicated to finding the suspect, not the AWOL witness.

Kate wondered if Angie might have seen the

spots on the news. She would have enjoyed the notoriety, the attention. She might secretly have pretended to believe someone actually cared about her.

"Why would you care what happens to me?" the girl had asked as they stood in the hall outside Kate's office.

"Because no one else does."

And I didn't care enough, Kate thought with a heavy heart. She'd been afraid to. Just as she had been afraid to let John back into her life. Afraid to feel that deeply. Afraid of the pain that kind of feeling could bring with it.

What a pathetic way to live. No—that wasn't living, that was simply existing.

Was the girl alive? she wondered, getting up from the couch to prowl the room. Was she dead? Had she been taken? Had she just left?

Am I being unrealistic to think there's even a question here?

She'd seen the blood for herself. Too much of it for a benign explanation.

But how could Smokey Joe have known where she was? What were the chances of his having spotted her at the PD and followed her to the Phoenix? Slim. Which would mean he would have to have found out some other way. Which meant he either had some in with the case...or an in with Angie.

Who had known where Angie was staying? Sabin, Rob, the task force, a couple of uniforms, the Urskines, Peter Bondurant's lawyer— and therefore Peter Bondurant.

The Urskines, who had known the first

victim and had a peripheral connection to the second. They hadn't known Jillian Bondurant, but her connection to these crimes had given Toni Urskine a platform for her cause.

Gregg had been there at the house Wednesday night when Kate had left Angie off. Just Gregg and Rita Renner, who gave all the appearances of being an Urskine puppet. Rita Renner, who had been friends with Fawn Pierce.

Kate had known the Urskines for years. While Toni might drive someone to kill, she couldn't imagine the couple practicing that hobby themselves. Then again, no one in Toronto had ever suspected the Ken and Barbie killers, and that couple had committed murders so hideous, veteran cops had broken down and wept on the witness stand during the trial.

God, what a sinister thought—that the Urskines might take women in using kindness and caring as a front for a sadistic hunting game. But surely they wouldn't be so stupid as to prey on their own clientele. They would be automatic suspects. And if the man Angie had seen in the park that night had been Gregg Urskine, then she would have recognized him at the Phoenix, wouldn't she?

Kate thought of the vague description the girl had given of Smokey Joe, the almost nondescript sketch, trying to make some sense of it all. Had she been so reluctant, so vague, because she was frightened, as Kate had suspected? Or because—as Angie said—it was dark, he wore a hood, it happened so fast? Or did her motivation lie elsewhere?

The task force had a hot suspect, Kate knew. Quinn was probably interviewing him right now. The caretaker from Jillian's town house complex. He had no inside connection to the case, but she supposed he could have known Angie if she had ever trolled for johns in the area around the Target Center, where he worked as a security guard.

But it didn't make sense for Angie to have a connection to the killer. If she knew him and wanted him caught, she would have given him up. If she knew him and didn't want him caught, she would have given a clear description of a phantom for the cops to chase.

And if she hadn't seen anything at all in the park that night, why would she say she had? For three squares and a place to stay? For attention? Then it would have made more sense for her to be cooperative rather than difficult.

Everything about this kid was a mystery inside a puzzle wrapped in an enigma.

Which is why I don't do kids.

But this one was—had been—her responsibility, and she would find out the truth about her or die trying.

"Poor choice of words, Kate," she muttered, heading upstairs to change clothes.

Twenty minutes later, she was out the back door. It had snowed another inch during the night, giving the landscape a clean dusting of fresh white powder, coating the back steps...where a pair of boots had left tracks.

Quinn had gone out the front this morning, to a waiting cab. The tracks were too small to be his, at any rate. They were more the size of Kate's feet, though that didn't necessarily establish gender.

Carefully staying to one side of them, Kate followed the tracks down the stairs to the yard. The trail led past the end of her garage and down the far side, down the narrow corridor between the building and the neighbor's weathered-gray privacy fence, to the side entrance of the garage. All the doors were closed.

A chill ran through her. She thought back to last night and someone defecating in the garage. She thought of the suddenly burned-out light, the feeling Wednesday night that someone had been watching her as she'd made her way from the garage to the house.

She looked around, down the deserted alley. Most of the neighbors had fences that hid the first stories of their homes from view. Second-story windows looked black and empty. The neighborhood was full of white-collar professionals, most of whom left for work by seven-thirty.

Kate backed away from the garage, heart pumping, hand digging in her bag for her cell phone. Moving toward the house, she pulled the phone out, flipped it open, and punched the power button. Nothing happened. The battery had died in the night. The inconvenience of modern convenience.

She kept her eyes on the garage, thought she

saw a movement through the side window. Car thief? Burglar? Rapist? Disgruntled client? Cremator?

She stuffed the phone back in her bag and pulled out her house keys. She let herself in, locked herself in, and breathed again.

"I need this like I need the plague," she muttered, going into the kitchen. She put her tote and her purse on the table and started to slip out of her coat, when the sound registered in her brain. The low, feral growl of a cat. Thor was under the table, snarling, ears flat.

The fine hair rose up on the back of Kate's neck, and with it the itchy feeling of being watched.

Options raced through her mind. She had no idea how close the person might be behind her, or how close they might be to the door. The phone was on the wall on the other end of the room—too far away.

Casually opening the tote, she looked inside with an eye for a weapon. She didn't carry a gun. The canister of pepper spray she had carried for a while had expired and she'd thrown it out. She had a plastic bottle of Aleve, a packet of Kleenex, the heel from the shoe she'd ruined Monday. She dug a little deeper and found a metal nail file, palmed that, and slipped it into her coat pocket. She knew her escape routes. She would turn, confront, break right or left. Plan set, she counted to five and turned around.

The kitchen was empty. But framed by the doorway to the dining room, sitting on one of

Kate's straight-backed oak chairs, was Angie DiMarco.

"HE CONFESSES TO having Jillian Bondurant's underpants, and you don't think he's the guy?" Kovac said, incredulous.

His temper had a direct effect on his driving, Quinn noticed. The Caprice roared down 94, rocking like a clown car. Quinn braced his feet in the floor well, knowing his legs would snap like toothpicks in the crash. Of course, it probably wouldn't matter, because he would be dead. This piece-of-crap car would crumple like an empty beer can.

"I'm just saying there are some things I don't like," he said. "Vanlees doesn't strike me as a team player. He lacks the arrogance to be the top dog, and the sadistic male is virtually always the dominant partner in a couple that kills. The woman is subservient to him, a victim who counts herself lucky not to be the one he's murdering."

"So this time it's reversed," Kovac insisted. "The woman runs the show. Why not? Moss and Liska say his wife had him pussy-whipped."

"His mother probably did too. And yes, it's often a domineering or manipulative or otherwise influential woman in his past or present a sexual sadist is killing symbolically when he kills his victims. That all fits, but there are holes too. I wish I could say I just look at him and like him for these murders, but I'm not feeling that bolt of lightning."

But then, that feeling had more or less deserted him in recent years, he reminded himself. Doubt had become more the rule than the exception, so what the hell did he know anymore? Why should he trust his instincts now?

Kovac swerved the car across three lanes to the exit he wanted. "Well, I can tell you, the powers that be like this guy fine. You talk about lightning. They're all getting a goddamn thunderstorm in their pants over Vanlees. He's got a history, he fits the profile, he has a connection to Jillian, access to hookers, and he's not Peter Bondurant. If they can find a way to charge him, they will. If they can, they'll do it in time for the press conference today."

And if Vanlees wasn't the guy, they ran the risk of pushing the real killer into proving himself again. The thought made Quinn ill.

"Vanlees says Peter was in Jillian's place predawn Sunday morning, and sent Noble on Monday to pay him to keep his mouth shut," he said, drawing a frighteningly long stare from Kovac. The Caprice began to drift toward a rusted-out Escort in the next lane.

"Jesus, will you watch the road!" Quinn snapped. "How do they give out driver's licenses in this state? You save up bottle caps or something?"

"Beer-can tabs," Kovac replied, returning his attention to the traffic. "So Bondurant was the one who cleaned up Jillian's house and erased the messages on the answering machine."

"I'd say so—if Vanlees is telling the truth.

And I think it's a safe bet then that Peter is the reason you didn't find any of Jillian's own musical compositions. He might have taken them because they revealed something about his relationship with Jillian."

"The sexual abuse."

"Possibly."

"Son of a bitch," Kovac muttered. "Sunday morning. Smokey Joe didn't light up the body until midnight. Why would Bondurant go to her place Sunday morning, wipe the place down, take the music, if he didn't already know she was dead?"

"Why would he wipe the place down at all?" Quinn asked. "He owns the town house. His daughter lived there. His fingerprints wouldn't be out of place."

Kovac cut him a glance. "Unless they were bloody."

Quinn braced a hand against the dash as a tow truck cut in front of them and Kovac hit the brakes. "Just drive, Kojak. Or we won't live long enough to find out."

WITH RUMORS OF a suspect in custody, the media circus had begun anew on the street in front of Peter Bondurant's house. Videographers roamed the boulevard, taking exterior shots of the mansion while on-air talent did their sound checks. Quinn wondered if anyone had even bothered to call the families of Lila White or Fawn Pierce.

Two Paragon security officers stood at the

gate with walkie-talkies. Quinn flashed his ID and they were waved through to the house. Edwyn Noble's black Lincoln was parked in the drive with a steel-blue Mercedes sedan beside it. Kovac pulled in behind the Lincoln, so close the cars were nearly kissing bumpers.

Quinn gave him a look. "Promise you'll behave yourself."

Kovac played it innocent. He had been relegated to the role of driver and wasn't to leave the car. He wasn't to cross Peter Bondurant's field of vision. Quinn had kept Gil Vanlees's revelation to himself, as an added precaution. The last thing he needed was Kovac bulling his way into this.

"Take your time, GQ. I'll just be sitting here reading the paper." He picked up a copy of the *Star-Tribune* from the pile of junk on the seat. Gil Vanlees took up half the front page—headline story, sidebar, and a bad photograph that made him look like Popeye's archnemesis, Bluto. Kovac's eyes were on the house, scanning the windows.

Noble met Quinn at the door, frowning, looking past him to the Caprice. In the car, Kovac had his newspaper open. He held it in such a way as to give Edwyn Noble the finger.

"Don't worry," Quinn said. "You managed to get the best cop on the case busted to chauffeur."

"We understand Vanlees has been taken into custody," the attorney said as they went into the house, ignoring Kovac as an unworthy topic.

"He was arrested on a DUI. The police will hold him as long as they can, but at the moment they don't have any evidence he's the Cremator."

"But he had…something of Jillian's," Noble said with the awkwardness of a prude.

"Which he says Jillian gave to him."

"That's preposterous."

"He tells a very interesting story. One that includes you and a payoff, by the way."

Fear flashed cold in the lawyer's eyes. Just for an instant. "That's absurd. He's a liar."

"He hasn't exactly cornered the market there," Quinn said. "I want to speak with Peter. I have some questions for him regarding Jillian's state of mind that night and in general."

The lawyer cast a nervous glance at the stairs. "Peter isn't seeing anyone this morning. He isn't feeling well."

"He'll see me." Quinn started up the stairs on his own, as if he knew where he was going. Noble hurried after him.

"I don't think you understand, Agent Quinn. This business has taken a terrible toll on his nerves."

"Are you trying to tell me he's what? Drunk? Sedated? Catatonic?"

Noble's long face had a mulish look when Quinn glanced over his shoulder. "Lucas Brandt is with him."

"That's even better. I'll kill two birds."

He stepped aside at the top of the stairs and motioned for Noble to lead the way.

THE ANTECHAMBER OF Peter Bondurant's bedroom suite was the showcase of a decorator who likely knew more about the house than about Peter. It was a room fit for an eighteenth-century English lord, all mahogany and brocade with dark oil hunting scenes in gilt frames on the walls. The gold damask wing chairs looked as if no one had ever sat in them.

Noble knocked softly on the bedroom door and let himself in, leaving Quinn to wait. A moment later, Noble and Brandt came out together. Brandt had his game face on—even, carefully neutral. Probably the face he wore in the courtroom when he testified for whoever was paying him the most money that day.

"Agent Quinn," he said in the hushed tones of a hospital ward. "I understand you have a suspect."

"Possibly. I have a couple of questions for Peter."

"Peter isn't himself this morning."

Quinn lifted his brows. "Really? Who is he?"

Noble frowned at him. "I think Sergeant Kovac has been a bad influence on you. This is hardly the time to be glib."

"Nor is it the time for you to play games with me, Mr. Noble," Quinn said. He turned to Brandt. "I need to speak with him about Jillian. If you want to be in the room, that's fine by me. Even better if you want to offer your opinion as to her mental and emotional state."

"We've been over that issue."

Quinn ducked his head, using a sheepish look to cover the anger. "Fine, then don't say anything."

He started toward the door as if he would just knock Brandt on his ass and walk over him.

"He's sedated," Brandt said, standing his ground. "I'll answer what I can."

Quinn studied him with narrowed eyes, then cut a glance to the lawyer.

"Just curious," he said. "Are you protecting him for his own good, or for yours?"

Neither batted an eye.

Quinn shook his head. "It doesn't matter—not to me anyway. All I'm interested in is getting the whole truth."

He told the story Vanlees had given him about the window-peeping incident.

Edwyn Noble rejected the tale with every part of him—intellectually, emotionally, physically—reiterating his opinion of Vanlees as a liar. He paced and clucked and shook his head, denying every bit of it except the idea that Vanlees had been looking in Jillian's window. Brandt, on the other hand, stood with his back to the bedroom door, eyes downcast, hands clasped in front of him, listening carefully.

"What I want to know, Dr. Brandt, is whether or not Jillian was capable of that kind of behavior."

"And you would have told Peter this story and asked Peter this question? About his child?" Brandt said with affront.

"No. I would have asked Peter something else entirely." He cut a look at Noble. "Like what he was doing at Jillian's apartment before dawn on Sunday that was worth paying off a witness."

Noble drew his head back, offended, and started to open his mouth.

"Save it, Edwyn," Quinn advised, turning back to Brandt.

"I told you before, Jillian had a lot of conflicted emotions and confusion regarding her sexuality because of her relationship with her stepfather."

"So the answer is yes."

Brandt held his silence. Quinn waited.

"She sometimes behaved inappropriately."

"Promiscuously."

"I wouldn't call it that, no. She would...provoke reactions. Deliberately."

"Manipulative."

"Yes."

"Cruel?"

That one brought his head up. Brandt stared at him. "Why would you ask that?"

"Because if Jillian isn't dead, Dr. Brandt, then there's only one logical thing she can be: a suspect."

33
CHAPTER

THE KID LOOKED LIKE HELL, Kate thought—pale as death, her eyes glassy and bloodshot, her hair greasy. But she was alive, and the relief Kate felt at that was enormous. She didn't have to bear the weight of Angie's death. The girl was alive, if not well.

And sitting in my kitchen.

"Angie, God, you scared the hell out of me!" Kate said. "How did you get in? The door was locked. How'd you even know where I live?"

The girl said nothing. Kate edged a little closer, trying to assess her condition. Bruises marred her face. Her full lower lip was split and crusted with blood.

"Hey, kiddo, where've you been?" she asked. "People were worried about you."

"I saw your address on an envelope in your office," the girl said, still staring, her voice a flat hoarse rasp.

"Very resourceful." Kate moved closer. "Now if only we could get you to use your talents for the good of humankind. Where've you been, Angie? Who hurt you?"

Kate was at the doorway now. The girl hadn't moved on the chair. She wore the same ratty jeans she'd worn from day one, now with dark stains that looked like blood on the thighs, the same dirty jean jacket that couldn't have been warm enough in this weather, and a dingy blue sweater Kate had seen before. Around her throat she wore a set of choke marks—purple bruises where fingers had pressed hard enough to cut off her wind and the blood supply to her brain.

A ghost of a bitter smile twisted Angie's mouth. "I've had worse."

"I know you have, sweetie," Kate said softly. It wasn't until she started to crouch down to take a closer look that Kate saw the utility knife in the girl's lap—a razor-blade nose on a sleek, thick, gray metal handle.

She straightened away slowly and took a half step back. "Who did this to you? Where've you been, Angie?"

"In the Devil's basement," she said, finding some kind of sour amusement in that.

"Angie, I'm going to call an ambulance for you, okay?" Kate said, taking another step back toward the phone.

Instantly, tears filled the girl's eyes. "No. I don't need an ambulance," she said, nearly frantic at the prospect.

"Someone's done a number on you, kiddo." Kate wondered where that someone might be. Had Angie escaped and come here on her own, or had she been brought here? Was her abductor in the next room, watching, waiting? If she could get on the phone, she could dial 911 and the cops would be here in a matter of minutes.

"No. Please," Angie begged. "Can't I just stay here? Can't I just be here with you? Just for a while?"

"Honey, you need a doctor."

"No. No. No." The girl shook her head. Her fingers curled around the handle of the utility knife. She held the blade against the palm of her left hand.

Blood beaded where the tip of the blade bit her skin.

The phone rang, shattering the tense silence. Kate jumped.

"Don't get it!" Angie shouted, holding her hand up, dragging the knife down inch by inch, opening the top layer of flesh, drawing blood.

"I'll *really* cut myself," she threatened. "I know how to do it."

If she meant it, if she brought that blade down a few inches to her wrist, she could bleed out before Kate finished the call to 911.

The ringing stopped. The machine in the den was politely informing whoever to leave a message. Quinn? she wondered. Kovac with some news? Rob calling to fire her? She imagined him capable of leaving that message, just as Melanie Hessler's boss had.

"Why would you want to cut yourself, Angie?" she asked. "You're safe now. I'll help you. I'll help you get through this. I'll help you get a fresh start."

"You didn't help me before."

"You didn't give me much chance."

"Sometimes I like to cut myself," Angie

586

admitted, face downcast in shame. "Sometimes I need to. I start to feel...It scares me. But if I cut myself, then it goes away. That's crazy, isn't it?" She looked up at Kate with such forlorn eyes, it nearly broke her heart.

Kate was slow to answer. She'd read about girls who did what Angie was describing, and, yes, her first thought was that it was crazy. How could people mutilate themselves and not be insane?

"I can get you help, Angie," she said. "There are people who can teach you how to deal with those feelings without having to hurt yourself."

"What do they know?" Angie sneered, her eyes shining with contempt. "What do they know about 'dealing with' anything? They don't know shit."

Neither do I, Kate thought. God, why hadn't she just called in sick Monday?

She considered and discarded the idea of trying to wrestle the knife away from the girl. The potential for disaster was too great. If she could keep her talking, she might eventually persuade her into putting it down. They had all the time in the world—provided they were alone.

"Angie, did you come here by yourself?"

Angie stared at the knife blade as she delicately traced it along the blue lines of the tattoo near her thumb, the letter A with a horizontal line crossing the top of it.

"Did someone bring you?"

"I'm always alone," she murmured.

"What about the other night, after I took you

back to the Phoenix? Were you alone then?"

"No." She dug the point of the blade into the tattooed blood droplets on the bracelet of thorns that encircled her wrist. "I knew he wanted me. He sent for me."

"Who wanted you? Gregg Urskine?"

"Evil's Angel."

"Who is that?" Kate asked.

"I was in the shower," she said, eyes glazed as she looked back on the memory. "I was cutting myself. Watching the blood and the water. Then he sent for me. Like he smelled my blood or something."

"Who?" Kate tried again.

"He wasn't happy," she said ominously. In eerie contrast, a sly smirk twisted her mouth. "He was mad 'cause I didn't follow orders."

"I can see this is a long story," Kate said, watching the blood drip from Angie's hand to her dining room rug. "Why don't we go in the other room and sit down? I can get a fire going in the fireplace. Warm you up. How's that sound?"

Distract her from her knife play. Get her out of sight of one telephone and near another, so that one way or another a call might get placed. The phone/fax in the den had 911 on the speed dial. If she could get Angie settled on the couch, she could sit on the desktop, work the phone off the hook, punch the button. It might work. It sure as hell beat standing there, watching the girl bleed.

"My feet are cold," Angie said.

"Let's go in the other room. You can take those wet boots off."

The girl looked at her with narrowed eyes, raised her bleeding hand to her mouth and dragged her tongue along one wound. "You go first."

In front of a psychotic with a knife, possibly going toward some waiting lunatic serial killer. Great. Kate started for the den, walking almost sideways, trying to keep one eye on Angie, one scouting ahead, trying to keep the conversation going. Angie clutched the knife in her hand, ready to use it. She walked a little bent over, with her other arm braced across her stomach, obviously in some pain.

"Did Gregg Urskine hurt you, Angie? I saw the blood in the bathroom."

She blinked confusion. "I was in the Zone."

"I don't know what that means."

"No, you wouldn't."

Kate led the way into the den.

"Have a seat." She motioned to the couch where she and Quinn had made love not that many hours before. "I'll get the fire going."

She thought of using the poker as a weapon, but discarded that idea immediately. If she could get the knife away from Angie by trickery, it would be preferable to violence for many reasons, not the least of which would be Angie's state of mind.

Angie wedged herself into a corner of the couch and began tracing over the bloodstains on her jeans with the point of the knife.

"Who choked you, Angie?" Kate asked,

going to the desk. A fax had come in. The call she hadn't answered.

"A friend of a friend."

"You need a better class of friends." She eased a hip onto the desktop, her eyes on the fax—a copy of a newspaper article from Milwaukee. "Did you know this guy?"

"Sure," the girl murmured, staring at the fire. "So do you."

Kate barely heard her. Her attention was riveted on the fax the legal services secretary had forwarded with a note saying *Thought you'd want to see this right away.* The article was dated January 21, 1996. The headline read: *Sisters Exonerated in Burning Death of Parents.* There were two poor, grainy photographs, made worse by the fax. But even so, Kate recognized the girl in the photo on the right. Angie DiMarco.

PETER SAT IN his bedroom, in a small chair by the window, the black duffel bag in his lap, his arms wrapped around it. He was wearing the same clothes he had worn in the night—black slacks and sweater. The slacks were dirty. He had vomited on the sweater. The sour smell of puke and sweat and fear hung around him like a noxious cloud, but he didn't care to change, didn't want to shower.

He imagined he was pale. He felt as if all the blood had been drained out of him. What flowed through his veins now was the acid of guilt, burning, burning, burning. He imagined it might burn him alive from the inside out, turn all his bones to ash.

Edwyn had come to tell him about the arrest of the caretaker, Vanlees, and had found him in the music room, smashing the baby grand piano with a tire iron. Edwyn had called Lucas. Lucas had come with a little black bag full of vials and needles.

Peter had refused the drugs. He didn't want to feel numb. He'd spent too much of his life feeling numb, ignoring the lives of the people around him. Maybe if he'd dared to feel something sooner, things wouldn't have come to this. Now all he could feel was the searing pain of remorse.

Looking out the window, he watched as Kovac nudged the nose of his car against the bumper of Edwyn's Lincoln, then backed up and turned around. A part of him felt relief that John Quinn was leaving. A part of him felt despair.

He had listened to the conversation on the other side of the door. Noble and Brandt making excuses for him, lying for him. Quinn asking the definitive question: Were they protecting him for his sake or for their own?

Time passed as he sat in the chair, thinking back, reliving all of it from Jillian's birth, on through his every devasting mistake, to this moment and beyond. He stared out the window, not seeing the news vans, the reporters waiting for an appearance by him, a sound bite from him. He hugged the duffel bag and rocked from side to side, coming to the only conclusion that made sense to him.

Then he checked his watch, and waited.

KATE STARED AT the fax, a chill running from the top of her head down her entire body. Her brain picked out key words: *burning deaths, mother, stepfather, drinking, drugs, foster care, juvenile records, history of abuse.*

"What's wrong with you?" Angie asked.

"Nothing," Kate said automatically, tearing her gaze from the article. "I just felt a little dizzy for a minute there."

"I thought maybe *you* were in the Zone." She smiled like a pixie. "Wouldn't that be funny?"

"I don't know. What's the Zone like?"

The smile vanished. "It's dark and empty and it swallows you whole and you feel like you'll never get out, and no one will ever come to get you," she said, her eyes bleak again. Not empty but bleak, afraid, full of pain—which meant there was still something in her to save. Whatever had happened to her in a childhood that culminated with the suspicious deaths of her parents, some scrap of humanity had survived. And it had survived the last days in "the Devil's basement," wherever that was.

"But sometimes it's a safe place too," she said softly, staring at the blood that ran in rivulets all over her left hand, back and front and around her wrist. "I can hide there…if I dare."

"Angie? Will you let me get a cold cloth for your hand?" Kate asked.

"Don't you like to see my blood? I do."

"I'd rather not see it dripping on my carpet," Kate said with a hint of her usual wry tone, more to spark some fire in Angie than out of any real concern for the rug.

Angie stared at her palm for a moment, then raised it to her face and wiped the blood down her cheek in a loving caress.

Kate eased away from the desk and backed toward the door.

The girl looked up at her. "Are you going to leave me?"

"No, honey, I'm not going to leave you. I'm just going to get that wet cloth." And call 911, Kate thought, moving another step toward the door, afraid now to leave the girl for fear of what she might do to herself.

The doorbell rang as she stepped into the hall, and she froze for a second. A face appeared at one of the sidelights, a round head above a puffed-up down jacket, trying to peer in through the sheer curtain. Rob.

"Kate, I know you're home," he said, petulant, knocking, his face still pressed to the window. "I can see you standing there."

"What are you doing here?" Kate asked in a harsh whisper, pulling the door open.

"I heard from the office you weren't going in. We need to talk about this—"

"You can't pick up a telephone?" she started, then caught herself and waved off the argument. "This isn't the time—"

Rob looked stubborn. He moved a little closer. "Kate, we *need* to talk."

Kate clamped her teeth against a sigh of exasperation. "Could you lower your voice?"

"Why? Is it a neighborhood secret you're trying to avoid me?"

"Don't be an ass. I'm not avoiding you. I've got a situation here. Angie's shown up and she's in a very fragile mental state."

His little pig eyes rounded. "She's *here*? What is she doing here? Have you called the police?"

"Not yet. I don't want to make things worse. She's got a knife and she's willing to use it—on herself."

"My God. And you haven't taken it away from her, Ms. Superwoman?" he said sarcastically as he pushed past her into the hall.

"I'd rather keep all my appendages attached, thanks."

"Has she hurt herself?"

"So far, it's just surface cuts, but one will need stitches."

"Where is she?"

Kate motioned to the den. "Maybe you can distract her while I call 911."

"Has she told you where she's been? Who took her?"

"Not exactly."

"If she goes to a hospital, she'll clam up out of resentment. It could be hours or days before we get the information out of her," he said in an urgent tone. "The police have made an arrest. The press conference is starting soon. If we can get her to tell us what happened, we can call Sabin before it's over."

Kate crossed her arms and considered. She could see Angie still sitting on the couch, drawing patterns with her fingertip on the palm of her bloody hand. If paramedics came and hauled her away, she would react badly, that was a sure bet. On the other hand, what would they be doing to her? Trying to drag what they wanted out of her while she sat bleeding and vulnerable.

Trying to catch a killer.

She heaved a sigh. "All right. We try, but if she gets serious with that knife, I'm calling."

Rob squinted at her. The toothache smile. "I know it pains you, Kate, but sometimes I *am* right. You'll see this is one of those times. I know exactly what I'm doing."

"WHAT'S *HE* DOING here?" Angie blurted out the words as if they gave her a bad taste in her mouth.

Rob gave her the toothache smile too. "I'm just here to help, Angie," he said, sitting back against the desk.

She gave him a long, hard stare. "I doubt it."

"It looks like you've had a little trouble since we saw you last. Can you tell us about that?"

"You want to hear about it?" she asked, eyes narrowed, her hoarse voice sounding almost seductive. She raised her hand and slowly licked the blood from her palm again, her gaze locked on his. "You want to know who did this to me? Or do you just want to hear about the sex?"

"Whatever you want to tell us about, Angie," he said evenly. "It's important for you to talk about it. We're here to listen."

"I'm sure you are. You like to hear about other people's pain and suffering. You're a sick little fuck, aren't you?"

A muscle ticked in Rob's cheek. He held on to his excuse for a smile, but it looked more like he was biting a bullet.

"You're trying my patience, Angie," he said tightly. "I'm sure that's not what you really want to do. Is it?"

The girl looked away toward the fire for so long that Kate thought she would never speak again. Maybe she'd gone to the Zone she'd talked about. She held the utility knife in her right hand, pressing the fingertips against the blade.

"Angie," Kate said, moving behind the couch, casually picking up the chenille throw from the back of it as she went. "We're trying to help you."

She sat on the arm of the unoccupied end, holding the blanket loosely in her lap.

Tears gleamed in Angie's eyes and she shook her head. "No, you're not. I wanted you to, but you're not. You just want what I can tell you." Her swollen mouth twisted into a bitter smile. "The funny thing is, you think you're getting what you want, but you are *so* wrong."

"Tell us what happened that night at the Phoenix," Rob prompted, trying to draw her attention back to him. "Kate dropped you off. You went upstairs to take a shower...Did someone interrupt you?"

Angie stared at him, slowly scratching the tip of the blade along her thigh over and over.

"Who came to take you, Angie?" Rob pressed.

"No," she said.

"Who came to take you?" he asked again, enunciating with emphasis.

"No," she said, glaring at him. "I won't do it."

The blade of the knife bit deeper. Sweat glistened on her pale face in the firelight. The denim shredded. Blood bloomed bright red in the tears.

Kate felt ill at the sight. "Rob, stop it."

"She needs to do this, Kate," he said. "Angie, who came to take you?"

"No." Tears streaked down Angie's battered face. "You can't make me."

"Let her alone." Kate moved off her perch. Christ, she had to do something before the girl cut herself to ribbons.

Rob's stare was locked on Angie. "Tell us, Angie. No more games."

Angie glared at him, shaking visibly now.

"Where did he take you? What did he do to you?"

"Fuck you!" she spat out. "I'm not playing your game."

"Yes, you are, Angie," he said, his voice

growing darker. "You will. You don't have a choice."

"Fuck you! I hate you!"

Shrieking, she came up off the couch, arm raised, knife blade flashing.

Kate moved fast, flinging the chenille throw to cover the knife and diving into Angie from the side almost simultaneously. The girl howled as they crashed to the floor, knocking into the coffee table and scattering the victimology reports.

Kate held her down as she struggled, the first wave of relief washing through her. Rob picked up the knife, closed the blade, and put it in his pocket.

Angie was sobbing. Kate moved onto her knees and pulled the girl into her arms to hold her.

"It's all right, Angie," she whispered. "You're safe now."

Angie pushed free, staring at her, incredulous and furious. "You stupid bitch," she rasped. "Now you're dead."

34
CHAPTER

"**THE SHARKS SMELL BLOOD** in the water," Quinn commented as they watched the mob gather for the press conference.

Kovac scowled. "Yeah, and some of it is mine."

"Sam, I can guarantee you, with Vanlees on the block, they could give a shit about you."

The idea seemed to further depress Kovac. It did nothing for Quinn either. Having Bondurant's people leak information about Vanlees to the press was bad enough, but to have the police talk openly to the press about Gil Vanlees at this point was dangerously premature. He'd said so to the mayor, Greer, and Sabin. That they were choosing to ignore his advice was beyond his control. And yet he could feel the anxiety singeing another hole in the wall of his stomach.

He was the one who had come up with the initial profile, which Vanlees fit, nearly to a T. In retrospect he thought he shouldn't have been so quick to offer an opinion. The possibility of tandem killers changed everything. But the press and the powers running the show had Vanlees now, and were all too happy to sink their teeth into him.

The mayor had chosen the grand Fourth Street entrance for the setting of the press conference. A cathedral of polished marble with an impressive double staircase and stained glass panels. The kind of place where politicians could stand on the stairs above the common folk and look important, where the glow of the marble seemed to reflect off their skin and make them seem more radiant than the average citizen.

Quinn and Kovac watched from a shadowed alcove as the television people set up and the newspaper people jockeyed for status spots. On the stairs, the mayor and Sabin conferred as the mayor's assistant brushed lint from her suit. Gary Yurek was deep in conversation with Chief Greer, Fowler, and a pair of captains who seemed to have come out of the woodwork for the photo op. Quinn would join the circus in a moment and give his two cents' worth to the throng, trying to give the announcement of a suspect in custody a cautionary spin, which almost no one would listen to. They would rather listen to Edwyn Noble spin lies for Peter Bondurant, which was almost certainly what he was doing standing with a reporter for MSNBC.

There was no sign of Peter. Not that Quinn had expected him—not after this morning, and not with the possibility of incest allegations seeping out into the news pool. Still, he couldn't help but wonder at Bondurant's mental state, and what exactly had brought Lucas Brandt running with his little black bag. Jillian's supposed demise, or the revelation of what might have happened all those years ago?

"Charm," Kovac said with derision, staring at Yurek. "Destined for a corner office. They love him upstairs. A million-dollar smile on lips he won't hesitate to use to kiss ass."

"Jealous?" Quinn asked.

He made one of his faces. "I was made for chewing ass, not kissing it. What do I need with a corner office, when I can have a crappy little desk in a crappy little cubicle with no decent file cabinets?"

"At least you're not bitter."

"I was born bitter."

Vince Walsh heralded his arrival with a phlegm-rattling coughing fit. Kovac turned and looked at him.

"Jesus, Vince, hack up a lung, why don't you?"

"Goddamn cold," Walsh complained. His color had the odd yellow cast of an embalmed body. He offered Kovac a manila envelope. "Jillian Bondurant's medical records—or what of them LeBlanc would release. There are some X rays. You want to take them or you want me to drop them off with the ME?"

"I'm out, you know," Kovac said even as he took the envelope. "Yurek's boss now."

Walsh sucked half the contents of his sinuses down the back of his throat and made a sour face.

Kovac nodded. "Yeah, that's what I said."

· · ·

PETER WAITED UNTIL the press conference was under way to enter the building. A simple matter of calling Edwyn on his cell phone from the car. Noble had no way of knowing he wasn't still at home. Peter had dismissed from the house the employees Edwyn had posted to keep an eye on him. They had gone without argument. He was the one who paid their wages, after all.

He came into the hall, holding the duffel bag in his arms, his gaze scanning the backs of five dozen heads. Greer was at the podium, going on in his overly dramatic way about the qualifications of the man he had chosen to succeed Kovac as head of the task force. Peter didn't care to hear it. The task force was no longer of any interest to him. He knew who had killed Jillian.

The press shouted questions. Flashes went off like so many star bursts. Peter worked his way along one side of the crowd, moving toward the stairs, feeling as if he were invisible. Maybe he was. Maybe he was already a ghost. All his life he had felt a certain emptiness in his soul, a hole nothing had ever been able to fill. Maybe he had been eroding away from the inside out for so long that the essence of what made him human had all leeched away, making him invisible.

· · ·

QUINN SAW BONDURANT coming. Oddly, no one else seemed to. No one looked closely enough, he supposed. Their focus was on the podium and the latest batch of bullshit they wanted to spread on the news and in the papers. And there was the fact that he looked vaguely seedy—unshaven, unkempt—not the Peter Bondurant of finely tailored suits, every hair in place.

His skin looked so pale, it was nearly translucent. His face was gaunt, as if his body were devouring itself from within. His eyes met Quinn's, and he stopped behind the camera people and stood there, a black duffel bag in his arms.

Quinn's instincts went on point—just as Greer invited him to step to the podium.

The glare of the lights blocked his view of Bondurant. He wondered if Kovac had spotted him.

"I want to stress," he began, "that the interview of a possible suspect does not end the investigation."

"Do you believe Vanlees is the Cremator?" a reporter called out.

"It wouldn't be prudent for me to comment on that one way or the other."

He tried to shift to an angle where he could see Bondurant again, but Bondurant was gone from the spot where he had last been. His nerves tightened.

"But Vanlees fits the profile. He knew Jillian Bondurant—"

"Isn't it true he had articles of her clothing

in his possession when he was arrested?" another asked.

Damn leaks, Quinn thought, his attention focused more on getting Bondurant back in his sights than on the reporters. What was he doing here on his own, and looking like a vagrant?

"Special Agent Quinn...?"

"No comment."

"Do you have *anything* to say about the Bondurant case?"

"I killed her."

Peter stepped out from behind a cameraman at the foot of the stairs and turned to face the crowd. For a moment no one but Quinn realized the admission had come from him. Then he raised a nine-millimeter semiautomatic handgun to his head, and awareness ran back through the crowd in a wave.

"I killed her!" Peter cried louder.

He looked stunned by his own confession—bug-eyed, stark white, openmouthed. He looked at the gun with terror, as if someone else were holding it. He went up the stairs sideways, eyes darting to the crowd, to the people near the podium: Mayor Noble, Chief Greer, Ted Sabin—all of whom backed away, staring at him as if they'd never seen him before.

Quinn held his spot at the podium.

"Peter, put the gun down," he said firmly, the microphone picking up his voice and broadcasting it to the hall.

Bondurant shook his head. His face was quivering, twitching, contorting. He clutched the duffel bag to him with his left arm. Behind him Quinn could see two uniformed officers moving into place with guns drawn and held low.

"Peter, you don't want to do this," he said quietly, calmly, shifting subtly away from the podium.

"I ruined her life. I killed her. It's my turn."

"Why here? Why now?"

"So everyone will know," he said, his voice choked. "Everyone will know what I am."

Edwyn Noble moved from the front of the crowd toward the stairs. "Peter, don't do this."

"What?" Bondurant asked. "Damage my reputation? Or yours?"

"You're talking nonsense!" the lawyer demanded. "Put down the gun."

Peter didn't listen. His anguish was an almost palpable thing. It was in the sweat that ran down his face. It was in the smell of him. It was in the air he exhaled too quickly from his lungs.

"This is my fault," he said, the tears coming harder. "I did this. I have to pay. Here. Now. I can't stand it anymore."

"Come with me, Peter," Quinn said, stepping a little closer, offering his left hand. "We'll sit down and you can tell me the whole story. That's what you want, isn't it?"

He was aware of the whir of motor drives as photographers shot frame after frame. The video cameras were running as well, some likely running live feeds to their stations. All of them recording this man's agony for their audiences.

"You can trust me, Peter. I've been asking you for the truth from day one. That's all I want: the truth. You can give it to me."

"I killed her. I killed her," he mumbled over and over, tears streaming down his cheeks.

His gun hand was trembling badly. Another few minutes and his own burning muscles would make him lower it. If he didn't blow his head off first.

"You sent for me, Peter," Quinn said. "You sent for me for a reason. You want to give me the truth."

"Oh, my God. Oh, my God!" Bondurant sobbed, the struggle within himself enormous, powerful, tearing him apart. His whole right arm was shaking now. He cocked the hammer back.

"Peter, no!" Quinn ordered, going for him.

The gun exploded. Shouts and screams echoed with the shot. A fraction of a second too late, Quinn grabbed hold of Bondurant's wrist and forced it up. Another shot boomed. Kovac rushed up behind Peter, the uniforms right behind him, and pulled the gun out of his hand.

Bondurant collapsed against Quinn, sobbing, bleeding, but alive. Quinn lowered him gently to the marble steps. The first shot had cut at an angle above his temple and plowed out a furrow of flesh and hair two inches long on its way to the second floor of the building. Gunpowder residue blackened the skin. He dropped his head between his knees and vomited.

The sound level in the hall was deafening. Photographers rushed forward for better angles. Edwyn Noble shoved past two of them to get to his boss.

"Don't say anything, Peter."

Kovac gave the attorney a look of disgust. "You know, I think it's a little late for that."

Ted Sabin took the podium and called for order and calm. The mayor was crying. Dick Greer snapped at his captains. The cops went about their jobs, dealing with the gun, clearing a path for the EMTs.

Quinn crouched beside Peter, hand still on the man's wrist, feeling his pulse race out of control. Quinn's own heart was pumping hard. A fraction of an inch, a steadier hand, and Peter Bondurant would have blown his brains out in front of half the country. An event to be broadcast on the nightly news with the disclaimer: We warn you—what you are about to see may be disturbing...

"You have the right to remain silent, Peter," he began quietly. "Anything you say may be used against you in court."

"Must you do this now?" Noble asked in a harsh whisper. "The press is watching."

"They were watching when he came onstage with a loaded gun too," Quinn said, tugging at the duffel bag Peter had smuggled the gun in. Bondurant, sobbing uncontrollably, tried to hold on to it for a moment, then let go. His body crumpled into a bony heap.

"I think people have already let too many rules slide where Peter is concerned," Quinn said.

He handed the bag to Vince Walsh. "It's heavy. He may have more weapons in it."

"You have the right to have your attorney present at questioning," Kovac continued the Miranda warning, pulling out handcuffs.

"Jesus God!" came the hoarse exclamation. Quinn looked up to see Walsh drop the duffel bag and grab the side of his neck, his face purple.

The paramedics said later he was dead before he hit the ground...right beside the bag that carried Jillian Bondurant's decapitated head.

35

CHAPTER

KATE STEPPED BACK from Angie, not trying to decipher what the girl had said. She was breathing hard, and she'd cracked her elbow on the coffee table on the fall to the floor. She rubbed it now as she tried to get her thoughts clear. Angie sat on her knees, keening like a banshee, hitting herself in the head with her bloody hands over and over again. Blood soaked the thighs of her jeans and oozed out through the slits she had cut with the knife.

"My God," Kate murmured, shaken by the sight. She backed into the desk, turned to the phone.

Rob stood three feet away, staring at the girl with a peculiar kind of interest, as if he were a scientist watching a specimen.

"Talk to us, Angie," he said softly. "Tell us what you're feeling."

"Jesus Christ, Rob," Kate snapped as she picked up the receiver. "Leave her alone! Go in the kitchen and get some wet towels."

He went instead to Angie, pulled a six-inch black leather sap from his coat pocket, and struck her across the back. The girl screamed and fell over sideways, arching her back as if to try to escape the pain.

Kate stood stunned, staring at her boss with her mouth hanging open. "W-what...?" she began, then swallowed and started again, her pulse racing. "What the hell is wrong with you?" she asked, breathless with astonishment.

Rob Marshall turned his gaze on her with undisguised hate. His eyes nearly glowed with it. The stare ran through Kate like a sword. She could feel the contempt roll off him in hot waves, could smell it rising, sour and vile from his pores. She stood there, time elongating, instincts coming alive even as she realized her phone was dead.

"You have no respect for me, Kate, you

fucking cunt," he said in a low, growling voice.

The words and the hatred behind them hit her like a fist, stunning her for a moment, then shaking her as the pieces fell into place.

"Who choked you, Angie? Did you know this guy?"

"Sure...So do you..."

"...It's all right, Angie. You're safe now."

"You stupid bitch. Now you're dead."

Rob Marshall? No. The idea seemed almost laughable. Almost. Except that the phone had been working before he showed up, and he was standing before her with a weapon in his hand.

She put the receiver down.

"I've had it with you," he said bitterly. "Picking, picking, picking. Bitching, bitching, bitching. Belittling me. Looking down your nose at me."

He stood on the victimology reports that had scattered on the floor. *Everyone is a victim of something.* She'd had that thought half a dozen times that morning when she'd been going over the reports, but she hadn't examined it closely enough.

Lila White had been a victim of an assault.

Fawn Pierce had been a victim of rape.

Melanie Hessler, another rape victim.

At some time or other they had all dealt with victim/witness services.

The only one who didn't fit was Jillian Bondurant.

"But you're an *advocate* for victims, for God's sake," she murmured.

An advocate who, because of his position, listened to account after account of people—largely women—being victimized, brutalized, beaten, raped, degraded....

How many times had he made her sit through the replaying of Melanie Hessler's interview tapes? Rob listening intently, running the tape back, replaying pieces over and over.

In her mind she was suddenly in Kovac's car at the Hessler crime scene, listening to the microcassette the killer had dropped. Melanie Hessler begging for her life, screaming in agony, begging for death.

She thought of Rob going to look at the charred body, coming back agitated, seemingly upset. But what she had mistaken for distress had in fact been excitement.

Oh, my God.

Bile rose up the back of her throat as every rotten thing she'd ever said to him scrolled through her memory.

Oh, God, I'm dead.

"I'm sorry," she said, options racing through her mind. The front door was just ten feet down the hall.

Disgust crossed Rob's face in a spasm. He squeezed his eyes nearly shut, looking as if he'd just caught wind of an open sewer. "No, you're not. You're not sorry about the way you've treated me. You're sorry I'm going to kill you for it."

"Angie, run!" Kate shouted. She grabbed the fax machine off the desk, jerking the power cord out the back, and flung the machine at Rob. It hit him in the chest and knocked him off balance.

She bolted for the door, slipping on one of the victimology reports—a mistake that cost her a precious fraction of a second. Rob grabbed at her, caught hold of a coat sleeve with one hand, and swung wildly with the sap.

Even through the thick wool of her coat collar, Kate felt the weight of it as it struck her shoulder. Heavy, deadly, serious. If he caught her in the head, she would go down like a rock.

She shied sideways, eluding his grasp, then used his own momentum to shove him into the hall. Grabbing his left arm and twisting it up behind him as he came past, she ran him into the hall table and bolted away before the crash was over, running for the front door that suddenly seemed a mile away.

Rob let out a roar and tackled her from behind. They hit the floor hard, Kate crying out as her right arm twisted unnaturally beneath her and she felt the sickening tear of muscles in her shoulder.

Pain swept through her like a fire. She ignored it as best she could as she tried to kick free and scramble to the door. Rob wrapped a fist in her hair and jerked her head back, hitting her with his fist on the right side of her head. Her vision blurred, her ear rang like a bell and burned like a son of a bitch. Knife-sharp pain shot out across her face and down her jaw.

"You bitch! You bitch!" he screamed over and over.

And then his hands were around her throat and he was choking her, and his screams faded from her head. She fought automatically, frantically, clawing at his hands, but his fingers were short and thick and strong.

She couldn't breathe, felt like her eyes were going to burst, felt like her brain was swelling.

With the last bit of sense she could grab, Kate forced herself to go limp. Rob continued to squeeze for seconds that seemed like an eternity, then slammed her head down on the floor. She knew he was ranting but couldn't make out the words as the blood roared back up to her brain. She tried not to suck in the great gulps of oxygen she wanted and needed so desperately. She tried not to let her mind stall out. She had to keep thinking—and not of the crime scene she had visited, not of the charred body of her client, not of the autopsy photos of four women this man had tortured and mutilated.

"You think I can't do anything right!" Rob raved, pushing himself up off her. "You think I'm an idiot! You think you're better than everyone and I'm just a nothing!"

Not able to see him, Kate inched her left hand toward her coat pocket.

"You're such a fucking bitch!" he screamed, and kicked her, too immersed in his ranting to hear her grunt of pain as his boot connected with her hip.

Kate ground her teeth together and concentrated on moving the hand, half an inch at a time, into her coat pocket.

"You don't know *me*," Rob declared. He grabbed something from her hall table and threw it. Whatever it was, it crashed somewhere in the vicinity of the kitchen. "You don't know anything about *me, about my True Self."

And she would never have suspected. God in heaven, she'd worked beside this man for a year and a half. Never once would she have thought he was capable of this. Never once had she questioned his motives for choosing his profession. On the contrary, his being an advocate for victims—so ready to listen to them, so ready to spend time with them—had been his one redeeming quality. Or so she had believed.

"You think I'm nobody," he yelled. "*I AM SOMEBODY! I AM EVIL'S ANGEL! I AM THE FUCKING CREMATOR!* Now what do you think of me, Ms. Bitch?"

He crouched down beside her and rolled her onto her back. Kate kept her eyes nearly shut, barely seeing more than a blur of colors between her lashes. Her hand was in her pocket, fingers sliding around the shaft of the metal nail file.

"I saved you for last," he said. "You're going to beg me to kill you. And I'm going to love doing it."

36

CHAPTER

"**WHAT HAPPENED** that night, Peter?" Quinn asked.

They sat in a small, dingy white room in the bowels of the city hall building, near the booking area of the adult detention center. Bondurant had waived his rights and refused to go to the hospital. A paramedic had cleaned the bullet wound to his scalp right there on the stairs where he had tried to end it all.

Edwyn Noble had thrown a holy fit, insisting to be present during questioning, insisting on sending Peter directly to a hospital whether he wanted to go or not. But Peter had won out, swearing in front of a dozen news cameras he wanted to confess.

Present in the room were Bondurant, Quinn, and Yurek. Peter had wanted only Quinn, but the police had insisted on having a representative present. Sam Kovac's name was not mentioned.

"Jillian came to dinner," Peter said. He looked small and shrunken, like a longtime heroin junkie. Pale, red-eyed, vacant. "She was in one of her moods. Up, down, laughing one minute, snapping the next. She was just like that—volatile. Like her mother. Even as a baby."

"What did you fight about?"

He stared across the room at a rosy stain on the wall that might have been blood before someone tried to scrub it away. "School, her music, her therapy, her stepfather, us."

"She wanted to resume her relationship with LeBlanc?"

"She'd been speaking with him. She said she was thinking of going back to France."

"You were angry."

"Angry," he said, and sighed. "That's not really the right word. I was upset. I felt tremendous guilt."

"Why guilt?"

He took a long time formulating his answer, as if he were pre-choosing each word he would use. "Because that was my fault—what happened with Jillian and LeBlanc. I could have prevented it. I could have fought Sophie for custody, but I just let go."

"She threatened to expose you for molesting Jillian," Quinn reminded him.

"She threatened to *claim* I had molested Jillian," Peter corrected him. "She had actually coached Jillie on what to say, how to behave in order to convince people it was true."

"But it wasn't?"

"She was my child. I could never have done anything to hurt her."

He thought about that answer, his composure cracking and crumbling. He covered his mouth with a trembling hand and cried silently for a moment. "How could I have known?"

"You knew Sophie's mental state," Quinn pointed out.

"I was in the process of buying out Don Thorton. I had several huge government contracts pending. She could have ruined me."

Quinn said nothing, letting Bondurant sort through it himself, as he had undoubtedly done a thousand times in the last week alone.

Bondurant heaved a defeated sigh and looked at the table. "I gave my daughter to a madwoman and a child-molester. I would have been kinder to kill her then."

"What happened Friday night?" Quinn asked again, drawing him back to the present.

"We argued about LeBlanc. She accused me of not loving her. She locked herself in the music room for a time. I let her alone. I went into the library, sat in front of the fire, drank some cognac.

"About eleven-thirty she came into the room behind me, singing. She had a beautiful voice—haunting, ethereal. The song was obscene, disgusting, perverse. It was everything Sophie had coached her to say about me all those years ago: the things I had supposedly done to her."

"That made you angry."

"It made me sick. I got up and turned to tell her so, and she was standing in front of me naked. 'Don't you want me, Daddy?' she said. 'Don't you love me?' "

Even the memory astonished him, sickened him. He bent over the wastebasket that had been set beside his chair and retched, but there was nothing left in his stomach. Quinn waited, calm, unemotional, purposely detached.

"Did you have sex with her?" Yurek asked.

Quinn glared at him.

"No! My God!" Peter said, outraged at the suggestion.

"What happened?" Quinn asked. "You fought. She ended up running out."

"Yes," he said, calming. "We fought. I said some things I shouldn't have. She was so fragile. But I was so shocked, so angry. She ran and put her clothes on and left. I never saw her alive again."

Yurek looked confused and disappointed. "But you said you killed her."

"Don't you see? I could have saved her, but I didn't. I let her go the first time to save myself, my business, my fortune. It's my fault she became who she did. I let her go Friday night because I didn't want to deal with that, and now she's dead. I killed her, Detective, just as surely as if I had stabbed her in the heart."

Yurek skidded his chair back and got up to pace, looking like a man who'd just realized he'd been cheated in a shell game. "Come on, Mr. Bondurant. You expect us to believe that?" He didn't have the voice or the edge to play bad cop—even when he meant it. "You were carrying your daughter's head in a bag. What is that about? A little memento the *real* killer sent you?"

Bondurant said nothing. The mention of Jillian's head upset him, and he began focusing inward again. Quinn could see him slipping away, allowing his mind to be lured to a place other than this ugly reality. He might go there and not come back for a long time.

"Peter, what were you doing in Jillian's town house Sunday morning?"

"I went to see her. To see if she was all right."

"In the middle of the night?" Yurek said doubtfully.

"She wouldn't return my calls. I left her alone Saturday on Lucas Brandt's advice. By Sunday morning...I had to do something."

"So you went there and let yourself in," Quinn said.

Bondurant looked down at a stain on his sweater and scratched at it absently with his thumbnail. "I thought she would be in bed...then I wondered whose bed she *was* in. I waited for her."

"What did you do while you were waiting?"

"Cleaned," he said, as if that made perfect sense and wasn't in any way odd. "The apartment looked like—like—a sty," he said, lip curling with disgust. "Filthy, dirty, full of garbage and mess."

"Like Jillian's life?" Quinn asked gently.

Tears swelled in Bondurant's eyes. The cleaning had been more symbolic than for sanitary purposes. He hadn't been able to change his daughter's life, but he could clean up her environment. An act of control, and perhaps of affection, Quinn thought.

"You erased the messages on her machine?" he asked.

Bondurant nodded. The tears came harder. Elbows on the table, he cupped his hands around his eyes.

"There was something from LeBlanc?" Quinn ventured.

"That son of a bitch! He killed her as much as I did!"

He curled down toward the tabletop, sobbing hard, a terrible braying sound tearing from the center of his chest up his throat. Quinn waited him out, thinking of Peter coming across Jillian's music as he straightened and tidied. The music may even have been his primary reason for going there, after the incident in his study Friday night, but Peter, out of guilt, would now claim Jillian's welfare had been the priority.

Quinn leaned forward and laid his hand on Bondurant's wrist across the table, establishing a physical link, trying to draw him back into the moment. "Peter? Do you know who really killed Jillian?"

"Her friend," he said in a thin, weary voice, his mouth twisting at the irony. "Her one friend. Michele Fine."

"What makes you believe that?"

"She was trying to blackmail me."

"Was?"

"Until last night."

"What happened last night?" Quinn asked.

"I killed her."

• • • •

620

EDWIN NOBLE WAS on Quinn the second he stepped out the door of the interview room.

"Not one word of that will be admissible in court, Quinn," he promised.

"He waived his rights, Mr. Noble."

"He's clearly not competent to make those decisions."

"Take it up with a judge," Sabin said.

The lawyers turned on each other like a pair of cobras. Yurek pulled aside the assistant prosecutor, Logan, to talk about a warrant for Michele Fine's home. Kovak stood ten feet down the hall, leaning against the wall, not smoking a cigarette. The lone coyote.

"Need a ride, GQ?" he said with a hopeful look.

Quinn made a very Kovac-like face. "I am definitely now a confirmed masochist. I can't believe I'm going to say this, but, let's go."

THEY RAN THE media gauntlet out of the building, Quinn offering a stone-faced "No comment" to every query hurled at him. Kovac had left his car on the Fourth Avenue side of the building. Half a dozen reporters followed them the whole way. Quinn didn't speak until Kovac put the car in gear and roared away from the curb.

"Bondurant says he shot Michele Fine and left her body in the Minneapolis Sculpture Garden. She'd been trying to blackmail him with some of Jillian's more revealing pieces of music, and with the things Jillian had allegedly

621

confessed to her. Last night was supposed to be the big payoff. He'd bring the money, she'd hand over the music, the tapes she had, et cetera.

"At that point, he didn't know she'd been involved in Jillian's murder. He said he was willing to pay to keep the story under wraps, but he took a gun with him."

"Sounds like premeditation to me," Kovac said, slapping the dash-mount light on the bracket.

"Right. Then Michele shows up with the stuff in a duffel bag. She shows him some sheet music, a couple of cassettes, zips the bag shut. They make the trade. She starts to go, not thinking he'll look in the bag again."

"Never assume."

Quinn braced himself and held on to the door as the Lumina made a hard right on a red light. Horns blared.

"He looked. He shot her in the back and left her where she fell."

"What the hell was she thinking, giving him the head?"

"She was thinking she'd be long gone before he called the cops," Quinn speculated. "I noticed travel magazines at her apartment when Liska and I were there the other day. I'll bet she would have gone straight to the airport and got on a plane."

"What about Vanlees? Did he say anything about Vanlees?"

Quinn held his breath as Kovac cut between an MTC bus and a Snap-on tool van. "Nothing."

"You don't think she was working alone?"

"No. We know she didn't kill on her own. She wouldn't have tried the blackmail on her own either. Willing victims of a sexual sadist are virtual puppets. Their partner holds the power, he controls them through physical abuse, psychological abuse, sexual abuse. No way she did this on her own."

"And Vanlees was in custody by the time this went down."

"They probably had the plan in place and she followed through without knowing where he was. She would have been afraid not to. *If he's the guy.*"

"They knew each other."

"You and I know each other. We haven't killed anyone. I have a hard time seeing Vanlees manipulating anyone at that level. He fits the wrong profile."

"Who, then?"

"I don't know," Quinn said, scowling at himself rather than at Kovac gunning the accelerator and nearly sideswiping a minivan. "But if we've got Fine, then we've got a thread to follow."

FOUR RADIO CARS had arrived ahead of them. The Minneapolis Sculpture Garden was an eleven-acre park dotted with more than forty works by prominent artists, the feature piece being a fifty-two-foot-long spoon holding a nine-and-a-half-foot-tall red cherry. The place had to be a bit surreal in the best of times, Quinn thought. As a crime scene it was something out of *Alice's Adventures in Wonderland.*

"Report from the local ERs," Yurek called as he climbed out of his car. "No gunshot wounds meeting Michele Fine's description."

"He said they met at the spoon," Quinn said as they walked quickly in that direction.

"He's sure he hit her?" Kovac asked. "It was dark."

"He says he hit her, she cried out, she went down."

"Over here!" one of the uniforms called, waving from near the bridge of the spoon. His breath was like a smoke signal in the cold gray air.

Quinn broke into a jog with the others. The news crews wouldn't be far behind.

"Is she dead?" Yurek demanded as he ran up.

"Dead? Hell," the uniform said, pointing to a large cherry-red bloodstain in the snow. "She's gone."

37

CHAPTER

ROB CAUGHT KATE by the hair and began to pull her up. Kate's fingers closed around the metal nail file in her pocket. She waited. This might be the best weapon she would get her hands on. But she had to use it accurately, and she had to use it at the perfect moment. Strategies ran through her head like rats in a maze, each desperate for a way out.

Rob slapped her face, and the taste of blood bloomed in her mouth like a rose.

"I know you're not dead. You keep underestimating me, Kate," he said. "Even now you taunt me. That's very stupid."

Kate hung her head, curling her legs beneath her. He wanted her frightened. He wanted to see it in her eyes. He wanted to smell it on her skin. He wanted to hear it in her voice. That was his thing. That was what he soaked up listening to the tapes of victims—his own victims and the victims of others. It sickened her to think how many victims had poured their hearts out to him, him feeding his sick compulsions on their suffering and their fear.

Now he wanted her afraid, and he wanted her submissive. He wanted her sorry for every time she'd ever mouthed off to him, for every time she'd defied him. And if she gave him what he wanted, his sense of victory would only further fuel his cruelty.

"I will be your master today, Kate," he said dramatically.

Kate raised her head and gave him a long, level, venomous stare, screwing up her courage as she sucked at the cut in her mouth. He would make her pay for this, but it seemed the way to go.

Very deliberately, she spit the blood in his face. "The hell you will, you miserable little shit."

Instantly furious, he swung at her with the sap. Kate ducked the punch and launched herself upward, bringing her right elbow up under his chin, knocking his teeth together. She pulled the nail file and stabbed it into his neck to the hilt just above his collarbone.

Rob screamed and grabbed at the file, falling back, crashing into the hall table. Kate ran for the kitchen.

If she could just get out of the house, get to the street. Surely he would have disabled her car somehow, or blocked it in. To get help, she had to get to the street.

She dashed through the dining room, knocking chairs over as she ran past. Rob came behind her, grunting as he hit something, swearing, spitting the words out between his teeth like bullets.

He couldn't outrun her on his stubby legs. He seemed not to have a gun. Through the kitchen and she was home free. She'd run to the neighbor across the street. The graphic designer who had his office in his attic. He was always home.

She burst into the kitchen, faltered, then pulled up, her heart plummeting.

Angie stood just inside the back door, tears streaming down her face, a butcher's knife in her hand—pointed directly at Kate's chest.

"I'm sorry. I'm sorry. I'm sorry," she sobbed, shaking badly.

Suddenly, the conversation that had taken place between Angie and Rob in the den took on a whole new dimension. Pieces of the truth began to click into place. The picture they made was distorted and surreal.

If Rob was the Cremator, then it was Rob Angie had seen in the park. Yet the man in the sketch Oscar had drawn at her instruction looked no more like Rob Marshall than he looked like Ted Sabin. She had sat across from him in the interview room, giving no indication...

In the next second Rob Marshall was through the door behind her and six ounces of steel packed in sand and bound in leather connected with the back of her skull. Her legs folded beneath her and she dropped to her knees on the kitchen floor, her last sight: Angie DiMarco.

This is why I don't do kids. You never know what they're thinking.

Then everything went dark.

THE TRAVEL MAGAZINES were still scattered on Michele Fine's coffee table with pages folded and destinations circled with notations in the margins. *Get a tan! Too $$$. Nightlife!*

The murderer as a tourist, Quinn thought, turning the pages.

When the police checked with the airlines, they might find she had booked flights to one or more of those locations. If they were very lucky, they would also find matching flights booked in the name of her partner. Whoever he was.

With the amount of blood at the scene in the sculpture garden, it seemed highly unlikely Fine had taken herself out of the park. Gil Vanlees had been in custody. Both Fine and the money Peter Bondurant had brought to the scene and subsequently walked away from were gone.

The cops swarmed over the apartment like ants, invading every cupboard, crack, and crevice, looking for anything that might give them a clue as to who Fine's partner in murder was. A scribbled note, a doodled phone number, an envelope, a photograph, something, anything. Adler and Yurek were canvassing the neighbors for information. Did they know her? Had they seen her? What about a boyfriend?

The main living areas of the apartment looked exactly as they had the day before.

Same dust, same filthy ashtray. Tippen found a crack pipe in an end table drawer.

Quinn went down the hall, glancing into a bathroom worthy of a speedtrap gas station, and on to Michele Fine's bedroom. The bed was unmade. Clothes lay strewn around the room like outlines where dead bodies had fallen. Just as in the rest of the apartment, there were no personal touches, nothing decorative—except in the window that faced south and the back side of another building.

"Look at the sun catchers," Liska said, moving across the room.

They hung from hooks on little suction cups stuck to the window. Hoops about three inches in diameter, each holding its own miniature work of art. The light coming through them gave the colors a sense of life. The air from a register above the window made them quiver against the glass like butterfly wings, and fluttered the decorations that were attached to each—a piece of ribbon, a pearl button on a string, a dangling earring, a finely braided lock of hair...

Liska's face dropped as she stopped beside Quinn, the realization hitting her.

Lila White's calla lily. Fawn Pierce's shamrock. A mouth with a tongue sticking out. A heart with the word "Daddy." There were half a dozen.

Tattoos.

The tattoos that had been cut from the bodies of the Cremator's victims. Stretched tight in little craft hoops, drying in the sun.

Decorated with mementos of the women they had been cut from. Souvenirs of torture and murder.

38

CHAPTER

HIS TRIUMPH is at hand. His crowning glory. His finale—for now, for this place. He has arranged the Bitch on the table to his satisfaction and bound her hands and feet to the table legs with plastic twine he has pilfered from the mailroom at the office. A length of it is wrapped around the Bitch's throat with long free ends trailing for him to wrap around his fists. For mood lighting he has brought candles down to the basement from other parts of the house. He finds the flames very sensual, exciting, erotic. That excitement is heightened by the smell of gasoline heavy in the air.

He stands back and surveys the tableau. The Bitch under *his* absolute control. She is still clothed because he wants her conscious for her degradation. He wants her to feel every second of her humiliation. He wants to capture it all on tape.

He loads the microcassette recorder with a

fresh tape and sets it on a black vinyl barstool with a ripped seat. He doesn't worry about fingerprints. The world will shortly discover the Cremator's "true" identity.

He sees no reason not to carry through with the plan. Michele might be out of the picture, but he still has Angie. If she passes her test, he might take her with him. If she fails, he will kill her. She isn't Michele—his perfect complement. Michele, who would do anything he asked if she thought compliance would make him love her. Michele, who had followed his lead in the torture games, who had encouraged him to burn the bodies, and reveled in her tattoo arts and crafts.

He misses her as much as he can miss anyone. With a vague detachment. Mrs. Vetter will miss her horrid little dog more.

Angie watches him as he unties the leather roll that holds all his favorite tools and spreads it out on the table. She looks like something from a teenage slasher movie. Her clothes are disheveled, the thighs of her jeans shredded and blood-soaked. She still holds the butcher knife from the kitchen and surreptitiously pricks the end of her thumb with the point of it and watches the blood bead. Crazy little bitch.

He looks at the choke marks on her throat, thinks about all the ways she has defied him during the execution of his Great Plan. Making him look stupid during her first interview, refusing to give the name of the bar where he'd picked her up that night to lend credibility to her story. Refusing to describe the Cremator to the sketch artist the way he had instructed her to. He had spent considerable time creating the image of a phantom killer in his mind. The girl had willfully given a description so vague it might fit half the men in the Twin Cities—including the hapless Vanlees. The idea of Vanlees getting credit as the Cremator makes him furious. And, even after the beatings he'd given her since Wednesday, she had refused him his perfect moment of revelation in Kate's living room.

"*Who came to take you, Angie?*"

"*No.*"

"*Who came to take you?*"

"*No. I won't do it.*"

"*Angie, who came to take you?*"

"*No. You can't make me.*"

She had been coached to say "Evil's Angel." No matter that he hadn't taken her, that Michele had been the one who'd saved the stupid little slut from slicing herself to ribbons in the shower, who'd cleaned up the mess and slipped the two of them out the back door of the house. The girl had her instructions and she defied them openly.

He decides he will kill her after all, despite her cooperation in the kitchen. She is too unpredictable.

He will kill her here. After the Bitch is dead. He pictures himself in a frenzy, wild with the euphoria of killing the Bitch. He sees himself throwing the girl onto the table, on top of the bloody, mutilated body, tying her there, fucking her, choking her, stabbing her in the face over and over and over and over. Punishing her exactly as he plans to punish the Bitch.

He will kill them both, then burn them together, here, and burn the house as well. He has already set the stage for the fire, pouring the accelerant—gas from a can he put in the Bitch's garage himself the night he shit on the floor.

The fantasy of the murders he is about to commit excites him as fantasies always have—intellectually, sexually, fundamentally. The pattern of the mind of his breed: fantasy, violent fantasy; then facilitators that trigger action: murder. The natural cycle of his life—and his victims' death.

Decision made, he turns his thoughts to the matter at hand: Kate Conlan.

CONSCIOUSNESS RETURNED FOR Kate in fits and starts, like a television with bad reception. She could hear but not see. Then she had some blurred vision, but nothing more than a horrific ringing in her ears. The only clear, constant signal was pain hammering at the back of her skull. She felt sick with it. She couldn't seem to move her arms or legs and wondered if Rob had broken her neck or severed her spinal cord. Then she realized she could still feel her hands, and that they hurt like hell.

Tied.

The ceiling tile, the smell of dust, the vague sense of dampness. The basement. She was tied spread-eagle on the old Ping-Pong table in her own basement.

Another scent—out of place—came to her, thick, oily, and bitter. *Gasoline.*

Oh, sweet Jesus.

She looked at Rob Marshall standing at the foot of the table, staring at her. Rob Marshall, a serial killer. The incongruity made her want to believe she was just having a nightmare, but she knew better. She'd seen too much when she was an agent. The stories were stacked up in her memory like files in a cabinet. The NASA engineer who had kidnapped hitchhikers and drained their blood to drink it. The electronics technician, a married father of two, who kept chosen body parts of his victims in his meat freezer in his garage. The young Republican law student who volunteered at a suicide hotline and turned out to be Ted Bundy.

Add to the stack the victim advocate who chose his own victims from the department's client list. She felt like a fool for not having seen it, even though she knew a killer as sophisticated as Smokey Joe was one of nature's perfect chameleons. Even now she didn't want to think of Rob Marshall as being that clever.

He had taken his coat off, revealing a gray sweater soaked at the throat with blood from where she'd stabbed him with the nail file. An inch in the right direction and she would have hit his jugular.

"Did I miss anything?" she asked, her voice rusty from the choking he'd given her.

She could see the surprise in his face, the confusion. Score one for the victim.

"Still with the smart mouth," he said. "You don't learn, bitch."

"Why should I? What will you do, Rob? Torture and kill me?" She tried desperately to keep the fear out of her voice. She felt as if it had her by the throat, then remembered with another jolt of adrenaline the ligature marks on the throats of his victims. "You'll do that either way. I might as well have the satisfaction of calling you a dickless loser to your face."

Standing to one side of the table, backlit by candles, butcher knife in hand, Angie sucked in a breath and made a pitious sound in her throat. She clutched the knife to her as if it were a treasured toy to comfort herself.

Rob's face hardened. He pulled a penknife from his pocket and jabbed it, all the way to the handle, into the bottom of Kate's right foot, and she learned very quickly and painfully the price he was going to make her pay for the strategy she'd chosen.

Kate cried out and her whole body convulsed against the restraints that bit deep into the skin of her wrists and ankles. When she fell back, the bindings seemed to have stretched to give her slightly more mobility.

She pulled her mind back together by focusing on Angie, thinking of the look she'd seen in the girl's eyes earlier, when she'd been struck by the thought that Angie's eyes weren't empty, that as long as there was some light in the darkness, there was still hope.

She thought of the way the girl had started to go after Rob with the utility knife.

"Angie, get out!" she rasped. "Save yourself!"

The girl flinched and glanced nervously at Rob.

"She'll stay," he snapped, stabbing the knife into her foot again, winning another cry from Kate. "She's mine," he said, eyes glowing with the intoxication he achieved from inflicting pain.

"I don't think so." Kate sucked in a sharp breath. "She's not stupid."

"No, you're the stupid one," he said, backing away a step. He pulled a long taper from the candelabrum he'd taken from her dining room and set on the clothes drier.

"Because I know the kind of pathetic, warped excuse for a human being you are?"

"How pathetic am I now, bitch?" he demanded, dragging the flame of the candle from toe to toe on her right foot.

Instinctively, Kate kicked at the source of her torment, knocking the candle from his hand. Rob pounced on it, swearing, disappearing from view at the end of the table.

"Stupid bitch!" he cursed frantically. "Stupid fucking bitch!"

The scent of the gasoline pressed over Kate's nose and mouth, and she shuddered at the notion of burning alive. The terror was like a fist in the base of her throat. The pain where Rob had already burned her was like a live thing, as if her foot had ignited and now the flames would shoot up her leg.

"What's the matter, Rob?" she asked, fighting the need to cry. "I thought you liked fire. Are you afraid of it?"

He scrambled to his feet, glaring at her. "*I am the Cremator!*" he shouted, the candle clutched in his fist. She could see his increasing agitation in his respiration rate, in the quick jerkiness of his movements. This wasn't going the way it had in his fantasies.

"*I am superior!*" he shouted, wild-eyed. "I am Evil's Angel! *I* hold *your life* in *my* hands! I am *your* god!"

Kate channeled her pain into her anger. "You're a leech. You're a parasite. You're *nothing.*"

She was probably goading him into stabbing her forty-seven times, cutting her larynx out and running it down the garbage disposal. Then she thought of the photographs of his other victims, of the tape of Melanie Hessler, of the hours of torture, rape, repeated strangulation.

She'd take her chances. Live by the sword, die by the sword.

"You make me sick, you spineless little shit."

That was the truth. It made her want to vomit to think she'd worked beside him day in and day out, and every time his mind wandered it wandered to fantasies of abuse and brutality and murder—the very things they tried to help their clients live through and get past.

He paced at the foot of the table, muttering under his breath, as if he might be speaking to voices in his head, though Kate thought it unlikely he heard any. Rob Marshall wasn't psychotic. He was perfectly aware of everything he did. His actions were a conscious choice—though, if he were caught, he would probably try to convince the authorities otherwise.

"You can't get it up without the domination, can you?" Kate pressed on. "What woman would have you if you didn't tie her down?"

"Shut up!" he screamed. "Shut the fuck up!"

He threw the candle at her, missing her head by three feet. He rushed up alongside her, grabbed a boning knife off the table beside her and jammed the point of it against her larynx. Kate swallowed reflexively, felt the tip of the steel bite into her skin.

"I'll cut it out!" he shouted in her face. "I'll fucking cut it out! I'm so sick of your bitching! I'm so sick of your voice!"

Kate closed her eyes and tried not to swallow again, holding herself rigid as he started to push the small, sharp blade into her throat. Terror tore through her. Instinct told her to jerk away. Logic told her not to move. And then the pressure stopped, eased away.

Rob stared at the tape recorder he'd left on the old barstool. He may not have wanted to hear her criticism of him, but he wanted to listen to her screams as he had listened to the screams and cries and pleading of all his victims. In fact, with her, he probably wanted it more. If he cut her voice out, he couldn't get that. If he couldn't get that, the act of killing her lost its meaning.

"You want to hear it, don't you, Rob?" she asked. "You want to be able to listen later and hear the exact moment I became frightened of you and gave you control. You don't want to give that up, do you?"

He picked up the tape recorder and held it close to her mouth. He put down the knife, picked up a pliers, and grabbed hold of the tip of her breast, squeezing brutally. Even through the buffer of her sweater and bra, the bite was sharp, then excruciating, making her scream. When he finally let go, he stepped back with a vicious smile and held up the cassette recorder.

"There," he said. "I've got it."

It seemed an eternity passed before the white noise faded from Kate's head. She was breathing as if she'd run the four-hundred-yard dash, sweating, shaking. The haze cleared from her vision and she was looking at Angie, the girl still standing in the same spot, clutching the knife to her. Kate wondered if she'd gone catatonic. Angie was her only hope, the weakest link in Rob's scenario. She needed the girl with her, lucid and able to act.

"Angie," Kate croaked. "He doesn't own you. You can fight him. You've *been* fighting him, haven't you?" She thought of the scene that had played out upstairs—Rob wanting Angie to decribe what he'd done to her after taking her from the Phoenix House, Angie refusing, defying him, taunting him. She'd done it before—in the offices.

Rob's face reddened. "Quit talking to her!"

"Afraid she might turn on you, Rob?" Kate asked with not nearly the attitude she'd had five minutes earlier.

"Shut up. She's mine. And you're mine too, bitch!"

He lunged at her, grabbed hold of the neck of her sweater and tore at it with his hands, trying without success to rip it. Swearing, sputtering, flustered, embarrassed, he fumbled for another knife among the array of tools he had so carefully laid out on the table.

"You don't own her any more than you own me," Kate said, glaring at him, straining against the bonds. "And you will *never, ever* own me, you toad."

"Shut up!" he screamed again. He turned and slapped her across the mouth with the back of his hand. "Shut up! Shut up! You fucking bitch!"

The knives clattered together and he came away with a big one. Kate sucked in what she imagined might be her last breath and held it. Rob grabbed the neck of her sweater again and cut through it with the knife, violently rending the fabric with big, jagged tears. The tip of the knife bit into her breast, skipped along her belly, nicked the point of her hip.

"I'll show you! I'll show you! Angie!" he barked, swinging toward the girl. "Come here! Come here, now!"

He didn't wait. He rushed around the end of the table, grabbed the girl by the arm, and dragged her back to Kate.

"Do it!" he said in her ear. "For Michele.

You want to do this for Michele. You want Michele to love you, don't you, Angie?"

Michele? Wild card, Kate thought, a fresh wave of terror flashing through her. Who the hell was Michele, and what did she mean to Angie? How could she fight an enemy she'd never seen?

Tears ran down Angie's face. Her lower lip was quivering. She clutched the butcher knife with both trembling hands.

"Don't do it, Angie," Kate said, her voice vibrating with fear. "Don't let him use you this way."

She couldn't know if the girl even heard her. She thought of what Angie had told her about the Zone, and wondered if she was going into that place now, to escape this nightmare. And what then? Would she act on autopilot? Was the Zone a dissociative state? Had it allowed her to participate in Rob's kills before?

She jerked again at the restraints, stretching the plastic another fraction of an inch.

"Do it!" Rob shouted against the side of Angie's face. "Do it, you stupid cunt! Do it for your sister. Do it for Michele. You want Michele to love you."

Sister. The headline went through Kate's mind like a comet: *Sisters Exonerated in Burning Death of Parents.*

Pig eyes popping from his ugly round head, Rob screamed with frustration and raised the knife he held. *"Do it!!"*

Light hit a blinding starburst off the blade as it plunged through the air and into the

641

hollow of Kate's shoulder just as she managed to twist her body a crucial few inches. The tip of the blade hit bone and glanced off, and the pain was like lightning striking her.

"Do it!" Rob screamed at Angie, striking her in the back of the head with the handle of the bloody knife. "You worthless whore!"

"*No!*" the girl cried.

"*Do it!!*"

Sobbing, Angie brought the knife up.

"WE GOT A HIT on Fine's prints in Wisconsin," Yurek said, stepping into the bedroom doorway.

The crime scene unit was removing the tattoo fetishes from the window, carefully folding tissue paper around each and sliding each into its own small paper sack.

"Her real name is Michele Finlow. She's got a handful of misdemeanors and a sealed juvenile record."

Kovac arched a brow. "Is skinning people a misdemeanor in Wisconsin?"

"The state that brought us Ed Gein and Jeffrey Dahmer," Tippen remarked.

"Hey, aren't you from Wisconsin, Tip?" one of the crime scene guys asked.

"Yeah. Menominie. Wanna come to my house for Thanksgiving?"

Quinn stuck a finger in his free ear and listened to Kate's home number ring unanswered for the third time in twenty minutes. Her machine should have picked up. He disconnected and tried her cell phone. It rang four times, then passed him on to her message service. Her clients called her on the cell phone. Angie DiMarco had the number. Kate wouldn't let it go unanswered. Not as responsible as she felt for Angie.

He rubbed a hand against the fire in his belly.

Mary Moss joined the group. "One of the neighbors down the hall says she sometimes saw Michele with a stubby, balding guy with glasses. She didn't get a name, but she says he drives a black SUV that once rear-ended the car of the guy in 3F."

"Yes!" Kovac said, pumping one arm. "Smokey Joe, you're toast."

"Hamill is talking right now with Mr. 3F to get the insurance info."

"We can bust the Cremator in time for the six o'clock news and still make Patrick's for happy hour," Kovac said, grinning. "This is turning into my kind of day."

Hamill hustled into the apartment, dodging crime scene people. "You won't believe this," he said to the task force at large. "Michele Fine's boyfriend was Rob Marshall."

"Holy shit."

Quinn grabbed Kovac by the shoulder and shoved him toward the door. "I have to get to Kate. Give me the keys. I'm driving."

"DO IT! DO IT!"

Angie let out a long, distorted scream that sounded very far away in her own ears, like a wail coming down a long, long tunnel. The Zone loomed up beside her, a yawning black mouth. And on the other side, the Voice had come to life.

You stupid little slut! Do what I tell you!

"I can't!" she cried.

"DO IT!"

The fear was like a softball in her throat, closing off her air, gagging her, choking her.

No one loves you, crazy little bitch.

"You love me, Michele," she mewed, not sure if she had spoken the words aloud or if they existed only in her head.

"DO IT!"

DO IT!

She stared down at Kate.

The Zone moved over her. She could feel the hot breath of it. She could fall into it and never come out. She would be safe.

She would be alone. Forever.

"DO IT!"

You know what to do, Angel. Do what you're told, Angel.

Her whole body was shaking.

Coward.

"You can save Michele, Angie. Do this for Michele."

She looked down at Kate, at the place on her chest where she was supposed to stick the knife. Just as Michele had. She'd seen her sister do it. *He* had made her watch as they stood on either side of the dead woman, one stabbing and then the other, making their pact, sealing their bond, pledging their love. It had frightened her and made her sick. Michele had laughed at her, then given her to *him* for sex.

He hurt her. She hated him. Michele loved him. She loved Michele.

Nobody loves you, crazy little bitch.

That was all she'd ever wanted, someone to care about her, someone to keep her from being alone. All she'd ever gotten was use and abuse. Even from Michele, who had kept her from being alone. But Michele loved her. Love and hate. Love and hate. Lovehate, lovehate, lovehate. There was no line between them for her. She loved Michele, wanted to save her. Michele was all she had.

"DO IT! KILL HER! KILL HER!"

She looked down at Kate, straining against the ties, terror in her face.

"Why do you care what happens to me?"

"Because no one else does."

"I'm sorry," she whimpered.

"Angie, don't!"

"Stab her. Now!"

The pressure inside her was tremendous. The pressure from outside was more. She felt as if her bones would collapse and the weight of it would crush her, and the Zone would suck up the mess and she would be gone forever.

Maybe that would be just as well. At least then she wouldn't hurt anymore.

"Do it or I let your fucking cunt sister die!" he shouted. "Do it or I'll finish Michele in front of you! DO IT!"

She loved her sister. She could save her sister. She raised the knife.

"NO!"

Kate sucked in a breath and braced herself, never taking her eyes off Angie.

The girl let out an unearthly shriek as she raised the butcher knife with both hands above her head, then twisted her body and plunged the knife into Rob Marshall's neck.

Blood sprayed in a geyser as she jerked the blade out. Blood on the wall, on the bed, on Kate, spraying like a loose fire hose. Rob jerked back, astonished, grabbing at the wound, blood gushing through his fingers.

Angie went on screaming, plunging the knife again, stabbing his hand, stabbing his chest. She followed him as he staggered backward, trying to escape. He tried to call out for help or for mercy and choked on his own blood, the sound gurgling in his throat. His knees buckled, and he fell against the clothes drier, knocking the candelabrum to the floor.

Angie stepped back then and stared at him for a moment, as if she had no idea who he was or how he had come to fall to the floor with the last of his life's blood pumping out of him as he gurgled and gagged. Then she looked at the knife, dripping blood, her hands covered and sticky with it, and slowly she turned toward Kate.

• • •

QUINN DROVE WITH no regard for the laws of the road or of physics, driven himself by a growing sense of panic in his gut. Kovac hung on, braced himself, screamed more than once as Quinn swept the Caprice around and between cars.

"If he's smart, he's already blown town," Kovac said.

"Smart's got nothing to do with it," Quinn said above the roar of the engine. "He brought Kate on the case as part of his game. He killed Melanie Hessler because she was Kate's client. He left a calling card in Kate's garage the other night. He won't leave town without finishing the thing between them."

He could see the hall light on as the car skidded to a stop in front of Kate's house. The light glowed through the sheers at the goddamn sidelights she should have known better than to have. Quinn slammed the Caprice into park before it fully stopped, and the transmission made an ominous sound. He was out of the car before it could stop rocking, running for the house as a pair of radio cars screamed up the street. He thundered onto the porch and pounded on the door, tried the handle. Locked.

"Kate! Kate!"

He pressed his face to the glass of one sidelight. The hall table sat askew. Things had tumbled over on it and off it. The rug was cockeyed.

"Kate!"

The shout that came from somewhere in the house went through him like steel. "No!"

Quinn grabbed the mailbox, ripped it off the wall, and smashed out the sidelight just as Kovac ran up onto the porch. Another few seconds and they were in. His eyes went to a smear of blood on the wall near the den.

"Kate!"

Her cry came from somewhere deep in the house. "Angie! NO!"

ANGIE TURNED THE knife in her bloody hands, staring at the blade. She let the tip of it kiss the fragile skin of her wrist.

"Angie, no!" Kate shouted, straining against the ties. "Don't do it! Please don't do it! Come cut me loose. Then we'll get you some help."

She couldn't see Rob, but knew he lay crumpled on the floor near the drier. She could hear gurgling sounds coming from his throat. He had knocked the candelabrum over as he crashed, and the flames had found some of the gasoline he must have poured around while Kate had been unconscious. It ignited with a *whoosh*.

The flames would follow the trail of fuel in search of more fuel. The basement was crammed with possibilities—boxes of junk her parents had saved and abandoned, stuff she'd been meaning to throw out but hadn't gotten to, the obligatory half-empty cans of paint and other hazardous chemicals.

"Angie. Angie!" Kate said, trying to pull the girl's focus to her. Angie, who stood looking into the face of her own death.

648

"Michele won't love me," the girl murmured, looking at the man she had just killed. She sounded disappointed in herself, like a small child who had written on the wall in crayon, then realized there would be a bad consequence.

"Kate!" Quinn's bellow sounded above.

Angie seemed not to hear the shouts or the thunder of big male feet. She pressed the blade of the knife lengthwise against the shadow of a vein in her wrist.

"Kate!"

She tried to shout "In the basement!" but her voice seized up so she barely heard herself. The flames caught hold of a box of clothes destined, oddly enough, for the Phoenix, and leapt with enthusiasm—far too near the table. Kate jerked at her bindings, succeeding only in pulling them even tighter around her wrists and ankles. She was losing the feeling in her hands.

She tried to clear her throat to speak. Smoke rolled thick and black from the boxes.

"Angie, help me. Help me and I'll help you. How's that for a deal?"

The girl stared at the knife.

The smoke detector at the top of the stairs finally blew, and the thunder of feet homed in on it.

Angie pressed the blade a little harder against her wrist. Tiny beads of blood surfaced like little jewels in a bracelet.

"No, Angie, please," Kate whispered, knowing the girl couldn't have heard her if she'd shouted.

Angie looked at her square in the face, and for the first time since Kate had met her she looked like exactly what she was: a child. A child no one had ever wanted, had ever loved.

"I hurt," she said.

"Call the fire department!" Quinn shouted at the head of the stairs. "Kate!"

"Joh—" Her voice cracked and she began to cough. The smoke rolled along the ceiling toward the stairwell and the new source of fresh air.

"Kate!"

Quinn led the way down the stairs with a .38 Kovac had lent him, his fear obliterating all known rules of procedure. As he dropped below the cloud of smoke, his focus was instantly on Kate, bound hand and foot on a table, her sweater cut open, blood pooling on her skin. And then his attention went to the girl beside the table: Angie DiMarco with a butcher knife in her hands.

"Angie, drop the knife!" he shouted.

The girl looked up at him, the light in her eyes fading away. "Nobody loves me," she said, and in one quick, violent motion slashed her wrist to the bone.

"NO!" Kate screamed.

"Jesus!" Quinn charged across the room, leading with the gun.

Angie dropped to her knees as the blood gushed from her arm. The knife fell to the floor. Quinn kicked it aside and dropped to his knees, grabbing the girl's arm with a grip like a C-clamp. Blood pumped between his fingers. Angie sagged against him.

Kate watched with horror, not even acknowledging Kovac as he cut her loose. She rolled off the table onto feet she could no longer feel, and fell in a heap. She had to scramble to Angie on her knees. Her hands were as useless as clubs, swollen and purple, and she couldn't make her fingers move. Still, she wrapped her arms around the girl.

"We have to get out of here!" Quinn shouted.

The fire had begun licking its way up the steps. A uniformed officer fought it down with an extinguisher. But even as he cleared the stairs, the flames were working their way across the basement, following the trail of gasoline, pouncing on everything edible in its path.

Quinn and a uniform took Angie up the basement steps and out the back door. Sirens were screaming out on the street, a couple of blocks away yet. He passed the girl off to the uniform and ran back to the house as Kovac came with Kate leaning heavily against him, both of them coughing as thick black smoke rolled up behind them, acrid with the smell of chemicals.

"Kate!"

She fell against him and he scooped her up in his arms.

"I'm going back for Marshall!" Kovac shouted above the roar. The fire had come up through the floor and found the river of gasoline Rob had poured through the house.

"He's dead!" Kate yelled, but Kovac was gone. "Sam!"

One of the uniforms charged in after him.

The sirens blasted out front, fire trucks bulling their way down the narrow street. Quinn negotiated the back steps with Kate in his arms and hustled down the side of the house to the front yard and the boulevard. He lowered her into the backseat of Kovac's car just as an explosion sounded from the bowels of the house and windows on the first floor shattered. Kovac and the uniform staggered away from the back corner of the house and fell to their hands and knees in the snow. Firemen and paramedics rushed toward them and toward the house.

"Are you all right?" Quinn asked, staring into Kate's eyes, his fingers digging into her shoulders.

Kate looked up at her house, flames visible now through the windows of the first floor. Behind Kovac's car, Angie was being loaded into an ambulance. The fear, the panic she had fought to keep at bay during the ordeal, hit her belatedly in a pounding wave.

She turned back to Quinn, shaking. "No," she whispered as the flood of tears came. And he folded her into his arms and held her.

39

CHAPTER

"I *NEVER* LIKED him," Yvonne Vetter said to the uniformed officer who stood guard outside Rob Marshall's garage door. She was huddled into a lumpy wool coat that made her look misshapen. Her round, sour face squinted up at him from beneath an incongruously jaunty red beret. "I called your hotline *several* times. I believe he cannibalized my Bitsy."

"Your what, ma'am?"

"My Bitsy. My sweet little dog!"

"Wouldn't that be *animal*ized?" Tippen speculated.

Liska cuffed him one on the arm.

The task force would get the first look around Rob's chamber of horrors before the collection of evidence began. The videographer followed right behind them. Even as they entered the house, the news crews were pulling up to the curbs on both sides of the street.

It was a nice house on a quiet street in a quiet neighborhood. An extra-large tree-studded lot near one of the most popular lakes in the Cities. A beautifully finished basement. Realtors would have been drooling over the opportunity to sell it if not for the fact Rob Marshall had tortured and murdered at least four women there.

They started in the basement, wandering through a media room equipped with several televisions, VCRs, stereo equipment, a bookcase lined with video- and audiotapes.

Tippen turned to the videographer. "Don't shoot the stereo equipment yet. I really need a new tuner and tape deck."

The videographer immediately turned the camera on the recording equipment.

Tippen rolled his eyes. "It was a *joke*. You techno-geeks have no sense of humor."

The camera guy turned his lens on Tippen's ass as he walked away.

A headless mannequin stood in one corner of the room decked out in a skimpy see-through black lace bra and a purple spandex miniskirt.

"Hey, Tinks, you could pick up some new outfits," Tippen called, eyeballing a sticky-looking residue on the shoulders of the mannequin. Possibly blood mixed with some other, clearer fluid.

Liska continued down the hall, checking out a utility room, moving on. Her boys would have loved this house. They talked endlessly about getting a house like their friend Mark had, with a cool rec room in the basement—where they could escape Mom's scrutiny—with a pool table and a big-screen TV.

There was a pool table here in the room at

the end of the hall. It was draped with blood-stained white plastic, and there was a body on it. The smell of blood, urine, and excrement hung thick in the air. The stench of violent death.

"Tippen!" Liska hollered, bolting for the table.

Michele Fine lay twisted at an odd angle on her back, staring up at the light glaring in her face. She didn't blink. Her eyes had the flat look of a corpse's. Her mouth hung open, drool crusted white in a trail down her chin. Her lips moved ever so slightly.

Liska bent close, laying two fingers on the side of Fine's neck to feel for a pulse, unable to detect one.

"...elp... me... elp...me..." Fragments of words on the thinnest of breaths.

Tippen jogged in and stopped cold. "Shit."

"Get an ambulance," Liska ordered. "She may just live to tell the tale."

CHAPTER 40

"I DIDN'T WANT to help," Angie said softly.

It didn't sound like her voice. The thought drifted through her drug-fogged brain on a cloud. It sounded like the voice of the little girl inside her, the one she always tried to hide, to protect. She stared at the bandage on her left arm, the desire to pull it off and make the wound bleed lurking at the dark edge of her mind.

"I didn't want to do what *he* said."

She waited for the Voice to sneer at her, but it was strangely silent. She waited for the Zone to zoom up on her, but the drugs held it off.

She sat at a table in a room that wasn't supposed to look like part of a hospital. The blue print gown she wore had short sleeves and exposed her thin, scarred arms for all to see. She looked at the scars, one beside another and another, like bars in a prison cell door. Marks she had carved into her own flesh. Marks life had carved into her soul. A constant reminder so she could never forget exactly who and what she was.

"Was Rob Marshall the one who took you to the park that night, Angie?" Kate asked quietly. She sat at the table too, beside Angie with her chair turned so that she was facing the girl. "Was he the john you told me about?"

Angie nodded, still looking down at the scars. "His Great Plan," she murmured.

She wished the drugs would fog the memories, but the pictures were clear in her head, like watching them on television. Sitting in the truck, knowing the dead woman's body was in the back, knowing that the man at the wheel had killed her, knowing Michele had been a part of that too. She could see them stabbing her over and over, could see the sexual excitement in them growing with every thrust of the knives. Michele had given her to *him* afterward, and he had taken her again that night in the park, excited because of the dead woman in the back and because of his Great Plan.

"I was supposed to describe someone else."

"As the killer?" Kate asked.

"Someone he made up. All these details. He made me repeat them over and over and over."

Angie picked at a loose thread on the edge of her bandage, wishing blood would seep up through the layers of white gauze. The sight would comfort her, make her feel less terrible about sitting beside Kate. She couldn't look her in the face after all that had happened.

"I hate him."

Present tense, Kate thought. As if she didn't know he was dead, that she had killed him. Maybe she didn't. Maybe her mind would allow her that one consolation.

"I hate him too," Kate said softly.

Facts about Rob and the Finlow sisters were coming out of Wisconsin and piecing together into a terrible, sordid story America received new episodes of every night on the news. The lurid quality of lover-killers and the fall of a billionaire made for juicy ratings bait. Michele Finlow, who had lingered for ten hours after being found in Rob's basement, had filled in some of the blanks herself. And Angie would supply what fragments her mind would allow.

Daughters of two different men and a mother with a history of drug abuse and assorted domestic misery, Michele and Angie had been in and out of the child welfare system, never finding the care they needed. Children falling through the cracks of a system that was poor at best. Both girls had juvenile records, Michele's being longer and more inclined to violent behavior.

Kate had read the news accounts of the fire that had killed the mother and stepfather. The general consensus of the investigators on the case was that one or both of the girls had started it, but there hadn't been enough evidence to take to court. One witness had recalled seeing Michele calmly standing in the yard while the house burned, listening to the screams of the two people trapped inside. She had, in fact, been standing too near a window, and was burned when the window exploded and the fire rolled outside to consume fresh oxygen. The case had brought

Rob Marshall into their lives via the court system. And Rob had brought the girls to Minneapolis.

Love. Or so Michele had called it, though it was doubtful she had any real grasp of the meaning of the word. A man in love didn't leave his partner to die a horrible death alone in a basement while he skipped the country, which was exactly what Rob would have done.

Peter Bondurant's bullet had struck Michele in the back, severing her spinal cord. Rob, who had been watching from a distance, had waited for Bondurant to leave, then picked her up and took her back to his home. Any gunshot wound brought into an ER had to be reported to the police. He hadn't been willing to risk that not even to save the life of this woman who allegedly loved him.

He'd left her there on the table, where they had played out their sick, sadistic fantasies; where they had killed four women. Left her paralyzed, bleeding, in shock, dying. He hadn't even bothered to cover her with a blanket. The payoff money had been recovered from Rob's car.

According to Michele, Rob had fixated on Jillian out of jealousy, but Michele had put him off. Then on that fateful Friday night Jillian had called from a pay phone after the battery in her cell phone had gone dead. She wanted to talk about the fight she'd had with her father. She needed the support of a friend. Her friend had delivered her to Rob Marshall.

"Michele loves him," Angie said, picking at

the bandage. A frown curved her mouth and she added, "More than me."

But Michele was all she had, her only family, her surrogate mother, and so she had done whatever Michele had asked. Kate wondered what would happen in Angie's mind when she was finally told Michele was dead, that she was alone—the one thing she feared the most.

There was a soft rap at the door, signifying Kate's allotted time as a visitor was up. When she left she would be grilled by the people sitting on the other side of the observation window—Sabin, Lieutenant Fowler, Gary Yurek, and Kovac—back in good graces after scoring news time as a hero at Kate's fire—a photo of him and Quinn carrying her out the back door of her house had graced the cover of both papers in the Cities and made *Newsweek*. They believed she was here at their request. But she hadn't asked their questions or pressed for the answers. She hadn't come to this locked psychiatric ward to exploit Angie Finlow. She hadn't come as an advocate to see a client. She had come to see someone she had shared an ordeal with. Someone whose life would be forever tied to hers in a way no one else's ever would be.

She reached along the tabletop and touched Angie's hand, trying to keep her in the present, in the moment. Her own hands were still discolored and puffy, the ligature marks on her wrists covered by her own pristine white bandages. Three days had passed since the incident in her house.

"You're not alone, kiddo," Kate whispered softly. "You can't just save my life and breeze out of it again. I'll be keeping my eye on you. Here's a little reminder of that."

With the skill of a magician, she slipped the thing from her hand to Angie's. The tiny pottery angel Angie had stolen from her desk, then left behind at the Phoenix.

Angie stared at the statue, a guardian angel in a world where such things did not truly exist—or so she had always believed. The need to believe now was so strong, it terrified her, and she retreated to the shadowed side of her mind to escape the fear. Better to believe in nothing than wait for the inevitable disappointment to drop like an ax.

She closed her hand around the statue and held it like a secret. She closed her eyes and shut her mind down, not even aware of the tears that slipped down her cheeks.

Kate blinked back tears of her own as she rose slowly and carefully. She stroked a hand over Angie's hair, bent, and pressed the softest of kisses to the top of her head.

"I'll be back," she whispered, then gathered her crutches and hobbled toward the door, muttering to herself. "Guess maybe I'll have to stop saying I don't do kids, after all."

The idea came with a wave of emotions she simply didn't have the strength to deal with today. Luckily, she would have a lot of tomorrows to work on them.

As she went into the hall, the door to the observation room opened and Sabin, Fowler, and Yurek spilled out, looking frustrated. Kovac followed with a look-at-these-clowns smirk. At the same time, a short, handsome Italian-looking man in a thirty-five-hundred-dollar charcoal suit steamed down the hall toward them with Lucas Brandt and a scowl.

"Have you been speaking with the girl without her counsel present?" he demanded.

Kate gave him the deep-freeze stare.

"You can't proceed with this until her competency has been determined," Brandt said to Sabin.

"Don't tell me my job." Sabin's shoulders hunched as if he might bring his fists up. "What are you doing here, Costello?"

"I'm here to represent Angie Finlow at the request of Peter Bondurant."

Anthony Costello, sleazeball to the rich and famous. Kate almost laughed. Just when she thought nothing could amaze her...Peter Bondurant paying for Angie's legal counsel. Retribution for shooting her sister in the back? Good PR for a man who would stand to face charges of his own? Or maybe he simply wanted to make up for the mess his daughter's life had become by helping Angie out of the mess her life had always been. Karma.

"Anything she told you is privileged," Costello barked at her.

"I'm just here to see a friend," Kate said, hobbling away to let the men duke it out.

A new act for the media circus.

"Hey, Red!"

She turned and stopped as Kovac came

toward her. He looked as if he'd fallen asleep at the beach. His face was the bright red of a bad sunburn. His eyebrows were a pair of pale hyphens, singed short. The requisite cop mustache was gone, leaving him looking naked and younger.

"How do you like them apples?" he croaked, fighting off a coughing fit. The aftereffects of smoke inhalation.

"Curiouser and curiouser."

"Quinn back yet?"

"Tomorrow."

He had gone back to Quantico for the wrap-up and to put in for his first holiday in five years—Thanksgiving.

"So you're coming tonight?"

Kate made a face. "I don't think so, Sam. I'm not feeling very social."

"Kate," he said on a disapproving growl. "It's Turkey Wake! I'm the damn bishop, for Christ's sake! We've got a lot to celebrate."

True, but a rousing, ribald roast of a rubber chicken with a mob of drunken cops and courthouse personnel didn't seem the way to go for her. After all that had happened, after the media she'd had to face in the last few days, interaction was the last thing she wanted.

"I'll catch it on the news," she said.

He heaved a sigh, giving up, sobering for the real reason he had broken away from the pack. "It's been a hell of a case. You held your own, Red." A hint of his usual wry grin canted his mouth. "You're okay for a civilian."

Kate grinned at him. "Up yours, Kojak."

Then she hobbled closer, leaned forward, and kissed his cheek. "Thanks for saving my life."

"Anytime."

A WARM FRONT had moved into Minnesota the day before, bringing sun and temperatures in the high fifties. The snow was nearly gone, re-exposing dead yellow lawns and leafless bushes and dirt. Ever conscious of the length of winter once it settled in with serious intent, the citizens of Minneapolis had emerged from early hibernation on bicycles and Rollerblades. Small packs of power-walking old ladies trooped down Kate's block on the way to the lake, slowing to gawk at the blackened exterior of her home.

Most of the damage had been contained to the basement and first floor. The house would be salvaged, repaired, restored, and she would try not to think too much about what had happened there every time she had to go to the basement. She would try not to stand at the washing machine and think of Rob Marshall lying dead and burned to a charred black lump on her floor.

There were tougher jobs ahead than selecting new kitchen cabinets.

Kate picked her way through the charred mess that had been the first floor. A buddy of Kovac's who had done a lot of arson investigation had gone through the structure for her, telling her where she could and couldn't go, what she should and shouldn't do. She wore the yellow hardhat he'd given her to protect herself from falling chunks of plaster. On one foot she wore a thick-soled hiking boot. Over the bandages on the other foot was a thick wool sock and a heavy-duty plastic garbage bag.

She sorted through the debris with long-handled tongs, for things worth keeping. The job depressed her beyond tears. Even with the timely arrival of the fire department, the explosion of paint and solvents in the basement had damaged much of the first floor. And what the fire hadn't ruined, the fire hoses had.

The loss of ordinary possessions didn't bother her. She could buy another television. A sofa was a sofa. Her wardrobe was smoke-damaged, but insurance would buy her another. It was the loss of things richly steeped in memories that hurt. She'd grown up in this house. The thing that now looked like a pair of burned tree stumps had been her father's desk. She could remember crawling into the knee well during games of hide-and-seek with her sister. The rocking chair in the living room had belonged to her great-aunt. Photograph albums holding a lifetime's worth of memories had burned, melted, or been soaked, then frozen and thawed again.

She picked up what was left of an album with pictures of Emily and started to page through, tears coming as she realized the photographs were mostly ruined. It was like losing her child all over again.

She closed the book and held it to her chest, looking around through the blur at the devastation. Maybe this wasn't the day to do this job. Quinn had tried to talk her out of it on the phone. She had insisted she was strong enough, that she needed to do something positive.

But she wasn't strong enough. Not in the way that she needed to be. She felt too raw, too tired, emotions too close to the surface. She felt as if she'd lost more than what the fire had taken. Her faith in her judgment had been shaken. The order of her world had been upended. She felt very strongly that she should have been able to prevent what had happened.

The curse of the victim. Second-guessing herself. Hating her lack of control of the world around her. The test was whether a person could rise above it, push past it, grow beyond the experience.

She carried the photo album outside and set it in a box on the back steps. The backyard was awash in yellow-orange light as the sun began its early exit from the day. The grainy light fell like mist on her winter-dead garden in the far corner of the yard, and a statue she had forgotten to put away for the season—a fairy sitting on a pedestal, reading a book. With nothing but dead stems around it, it looked far too exposed and vulnerable. She had the strangest urge to pick it up and hold it like a child. Protect it.

Another wave of emotion pushed tears up

in her eyes as she thought again of Angie looking so small and so young and so lost sitting in the too-big hospital gown, her gaze on the tiny guardian angel statue in her hand.

A car door slammed out front and she peered around the corner of the house to see Quinn walking away from a cab. Instantly her heart lifted at the sight of him, at the way he looked, the way he moved, the frown on his face as he looked up at the house without realizing she was watching him. And just as instantly her nerves tightened a notch.

They hadn't seen much of each other in the days since the fire. The wrap-up of the case had taken much of Quinn's time. He'd been in demand by the media as they had insisted on rehashing, analyzing and re-analyzing every aspect of it. And then the official summons back to Quantico, where he had several cases coming to a head at once. Even their phone conversations had been brief, and both of them had skated around the big issues of their relationship. The case had brought him to Minneapolis. The case had brought them together. The case was over. Now what?

"I'm out back!" Kate called.

Quinn fixed his gaze on her as he came up the walk beside the house. She looked ridiculous and beautiful in a hardhat and a green canvas coat that was a bit too big for her. Beautiful, even battered and bruised and shaken from the inside out.

He'd almost lost her. Again. Forever. The idea struck him with the force of a hammer to the solar plexus about every five minutes. He'd almost lost her in part because he hadn't been able to see right in front of him the monster he was supposed to know as well as any man on earth.

"Hey, pretty," he said. He dropped his bags on the ground, took her into his arms, and kissed her—not in a sexual way, but in a way that gave them both comfort. The hardhat tipped back on her head and fell off, letting her hair cascade down her back. "How's it going?"

"It sucks. I hate it," she said plainly, Kate-style. "I liked my house. I liked my stuff. I had to start over once. I don't want to have to do it again. But life says, 'Tough bounce,' and what are my options? Take it on the chin and keep marching."

She gave a shrug and broke eye contact. "Better than the deal Angie got. Or Melanie Hessler."

Quinn took her stubborn chin in his hand and turned her face back to his. "Are you beating yourself up, Kathryn Elizabeth?"

She nodded and let him wipe the tears from her cheeks with his thumbs.

"So am I," he confessed, and found a wry smile. "We're a pair. Think how great the world would be if you and I really did control it."

"We'd do a better job of it than whoever has the job now," she promised, then shivered. "Or I'd blow it, and people I cared about would get hurt."

"Well, here's an ugly rumor I heard today: We're only human. Mistakes come with the territory."

Kate knitted her brow. "Human?" She took his hand and led him to the old weathered cedar garden bench. "You and I? Who told you that? Let me go melt their brain with death rays."

They sat, and his arm automatically went around her shoulders, just as her head automatically found his shoulder.

"Hey, you. You're early," she said.

"Well, I didn't want to miss Turkey Wake," he said, deadpan. "Happy to see me?"

"Not after that answer."

He laughed and brushed a kiss against her temple. They sat in silence for another few minutes, staring at the blackened back door of the house where Quinn and Kovac had carried her out.

"I came back here and built this very specific life," Kate said softly. "Thinking if I did it that way, I could have control of it, and bad things wouldn't happen. How's that for naive?"

Quinn shrugged. "I thought if I could grab my world by the balls, I could ride all the demons out of it. But it doesn't work that way. There's always another demon. I can't count them all anymore. I can't keep them straight. Hell, I can't even see them right in front of me."

Kate could hear the hint of desperation underlying the toughness, and knew his faith in his abilities had been shaken too. The

Mighty Quinn. Always right, always sure, moving forward like an arrow. She had always loved his unfailing strength, had always admired his bullheadedness. She loved him as much for his vulnerability.

"No one saw this coming, John. I hated the guy from the day he took the job, and not even I suspected *this*. We see what we expect to see. Scary, considering what can lie beneath the surface."

She stared at the garden, dead and brown, surreal in the fading light. "Imagine the most horrific, repulsive cruelty one human being can commit against another. Someone's out there doing it right now. I don't know how you stand it anymore, John."

"I don't," he admitted. "You know how it is when you first come on the job? Everything gets to you. You have to toughen up. You have to get that emotional armor on. Then you reach a point when you've seen so much, nothing gets to you, and you start to wonder about your humanity. Stay at it long enough, the armor starts to corrode, the evil starts to eat through it, and you're back where you started, only you're older and tired, and you know you can't slay all the dragons no matter how hard you try."

"And then what?" Kate asked quietly.

"And then you either step aside, or you eat your gun, or you drop in your tracks like Vince Walsh."

"On the surface that choice would seem like a no-brainer."

"Not when the job is all you've got. When you bury yourself in it because you're too afraid to go and get the life you really want. Portrait of me for the last five years," he said. "No more. As of today, I am officially on leave. Time to drain the strain, get my head screwed on straight."

"Decide what you want," Kate offered to the list.

"I know what I want," he said simply.

He turned to her on the bench and took her hands in his. "I need something good in my life, Kate. I need something beautiful and warm. I need you. I need us. What do you need?"

Kate looked at him, her destroyed home in her peripheral vision, and thought, of all things, of the phoenix rising from the ashes. The events that had brought them to this place in this time may have been devastating, but here was their chance for a new beginning. Together.

For the first time in five years she felt a sense of warm, sweet peace in place of the hard, aching emptiness she'd grown almost numb to. She had spent the years without him, merely existing. It was time to live. After all the death, literal and metaphorical, it was time for both of them to live.

"I need your arms around me, John Quinn," she said, smiling softly. "Every day and every night of my life."

Quinn let out a pent-up breath, a grin splitting his handsome face. "Took you long enough to answer."

He took her into his arms carefully, mindful of her wounds, and held her close. He imagined he could feel her heart beat even through the heavy canvas of her coat.

"You've got my heart, Kate Conlan," he said, burying his cold nose in the thick silk of her hair. "You've had it all this time. I lived too long without it."

Kate smiled against his chest, knowing *this* was home—his embrace, his love.

"Well, tough, John Quinn," she said, gazing up at him in the last light of sunset. "I'm not giving it back."